The Woman in Beige

V.G. LEE

DIVA

By the same author:

The Comedienne

First published 2003 by Diva Books,
an imprint of Millivres Prowler Limited,
part of the Millivres Prowler Group,
Spectrum House, 32–34 Gordon House Road,
London NW5 1LP UK

www.divamag.co.uk
www.divamailorder.com

Copyright © V.G. Lee 2003

Part of this work appeared in a different form in *Groundswell:
The Diva Book of Short Stories 2*, edited by Helen Sandler (2002).

The moral right of the author has been asserted.

A CIP catalogue record for this book is available from the British Library

ISBN 1-873741-80-4

Distributed in the UK and Europe by Airlift Book Company,
8 The Arena, Mollison Avenue,
Enfield, Middlesex EN3 7NJ
Telephone: 020 8804 0400
Distributed in North America by Consortium,
1045 Westgate Drive, St Paul, MN 55114-1065
Telephone: 1 800 283 3572
Distributed in Australia by Bulldog Books,
PO Box 300, Beaconsfield, NSW 2014

Printed and bound in Finland by WS Bookwell

Spring 1994

Blessed are the meek...

Dear Pat,

Received your postcard this morning. That could almost be you on the water-skis, except your hair is blonde and short. Where are you? Obviously this letter will go to your home address and it will become a case of "Where were you?" I'm bewildered. Your card says "Printed in Italy", yet actual printed matter is in Greek characters, with a silhouette of our own dear queen in place of a foreign stamp. Didn't you say you were off to Florida?

I'm sorry to hear that you're depressed and missing Harry, but your very nice neighbour, Avril, tells me he's still swimming the right way up and seems pleased to see her when she pops in to deliver his daily pinch of fish food.

Your P.S. – "Parga swings" – seems hopeful. No mention of Parga in my Oxford Dictionary of the World. Is Parga, perhaps, a new acquaintance?

What books am I reading? None at present. I'm dipping into the Vitamin Bible by world famous nutritionist Earl Mindell. There is a complete chapter devoted to the individual requirements of specific groups. I enclose photocopies of "Runners, Joggers, Athletes and Tennis Players" for yourself. Avril said you're thinking of taking up golf. You're a dark horse, you never said. Earl Mindell advises that "the stress and tension of golf can use up Vitamin B at a rapid clip," so be warned.

Guess what? I come under "Excessive TV Watchers". Surprisingly I need Vitamin A with breakfast for eye-strain and Vitamin D if I go for long periods without seeing the light of day.

Have been visiting Edna and Lily – they are still ghastly...

At that point, I paused and looked up, trying to focus on the woman opposite me on the other side of the train gangway, which was difficult with my reading glasses.

There was a blurred impression of head-to-toe beige – not a favourite colour. I hadn't noticed her before. Had she boarded at Haywards Heath while I was in the buffet car negotiating the number of bacon rashers that warranted two slices of limp bread being called a bacon sandwich? I returned to letter writing.

Now what else might Pat want to know? And why exactly was I writing to Pat, who would no doubt be on the telephone as soon as she got home? Or would she? For the last few months, Pat hadn't been herself, as in, bosom friend to be relied on in and out of a crisis. Pat had been distant. Pat had owned to vague unspecified yearnings.

Helen, a mutual friend, had said Pat was a cold fish. Or had she said, "Pat has a goldfish"? She'd certainly said, "Harry is a strange pet for a grown woman to be so fond of, although I can't deny he has winning ways."

I was aware of some repetitive movement from the woman's corner as if she might be signalling out of the window to someone, which was unlikely on a fast train in the middle of a stretch of countryside, but worth investigating. Surreptitiously I slid the letter to Pat inside my *Vitamin Bible* and changed over to long-sighted spectacles. The woman came into focus; she was sitting perfectly still, staring unseeingly at the back of her hands. At first glance, not very interesting – more interesting was the large grey plastic pet-carrier perched next to her on the seat. Inside was something almost too large for its container; long straggling hanks of fur stuck out of the grille door and through the horizontal ventilation gaps.

"Fur quality, poor and unkempt," I wrote in my pocket notebook, "at odds with owner who is extremely tidy and colour co-ordinated."

Just before Clapham Junction, the woman stood up and began to pull on a beige raincoat. So far she hadn't said a word to the hairy creature next to her, and the hairy creature hadn't said a word to her –

2

I'd been watching both of them closely, while feigning an interest in the patterned seat upholstery which I'd assessed as circa 1973. This was an old and well-tried subterfuge, and was why I never left home without a set of coloured felt-tips and my notebook. Many were the times that my small studies of seat coverings on bus, tube and train had prompted cheerful exchanges, or an invigorating debate on just when was the golden age of transport. On one occasion such a debate had even formed the basis for a three-week relationship.

But no interest in upholstery patterns was showing here; the woman continued to stare out of the window as she slowly, thoughtfully buttoned her coat. She had an attractive, tanned face, slightly hooked nose which I found rather distinguished, beige trousers, beige suede boots.

Go for Ploy 2 before woman gets off train and disappears forever: assume pose of inquisitive sentimental animal lover.

"Puss is remarkably good," I said sweetly, "not so much as a murmur."

The woman glanced across at me – no, the woman looked down her elegant hooked nose at me and I felt the full impact of tanned face, cold green eyes and a weight of beige. As I said a week later, when a bronzed Pat called in to deliver a small bottle of Metaxa brandy and a jar of Pargan olives: "Time stopped for me, Pat. That was it. I'd never liked beige before, but this woman looked fantastic in it."

Back on the train, as time and the train were stopping, the woman said coolly, "It isn't a cat – it's a Highland Terrier. I'm taking him home to bury."

"Good heavens, I'm so sorry."

"No need. He's not my dog. He belonged to… a friend." That faint pause, the bitter smile denoting… heartache, a personal tragedy?

Clapham Junction and the woman got out.

"Don't go," I wanted to shout. "Here's my name and phone number," scrawled on the back of Seat Cover no. 122. The train moved on, I saw a straggle of fur, a beige boot and the buckle of a flying raincoat belt disappearing into the crowd on the platform. I fell back into my seat, my heart beating fiercely. How odd. How appropriately odd. Who was the woman? Why was she ferrying a friend's dead dog from Haywards Heath to Clapham Junction? Friend not got a garden, perhaps?

"Look Mavis, don't worry, I'll take him – pop him down in between the ornamental pear and Lord Napier nectarine – the little chap will be fine and dandy. I'll have a plaque engraved: 'For the precious link in the chain of our love.'"

Was that ridiculous? Yes, it was ridiculous. Suddenly I remembered an incident from my childhood: burying Gran's dog, Peppy 6, snappy but loyal Pomeranian. All in all, over a thirty-year period, there were Peppys 1 to 8, all snappy and nervous, which I think (now that I'm older and more reflective) had more to do with Gran than the Pomeranians; although Pat had a theory that Pomeranians came out of their mothers' wombs in a bad temper.

I was seven years old, my brother David eight, when Peppy 6 died. David and I laid him out on the kitchen table – David spent some time tweaking at his upper lip which had rigor mortised into an aggressive snarl, then wrapped him in a scarlet blanket and arranged him in his wicker basket ready for the grave Gran was digging on the far side of the rockery. Earlier she'd said, "Digging graves is too much like bloody gardening and I'm not made of money." This last was an oblique reference to burying the blanket and basket with the dog, which we'd thought only right and proper.

It was pouring with rain as the small funeral procession set off across the garden. The grave was too small for the basket, and we had to put Peppy 6 under a bushy camellia while we all dug around the edges: me using the hand trowel, Gran the spade and David a silver tablespoon. I don't recall Gran crying, although with all the rain that fell on us that afternoon, I couldn't be absolutely sure.

All done, and Gran smoothed the earth with her boot, using my lolly stick as a temporary marker.

She said, "Blessed are the meek for they shall inherit the earth," which I approved of in theory, but thought inappropriate as Peppy 6 had been anything but meek.

The rest of the journey home passed quickly – very little incident worth reporting. A small skirmish with the ticket collector who insisted belligerently that my ticket required me to travel between ten a.m. and four p.m., and it was now six-thirty – nothing I couldn't handle.

Autumn 1995

Enter the charlatan

Tetley and Typhoo weren't good enough for Pat these days; it had to be herbal – and not just any herb. Sandra, the new girlfriend, knew a special shop selling 'nature's products' in the Cotswolds. Pat carried a small tin – one of a series of dainty presents she'd had from Sandra last birthday – which was divided into five airtight compartments, a different variety of herbal tea bag in each. I remembered the days when Pat carried an airtight tin of Golden Virginia and always kept a card of five-lighters-for-a-pound about her person.

"So," I continued, "I told her she was a stuck-up bigot."

"You didn't?" Pat said, open mouthed over her tea cup.

"Well as good as…"

"But last week you said you thought there was a definite spark flickering between the two of you."

"That was last week. A week's a long time in affairs of the heart," I replied glibly.

"Lorna, what is the matter with you? You say these things, yet you don't really mean them. Why can't you just be yourself?" – which was rich coming from Pat, who'd been herself for thirty years and then overnight, some eighteen months ago, become a very different kettle of fish.

"I'm trying to be myself," I said, "which is why I'm seeing a counsellor, only as you know we're still at the boundaries and personal contract stage."

Pat sniffed dismissively and we drifted into the new and thus relatively lively debate of her counsellor versus mine. On my initial visit, my 'opportunity to dip in my toe and test the water' visit, Jenny

Salter, my counsellor, had said, "We'll be like two close friends, only I will know more about you, Lorna, than you will know about me. We will unlock doors and go through them together."

Pat said this was outrageous and that her counsellor, who was a proper counsellor with her own Victorian cottage in a desirable road in Walthamstow Village populated by similar intense and worthy women, would never encourage such familiarity. Pat did admit to a certain personal bewilderment that after nearly two years, her counsellor still seemed underwhelmed by her attractive personality and other unique qualities, e.g. her sex-appeal – which to be honest I'd never particularly noticed although I'd known Pat since secondary school. Of Jenny Salter, Pat said, "How like you to get mixed up with a charlatan," pursing her lips and dunking her fennel tea bag virtuously.

I was sorry when she went home to Sandra, who was making one of her leek and parmesan risottos; leaving me to work on my epic poem of star-crossed lovers set in Abney Park Cemetery. Hard to stop resentment creeping in (regarding Pat and Sandra, not the lovers). Pat and I had been best friends since the day in the fifth form when my brother David asked her out and she replied, "No thank you, David – no offence meant, but the opposite sex make me queasy," which had seemed a very sophisticated response at the time, although I'd felt sorry for David. One of those difficult things about being related – even when the relation appears perfectly cheerful, you can tell deep down they've been hurt. David spent the next week studying his face and profiles in Gran's three-way dressing-table mirror, practising casual smiles and sneering disinterest to deal with Pat the next time they met. I don't think she even noticed. She has a thick skin, has Pat.

Regarding Pat and Sandra and the desirable risotto, I'd said, "Oh, leek and parmesan risotto, sounds good, Pat."

"It's easy. Put it in that cookbook you're writing. Even you could do it on your Baby Belling."

"Is that strictly necessary?"

"Just write."

Sandra's Leek and Parmesan Risotto

One pound wild organic rice, 1 organic leek, 1 small onion (organic), 3 ozs unsalted free-range butter, 2 pints of vegetable stock, quarter pint of Sancerre or similar, half level teaspoon of fresh saffron, 3 ozs of FRESH parmesan and not that stuff in cellophane packet that you, Lorna, let go mouldy at the back of your minuscule fridge!

1. Put the lot, bar the stock, into a pan and fry.
2. Stir stock into boiled rice. Ooops. If you haven't already put the saffron in with 'the lot', it goes with the rice, et voilà.

"Sounds quite a lot for the two of you," I said.

"Far too much. We've four friends coming to share it."

"So, I'm not counted as a friend?"

"Four friends other than you, stupid. You're *my* friend, not an 'our' friend. Sandra says…" she paused, rummaging amongst the muddle on my desk for her tin of herbal teas.

"What does Sandra say?"

"That you've got a smart mouth. Take it as a compliment."

For the moment, I'm not going to tell you what Sandra's like. I may never tell you. You'd probably think she sounded an attractive intelligent woman, who cooked well and had a weather eye open for her partner's disruptive friends. Yes, I know I should have beeen pleased that they'd found each other, as Pat kept telling me. Reverend Joseph, my next-door neighbour, said, "Lorna, we should rejoice when the good Lord smiles on our nearest and dearest. Your time will come, my dear."

The worry was, my time might have been.

Pat's parting shot as she shrugged into her jacket was: "All your lovers are star-crossed. In real life, Lorna, you meet the love of your life and set up home in a two-bedroomed terraced house."

I said, "Not everybody's lucky enough to meet the love of their life every three years. Some of us are like swans, we mate for life."

"Well, I hope you don't intend to mate for life with this Stowell-Parker woman. I don't quite like the sound of her."

"I told you, I was extremely cool when we met at Sarah and Jane's camcorder evening."

I hadn't been scrupulously honest with Pat, what I'd actually said to TSP was, "I think Theresa Stowell-Parker is a delightful name. Yes, it has a certain ring to it," and I'd looked into her tawny eyes in what I hoped was a scintillating manner.

TSP had simpered most attractively and said, "Do you really think so, Lorna? I'm always rather self-conscious of admitting to the double barrel, especially in this grisly part of London." This last with a girlish shudder which I admit was offensive, yet somehow charmingly offensive. However, although she then promised to call me *tout de suite*, I had heard nothing more from Theresa in ten days. Just what did *tout de suite* mean to west Londoners?

From my window, I watched Pat until she turned the corner onto the High Street – she walked in a brisk, thoroughly pleased with life, style. "I'm thoroughly pleased with life, as well," I said, and settled down to watching a line of brownish birds loitering on the telephone wires. Every now and then, one raised an impatient foot as if to emphasise its point. Foot or claw? Foot or claw? I did quite a bit of watching out of windows, when I wasn't in a Portakabin in Spitalfields weighing and packing organic fertiliser for Green Bees Garden Products, which was Thursday, Friday and Saturday afternoons. Why wouldn't someone pay me to look out of windows? I didn't get bored or fall asleep. I was a very alert person with her own camera and a pair of orange opera glasses – a present from David when he took me to see *The King and I* on my birthday.

At parties: "And what do you do, Lorna?"

"Actually, I'm in surveillance. Very hush-hush."

TSP's eyes widen admiringly.

To put you in the picture

What do I look like? How old was I at this point? I was thirty-eightish but looked a lot younger (although my enemies would disagree). I am tallish, widish, with straight brown hair worn behind my ears for everyday purposes, or framing my face for special occasions. As well as being bodily widish, I have a wide forehead and a wide face, hence the need of hair forward when trying to impress. Pat said re. me: "All that face can work against you on first acquaintance, old chum."

My flat was on the second floor of a three-storey house in north London. My brother David and Julie, his wife, had the ground and first floor. We were supposed to share the garden, however, slowly over the years, Julie had taken over, which David said was only right and fair, since she had done all the hard work.

"But David, nobody asked her to uproot a perfectly lovely country-cottage-style garden and lay decking, wire up electric lights, plumb in water features, manhandle large boulders, construct arbours and conversation pieces, hang wind chimes..."

David held up his hand, which he often did to indicate that he wanted me to pause without his having to raise his voice or lose his temper. "The garden was old fashioned, and Julie likes contemporary."

"Wind chimes?"

"Positive emanations."

"Positive emanations, my backside."

This made David wrinkle the family brow – his brow being even wider than mine, his hair in the process of receding like the tide going out at Southend. He didn't like toilet humour, or anything even vaguely connected to toilet humour: backsides, bottoms, bums, 'Carry on at your Convenience' type words embarrassed him. As far as I knew, he and Julie had never used their lavatory; they had another, more spiritual way of organising their bodily functions.

"If you're not happy with the garden, take it up with Julie." End of discussion. Julie was a force to be reckoned with. I was building up towards this moment of reckoning, not there yet. When Julie made a suggestion, David hopped to it. He was a big man and it was not a pretty sight. It was all very different when we were children. In those days, we were on each other's side – we needed to be.

I made myself a mug of coffee and took it out into the garden, picking my way past the trays of red, white and pink cyclamen waiting for Julie to plant them in her tubs and window boxes. It was a bitterly cold autumn day. Through the wire netting fence (estimates expected for a brick or slatted wood alternative), Mr. E, our other neighbour, stood very still, considering a newly dug grave. Squatting at his feet sat Alfred the Great, his giant albino rabbit. Alfred was a character. If I met any of the E family on the street, I always asked after Alfred, and more often than not there was an adventure to report: Mrs. E's capacious brassiere had been run off with, or he had chewed through the washing machine cable while it was switched on and lived to tell the tale. For once Alfred was sitting quietly, looking a little perplexed, as if such inactivity was a new and not completely enjoyable experience.

"It's a bit big for Alfred," I quipped.

Mr. E raised a very faint smile. "It's for the sweetpeas, Lorna: Little Sweetheart and Peter Pan. You've got to get the ground dug and fed early with sweetpeas." He began emptying small bags of John Innes multi-purpose compost, which he bought two at a time from Woolworths, into the trench.

"Why don't you let David get you horse manure from the stables?"

"I don't want David straining himself."

"He doesn't have to carry it. He has minions to put it in the boot of his car and me or Julie to take it out this end."

Mr. E gave me the silent treatment, which wasn't always effective, as he was such a silent man anyway. He liked David. All the E children were girls and as soon as they could talk they bossed him about, as did Mrs. E. He wouldn't ask my brother to do anything, didn't want to be a nuisance. David got away with blue murder. When he was a little boy, he had asthma; now that he was older, it was cholesterol – and he still mustn't be upset.

"What do you think the weather's going to do?" I asked.

Mr. E shrugged. "Maybe rain."

We both stared up at the sky which was made up of several threatening shades of grey cloud. Against this, the treetops carried golden tatters of autumn leaves. I could almost imagine we lived in the country, apart from the persistent wail of sirens out on the main road. Otherwise it was so peaceful, even a few birds trilling. Mr. E began fidgeting with another bag of compost and the moment passed.

Two messages on my answerphone: first a ringing off; second, message from ex-friend Kate to say she and Tina were thinking of breeding clumber spaniels. I'd been remarkably silent all year. Had she offended me?

Well no, of course I wasn't offended. I thoroughly enjoyed being dumped three years ago on my thirty-fifth birthday in front of all our many friends – appreciated her generous gift of giving me access to a precious learning experience.

I resented the way Jenny Salter plonked an open box of Scotties Tissues onto the table next to my elbow the moment I sat down.

"I don't cry every week."

"I thought you might find it stressful having to ask for a tissue," Jenny said, settling herself into her chair like a golden eagle on its nest – not that I've ever seen an eagle, golden or otherwise, settling on a nest, but I like to think I have a vivid poetic imagination where wildlife is concerned.

Jenny Salter had long brown hair with a copper glint to it, undeniably lovely burnished hair – but a small mean voice in my head, probably planted by one of Pat's negative remarks, whispered that it would be more appropriate tied back. Then another small voice, the one that liked and admired Jenny Salter, wondered if she used her curtain of hair to hide behind. Jenny's face was not a modern face. She reminded me of a drawing I'd once seen of Mary Queen of Scots – long straight nose, clever eyes with heavy eyelids and a small thin mouth – but possibly Jenny didn't appreciate the sum of these singular features as I did.

Incongruously, considering how cold it was outside, Jenny wore brown leather sandals. She took my quick look of surprise as a sign of approval, because she then wiggled the unpainted toes of her left foot, and swung her ankle so she could better admire the sandal.

"New sandals?" I asked.

"Yes," she dunked her Earl Grey tea bag several times into her cup before placing it delicately in the saucer. The small cubbyhole of an office was filled with its slight aromatic smell. For a moment she seemed lost in her own private thoughts.

"Penny for them, Jenny?" I said affably, but with an edge. After all, I wasn't paying thirty pounds for fifty minutes for Jenny Salter to daydream or deal lovingly with tea bags.

"I was wondering, Lorna, where your anger was coming from?"

"I'm not angry. Aren't your feet cold in those sandals?"

"I rarely feel the cold," Jenny said and tucked her sandalled feet away under her chair. "Do you?"

I blinked – I had a sudden very clear image of myself and David standing in what had once been our grandmother's kitchen; we were ten and eleven, the year that David started grammar school. We wore striped pyjamas (wherever possible Gran dressed us both the same for economy); our backs were turned to the open oven, set at Regulo 3, bum (sorry David) -warming temperature. In the hall, Gran put down the telephone. David said, "They're not coming, are they?" We both felt it; a feeling of relief mixed with the underlying chill of disappointment.

I shivered. "Yes Jenny, I do feel the cold."

Introducing George and Della

The bungalow on the outskirts of Hornchurch was arranged for George and Della's convenience, which was how it should be – their home had always been their own private world, because as George so often said, "There's no privacy in army quarters – no sooner had we hung up the curtains, down they came and off we moved again."

By all accounts – well, his and Della's – George, who was a chef in his army days, was still an excellent cook, something of a wine buff, appreciated a good cigar, a round of golf... "Your dad's a bon viveur and no mistake," Della had often told her children, and George would respond complacently, "No argument, I like the good things of life but I've never been afraid to share." Hmm.

In the lounge (Della said 'sitting room' was so fifties, screamed brown moquette three-piece suites and utility furniture) they had a picture window front and back, a settee for Della, and a choice of two large squashy armchairs with *en suite* pouffe for George – background colour Chinese Coral with a raised floral pattern in maroon Dralon. Against the long wall was a large flat-screen television and video. It was positioned just so, for when they put up their slippered feet and settled with maroon and Chinese Coral brocade cushions behind their heads and shoulders. "Getting comfy," they called it. Then there was a central coffee table for Della's coffee-table books on stately homes and one on National Trust Gardens that had been there forever, plus large storage compartments for videos of the moment. Within easy reach were two G Plan occasional tables that they used constantly for their coffee cups, tea cups and, moving along into early evenings, vodka and tonic for Della, gin, tonic, ice and lime slice for George, and finally brandy nightcaps (wine at the dining table only). They were creatures of habit, moulded into shape by army life where every hour of every day was accounted for.

There was a guest bedroom that in fifteen years had never been used but was kept immaculate with fresh flowers on the wide windowsill. George and Della's own bedroom was spacious and also welcoming, decorated in shades of peach which they both agreed was a flattering shade, reflecting warm colour into their faces. There was plenty of room for their two three-quarter beds with a cabinet in between bearing a lamp with a fringed peach-coloured shade, their monogrammed spectacle cases and their books: Deighton and Le Carré for George, any fiction recommended by *She* magazine for Della, which frequently left her frustrated and annoyed.

"Once again, I've wasted good money on two novels about wicked mothers and their angelic bloody daughters," Della said for the umpteenth time over a fifteen-year period. She was sitting up in bed wearing a cream cotton nightdress in a Victorian style, small pearl buttons at her throat and wrist. "When's the boot going to fit the other foot? Daughters can be absolute beasts. I don't think Lorna's ever made one single attempt to please, yet I'm expected to dole out love, whatever curve she chucks at me."

"Hear, hear," murmured George from behind his own book, which was *Enigma* by Robert Harris, a divergence from his usual tried and tested. "This is pretty baffling."

"Wait till this Margaret Forster woman has daughters of her own." Della threw the book down in disgust. "Do you remember the two-tone trousers Lorna turned up in that time at the Strand Palace Hotel?"

"I do indeed. Shall I ever forget it?" A thought struck George and he took off his reading glasses. "I'm tempted to pay a flying visit next time we're in London. Cause a bit of disruption. Any recent news from Camp David?"

"All I've had is a postcard from Lorna, telling me about some job at the *Hackney Echo*."

"A reporter?" George looked unwillingly impressed.

"I doubt it. God knows what the postman thought – the picture was of an over-developed young woman breast-feeding a baby, with the caption, 'And it's a man's world?'"

George returned to his book, Della began rereading that month's *She*. The minutes ticked by, the only sounds in the room were the click of the digital clock and the turn of pages. Finally Della lowered the magazine and smiled at her reflection in the mirror of the wardrobe opposite. "Are we an awful pair, George?" she asked.

He also smiled fondly at her reflection. "I don't care if we are," he said, and for a moment they linked hands between the two beds and George stopped smiling and a shadow crossed his plump, healthy face.

"I know what you're thinking," Della said with a soft sigh.

"Sorry."

"But that house belongs to them. By rights it should be yours, but George, it isn't. It's been twenty years since your mother died, time to put the past behind you."

"The trouble is, I can't. Gets worse as I get older. We had some good times in the old days."

From an early age, David and Lorna had known they were not as other children. Their parents were absentees; and neighbours, teachers, their grandmother's friend Edna, all felt sorry for them.

"Their childhood's been blighted," Edna said. "They've developed old heads before the time for old heads."

George with disarming frankness asserted, "They cramp our style, Mother. Della and I aren't kiddy people and as you dote on them both, it would be a crime to drag the little tykes overseas. An absolute bloody crime. Of course Della's heart-broken, aren't you, darling?"

Della said, nodding and dabbing prettily at her dry eyes: "Heart-broken, but my place is at George's side. I love your son more than life itself, Irene."

Irene retired to her kitchen muttering, "Well, bully for the two of you, you selfish buggers," but not altogether displeased to be left with her two grandchildren.

While she was still in good health, she put the house into David and Lorna's names because as she'd said to her friend Edna, "Who else will look after them once I'm gone? You can't depend on that feckless pair." She generally referred to George and Della as 'that feckless pair', as if they were nothing much to do with her; as if they weren't her son and daughter-in-law. Even so, George and Della still continued to seem dangerously attractive to the children when they did turn up, even though their visits, as Irene cannily predicted, always ended in somebody else's tears.

By the time his mother died, George had taken early retirement from a lifetime of overseas postings and they were living comfortably on an army pension in a large bungalow on the outskirts of Hornchurch. 'When Mother dies' had been a subject much discussed between them, which might seem callous of George, but he *was* callous – and why shouldn't he be, Della maintained, having never been the favoured son? This in itself was a long and tortuous story of several versions, worthy of being ranked next to Cain and Abel, Castor and Pollux and Don and Phil Everly. Whatever the rights and wrongs of George's background, as only surviving son he had high expectations of 'Mother coming good', in the end or at her end.

And then Mother did die.

"I'm sorry Dad, but Gran died late last night," Lorna said on the telephone.

"I see. Did she mention me?"

"No. She was unconscious, otherwise I'm sure she'd have had something to say."

George didn't much care for Lorna's tone. He'd tackled her about tone before and been told she was being ironic.

"How's your brother taking it?" he asked.

"We're both very upset, but it wasn't unexpected."

"It was as far as I'm concerned."

"We told you at the weekend."

"You said the end was in sight, which is very different from 'falls into a coma and dead two days later'."

No reply from Lorna.

"So when's the funeral, or was she buried this morning?"

Finishing with Lorna he went in search of his wife, found her in the conservatory manhandling her sunbed out onto the patio. "Hell's bells, Della, Mother's dead."

Della's eyes immediately filled with tears. She left the sunbed wedged in the doorway and ran, literally ran to George. "Are you all right, George? Not too upset? I couldn't bear you to be upset."

"I am a bit. It's a shock but it was expected. She didn't mention me at the end."

"Old bag."

George stared up at the glass ceiling, blinking rapidly. "No, she couldn't help it. Fish of one and fowl of the other."

They came into London on the train, leaving their maroon Rover parked at Hornchurch Station because, as George said, "There's nowhere safe to leave a car in London. We'll be in the crematorium five minutes and come out to find the bloody car stripped down to the paintwork."

David and Lorna were now nineteen and eighteen. It was three years since they'd last seen their parents.

"We're not children any more," David said the night before the funeral. "They've been lousy parents. However attractive and amusing they seem, it's not real, it's nothing to do with us."

"It's a shame though, isn't it? George at his best is so funny…"

"Yes, well, see how funny he'll be if you tell him you've decided to be a lesbian and have been recently seduced by your driving instructress! And Mother's lethal whatever the situation."

"Point taken, David. We must support each other."

"Edna says they'll be after money."

"They've got money."

"We mustn't weaken."

"I won't weaken – if anybody's likely to weaken it's you."

"Thanks very much, Lorna."

"What I meant is, Dad will pick on you because you're the boy. Girls don't matter to either of them."

*

After the funeral, the mourners, consisting of George, Della, David, Lorna, Pat and the E family from the other side (as in 'other side of Gran's house'), plus several ladies from her indoor bowling club, all went into the Reverend Joseph's for sandwiches and Harvey's Bristol Cream. After several Bristol Creams and George saying jovially, "Steady on Della – that's almost pure alcohol you're imbibing," Della began telling everyone that the deceased would have a ruddy cheek if she hadn't left her one surviving son well provided for, and they'd carry it to the highest court in the land if there proved to be a problem – by 'problem' she meant David and Lorna. George was forced to take her firmly by the arm and hiss, "I couldn't agree more darling, but could you please moderate your voice?"

David and Lorna said little, kept their old heads down, and much appreciated encouraging pats on their backs from Rev. Joseph and Mr. E.

"Keep on the move, tire them out," was Mrs. E's advice, "and keep topping their schooners up. If they pass out, Mr. E and I will take them down to the canal in the car and let nature have its way."

"Mrs. E, they are our parents – we can't kill them."

"I wasn't intending to kill them – I was putting their fate in God's hands."

"That's enough blasphemy, Glenda," the Reverend Joseph said. It always surprised Lorna when the Reverend Joseph called Mrs. E 'Glenda' – nobody used her name, not even Mr. E, and never with that gentle, affectionate tone of voice which made her eyes soften.

Lorna joined Mr. E over by the window. He was wearing two black armbands.

"Everything OK, Mr. E?"

"You know, Rusty died on Tuesday as well. Your gran was very fond of Rusty."

"I know she was. I thought I hadn't heard him barking at the postman recently."

"I won't get another dog. It's worse than children – dogs break your heart. Your grandmother called him the devil dog, but it was a term of endearment, like 'that old devil moon' in the song."

Lorna wasn't so sure.

However...

"Quite apart from everything else, David, I hope we'll be allowed some sentimental pickings," George said, finally cornering David in Rev. Joseph's kitchen. When George was with his son, he often felt filled with an incredible power, felt almost god-like... it was worth doing the trip into London for. He was a valuable inch taller than David, his stomach was as flat as a board while David, he'd noticed, carried quite a bit of flab. What he'd like to suggest one day was for the two of them to go several rounds of boxing at a local Hornchurch gym, just so that David would know, once and for all, who was head honcho of the family.

"As I recall, the old lady had some nice paintings in ebony frames, a highly desirable creamware jug that I know your mother would like, and jewellery, wasn't there jewellery? Lorna won't want it. I can see she's going to be the wooden beads and Jesus boots type of gal. I don't want you getting rid of anything before the will's read."

At that moment Lorna came into the kitchen. David's voice almost broke for the second time in his life. He looked at Lorna, he avoided looking at George and said, "I'm sorry, Dad, everything's been sold."

George stepped back a pace and looked sternly at his son. "Not possible. What about probate? The house must be worth a hundred and fifty grand alone."

"The house is ours," Lorna said.

"Young lady, this house isn't yours. You don't know what you're talking about."

"Gran put it in our names."

"She can't do that. It's illegal. An avoidance of death duties." George's voice started to rise. In the Rev. Joseph's sitting room, the guests were quieting.

"Ten years ago," David said. "Her will specified that certain items were to be sold and the rest of the furniture given to her friend Edna."

George's face was purple. "Edna? Is that the tanned weasel of a woman who smokes a clay pipe? Where is she, this paragon, this lifelong friend? I don't see her."

"She's having an operation for carpal tunnel syndrome."

"A likely story. That woman never had a syndrome in her life."

"It's a physical condition – it's been aggravated by building a concrete coal bunker."

"I don't want to listen to this – I couldn't care less if a concrete coal bunker had fallen on her head – she's been turning my mother against me for years and now she and you two walk off with the spoils. I've had all the pain and bloody grief, been shat on from afar..."

"Easy, George," said the Reverend Joseph.

At this point, Della managed to disentangle herself from Mrs. E, who'd been regaling her with tales of her mother-in-law's endearing eccentricities. "I'm sorry, Mrs. E, delightful... another time, must have a word with George and the kids..." She erupted into the kitchen: "Do you two little beasts realise we could take you to court on a variety of grounds?"

"You couldn't, Mum. Gran sorted her finances out years ago with her solicitor. She didn't want you and Dad to have a thing. She cared about us, while you two thought we were bloody nuisances."

"What did you ever achieve in life?" This was one of Della's surprise tactics: change subject and get personal.

"Mum," Lorna said mildly, "I'm eighteen – my life's hardly started."

21

Autumn 1995

Those water retention days

Around two-thirty each Saturday I took a late lunch at the Vortex Jazz Bar in Stoke Newington Church Street. Nothing much: a bowl of soup, a fresh baked roll and a glass of chilled white wine, maybe a sliver of walnut and fudge cake with a dash of cream. I took my notebook in case I had a flash of inspiration, and also as a ploy to secure the interest of any passing unattached – which was how I'd met Theresa. In fact I was thinking as I set out for the Vortex on this particular Saturday, "I may meet Theresa." Unfortunately, instead, I was kidnapped by Mrs. E, our left-hand neighbour, and her family. (A point to clarify: Mrs. E was a trainee deacon on behalf of the English Martyrs and Unitarian Church, while the aforementioned Reverend Joseph was our right-hand neighbour and Pentecostally inclined.)

I'd just reached the Victorian postbox on the corner of Duxford Road and was wishing I'd worn a woollen scarf, when Mrs. E's old white Datsun swerved to my side of the road and pulled up at the kerb in front of me. I'd forgotten, still don't recall, am convinced it was one of Mrs. E's fictions, like her being a size ten, but apparently I'd agreed to support her church jumble sale at an unspecified address in the Woodberry Down area.

"A promise is a promise, Lorna," said the smallest child piously as the E Family Robinson swarmed around me, gathered me up and cramped me into the back of their car.

"So how's Julie?" Mrs. E yelled from the front seat, lighting a small cheroot while steering with her knees. "I heard her shouting in the night again. Who's Barry?"

"A teenage love affair. For some reason she always shouts for Barry."

"Did he take her virginity?" asked Esther, who was fourteen and thought herself sophisticated. She smirked across at her twin sister Estelle who was painting her lips mulberry in the cracked wing mirror.

"So I believe," I said, "but don't tell her I told you." And we lurched to a stop outside the church.

"This is my neighbour, Lorna," Mrs. E said to the benignly serene vicar, who smiled, shook my hand and then affably counted heads as they filed past us into the church hall.

"That will be seven at twenty pence," he said. No sign of Mrs. E, so I broke into my soup-of-the-day-etceteras money. Almost immediately, Mrs. E materialised and introduced me to several of her close friends: large ladies in aprons who pressed cakes and jars of liquid jam on me, than charged me fifty pence for each item I'd accepted. On foolishly admiring a lady's apron, murmuring, "How pretty and useful – you can't get a decent apron for love nor money these days," I was coerced into buying two: a bib-fronted gingham and a waist one with aubergines appliquéd on the pockets.

"For cleaning the house. Matching oven gloves, Lorna?"

"Good stock of oven gloves, thank you, Mrs. E," but Mrs. E was moving away towards the underwear stall.

"Lorna, look at these –" she waved towards a pack of three pairs of extra-large Aertex knickers – "a bargain at two-pounds-fifty."

"They're too big," I said.

"Nonsense – take them for those water retention days. Your friend Pat said you blow up like a balloon each month." Thank you, Pat.

At that point, I cut and ran – left them crowding around the tombola where Esther was trying to win a bottle of Liebfraumilch.

At the bottom of my road, I met Mr. E on his way back from visiting the greengrocer's. He walked very slowly as he had to drag an old home-made trolley behind him, which kept tipping over as the rubber on the tyres had perished. He went to the grocer's twice a week to collect over-ripe vegetables and fruit for his rabbits. We talked about rabbits and his old dog Rusty that died years ago and I agreed that

"Yes, he was a lovely old dog," although I remembered mad angry eyes and a grey muzzle pulled back and up in a vicious snarl, a permanent trail of white saliva. If there hadn't been a high wire fence between us, he'd definitely have lunged for my throat.

"No evil in him, Lorna," Mr. E said gently, as we parted company at my gate. I did like my neighbours.

I'd taken on an extra job, one afternoon a week, delivering the *Hackney Echo*. This was as a direct result of an argument with my brother regarding 'High time Lorna brought in a decent wage, settled down to a proper job etc...'

He was, however, unimpressed. In fact, everyone I'd told was unimpressed except, surprisingly, Mr. E, who said, "The fresh air will do you good, Lorna, you're looking peaky. Too much time spent watching the world go by."

Every Tuesday, I sat at my kitchen table and folded the newspapers. They needed two creases to be narrow enough to go easily through the smallest letterbox, plus there were several batches of leaflets advertising toothpaste and the delights of Dalston Shopping Centre, which had also to be folded and put inside the newspaper. The *Echo* had issued me with a large orange bag which must be returned should I ever leave their service.

I met friend Helen in the street, looking very well and prosperous, clothes obviously from a proper shop, as opposed to my outfit which consisted of a twenty-five-year-old school shirt plus a gigantic pair of khaki shorts from before David went on his high-fibre diet. She looked pityingly at my loaded shoulder bag and said, "How much are you getting for this paper round?"

"One-pound-sixty a hundred."

"God, that's only one-point-six pence per copy. It was a penny a copy when I did a paper round, twenty years ago."

"Oh well," I shrugged (not easy with a bulging bag weighing several stone slipping off my shoulder).

"Anyway, nice to see you, Lorna, must run. Watch out for vicious dogs and muggers. The small ones are the worst."

Similar warnings from Pat, Betty from Londis, and Mrs. E, so was watching out for small muggers and vicious dogs. Unfortunately nobody warned me about neighbours, and on my first outing with paper sack, the Reverend Joseph asked me to sponsor a church elder at fifty pence per length of the local swimming baths now that I had a job. By 'elder', I ignorantly thought 'elderly'. Wrong. The 'elder' was a man in his early thirties, winner of a bronze medal freestyle in the last Commonwealth Games. He swam one hundred and four lengths.

Final words on my paper round came from brother David, who kept repeating, "Are you mad, are you completely mad?" Then stormed out into the garden and shouted at Julie, "Is she mad, is she completely mad?"

Julie did not know, but said, "For God's sake, calm down, David, before you have a heart attack. Gentle reasoning is what Lorna needs."

Did they think I was deaf? I was sitting in my back bedroom with my windows wide open. I yearned for a pea-shooter to sting the backs of their clean pink necks, shouting, "Yes, it's me, Lorna. I'm a flat owner and a grown-up. I won't be manipulated by you two conventional nine-to-fivers. Yah, boo, bugger off." Closes window and goes off to chortle and find more dried peas.

David and I hadn't been getting on. It had all started a couple of weeks earlier when I rang him up at work and asked him to buy a packet of Hoover bags. (Julie did the garden, front and back, David bought the shopping, and I hoovered the common parts and wiped down all wooden surfaces.) I had the make and number, I'd even noted down the approximate price.

"David, I think it's best to buy a couple of packets as we get through them at a rate of…"

He stopped me. "Hold it right there, Lorna."

"Sorry, do you want to get a pen and paper?"

"No. Do you want to get your own Hoover bags?"

"They're not *my* Hoover bags, David, they're house Hoover bags."

"Listen Lorna, I can't talk now, I'm due in a planning meeting. I'll come over this evening."

"I may be out," I said, but he'd already put down the phone.

Dead on eight o'clock, I heard David let himself in, tracked him into their front room, listened to the hum of voices as the television was turned down, then his footsteps into the kitchen. Water in the kettle.

I moved two dirty mugs from my desk to an empty shoe box under my bed and put the portable television onto the bulging dirty-washing basket to stop it exploding (the basket, not the television), just as his footsteps hit my uncarpeted staircase.

He kicked at my door. "Lorna, open up, I'm carrying a tray."

He'd made two mugs of tea and brought a packet of peppermint Viscounts. My stomach rumbled; were they for him alone, or us?

He sat on Pat's chair. (I called it Pat's chair because she was the only one who ever came up here.)

"So," he began, pushing a mug and a Viscount in my direction, "How goes it with the major opus?"

"Quite well. How goes it yourself?"

"Pretty good. We should start building on schedule. It's a nice site; inner city for a change. But the novel, going to be a money spinner, is it?"

"It's not a novel; it's an alternative cookbook."

"Alternative to what – hard work?"

I'd walked into that one. "Alternative to all those polished recipes you get in most cookery books. I thought I'd put Gran's rectangular fried eggs in."

"Very praiseworthy –" he didn't sound sincere – "but rather self-indulgent. I mean, do they pay you income support to write cookery books? I wasn't aware that they did. Of course I may be wrong." He popped the whole Viscount into his mouth.

"You're not wrong."

"And Green Bees? Still keeping the fertiliser flowing?"

"I've had no complaints."

"Tell me..." David pretended to be concentrating on unwrapping his next Viscount. "How do they pay you?"

"Cash in hand. I'm part of the green black economy," I said loftily. "Small firms like Green Bees have to start somewhere, they can't afford all the taxes..."

David was holding up his hand signalling for me to be patient, that as soon as he'd finished crunching and munching, he had more to say on the matter. He surprised me by using one of Mum's tactics and setting off on a different route.

"Julie and I really appreciate the way we can rely on you to keep the hall and stairs clean. As Julie says, 'First impressions count,' and you make a first-rate job of the brass door furniture."

"Thank you," I said. A little recognition goes a long way to smoothing ruffled feathers, and that door furniture was a bugger – we had so much of it. I called it the 'Julie Disorder', which was based on the presumption, 'Why have one item, when several alternatives are available?' We had a letterbox and a letter box, a door knocker and a purely decorative bell-pull, we had our numbers on the door and on the wall and we had a brass pineapple in the centre of the door itself, to facilitate pulling the door shut – or pushing it open if feeling particularly fragile.

"Only –" pause to check fingernails for traces of chocolate – "it's not necessary to polish the door furniture every other day. You're rubbing off the varnish, which means the brass then tarnishes that much quicker. You're making more work for yourself, when you might instead go out and buy Hoover bags. You are at home a good part of the week."

"I'm busy."

"Hoovering and polishing. You search out dust, you hoover for the sake of hoovering."

"That's your opinion."

"It's my Hoover. The constant noise sets Julie's teeth on edge when she's trying to work."

"She hasn't got any teeth."

"That isn't funny."

"Why must she work at home? She's started playing Jazz FM in the mornings. I can't concentrate on my writing."

"Lorna, she can do what she likes. It's our house also. Look, here's a recipe for your bloody cookbook: hard work, honest toil, regular hours, cook for at least a year and you have money in the bank and self-respect."

"Are 'hard work' and 'honest toil' a little like leek and celery – similar but not quite the same?"

"Very funny. If you're signing on and working at the same time, you should be ashamed of yourself."

The tea party degenerated into a slanging match – not that David put up with it for long, as his cholesterol levels had to be safeguarded. He soon went thumping back downstairs. I ate the remaining three Viscounts, and made perfect silver balls with the paper.

Jenny Salter and I sat for twenty-two minutes without speaking. On an earlier occasion we'd discussed the qualities of silence: that if I wished, I need not say a word; I should learn to accept silence, to feel at ease with it when shared. Jenny Salter looked at ease. The lines of her face had drooped a little, only her eyes remained bright and attentive. I felt sad and dull like a poor guest at a dinner party of whom much had been expected.

Finally I took from my pocket a square of folded paper and laid it between her saucer with its tea bag and her empty cup. On one side of the paper was an illustration of brown, orange and black upholstery, underneath scrawled, "Great Western Railway 1963." From the other side she read: "'I want to say this very moment, while you still care to listen, that any words I have, may only be written down.' Well, that's OK by me, Lorna, write away."

With difficulty, I said, "I can talk now."

A very little about my ex-friend Kate

In case you're thinking I'm a lonely misfit desperate for a relationship, the Bridget Jones of lesbian land, let me remind you that up until three years ago I was one half of an idyllic relationship with my ex-friend Kate.

Perhaps 'idyllic' is stretching a point – nothing could be truly 'idyllic' where Kate was concerned. Whatever, we shared a deep and, I thought, meaningful friendship that often, *correction*, from time to time, found us in bed together; not a day went past without meeting up or a telephone call; we were invited everywhere as a couple. Friends enviously said we had the best of both worlds, i.e. our freedom and an easy-going, affectionate relationship. Like Pat, and indeed like most women I was drawn to, Kate knew how to make me laugh; unlike Pat she was tall and reassuringly big boned (Pat was short and irresponsibly thin).

I hadn't thought about Kate for some time. One further message had been left on my answerphone saying, "If Poppy has a litter, do you want a pup? Clumber spaniels make adorable pets." I'd considered returning the call with a stiff response along the lines, "Only you could be so thoughtless as to imagine a clumber spaniel would thrive in an upstairs flat in Hackney." However, she was the sort who would have a laughing, smart reply. I'd be informed that clumber spaniels were ideal town dogs, voted Best Urban Mutt by the Kennel Club, and "Really Lorna, don't you know anything?"

It being a Wednesday and no Green Bees to go to, I had some free time on my hands. I made myself a cup of hot chocolate with lashings of Elmlea pretend cream. Write it down, Lorna! This is the sort of everyday refreshment that needs a mention.

<u>Lorna's Chocolate Supreme</u>

Full cream milk, Cadbury's drinking chocolate, cube white sugar, Elmlea pretend cream in aerosol, chocolate flake.

Boil milk in pan. Put one and a half teaspoons of drinking chocolate in mug, add little of the milk and stir vigorously. Add remainder. Spray Elmlea pretend cream to a height of two inches above rim of mug, scatter pulverised chocolate flake on cream and balance as many cubes of sugar as possible onto whole mixture. Approach with care.

One day I was going to confuse the Elmlea aerosol with my hair mousse aerosol; they were very similar, felt the same, cool and metallic. Would be an excellent trick to play on an enemy. *Julie, your curls would look... more bouncy... David, you know it adds volume to wispy hair...*

I carried the mug of chocolate into my bedroom which, as opposed to my work room, I kept scrupulously tidy. No point having a glamorous seductive bedroom if there was a week's worth of socks and knickers draped everywhere. The walls were a deep blue and I'd picked out bits of the ceiling rose and the cornices in gold leaf, carrying the gold theme into picture frames and scatter cushions on the bed. In front of the window there was a small cream (and gold) spindly table I'd bought from a second-hand shop in the High Street. On it was a vase of overblown silk peonies which I thought looked rather lovely and required only a good shake out of the window once a fortnight to retain their fresh beauty. On the bed, covering the duvet, was an embroidered throw, very expensive, from Covent Garden and purely decorative. At night I folded it over a coat hanger and hung it in the wardrobe.

Kate, who in another incarnation used to work in John Lewis's soft furnishing department, said it looked like a tart's boudoir. But what did she know, going out with agricultural students and land girls, bare boards and straw between their toes. Her own bedroom was a tip. I needed a piece of string tied to the door handle, the other end around my waist, to guarantee finding my way out again.

"Women don't usually want to find their way out again," said Kate.

Jenny Salter had instructed me to think through my anger, which apparently I had a lot of, and take time out to reflect, which I'd also been trying to do. Not necessarily that easy with an antagonistic brother and his wife...

And Kate bombarding me from deepest Yorkshire trying to palm me off with her and Tina's spaniel offspring as if that made everything all right between us, and it was nearly November again...

And talking of Pat (which I wasn't), having initially spotted Sandra while on holiday in Parga but never getting the chance to speak to her as she was inside a coach going in the opposite direction to Pat's coach, then bumping into her six months later in Hackney and starting to see Sandra every night of the week, sharing leek and parmesan risottos while telling me that both still treasured their own personal space...

And most definitely insisting that they were not even thinking of moving in together, although "Who knows where we'll be this time next year?" ...

And this *was* next year...

And they'd just finished stripping and polishing their first jointly owned lounge/dining-room floor.

Phew. This thinking through my anger was exhausting!

A faithful friend is the medicine of life

What can I say in defence of Mr. E's garden? You needed imagination and a certain amount of empathy to see behind the rusty blue shell of a Morris Minor, the untidy stacks of used tyres and the rabbit huts made of scrap iron to appreciate that here was a man who truly loved the great outdoors – which was fortunate, as Mrs. E would rather have him out than in. As children, we built stories around Mr. E and his projects. He was the man who dug to Australia, or that was how it seemed, in the year when his project was Operation Cesspit. Gran never got to the bottom of why he should begin to dig a cesspit, and then keep on and on digging as if his life depended on it – she knew the E Family had all the in-house Water Board facilities required. Then there was the Pipe Laying Project, when he dug up the kitchen floor and left it for an entire summer, so that Mrs. E had only an eighteen-inch-wide ledge of floor left around her kitchen perimeter – one false move and she fell down into a three-foot drop. Many of his projects were to do with digging or water. He began building an outside toilet on the site of the outside toilet he'd knocked down several years earlier, became disheartened and left it as a three-sided, roofless extension, which one day, when he had less to do, would be given a glass roof and called the conservatory. We loved Mr. E then – still did now, in a grown-up, no-nonsense kind of way. Even Gran, who kept herself to herself, had a soft spot where he was concerned and initially helped him, David and me to manhandle the Morris Minor around the side of the house – a favour that left Gran and Mrs. E not speaking for nearly two years. I regretted that Gran never met Alfred the Great who was indeed an admirable rabbit and good friend to Mr. E.

However, laying sentiment aside, David (as official part of David and Julie unit) was increasingly unhappy about Mr. E's garden, as seen from our side of the wire netting fence. We had all lived in perfect harmony for years and then David and Julie, as befitted a married couple (or so they said), started having drinks parties, or what Julie referred to as her 'evening/afternoon soirées'. I was usually invited, although at some point before the party got under way, David would take me aside and say, "Try and keep a low profile, Lorna, and steady on the drink," as if I was a badly behaved teenager, instead of exactly one year younger than him.

I almost enjoyed these do's, using my eyes and ears to pick up snippets of gossip, finding out what these people really thought of David. Was he as dynamic and hard working as he told me he was? Sadly, it seemed so.

The last summer, in particular, I'd noticed a change in the conversations: everyone was discussing house prices and locations, loft conversions, extensions, and garden makeovers. Most of these friends were from south of the river – Julie's home territory (she once told me she'd left her heart behind in Peckham Rye, which seemed an extraordinary place to leave something so important). Frankly, the south of the border friends weren't my sort at all, wouldn't have been Gran's sort, most definitely not Mr. E's sort.

"When's matey going to clear it?" man in ironed Gap jeans and T-shirt mouthed, while girlish partner in sleeveless frock squeezed his arm and trilled, "Shush, he'll hear you. I'm sure he's sitting in the car." Julie and David shrugged their 'God only knows what he's up to' shrugs.

"Mr. E has plans," I told the bloke later. He wore tortoiseshell spectacles and I gave him and his glasses a hard accusing stare. "Mr. E used to keep tortoises."

"Did he? What happened to them?"

"They ran away."

Man looked puzzled. Was I being funny or was I weird? Decided weird and edged away from me, tapping his half-empty glass by way of explanation.

What this lot with regular incomes didn't understand was that not everybody wanted it all perfect – THIS MINUTE – NOW! Mr. E, to name but one, saw the joy in long-term planning, dreams… pipe dreams, maybe. So what? One day, perhaps, those tyres would be painted bright primary colours and made into containers for his Tom Thumb tomatoes and Little Gem lettuce. Those grey rabbits with their mournful navy eyes had only been locked away because David and Julie had guests who were likely to stampede at the sight of something of middle size and furry scuttling about. Normally, the rabbits were out gambolling in their boy and girl pens, and very charming they looked.

And let's not forget Mr. E's fruit trees (apple, pear and cherry), the long green grass dotted with wild garlic ("For Christ's sake, David old man, whatever's that ghastly smell?"), renegade onions, self-seeded purple broccoli and towering spring greens. Mr. E could live all year outdoors, with a small camp fire and a billy can. He loved his garden, was at one with it, which was why so often it came as a shock when he moved out from the shadow of a tree where he'd been standing, quietly drinking in the beauty of a combination of nature and scrap metal. Not for one minute did he envy David and Julie and their distressed stonework.

Julie, Julie, Julie – high time I touched on Julie, can't live with her, can't live without her, as David says fondly.

This particular early afternoon at the end of November, she was out in the garden, cutting what was left of the oregano from one of a line of herbal urns she'd planted up on the decking. I was in my bedroom, which looked out over all the back gardens, and I was drawn to the window by the click-click of her heels on the mahogany-stained wood.

Julie was a very little like Jenny Salter in that she refused to acknowledge the colder seasons. Apart from this they were chalk and cheese. No way could Jenny Salter double as a golden eagle were she wearing pink pedal-pushers and a white satin blouse knotted at her waist. Jenny Salter's sandals were 'salt of the earth' style sandals; she'd never wear a thin high heel and ankle straps, never mind the frosted toenails. There were few who dressed like Julie around here, which David said was great – he liked a woman to look like a woman – and even Pat and my ex-friend Kate used to sometimes say, "Blimey," "Phew," and "Hasn't she heard of Damart?"

Once a month Julie had her hair dyed auburn. She tried to keep it straightish but it puffed into fluffy curls the moment she stepped out of the hairdressers. What else can I tell you? Aided and abetted by Estée Lauder, she had a doll-like complexion and rosebud lips which belied her will of iron and the fact that she was physically stronger than David and myself put together.

When the stone urns were delivered and left at the front door, she pushed David and me aside as we struggled to get a grip on one of them, saying, "Give it here, you two useless articles."

"She's incredibly strong, David," I said admiringly as she carried the last one through the house, ruining that day's eau de nil ensemble.

"She can lift me up," he said.

"Really?" – wondering what kind of an intimate relationship required a six-foot man to be carried around the house by a five-foot-two woman.

I watched her fondly as she walked among her plants, administering Julie's brand of 'tough tenderness', i.e. "If they don't do the job I've paid good money for them to do, then they're on their bikes via the dustbin." I was ready to lean out of my window and apologise for the way I'd been treating her door furniture for weeks. I'd known what I was doing – making my point because I wanted Gran's old-fashioned letterbox and number plate put back.

"They're original features," I'd appealed while she unscrewed them.

"As far as I'm concerned," she'd gritted through a mouthful of brass screws, "original features have been done to death."

*

Oregano, rosemary, thyme, lavender; whatever was she thinking of cooking? She meandered with a purpose towards Mr. E's six-foot-high wire netting fence. He'd put it up when we were still children. Gran brought out celebratory shandies and bowls of crisps and peanuts on her precious old Coronation tray, glasses and bowls arranged around the Queen's hair and crown like a halo.

"Doesn't seem right putting glasses of shandy on her face," Gran said. We could rarely bring ourselves to use the tray after that.

"You can't beat wire netting, Mrs. Tree." (Tree's the family name.) He rattled the fence from his side. Sensibly he'd left a gap for just such occasions of passing over glasses and bowls – and that gap had been used so many times since.

Julie had come to a full stop at the section of fence where a little woody nightshade was making its way determinedly through the diamond-shaped wire. She bent forward and sniffed it dubiously, then straightened up, stiffened her shoulders for battle, her heels sinking into what remained of the lawn (a much-reduced kidney shape cuddling the small circular pond).

Mr. E suddenly materialised like a wild animal flushed out of the brush, a second too late to make a successful dash for safety.

"Could I have a word, Mr. E?" she asked sweetly.

I may have painted Mr. E as a quiet passive child of nature but he's no fool, he can smell trouble a-coming from fifty yards. "Got to go, I'm afraid. That damn Alfred's gone indoors and he'll be up to his old tricks if I don't get in after him."

"You're all right. I can see him. He's gone behind the Morris Minor."

Even Julie knew better than to give Morris Minor anything less than its proper name, no 'eyesore, wreck, lump of scrap'.

Mr. E wasn't finished. "I hate him going in behind Morris Minor. He's so fat, it will take three of us to lift it off him if he gets stuck," and he took one and a half long strides away from Julie.

"Wait," she barked. Had to hand it to her, she was wasted in marketing. Julie should have been used against bank robbers and kidnappers: *"Drop that gun – now."* They would. Mr. E, one leg raised, waited as ordered.

"I wanted to tell you, just as a courtesy, that David and I are taking down this wire netting and replacing it with a lovely new wooden fence. The fence posts do fall on our side, you know."

"But the wire netting belongs to me," Mr. E said, lowering his foot into the long grass.

"Of course it does. And you're very welcome to keep it. I'm sure it's very useful. It's done a wonderful job for many, many years." She shook it almost lovingly, as if it were a dearly beloved relative when the sad moment had come to consign them to a nursing home. "But you'd surely much prefer a solid wood fence?"

Upstairs, I shook my head and tutted. Never ask Mr. E a question; he may not answer in your lifetime. He sighed and sunk his hands into the baggy pockets of his baggy corduroy trousers, sighed again.

"Thing is, Julie, wire netting lets in the air and the light. There's no light will get through your wooden fence and then again it requires maintenance and life's too short" – a long speech for Mr. E, said in his slow gentle voice. Not a wonder Gran got on with him. Hard to take offence with Mr. E, or even take a fence off Mr. E. Chuckle, chuckle.

"It will look better," Julie said defensively.

"Looks aren't everything."

Well done, Mr. E, round one goes to you. With dignity he walked away towards his house. "Come on, Alfredo," he called, and Alfred lumbered out from behind the Morris Minor where he'd been secretly listening and willing Mr. E success. Without a backward glance at Julie, they passed by the Nissen huts where the small grey rabbits were peeping curiously out: "What's all the noise about? Don't often see dejection registering on the lady wearing pink's pretty face."

Julie stood her lonely ground a moment more, in a pretence of searching for koi carp wintering underwater, then she turned quickly and looked straight up at my bedroom window as, too late, I made to duck out of sight.

"Lorna, could I have a word? Down here, please."

As I came into their kitchen, Julie was just dropping all the herbs she'd picked into the pedal bin. I sat down at their pine table and waited.

"Tea?" she asked, already pouring tea into the cup in front of me. "Lorna, I've ordered the fencing. It's arriving on Friday. What do I do about Mr. E?"

Rather pleasant to be consulted for once. I felt as if I might be one of Julie's work colleagues, subordinate of course. *"A sticky problem on the shop floor, little oik and his rabbit refusing to accept the march of progress. Should we sack him, shoot him, or kill the rabbit and stick it in the bed between him and Mrs. E? I'd value your opinion, Lorna. Could be a promotion in the offing."*

"You see, Julie," I began, "If you put your fence up, you won't only offend Mr. E, you'll offend the whole family. They have looked at us and we have looked at them for years and years. We've always had a kind of friendship. They'll think we're trying to block them out. They're good neighbours."

"I don't want good neighbours, I want tidy stylish neighbours!" But she laughed. "Oh bugger it, Lorna, I can't go year after year looking at Morris Minor and Alfred the Great."

"What about trellis? Mr. E mightn't mind trellis used in moderation. He could grow runner beans up his side. You could plant honeysuckle... Well, you'd know what to choose, you being the gardener," I said tactfully. "We could still all peek through if we wanted a word."

"It's so long term. I'll be an old woman by the time their garden is obliterated," she wailed.

"You'll be two years older. In your prime."

"I'll have to cancel and change the order."

"You're always cancelling and changing the order."

She leant her chin thoughtfully on the palm of her hand. "Will you speak to Mr. E? He likes you."

"He likes David more, but probably I am best at speaking to him. I don't know why, but even when I was a little girl I think I made him nervous."

"You have your ways, Lorna. You're no pushover." Quite a compliment coming from Julie. We sat opposite each other, drinking our tea in companionable silence. Julie was the first to break it.

"Sorry I complained to David about the Hoover," she said.

Do you know, I'd completely forgotten about the Hoover, I'd been so incensed over the door furniture.

"And *I'm* sorry I rubbed the varnish off the brass. I'll revarnish it at the weekend."

We'd never behaved in such a civilised fashion before.

"How's your friend Pat and her girlfriend?"

"Ecstatic. Last week Sandra cooked risotto for six but I wasn't invited."

"Bloody cheek. We're having fish and chips, more than enough for three, if you care to join us."

At seven, David came in to find us finishing a bottle of white wine, our cheeks rosy, going through Julie's gardening encyclopedia in search of climbers and original ways with trellis.

It was after midnight when I went back upstairs to my own flat. Felt cheerful. Felt as if I'd turned some corner, and yes, for the time being perhaps I have. Three calls on the answerphone, another ringing off; 'ringing off' being my most regular caller these days. Message from Pat: "Pat and Sandra request the presence of Lorna Tree for dinner. Telephone and we'll fix a date. There. Satisfied, you old bag?"

The return of the woman in beige

I want to take you back to the beginning of this year. Sorry to dot about but I keep remembering incidents I need to share, as J. Salter would put it, i.e. my next sighting of the woman in beige and how Pat and Sandra met again and they became a house-owning item. Why go over old ground, Lorna? My only excuse is that the human mind is not a reliable vessel – or is that the human heart? Whatever, when something important happens, it's generally as a repercussion or it has repercussions and the whole bloody lot links up like a huge daisy chain.

So, not a word from Pat over Christmas, not even a card. On the fifth day of the new year I heard David letting her in downstairs, "Happy New Year, David, you too, Julie! OK if I go up and see misery guts?" Up she thundered. Something cataclysmic had happened to her, I could tell by the exuberant noise her feet made on my uncarpeted stairs, catapulting onto my landing wearing an unfamiliar reversible fleece in black and red and a new short sharp haircut with her face 'wreathed', as they say, 'in smiles'.

"Happy New Year, Lorna," she said kissing me exuberantly on the cheek – another break with tradition. Pat and I pride ourselves on our emotional control, our cool air kisses. Secretly we both look forward to the return in popularity of the brusque handshake.

"New Year was last week," I said. "Come on into the sitting room."

"Sorry about missing the festive season." She followed me in, throwing her car keys and rucksack onto the settee. "I opted out this year, thought I'd pamper and hone the old bod for the New Year do at the pub." She smiled admiringly at her reflection in the mirror above the mantelpiece. I recognised all the signs: the profile and double-chin check, the sucking in of her cheeks to give herself interesting cheek-bones – she'd met someone.

"So, what's been going on?" I asked, aware that the addition of 'you old dog' would have mightily pleased her. I couldn't quite manage it.

"What hasn't been going on, more like." Then she remembered her manners. "First of all, how was your New Year? Any news from the errant Kate? Did David carry in the coal, same as usual?"

"Nothing from Kate. I could have been dead as far as my two best friends were concerned and David only ever carried in the coal on one occasion. As a matter of fact, they went to bed early, and I went in next door for Mrs. E's sing-song."

"She's a case, your Mrs. E. How's her piano-playing? Added any more to the repertoire or is it still 'The Bonny Scotsman' followed by 'The Bonny Scotsman'?" Pat flopped onto the settee next to her belongings. "However, to change the subject ever so slightly, I've met a woman. No, I've remet *the* woman. *She is the sunshine of my life...* I want the two of you to meet. I've told her all about you: my oldest living friend."

"Very amusing. I'm two months younger than you are."

"Joke, Lorna. Sense of humour gone AWOL? I've promised we'll meet her and some mutual friends – who you don't know – in the pub. It's her birthday. You don't mind, do you? We can talk any time."

My heart sank. I thought of my plate of yoghurt dips waiting on the draining board, the fan of chopped celery and carrot, the bottle of white wine chilling in the fridge... Instead it would be the whole evening spent in Pat's special pub, emphasising the fact that Lorna would be going home alone for another night curled up with Patricia Highsmith. I retired to the bathroom and ran cold water over my wrists to calm me down.

Outside it was freezing. Pat fumbled with the lock on the passenger side.

"I'll have to climb in via your seat, Lorna – someone hit my door while I was parked in Sainsbury's car park. *Parked*, mind you. I was actually sitting in the car. Would you believe the joker just reversed into my side and then drove off waving?"

I could believe it. She got in. I followed, adjusting the seat to fit my longer legs. She grinned. "You'll like Sandra. She's not like my usual – she's a high achiever."

"Is she? In what way?"

"You name it – she achieves it. Turns her hand to anything – car maintenance, plastering, cordon bleu cookery, softball, mountain biking – I wouldn't be surprised if she could give you some pointers on poetry. Sorry about the mess." She shifted maps, cigarette cartons, sweet papers and gloves from the dashboard and threw them all onto the back seat next to a bouquet of red roses and pink freesias plus large birthday card.

"Where did you meet this time?" I asked as we moved off.

"Usual New Year's do. You should have come."

"I wasn't invited."

"Point taken but let's not be bitter. Where was I? There was Maisie and Chris and all their friends. Now do I go left or right here? Yes, of course it's right."

"Left," I said.

"Anyway, there were two women I hadn't seen in the pub before, both nurses. I always end up with nurses, don't I? Must be something psychological. One was too tall for my taste – about your height – and I could see the other woman was a heavy drinker, you know how the eyes get, so I told myself, 'No Pat, you've been down that particular road too many times before.' Now, I want to turn right, but there's no right turn, I'll have to go on, turn in the garage, come back on myself and turn left."

"Right. And then what happened?" I prompted.

"In walks Sandra, as large as life – you remember, my lovely lady from Parga! I thought, 'Pat, this is your lovely day – this is the day you'll remember the day you're dying.' God, I love that aria. We ended up in bed together."

"Sandy – that's a nice name."
"Sandra. She's a very nice woman."

It was a popular pub on the outskirts of Hackney, packed every night of the week. I ordered a lemonade spritzer for myself, lager top for Pat.

"Crowded in here tonight," she observed from behind her bouquet. "Now where is everybody?"

'Everybody' was just behind where we stood.

"Happy birthday, darling." Pat, almost crying with emotion, grasped Sandra, who sat perched on a high stool, and crushed her to her fleece. "These are for you. Sniff that – roses and freesias, for the sweetest-smelling woman in the world."

Sandra smirked, and said romantically, "Better leave them in the car, mate, bit crowded in here."

"Open the card, open the card."

"That's great, Pat. 'Best Babe.' Am I really?"

"You are, Sandra. It's a collage. Took me over an hour to make."

Exit Pat with flowers and card. I pulled up a chair. "I'm Lorna," I volunteered.

"Angela, Debbie, me Sandra," Sandra said unsmilingly. I arranged my jacket across my knees and gave her a secret assessing glance. She looked efficient, and confident, and world weary, and a proficient plasterer. We lapsed into silence.

"Known Pat long?" I inquired of the table in general.

"Not long. Couple of years," replied Angela. "And you?"

"We went to school together," I said.

Back Pat bounced, carrying a stool, squeezing it in between Sandra and Debbie, then squeezing herself onto it with considerable suggestive giggling. I watched Sandra carefully to see how she responded to Pat in the sober light of several days later. Did she regret her hasty seduction? She didn't look the type to do anything hastily. Her hand moved from her own thigh and rested possessively on Pat's; she gave it a reassuring squeeze and Pat blossomed as only Pat can blossom. Snippets of her conversation drifted across the table; subject – Pat's watercolours.

"It's no easy business reproducing an autumn sky."

I hoped she hadn't brought her sketchbook showing the Canada geese at Kew Gardens under six different weather conditions. Angela looked at me from under her aggressive fringe.

"You'll have seen Pat's pictures?"

"Er, yes."

"They're fucking marvellous."

"Her Greek landscapes are rather good," I murmured.

"And what about the nudes, eh?"

"Yes, they're... very solid."

"Solid," Angela agreed, "they're bloody solid." She looked disbelievingly at Pat, shaking her head in wonderment.

"Another round?" said Debbie. We all nodded.

My eyes glazed, then focused. I rummaged in my rucksack for my long-sighted glasses. *Yes, Jenny Salter, I realise it's a sign of personal insecurity that I don't want people to know I depend on glasses.* On the other side of the horseshoe bar, it seemed I'd seen a rectangle of beige; something familiar about the jerky action of a hand and head. By the time I'd put my glasses on, the woman was walking away, carrying two wine glasses. I started to stand up.

"Don't get up, Lorna, I can manage," Debbie said.

"No, I..."

"There you are. Get your laughing gear round that." Pat pushed my spritzer across the table and I sank back in my seat.

Angela was talking to a rapt Pat and Sandra: "Do you know, I was going out with this woman for three and a half years. She wanted a baby, and I said, not fucking likely. So she left me, took every stick of furniture, cleared out our joint bank account. I was utterly destroyed." Her head zoomed in my direction. "Do you know what I mean?"

"Oh yes," I said, scenting an opening for me to discourse on utterly destroyed moments in my own life.

"Then this bloke got me drunk, said he didn't believe in lesbians and I didn't know what I was missing until I tried it. My one and only time – and nine months later, out pops Baby Tonia. I believe in happy endings, don't you, Lorna?"

I nodded my head vigorously and turned my attention to Debbie, who looked less than happy. She wore a rather striking jean-style suit in scarlet, the type I'd admired in Gran's catalogues when I was about eleven: models accessorised with a sun visor and navy deck-shoes, a blue and white yacht and Mediterranean sea in the background. Not the outfit for a cold January evening. At this point I'd better mention that Angela, the proud mother of Tonia, wore a similar suit, but in a denim denim. Had they perhaps shared the same catalogue at one time, or was this an incoming fashion I'd been unaware of?

"I must say your trouser suit's a nice cheery colour," I said.

Disaster. Debbie's eyes filled with tears. "Yes, it is a cheerful colour, isn't it? For Christ's sake, I need something to cheer me up. It was a year ago today that Myra left. I mean, Ange can talk about three-and-a-half-year relationships, but this was fourteen years. We'd been inseparable. Debbie and Myra – *that's who we were.*"

"I'm so sorry," I said. I was certain that somewhere behind Debbie's head, the woman in beige was playing a game of darts. If Debbie would only stop crying and talking, and duck down below the table.

"And if that wasn't bad enough, just as I was getting back on my feet, I met this woman called June. She was really nice. Said she'd help me to forget." She looked mistily into her empty glass. "It lasted six months, then she went off with the barmaid of the pub we were running."

"Pat," Angela cut loudly across our conversation, "I want you to do an oil painting of my little love. I'll pay you."

Pat beamed, chest expanding under her substantial fleece. "I don't advise an oil painting, Ange – kiddies won't sit still long enough. You want a watercolour or a charcoal sketch, doesn't she, Lorna? Lorna did a course in graphics at the tech," she said graciously, not waiting for my reply. She went straight into Greek reminiscences.

"Which reminds me of a woman who wanted me to sketch her child when I was in Lesbos, a couple of years ago – did I tell you, Sandra?"

Sandra nodded adoringly. When had that been? They'd only met each other once before, and gone straight to bed.

"Sandra, you are a fabulously erotic woman, and you put me very much in mind of this Greek mother who wanted me to do a watercolour of her kiddy the other year..."

"It was the best thing I ever did."

They all looked impressed. I took another gulp of my spritzer... Yes, it definitely was her! Yet again, time had stopped, the *kerpow* impression she'd made on me that first time I'd seen her on the train... astonishing that I'd let her slip from my thoughts. I must at least speak to her...

"Another drink, anybody?" I asked.

"I think this round's mine." Sandra strutted to the bar, admiring glances aimed at the creased back of her jacket.

"The dreadful thing was," continued Debbie, pulling deeply on her cigarette, "I had a nervous breakdown in the June, last June in fact; both June and Myra knew but they never came to see me." Her eyes filled up with tears again.

I finished my drink quickly. Back came Sandra with a tray of refills and received a kiss from Pat for being so clever. I shuddered. This was a Pat I didn't want to see – a Pat I felt I didn't know.

Debbie was clutching at my arm again. "Do you think if I wrote to both of them, I'd at least stand a chance of one of them replying? June did send me a Christmas card saying, 'love June'."

"There's no harm in trying."

"I could play the guitar by the time I was four," Angela said to nobody in particular. "I begged and begged my dad for a piano as well, but he bought me a squeeze-box instead."

"You could get good money for that now," Pat said, breaking suction contact with Sandra.

"I was a bit of a child prodigy. When I was eight I won a competition judged by a world-famous squeeze-box player."

I nodded my head agreeably, unable to immediately pinpoint any world-famous squeeze-box players. There was Jimmy Shand who'd played the accordion. Gran had a recording of his, 'Bluebell Polka', where he was referred to as Scotland's accordion wizard on the record sleeve.

"Then my fucking father, in his wisdom, made me play at my cousin's wedding – wanted me to get up and play there and then, no bloody rehearsal, them all shouting out for 'When a Man Loves a Woman'. I made a right mess of it. After that I thought, fuck that for a game of soldiers. I'm not playing any more."

Debbie opened her mouth to say something but I stood up quickly: "Another drink, anybody?"

Apart from Debbie, they'd been drinking halves of lager. Sandra had been alcohol-free. "I'll have a Remy Martin," she said now.

"A Bacardi and Coke, no ice," said Debbie.

"Make ours pints." Angela held up her and Pat's glasses.

"What lager do you want?" the barmaid asked sullenly.

"I don't care," I said. "I'll be back."

Nobody at the dartboard. I walked the length and breadth of the pub, took a look outside in the garden, went back into the pub and finally down into the basement where the pool tables were kept. There she was: beige jeans, beige shirt, sleeves rolled up to the elbows. I felt sick with love and lust, which was so unlike my usual state as to make me feel strangely dizzy. She faced me from the other side of the table, her cue poised to pot the black. I didn't move, I said nothing, stood there, my heart drumming... Her eyes flicked upwards and met mine.

"Come on, Dan," someone said. Dan. Now I knew her name.

"Lorna, what are you doing down here?" Pat nudged my elbow. "The drinks are getting warm."

Dan potted the black, neatly and smoothly. She chalked the tip of her cue, looked at us, said, "If you're not waiting to play, do you mind not hanging about down here?"

"Fair enough," said Pat. "Come on, Lorna, you're missing out on one of Angela's stories."

She led me away like a prisoner. "Here she is, I found her loitering around the pool table."

Angela was now seriously into crystals. "And I mean 'seriously', as in 'seriously'," she said as she poured the remains of her original glass into the full one.

"I've got a crystal – and a rose quartz for harmony," I interjected desperately, "and I keep a kunzite in the bathroom to stimulate my inadequate self-love." But all eyes were on Angela, who ignored me.

"Real crystals. Crystal balls. Telling the future." She looked intently around the table. "Put a personal possession in my hand for an hour and a half and suddenly I'm babbling out all this stuff. And do you know –" we shook our heads – "it's all true! Now isn't that weird?"

"You should do that for a living," Sandra said. "You might get on television."

"No thanks, it's too weird. Frightened the hell out of me. In the end I thought, fuck it, I'm not doing this any more. The spirit world is a really dangerous place to go."

Debbie stood up abruptly, banging against the table and spilling our drinks.

"Sorry folks," she said. "I'll have to love and leave you. Touch of the PMTs coming on."

"She's such a nice woman. Been so fucking unlucky," Angela said.

We all nodded and stared at our drinks, observing a moment's silence. Sandra even stopped massaging Pat's leg.

I saw Dan coming up from the pool room, putting on a leather jacket; she was on her own. She was going to pass our table. My heart, as I think they say, was in my mouth – also, I'm certain, in my eyes. She walked past and then, suddenly, a tanned hand reached across from behind me and picked up my spritzer. I looked up. We all looked up. Dan had a mouthful, grinned, and said as she put it back on the table, "That's a foul drink, Lorna. See you around."

"Well, cheeky so-and-so," said Pat, "I can't stand that type, can you, Sandra? They think they own the pub. Now that was very interesting, Ange, about the crystals. Wasn't it, Lorna?"

I hadn't seen Dan, my woman in beige, since that night, but then I hadn't been out much. Pat, my usual accomplice, had Sandra and house-buying on her mind. Do I sound bitter? At the time, Pat said I sounded bitter – "Not like you to be unkind about me finding a little happiness" – which made me feel guilty. Oddly enough, I didn't mention Dan. I didn't mind Pat thinking I was keen on the TSPs of this world – and I was keen in a mild, not-a-matter-of-life-or-death way – but something serious was another matter. That kind of feeling was fragile, precious – very different from what I shared even with Kate.

The positive news was, since Jenny Salter arrived on the scene, I was able to see myself in a different light. Good old Jenny Salter, maybe she was a charlatan, but she was my kind of charlatan.

She said, "No Lorna, this isn't bitterness you're expressing. Reflect, this is historical hurt. You are in mourning. Your closest friend Pat, Kate your ex – they represent 'family'. They have rejected you, as did your parents all those years ago. This Dan person [Jenny was the one and only person I'd trusted to tell], whether you see her or not in the future, perhaps she represents hope."

To give Pat her due, when I repeated part of Jenny's fresh take on my life, she looked a little thoughtful, eventually saying, "Actually, yes. She's probably right. Poor old you."

Life moves on

The *Hackney Echo* was taking advantage of my passive good nature. That was what all of us keepers of the flame, carriers of the orange shoulder bag, must be – passive. The odd thing was, I felt as if I was the only *Echo* employee – had never crossed paths with another, apart from the suavely sophisticated, previously mentioned Helen. Did they employ just one of us at a time and push the poor devil to breaking point? They'd discover that we Trees were a sturdy bunch. We rarely broke, were capable of a good deal of bending before flying back into the faces of our enemies. I was nearing 'flying back' stage, had even tried telephoning head office to voice my complaints, but no answer, no answerphone. How did they get their news? What would happen if I had an important scoop to impart? "Hold front page. *Echo* employee – witness to gangland murder."

Perhaps if I showed loyalty for another three months, I'd be issued with a secret telephone number, direct line to the news desk; man in green visor and overflowing ashtray. For the moment I was isolated in more ways than one. David and Julie had left me in charge of monitoring their central heating thermostat and were taking a 'winter break', as opposed to their other seasonal breaks, bank holiday breaks, *bon anniversaire* breaks, therapeutic breaks, and 'relocating each other's centres' breaks. These last followed arguments – or 'differences of opinion' as David called them when he came up to my flat to apologise for the shouting the night before.

Plus, and added to that, Pat had gone off 'food shopping' with Sandy several days ago and hadn't been heard of since. Which brings me back by circuitous route to my original complaint about the *Echo*.

"For Pete's sake, change the record, Lorna." That's what George would

say. Who is Pete? Why should I change the record for the sake of a man I don't even know?

... The *Echo*, in their wisdom, had last week added six different leaflets to be included inside the newspaper, also a new 'invisible' sanitary towel, wrapped in blue tissue. It wasn't invisible, it was a solid rectangle adding the weight of two king-size duvets to my already heavy load. My round had to be split into three: Tuesday afternoon and evening, plus Wednesday morning, thus eating into my 'long poem' working time.

On my explaining to the Reverend Joseph why I was out delivering newspapers at ten o'clock at night, he suggested I form my own one-person neighbourhood watch.

Initially I thought he was joking. "You are joking, Reverend Joseph?" I said.

He gathered his vestment – paint-spattered cardigan worn every day except Sunday – around his bony shoulders and said, "No Lorna, I'm absolutely serious. You'd be putting something back into the community."

"I haven't taken anything out of it yet," I said tartly, which only confirmed his and David's opinion that I was capable of being a nasty piece of work.

And now, today, of the following week, I'd taken delivery of a) my four usual bundles of newspapers, b) a stack of brightly coloured broadsheets proclaiming, "This Saturday, meet Barbara Windsor in person, at Sainsbury's," and c) two large cardboard boxes containing two hundred of each of Timotei shampoo and Timotei conditioner. I rang Helen.

"Helen, did you have to deliver freebies when you delivered the *Hackney Echo*?"

"Who is that?" Helen asked.

"Lorna. Lorna Tree. Who does it sound like?"

"Could have been a number of people. You and I haven't spoken in two months. Life moves on. Voices get deleted from memory banks.

Vis-à-vis freebies – deliver only one of anything to houses of multiple occupation, which should take care of most of your route. Keep the rest. I had enough Nescafé to last a year."

"I thought coffee gave you headaches."

"It does – now. Too much, too soon." She sniggered in the 'I'm very well catered for, thank you' manner that Helen had, giving me an inkling she might not be alone.

"Another Nescafé, darling?" Helen opens minimalist Ikea kitchen cupboard and out tumbles a hundredweight of coffee sachets. I had a sudden vivid image of Jenny Salter that required my immediate attention, so said, "Good on you, Helen," in my best Australian accent, which might just leave Helen pondering, *"What was that all about? There's more to Lorna Tree than meets the eye."*

Every single week, on a Tuesday, the sun shone brilliantly until I stepped out onto the pavement. The winter winds were blowing, even though it was only the beginning of November; however, must persevere – no gain without pain, as Pat liked to tell me when she jogged back from her bi-weekly workouts at Sunstone Gym.

Strange occurrences: while out on paper round, I was stopped for the second week running by the same middle-aged man on a bicycle, asking for a copy. This time I wasn't quite so quick to hand one over, especially when he added, hand outstretched, "I hear the *Echo* are giving away free sachets of Timotei." Word had got around. Why had word got around? Not as if the *Echo* were giving out drugs, or a new car, or a Marks & Spencer voucher. He looked a little shifty, unable to meet my clear steady gaze. "Of course, it's only a rumour," he said with a dry nervous cough.

Although I would have hated to be mugged for a sack of shampoo, I stood my ground, determined to defend my proprietor's property. "I'm afraid I could get into serious trouble handing out free gifts willy-nilly; they're strictly customers only."

"I'm a customer," he said.

"Customers in houses, with letterboxes."

"I've got a letterbox."

"In this area?"

"In Dalston."

"You'll have to apply to that branch, I'm afraid. More than my job's worth. I took a risk letting you have a paper last week." I warmed to my role as courageous lone woman – the final frontier between established letterbox owners and chaos.

"Fair enough," he said meekly (which was rather disappointing) and cycled off. Thoughtfully I recommenced my deliveries. Could he have been sent on behalf of the *Echo*, to spy on me, making sure I was adhering to company policy? And if so, did he earn more or less money than I did? Probably more, plus unlimited mileage on official bicycle.

It was hard work. Kept you fit. Down the steps into each basement, up steps to main front door; deliver to all houses, except those bearing notices saying, "We don't want the *Echo*." With relief I turned into Neville Road where most of the doors were at street level – a clear run up to Milton Grove, where the flights of steps began again.

It was early afternoon now and the roads between the High Street and Albion Road were quiet. The kids hadn't spilled out of school yet and the weather was too bad for men to lie under cars and tamper with their engines. I virtually had the road to myself. It was like a stage set in its stillness. I was used to the subdued sounds: distant music, police alarms, the clang and clatter of scaffolding being taken down or erected a street away, bark of a dog, cry of a child – every noise slightly muffled as it should be at this time on an early winter's afternoon – nothing much stirring.

It started to rain. I put up my hood which, quite apart from impairing my side vision, was unflattering. My waterproof was long, black and all-encompassing – with the hood up, I resembled Darth Vader, although the muddy white trainers struck a reassuring note.

I plodded stoically onwards through a glittering mist of rain;

behind me I heard that particular sound of car tyres on a wet road, the car slowing down but not stopping. An ominous sound. Not a soul, not another movement in the road, just me and the lone car.

"This is it," I thought. "Man on bike tips off kidnappers in car about woman on foot carrying pharmaceutical swag in bag."

The car, a navy Mercedes, nosed past me. Long sloping bonnet, raindrops ricocheting off the gleaming paintwork. I couldn't see the driver. On the passenger side, the window was rolled right the way down; I saw a profile, heard a muttered, "Pull up here."

I pulled my hood further forward. About fifteen yards ahead of me the car stopped – motor still running, a tall woman wearing a beige raincoat got quickly out, her collar turned up to hide the lower half of her face. She opened the back door of the car and slid a large pet-carrier off the seat; hurried up the steps of a smartish house, pebbledash recently painted a warm peach colour. (These decor details I noted down later for my own *aide-mémoire* and the benefit of Julie.) The front door opened before the woman had even reached the top step; a hand reached out and took the pet-carrier, another hand held out a long white envelope. Woman in raincoat took envelope, front door shut and woman in raincoat ran back down steps, stuffing envelope into inside pocket. I stepped forward out of the rain.

"Would you like a copy of the *Echo*?" I said brightly. "This week we're giving away free sachets of shampoo and conditioner..."

"Get lost." She tried to push past me.

"Don't push me. Have a little respect."

"Why?" she asked.

"Because I'm a woman doing an arduous job for very little money."

She laughed, quietly but with great good humour. "More fool you," she said. She tilted her head to one side, a slight frown playing across her forehead – she knew me, but for the moment couldn't place me.

Still couldn't see the driver, even when she leant across and pushed open the passenger door: "Come on, Dan, it's getting late." Woman's voice – was it familiar?

In Dan got. The car moved off at speed. I swear Dan looked back at me. Once the car turned the corner into Milton Grove, I made a note of the number on the back of my hand.

I felt inclined to whoop, a little drunk, a little traumatised, I felt as if I'd touched her skin, or she'd touched mine – contact had been made – again. For less than two pins, I'd have ditched my bag and gone home to mull over this third, strange, momentous sighting.

Gran's voice came from far away, from a tiny Gran figure leaning out of a window at the top of a very tall building: "Lorna, hold steady. You've always wanted to be in surveillance – here's your chance – an adventure – a mystery with you in mind. In your shoes I'd have leapt at it." I looked down at my trainers. I would leap at it. For Gran, just supposing (and apologies for sentimentality) she was watching, I jumped into a small puddle. It was initially satisfying, then I felt the first trickle of water soaking my socks.

I carried on with my round, making a mental note of the relevant house number. I'd be back the following week, when once again I'd become an invisible delivery person. I'd peep through that letterbox before shoving in the newspaper – see what was what in the way of small animals. For all I knew, it could be a monkey, a raccoon, a snake, or a koala bear – but would not be a polar bear, horse or elephant. Or camel, or rhino, I thought; then, just how small are camel and rhino babies? In a silly, over-excitable mood.

"You're soaked," Julie said unnecessarily. "Come into our kitchen and dry off."

Nothing better than drying off in Julie and David's kitchen. There was guaranteed warmth. They had the Aga on most of the time, a supply of warm fluffy towels in pink, white or citrus, and Gran's rocking chair, which neither of them would use because they thought it made them look elderly.

"That is very ageist," I would say.

"We don't care," they would reply. Sometimes they bore some

worrying resemblances to George and Della, but I tried to keep them on the straight and narrow.

"Have you finished for the day?"

"I'll do the rest tomorrow." I took off my trainers and warmed my damp feet against the scarlet Aga.

"Julie," I said, when she'd handed me a scalding hot cup of tea laced with medicinal whisky, "what would you think, if you saw a woman on a train carrying a friend's dead dog home to bury, and then saw the same woman some months later, delivering something in another pet-carrier to a nearby house?"

"I'd assume she was a vet."

"Hmmm." That would be a very mundane and disappointing reason. "Do vets drive around in new Mercedes?"

"Celebrity vets might. You'll have to shift in a minute, I've got to get the boeuf bourguignon started."

"I thought we weren't eating beef," I said plaintively.

"You aren't. We are. David and I decided unanimously to support British beef."

"You wouldn't like to reconsider? I have some tofu, upstairs."

"No thank you."

She added more whisky to my cup; the contents were now whisky laced with medicinal tea. Julie wasn't my type but, objectively, she was a joy to watch: the way that, while making important 'lifestyle statements', she had still managed to created a colourful, congenial home. She could be snobbish with her Aga and her Heals this and Heals that, and one perfect orchid positioned on the bathroom windowsill amongst all her expensive beauty products; but the nips of whisky and their equivalent redeemed her, hinted at her... intrinsic... warmth. Yes.

I left her pouring good red wine into a green enamelled cookpot. Wouldn't ask her for her boeuf bourguignon recipe. Definitely not alternative enough for my alternative alternative cookbook.

Three messages on my answerphone – Lorna was a popular woman! First it was Helen asking if I'd got any Timotei Shampoo and

Conditioner left as she could shift a couple of dozen. Then it was Kate to say she and Tina were opening a bed and breakfast operation to supplement their incomes from the kennels – spread the word! Finally it was George asking whether I'd died.

Examining the contents of my fridge, and finding it wanting, reminded me of our childhood fry-ups and Gran's special frying pan. I never saw another one quite like it: rectangular, divided into two small squares, and a double-width rectangle in which two steaklets sat comfortably, shoulder to shoulder. (Steaklets were an early form of beefburger, before someone decreed that circular was the optimum shape.)

The real joy came with the eggs, when the whites hardened into perfect squares. Pat turned up, particularly at tea time during our teens, just to witness the wonder of square fried eggs.

I did most of the cooking, while David slept in the armchair in front of the gas fire. He was a lethargic boy, said school wore him out, he couldn't cope with such long hours.

Our gran worked till she was seventy-five – she lied about her age, took ten years off – she was such a good secretary that the accountancy firm she worked for chose to believe her. I don't think they'd do that now, when there's such emphasis on looks and dynamism. Gran was never dynamic, she was efficient – looked older than her age because, as she told us often, she'd had a hard life – but she was the fastest shorthand typist they'd ever had. She revelled in her work, took to audio-typing, electric typewriters... would have conquered word processors, no problem. Sorry to go on about Gran, but the more I think of her, the more proud I am of her achievements. I never gave Gran or her achievements a thought when she was alive. I wonder if David thinks the same way?

At home, she hated cleaning and cooking, and did the minimum. Mrs. E came in twice a week and dealt with the kitchen, bathroom and washing; I did the hoovering even then, David the dusting. The neighbours liked Gran, but she maintained a reserve with them, although she could soften in an emergency. We knew without thought that, unlike Mum and Dad, she put us first.

David and I were old-fashioned children, children of habit, compulsive about who did what, what went where; weekdays with our steaklets and eggs with tinned tomatoes, or tinned ravioli, or Heinz spaghetti, or Crosse and Blackwell baked beans. The tea table must be laid just so. Whatever the meal, the gnome and pixie condiment set stood in front of the taller mustard, ketchup and HP sauce bottles – how else would they be able to see what was going on? They were only little. At the weekends, if visitors came, I made sandwiches from tinned pink salmon mixed with Heinz salad cream, garnished the plate with vandyked tomatoes, put white paper doilies on a cake stand, and cut thin slices of Battenburg cake and thick slices of chocolate Swiss roll. Then David must wash up immediately so he could reclaim the armchair and his comics; I must read for half an hour before picking up a tea towel.

He said, "The fat congeals on the plate if I don't wash up straight away. My fingers will feel greasy all evening." He kept a jar of Pond's moisturising cream, which Gran bought especially for him, at the back of the draining board. He still moisturises his hands; says it would make him feel lopsided all day if he didn't.

I said, "The plates and pans need time to drain, otherwise the tea towel gets soaked and smells of stagnant water." I still sniff tea towels – my own and other people's – and if I find a pungent tea towel, I'll make a mental note to buy a fresh cheerful new one. I am known for visiting with a bottle of wine, box of After Eight mints, and an Irish linen tea towel.

Lorna Tree's Childhood Tea (for two)

1 packet of Bird's Eye Steaklets, 4 eggs, 1 large tin plum tomatoes or similar, quarter pound of lard, 4 slices of stale Vitbe or Hovis bread, Gran's rectangular frying pan.

1. Open tin of tomatoes with rusty can opener and tip contents into milk saucepan (as opposed to dog-food saucepan which, although same shape and size, always had a ring of congealed fat stuck two-thirds of the way up on the inside).
2. Put large blob of lard into each egg compartment of Gran's frying pan, 2 blobs of lard in wider section.
3. Drop in half of the ingredients, i.e. 2 steaklets and 2 eggs, and cook rapidly till all food is either dark brown or speckled dark brown. Serve on buttered toast. Repeat.

Gentlemen present

Some months ago I had joined a poetry workshop, one evening a week. It was a mixed class and I was surprised to find myself enjoying it. They all seemed quite amenable to listening to large chunks of 'Faith, Hope and Tragedy'. The tutor, a kindly man in good-quality patterned pullover, had said after my last rendition, "It's rather finely done – quite atmospheric – only, try not to over-egg the pudding"; an insightful remark as 'over-egging puddings' is a phrase often applied to yours truly.

So far, my only serious irritation was a Dane called Ragnar: very large and unfamiliar with soap, hot water and deodorant. Every week he sat at the front of the class rocking back and forth in his seat, rustling and chomping on a giant bar of Toblerone balanced on his lap – open end protruding in an obscene, suggestive manner. As the evening progressed the Toblerone grew smaller and smaller with his realisation that the tutor, once again, wasn't going to let him read his reworking of 'The Bent Copper', which was written in a mystifying broken English, yet with a strange dated resonance to *Dixon of Dock Green*.

Every now and then, he would shout to the class at large, "You English don't know what your coppers get up to," and the tutor would gently reply, "Oh, I think we do, Ragnar."

I was savouring disliking Ragnar. He was a joy. Might he never leave. At the end of last week's session, he had come out with a three-minute rant along the lines of, "You English, don't you see, your English poetry is a heap of shit?" Donald, another decent chap with leather elbow patches, had said, "Steady on Ragnar, ladies present."

What with the weather being so wet and stormy, on some evenings as we walked en masse down to our favourite pub on Drury

Lane, I felt as if we were actors in an old black and white Second World War film. Kindly tutor could be Jack Hawkins in windswept duffel coat and captain's cap, teeth clenched on a venerable briar pipe; the rest of us filling up the ranks – although for myself, I rather favoured chirpy Cockney Gunner Tree, "Look out, skipper, submarine rising to starboard."

Any women not wishing to be in the crew, I'd cast as either anxious-faced Wrens or stalwart Gracie Field types wearing knotted headscarves and belted raincoats warbling, "Sing as we go," as they pushed old prams through war-torn London.

In the pub, I gazed dreamily into the regular flames of the artificial log fire. An intrusive unpleasant aroma in the human shape of Ragnar sidled up to me.

"So Lorna," he breathed, "did you know that I was named after Ragnar Lothbrok, or 'leather breeches', whose death in Northumbria in 865 triggered off the main Viking attack on this island heap of shit?"

Took a leaf out of tutor's book and replied gently, "Actually Ragnar, I don't think I did."

So many men around: my jolly evening-class blokes being hearty and pleasant – the tutor, Donald, Ken, Michael... old-fashioned words like 'kindly', and 'gently' kept cropping up. I added my brother David (although brothers hardly count), and Mr. E and Reverend Joseph, Duxford Road's residential spirit guides – Reverend Joseph in his old cardigan casting a protective eye front of house, while Mr. E was out back reminding me of life's simple treasures under the bleary-red eyes of friend Alfred. And of course, my father George, who, although rarely seen in the neighbourhood, seemed to float like a small grey cloud, never allowing me to feel quite free to dispense with an umbrella. All of them prompted a mixed memory of childhood...

"Poor wee bairns," Mrs. Turner from Turner's Corner Caff, Stamford Hill, called us. She wasn't Scottish, only a great fan of Janet, the housekeeper in *Doctor Finlay's Casebook*.

"Aye, the poor wee bairns," Gran agreed. She wasn't Scottish either but liked the sound of the phrase – also admiring Molly Weir, the middle-aged Scottish actress who did the Flash floor and wipe-clean surfaces advert.

"Would you be from north of the border, Mrs. Tree?" Mrs. Turner asked.

"Och weel, we Trees spring up everywhere. I'll settle up at the end of each fortnight. Is that all right by you?"

"It is, Mrs. Tree."

"Stand no nonsense."

"I've never stood for any nonsense."

We loitered behind Gran, eyeing the tiered wooden rows of sweets greedily.

Everyone knew that Mrs. Turner stood no nonsense – she was very tall with very black hair, very black eyebrows and a lipless mouth. Her looks were admirable rather than unattractive. She'd have looked impressive on a warlike steed, wearing a suit of armour and a plumed helmet; instead she wore a spotless overall and ruled over the caff and confectionery-cum-bakery-cum-tobacconist with a firm but fair hand. Only two children at a time allowed near the sweets, school bags to be left outside, adults took precedence, no raised voices or out you go.

I peered past her and Gran into the gloom at the back of the caff. It was late afternoon, near closing time, and there was only Ron the station master sitting over a cup of tea and a full ashtray. The other tables were laid up for the following morning: gingham oil-cloth tablecloths, white plastic menus wedged between the sauce bottles.

"Thank you, Mrs. Turner, that's a weight off my mind. They're getting to an age when they can do damage indoors. Having their lunches here breaks up their day and expends energy. I'll take twenty Consulate while I'm here and a box of matches. Say thank you to Mrs. Turner, you two."

"Thank you, Mrs. Turner," David mumbled, his head down.

I'd intended to ingratiate myself with Mrs. Turner. I would be the only one of my school friends she would smile for. I would be enchanting. When Gran came in to settle up, Mrs. Turner would say, wiping a tear from the corner of her eye with the end of her tea towel, "That's a dear little girl you have there, Mrs. Tree. I shall be quite forlorn when the angel goes back to school." I'd recently read *Pollyanna*, the bit where she strung glass beads around the home of a miserable old biddy and filled the place with rainbow prisms. Instead of biddy saying crossly, "Bloody dust traps, if one of these beads hits me in the eye, you're for it, Pollyanna," biddy instantly became younger and prettier and married her first real love, while Pollyanna secured a place for herself in both their hearts.

"Go on, Lorna," Gran was saying.

"Thank you so much, Mrs. Turner," I said in a high, sing-song, southern belle voice.

Mrs. Turner blinked, David sniggered and Gran lifted her eyes and eyebrows ceilingwards and said with a heartfelt sigh, "Bye-bye, Mrs. Turner."

David and I dawdled along behind Gran as far as Dewhurst's the butcher, where she stopped and turned. She bent down and tightened my woollen scarf roughly around my neck.

"Lorna, you don't amuse me in the slightest. You may think you're funny, putting on silly voices, but that won't endear you to Mrs. Turner or her customers – people don't like show-offs."

More sniggering from David.

"Nor do they like little boys who slouch and can't look them in the eye. Take your hands out of your pockets, for the ninety-ninth time."

"But Mrs. Turner's a giantess. My neck aches having to look up as far as her eyes," David said.

"She is not a giantess – she's taller than average. We don't make personal remarks. What's happened to your manners?"

(Gran was always wanting to know what had happened to our manners. We could spend an enjoyable hour amusing ourselves with possible explanations: "They've gone for a lie down", "They're in the toilet", "They've hurt their leg".)

"Don't know, Gran."

"Well, you'd better locate them, PDQ. Manners maketh man, remember?"

"What about Lorna?"

Gran tapped her rolled newspaper against the back of David's head.

The caff was a 'working men's caff', another phrase dear to Mrs. Turner and Gran. Gran's dad had been a 'working man', as had her husband, Tom, who'd died when we were babies.

"Tom worked. By God, that man knew how to work."

Gran had had another son, Steven, who'd been a 'grafter', as opposed to a 'working man', which was still pretty good but meant he'd had an office job. 'Graft' in Gran's lexicon meant working hard. 'Working men' worked hard at hard work – even better. Very different to our own dear father, George, who'd been known to produce herons and swans made of ice for his brigadier's birthday. Gran said, "Your father doesn't know the meaning of hard work."

What happened to Steven? She said he'd drowned trying to save a family of kittens from a swollen river, although in Dad's version, Steven died trying to *drown* a family of kittens in a swollen river.

As far as we were concerned, those first few lunch times were purgatory. David and I with our 'old heads' were painfully shy, taken out of our usual safe environment of home and school. We walked through a sea of dark and dusty flat caps, the air heavy with the mingled smell of cooking fat and coal dust. Behind the deep rumble of men's voices was the background clattering of cutlery and chair legs scraping on the stone floor. We made for the only vacant table laid for two. Eventually this became our table – Lorna and David's, Mrs. Tree's grandchildren's – the special table, the one under the yellowing film poster of *Breakfast at Tiffany's* showing Audrey Hepburn with a cute ginger cat on her shoulder and long, long cigarette-holder.

Nobody spoke to us. Nobody looked at us. We reached the table, sat down facing each other and read and reread the menu.

"What will you have, then?" Mrs. Turner asked after giving us ten minutes. She was thin but with big bones which made her look even taller. Gran called her a 'workhorse', which was a compliment. She liked women to be workhorses but thought I was 'work-shy like my father' – which, in retrospect, I prefer. David, for all his rebellious mutterings as a boy, would now certainly get the accolade of 'grafter'. I can't imagine what Gran would make of Julie – probably 'a little madam who gets too much of her own way'.

"What will you have, then?" Mrs. Turner was saying.

"Egg, chip and pea, for two," David said, and the room rocked with a huge gust of laughter.

"One egg or two?" she continued, straight faced.

"Two please."

"And to follow?" – which I see now was quite an upmarket way of asking us what we wanted for pudding. Almost, "Would Madame prefer the cheese board to the sweet trolley – I can heartily recommend the Stilton..."

"Vanilla ice cream, please."

"Drink?"

"Coca-Cola."

Every single day, every school holiday for the next two years, we ordered the exact same lunch. It was another ritual to keep us safe and give us confidence. After the first week, we started spooning our ice cream into the Coca-Cola. Mrs. Turner said nothing, just changed our thin paper straws to chunky candy-striped plastic ones.

We got to know our fellow diners and they got to know us. There were the men who checked the railway lines in their donkey jackets with warning Day-Glo stripes front and back; binmen in leather waistcoats, with leather gauntlets tucked into the pockets of their trousers; but mostly we got on best with the coalmen who parked their lorries down by the railway station. Their skin and clothes were engrained with dust from the coal and coke they collected out of the huge wooden pens running alongside the railway track and shovelled into rough sacks made of gunny cloth. They had the best tempers and when they smiled, their teeth showed up white against their grey skin.

"What ho, David. What ho, Lorna," they'd say gruffly, looking over their newspapers at us.

"What ho," we'd return. We'd even started saying, "What ho, Gran," and she'd said, "Never ever say that in front of your mother and father."

It was like being part of a family where everyone liked us and found us incredibly amusing. Even Mrs. Turner, who never gave a smile or a softened word – we knew she liked us as well. Sometimes, not every day, as she cleared away our plates, she'd lay a Kit Kat or a bar of Aero between us.

"Thank you, Mrs. Turner," and Mrs. Turner would jerk an acknowledging nod.

"Why doesn't Mrs. Turner ever smile?" David asked Gran.

"Nothing much to smile about," Gran said, adding after some consideration, "And possibly the men would try to take advantage."

"Why?"

"It's what men do."

"Even Grandad Tom?"

"You've got big eyes and ears for such a small boy," she said, which David didn't like at all.

*

So all went well for us. It was the longest period Dad and Mum had ever stayed away. We relaxed... then suddenly, with just a telephone call to Gran, they came back.

Our parents were glamorous in the way film stars were glamorous and we were proud of them, idolised them... then. It seemed they always arrived in pouring rain, sliding out of sleek cars and overwhelming Gran's small front garden. David and I would have been waiting and watching at the window for hours. In they came, both deeply tanned from postings in Cyprus, Aden or Germany: Dad still in his uniform (which Gran said was sheer affectation), worn under a cashmere overcoat with wine-coloured velvet collar; Mum, whatever the weather, in summer clothes. She favoured thin white cardigans draped over her brown shoulders, low boat-necked dresses with full skirts, multiple net petticoats that rustled when she moved.

"She's at least ten years out of date," Gran said. "That style went out with Bill Haley." Slyly to Della she said, "Della, dear, you know, you're still just about young enough to get away with this shift dress fashion. Cuts out the ironing – we're all drip-dry here in England."

"Shift dress, sack dress. No bloody thank you. George likes a real woman, not a skin-and-bone, glorified clothes horse. Now a sheath dress, that's a different matter." And so this time, as they ran in from the rain-soaked car, she wore a white silk sheath – the white spattered with a pattern of navy paw-marks as if a tiger had walked all over it. A tigress was wearing it – we knew it in the way she watched Dad. He was hers and she didn't intend to share him with anyone else – which was just fine with him. They dwarfed the house, Gran, David and me, and we dwindled. All our interests, all the many topics we'd hoarded up to share with them when they finally arrived – we knew they wouldn't want to know.

David had been so pleased, that morning, with his flowery kipper tie and corduroy jacket from the jumble sale. I wore David's borrowed best shorts and my favourite fawn cardigan with the cream ruffle down the front. But in front of our bird of paradise parents we became as pale and washed out as a couple of child ghosts.

"Don't these kids ever see the sun, Mother? Let's look at you both. Good God, who'd have thought we'd have such a colourless pair? Give your old dad a kiss."

"They're not ill, are they? They look tubercular. Can't you put some heating on, Mum? This bloody British climate gives me the pip."

"It's almost June," Gran said, "and they're perfectly healthy." But she manhandled the spare electric fan-heater from the cubbyhole under the stairs.

"I can't bear rain."

"For God's sake, Della, that complaint's grown whiskers." Dad was laughing, genial, pleased with the impact they made, rumpling Mum's dark hair as if she were his favourite cabin boy and not the next best thing to Elizabeth Taylor.

The next day was Saturday, sunny and warm. Dad decided he'd like to wander around his old neighbourhood so they could show themselves off and pop into a pub. They planned to park David and me outside on the bench with lemonade and crisps. They would have a couple of gin and tonics, then back home for lunch – Gran was doing a roast.

"Nothing beats your roast, Mother," Dad said, as Gran stood at the sink, grimly peeling potatoes.

"Pick me up some cigarettes while you're out," she said.

"How many do you smoke, these days? There was a full pack of twenty last night."

"Sixty a day."

"Good God, you don't?"

"I do when you're here."

We walked along in the sunshine. Dad had changed out of his uniform into a pale grey double-breasted suit and Mum opted for a black and white check dress with wide black patent belt. Everyone stared at them. They looked prosperous and out of place, which Dad loved. He swaggered along with Mum on his arm, click-click-clicking on her high stiletto heels. Nobody noticed us tagging on behind.

Suddenly Dad started to run. "Come on, we'll hop on a bus," he called, and we hopped on a bus and it took us right up to Stamford Hill. Dad caused a huge fuss, claiming he only had a ten-pound note and what sort of a bus company was Great Britain Limited running if they couldn't change a note of the realm?

In the end, David paid with that week's pocket money and I envied him and wished I hadn't spent all mine in Woolworths on a plastic dining-room suite for my dolls' house. We walked up to the station because many years earlier when Dad left school he'd worked in the ticket office for six months, and he wanted to show the staff just how well he'd got on.

"Ron about?" he asked at the kiosk.

"Ron's in Turner's caff having his lunch."

"That wouldn't by any chance be Betty Turner's caff, would it?" Dad asked, stroking his chin.

"It would be."

David pinched my arm. We'd been warned not to mention our lunches at Turner's.

"It's nearly lunch time, Dad. We'll need to hurry if you're stopping at the pub," David said.

Dad looked at his watch. "Bugger the pub, we'll pick up a bottle of Gordon's and some tonic on the way home. Well, well, Betty Turner. Used to be Betty Bridges before she married. Strapping woman. Did you know Betty Turner was in the year ahead of me at school?"

"And who's Betty Turner when she's at home?" Mum asked.

"Betty Turner was the fastest sprinter in the south-east. Her record's never been broken."

"Sporty," Mum said damningly.

"Oh yes, she was sporty all right," Dad grinned.

Mum removed her hand from his arm.

*

"They're smashing kids, ain't they, Mrs. Turner?" Ron was saying. He was about a foot shorter than Dad, tubby and jocular. We liked Ron.

"Very well behaved," Mrs. Turner said without smiling.

"Glad to hear it, Betty. And how about you? I imagine this place is a little goldmine?" Dad said. "The joint's really hopping." He peered slyly at Mrs. Turner to see if she'd been impressed by his American slang.

"It's very hard work for one woman," Mrs. Turner said sourly.

"What happened to your husband? I remember him, little chap, balding but pleasant."

Mum twitched at her white cardigan and stared out of the window.

"What ho, Lorna. What ho, David," said Rory, one of the coalmen on his way through for his lunch. David kicked my shoe and we both nodded at Rory.

"Died several years ago," Mrs. Turner said.

"Not an ounce of trouble, are you, young David? Lorna? We don't play favourites here," Ron said.

"I'm very glad to hear it, Ron. Well, I'll have twenty Consulate for Mother – she's still smoking herself into an early grave, but what can you do? A tin of Tom Thumb cigars for myself. How about you, Della, anything take your fancy?"

Mum shuddered. "No."

"We all love them. They're so solemn and old fashioned, I crease up, don't I, Mrs. Turner? 'Egg, chip and pea for two, please Mrs. Turner.' This place seems empty when they go back to school."

"What ho, David. What ho, Lorna," said Steve, one of the dustmen, on his way out. He winked at Mum; we nodded at him.

Dad, who'd been trying to vanquish Mrs. Turner with the full force of his tanned and glossy personality, looked perplexed. Had that grimy chap just winked at his wife? Why did men keep 'what-ho-ing' his children? What the hell was Ron making such a fuss about and what was this about chips and peas?

"Ron, I don't know that I'm following you..."

"Over there, George." Ron pointed to our table under the poster.

Dad and Mum stared in a bemused fashion. "That's theirs at the back. When they're in school or at the weekends, Mrs. Turner makes it over to sauces and cutlery, because we customers don't like it used. Seems almost sacrilegious. We love 'em, you see."

"Yes, I think I do see," Dad spun on a fine leather heel towards Mrs. Turner, his eyebrows raised in 'genuine' bewilderment. "So, David and Lorna come in here for their lunches?"

"In the holidays. Keeps them out of trouble," she replied tersely, sniffing at Dad's proffered ten-pound note.

"We had no idea, Betty," he said in a sombre tone as if just finding out that Betty was suffering from some infectious terminal complaint. However, he managed to keep his smile in place – he liked to be liked, Mum was the one with the nasty temper. She insisted that tempers were a required facet of a beautiful woman's personality, citing Maria Callas and her own heroine Elizabeth Taylor, to name but two. Storm clouds were gathering, the sharp toe of one of Mum's high-heeled shoes was tapping ominously, there was a frown spoiling her smooth powdered forehead.

"Well, Betty, better get on. Good to see you – you don't look a day older, nor you Ron. Amazing." Dad paused for them to return the compliment in spadefuls, but they didn't.

Ron gave us an Aero each and pulled David's ear. "Ta-ta, you two, be good."

It was a long way back. No useful bus appeared and we had to walk. The sun had gone behind a cloud and by the time we reached the corner of our road, we felt the first spots of rain.

"Bloody weather," Della said. "My hair will be ruined."

Dad said nothing. He was striding some yards ahead of the party, his face grim and determined. Nearing the house, he broke his silence and turned on us: "Come on you lot, don't dawdle."

"I hope you're not including me in the 'you lot', George," Della said icily, adding, "My cardigan reeks of chip fat."

"You should have stood outside. After all, it is a caff, not the Savoy Grill; and ever since, you've been walking along at a bloody snail's pace."

"I am not your Betty Turner. I've never pretended to be the fastest sprinter in the universe."

"The south-east, Della. Don't get aerated. Now listen up, we'll go in together – show Mother a united front."

"Why, Dad?" David asked.

"Because I say so. Nobody mentions Mrs. Turner, etc. I'll bring it up when I'm good and ready. We will paste cheerful, family day out smiles on our faces. OK by you, Della?"

Mum's face crumpled a little. "My feet hurt, George."

"Of course they do, darling." He smiled fondly and tucked Della's small hand under his arm. "You shall go indoors and slip into a pair of Mum's comfy, fluffy boats – that will go well with your frock, won't it?" And he roared with laughter.

Della pulled her hand away. "You can be so cruel."

"I'm sure I can, but keep smiling, dear."

Funnily enough, we loved Dad when he was like that and we knew Mum loved him too. That cruel yet playful streak that could also be amusing and boyish. It took David and me a few more years to see what Gran saw and stop being quite so easily pleased.

The house welcomed us as soon as we stepped into the hall with the thick brown smell of Gran's roast lamb and gravy, the tang of her mint sauce, the cosy, autumnal scent of apple crumble made from the first-ever crop of Mr. E's Bramleys.

In the sitting room, the fire roared away up the chimney. Gran had opened up the connecting double doors to the dining room and the mahogany table was laid with her own grandmother's dinner service. Pink paper serviettes sat cheerily in the glasses and she'd put out the best place mats with scenes of Dartmoor ponies through the seasons. With candles in the gilt candle sticks, it was better than Christmas.

David and I were dazzled and even Mum and Dad quietened down – they knew the effort she'd made.

It was a good dinner, with everybody jolly and laughing. I remember it as the last of the good family dinners. Mum pretended to like everything and Dad made Gran chuckle with his fantasies about the young E couple, who'd moved in next door.

"I've seen you ogling him from the back bedroom window, Mother."

"Get on with you. He's young enough to be my grandson."

"He's a fine-looking bloke. What's he digging – an escape tunnel? Watch out he doesn't come up under your deckchair one of these fine afternoons."

Della got up, like a good daughter-in-law. "I'll wash up, you sit there. George will dry."

"George will not dry," Dad said. "George hasn't handled a tea towel in over twenty years and he's not about to start now. Lorna, I'll give you two bob if you do it."

"I'll do it, Dad," David said.

"You sit still. Go on, Lorna."

By the time I got back from the kitchen, he'd forgotten all about my two bob. Mum (who'd given up on the washing once we reached the saucepan-and-roasting-dish stage) was tucked in next to him on the settee, David was slumped in his usual armchair and Gran was nodding off over the newspaper in the other. I pulled the leather pouffe up to the fire.

"Don't nod off, Mother, I want a word," Dad said.

Gran blinked and looked momentarily confused.

"You know, these two are turning into a pair of bloody Cockneys. I'm the last person to criticise but you're letting them hobnob with all and sundry. I mean, Betty Turner and Ron from the station aren't my idea of companions for my children," he said. "Yes, you know what I'm talking about – I went in to Turner's Caff today. That little oik Ron pawing my arm, telling me what good kids I've got, the patronising bugger, and some other big hairy chap smelling of bins had the damn sauce to wink at Della."

"What do you suggest, George? I have to go out to work and these children need their lunches. Mrs. Turner keeps an eye on them. They're amongst decent working folk."

"Decent working folk, my backside."

"Language, George," said Della lovingly.

"I've spent my life listening to that old cracked tune of yours Mother. I don't want my children mixing with decent working folk."

"Perhaps you'd like to look after them yourselves for a change. Give you both a chance to get to know them…"

"No need to adopt that attitude. I'm just saying…"

"Mum, George is just saying, it's for their ultimate good. They could pick up anything in a place like that – disease, infestation – before we know where we are, they'll be swearing like a couple of troopers."

"Don't be ridiculous, Della, Mrs. Turner runs a…"

"Working men's caff, top and bottom of it. It's not on, Mother. It isn't what we've envisaged for these two."

"And just what would that be?"

This stumped Dad. He stared at us both as if registering us for the first time. Were we up to fulfilling his grand plans? On David's kipper tie was a dark grease stain – I had a feeling it had been there when he'd paid his three pence for it in the jumble sale. My hand brushed self-consciously at my knee, where I'd half peeled away a large scab. There was a trickle of dried blood on my leg, reaching almost to the rib of my sock.

"It's just not on, Mother," George said in a deadly tone.

"No, I'm sorry, Mum, it's not on," Della agreed.

We didn't go back.

At home with Edna and Lily

It was midday by the time I reached Brighton and it took me a further fifteen minutes to arrive at Druce Court, an ugly block of flats tucked away at the back of Bartholomew Square.

The last time I'd visited Edna was well over a year ago, the day of my first momentous encounter with Dan. Haywards Heath and Clapham Junction meant something very special to me now – they'd formed a giant tacking stitch in the fabric of my life. Dan boarding the train, getting off the train – incredible. Fate is so dependent on the trivial – I might never have looked up from my letter to Pat, might never have spotted the love of my life. Of course, Pat had been her usual sarcastic self and poured cold water over my fantasies: "You can't possibly love someone you don't even know."

"But I can. People do it all the time."

"People, Lorna, not you. You're abnegating the business of living."

"I'm doing what?"

"Abnegating, in denial. Pinning your hopes on the impossible to avoid dealing with reality." She squeezed my shoulder, which was quite a declaration of friendship coming from Pat.

"I need to have hope," I said.

She snatched her hand away. "Now you're being maudlin and self-indulgent. What's happened to Theresa Parker Bowles?"

"Stowell-Parker. Rumour has it she's been spotted several times on the back of a Harley Davidson. Informant can't be absolutely sure because of helmet and swathed pashmina."

"Somebody's got money – pashminas don't come cheap. I wouldn't want one. Don't ever buy me one!"

"I wouldn't dream of it. You're the last person I'd buy a pashmina for."

"And what's wrong with me? I'm every bit as attractive as Theresa Huijamaflip. Sandra says I've a lot going for me in the looks department."

"Hmm, Sandra needs her eyes tested."

And so we went on. Pat and I, when time and Sandra allowed, could talk for days and days about nothing much.

Let me return to Dan, before I return to Edna and Druce Court, because frankly Dan filled my daydreams and Edna and her girlfriend Lily did not.

I'd seen the navy blue Merc several times around Stoke Newington, often parked on double red lines which implied haste.

"Doctor, this cat's going to have kittens – there's no time to lose."

"I'll be right there – make sure there's plenty of boiling water and fresh towels, disinfectant and at least two sterilised buckets, a darning needle and some garden twine."

Dan's driver (celebrity vets warrant chauffeurs) pulls up to the kerb. Dan to driver: "Damn it, Clarice, more double red lines. Never mind, the kindly traffic warden will understand. I'm going to need you by my side for this one. The little mother won't wait, God bless her."

For two of the sightings, regretfully, I'd been on the bus on the way to the Green Bees outlet, but on the third occasion it was a wet Sunday evening and I was coming back from the late night Turkish supermarket, where I'd been sent by Julie for an urgent tin of prunes. There was the car, parked on the High Street on the opposite side of the road. Casually, I sauntered across and gave it the once over. No doctor's stickers, nothing – not a cushion, a box of tissues, or a nodding dog. The interior was of navy upholstery with a fine grey pinstripe – by the light of the street lamp, I'd have said recently hoovered, which wasn't much of a clue.

I recrossed the road and took up surveillance position between the bus stop and Shoe Fayre's window. I waited nearly an hour, alternating between ten minutes standing at bus stop staring at each arriving bus in enraged manner, muttering, "How many more 67s before the garage sends out a 149," plus bewildered squinting at timetable; and ten minutes considering the shoe-shop window and taking notes as if I might be checking out, say, slippers or sandals as a possible birthday present. Not for David or Julie, nor Pat for that matter – they wouldn't wear polyurethane. I became so engrossed counting shoes which boasted leather uppers that I didn't notice the Mercedes snake smoothly away behind me. What a life. Such excitement. Who'd want to sit snuggled against a beloved watching early evening television, when instead you could get soaking wet and increase your product databanks?

Dan, oh Dan. Forget Desperate Dan or Dan Dare – wouldn't you agree that Dan is a fine name? Heroic, mystical, capable of anything larger than life? Isn't it only to be expected that a woman called Dan could so efficiently pot the black, would bury her dear friend's dog in her own garden, could wear the abysmal beige with complete self-assurance? Dan – possible celebrity vet, probable caring friend, possible... hoodlum. Now why ever did that pop into my head? Must have been the navy Merc, her turned-up raincoat collar, the driving rain... I associated bad, sad times with rain.

"Rain can be beautiful," Jenny Salter said.

"Not for everybody," said I, and it was a tribute to J. Salter's sterling sensibilities that she refrained from elaborating as Reverend Joseph elaborated: "We need the rain to grow our crops. *["Oh really?"]* Lorna, all over the world, even as we speak, people are praying for rain."

"It was only a throw-away remark, Reverend Joseph, I fully appreciate the necessity for rain." Sometimes, he did insist on taking a simplistic view of life.

"There is no such thing as just 'a throw-away remark', Lorna. Every single phrase we utter is weighed in the hands of God."

He said this so seriously, with such conviction, that initially I was dismayed. I too saw God – usual chap in white robes – he was scrutinising several of my more flippant remarks and wore the disappointed expression of a man who'd been short-changed in the tobacconist. But what did Reverend Joseph know? Why should I believe in his direct line to God?

"I think it's perfectly acceptable to make a throw-away remark," I insisted stoutly. "One can't spend every minute of one's day weighing words before one says them."

"There would be peace in this world if we did," he said solemnly and shut his front door.

Phooey to the Reverend Joseph. Lucky I didn't pay *him* thirty pounds for fifty minutes' supportive insight, as we'd never get further than "Now Lorna, let's consider carefully what we think the phrase 'Hello, Reverend Joseph' might mean to our heavenly father?"

"No, let's not. Can't we please move on?"

Back to Druce Court, home of Edna and Lily. As you may recall, Gran had left the contents of her house to Edna. To this day, I'm unsure just why she did that. Was it an act of vengeance or reconciliation? You see, Gran's possessions filled a four-bedroom house and two outside sheds and all Edna had was a one-and-a-half-bedroom flat with own concrete coal bunker and dustbin area. Edna could have stuck the lot in at auction, that's what David suggested, but instead she and Lily absorbed it, stacked it, put small items into larger items, wedged trunks under beds, footstools into the airing cupboard... leaving themselves seating niches with a china cabinet or Welsh dresser shelving for a headrest.

Edna was seventeen years younger than Gran. They got to know each other soon after Grandpa died. As I've said, Gran was always a reserved woman with no real friends apart from Edna, whom she treated as if she were her daughter, having been unimpressed when George brought Della home.

We didn't see much of Edna. Gran usually went to Edna's house for somewhere to walk Peppies 6–8, as Edna said she preferred dogs to small children. This must have gone on for several years if three Pomeranians were involved but David and I were self-absorbed kids;

we didn't look up from the television or our books when Gran said, "I'm just walking Peppy over to see Edna – back in an hour or two." "Gran and Peppy are at Edna's," we'd say if anyone rang for her.

No, Edna hardly ever came to our house unless she and Gran had an argument, and then she'd arrive with an armful of 'flowers from my garden', which consisted of branches of drooping privet and earwig-infested dahlias. "Sorry Irene – I've got a big mouth. Take no notice." And Irene would agree that yes, she had got a big mouth and she hadn't taken any notice and had Edna noticed there were earwigs crawling all over the kitchen table?

All good friendships, as I can testify, pause, come to a natural end, lose momentum, and with the death of Peppy 8, Gran seemed in no hurry to order a Peppy 9 – she went less and less to Edna's.

One afternoon Edna just turned up, flowerless. I could see Gran was flustered. "You'd better come in," she said as if Edna was a police constable arriving to make an arrest. They went into the kitchen and talked sotto voce for over an hour and then Edna left without shouting goodbye and Gran stayed in the kitchen with the door shut.

"Do you think Gran's all right?" David asked without taking his eyes off the television screen.

"Who knows?" I said – which was my favourite response that year.

Gran came in to watch the nine o'clock news. She was quiet but then she generally was quiet.

"All right, Gran?" David asked without taking his eyes off the television screen.

"Quite all right, David, but thank you for asking" – which wrong-footed me for not asking.

Edna dropped out of my consciousness. Gran had joined a women's indoor bowling club in Finsbury Park. The next time I saw Edna was on Gran's birthday in the following year. "Edna will be bringing a friend," Gran said, scrutinising me narrowly – I knew she was wondering whether I was too old now to be given a warning regarding manners and what she called 'precocious remarks'. She said nothing.

I didn't think much of Lily when she arrived, clinging on to Edna's arm as if otherwise she'd topple over. I get it off Gran, my aversion to fluffy feminine women (with the exception nowadays of Julie, who's grown on me since I've seen the steel behind the dinky heels and pastel-coloured clothing). David was away on a school trip, so the socialising fell to me as Gran seemed to be in one of her even more silent than usual moods. I was assiduous in offering more salad, more salad cream, more boiled potatoes, more beetroot, perhaps a pickled onion?

"I couldn't possibly eat pickled onions," Lily said in a high squeaky voice. "My breath would smell."

"Only of pickled onions," I said, "and everybody loves them, don't they?"

"That's enough, Lorna," Gran said. "I've baked a queen of puddings for afters." She gathered up the plates. "Lorna, I think Lily would like more lemonade."

Gran brought in the queen of puddings and put it on a raffia mat next to the budgerigar's cage to cool – there was so much steam coming off it, the glass walls of the conservatory were misting up. Outside it was a grey day anyway – I had a vision of this being the last meal on the *Marie Celeste* and was just about to share my insight with the guests when Lily produced a small package from her cream crocheted hold-all and put it next to Gran's pudding plate.

"I made these for you, Irene. Edna said you suffer from cold feet."

Well, I thought, this beats the band – which you might think is a rather old-fashioned thought for a burgeoning teenager to come up with as late as 1970 – put it down to the 'old heads' complaint.

Gran looked... as if some enormous unhappy conflict was raging inside her. She stared at the package as if it might contain a wedge of poisoned Kendal Mint Cake.

"Open it up, Irene. You'll like them. Lily's an ace knitter," Edna said.

I noticed that Gran's mouth had changed suddenly – from its

normal pretty if faded rosebud to a thin cold line of purple. I stared fiercely at Edna, at Lily. For once I wanted my brother David there so we would outnumber the enemy. Edna was just smiling stupidly, her gaze flickering between Gran and Lily, and when it rested on Lily I recognised a besotted warmth.

Gran opened up: "Thank you, Lily – how very thoughtful," she said in a strained voice as she held up a pair of lavender-coloured bedsocks.

"Try them on, Irene," Edna said.

"Gran doesn't want to try them on," I said. "She has a hot-water bottle. She doesn't need bedsocks."

"That's enough, Lorna. If you don't mind, I'll try them on later – my feet are rather swollen at the moment. That pudding should be about ready, I'll just get the cream. Lorna, I think Lily would like more lemonade."

"I think Lily's had more than enough lemonade," I said.

There was a moment's silence, then Edna said, "What's your trouble, little girl?"

"Lorna, leave the table please."

"No Irene, she's old enough to speak for herself. Lily is your grandmother's guest, so why are you being so rude?"

"Lily's drunk all the lemonade," I said stubbornly.

"What a funny child," said Lily. "Take no notice of her – she's having a tantrum."

"Lorna, leave the table – now."

"I'm going. I don't want to sit here and coo over old bedsocks. My gran can afford to buy her own bedsocks if she wants them, she doesn't need..." At that point Edna stretched across the table and slapped me.

"Edna! Lorna, go to your room," Gran said.

"I'm not having Lily insulted after all the trouble she's gone to," Edna said.

"No trouble. Took me an afternoon. I could knit them in my sleep.

I'm a top outworker for a famous hand-knitwear company based in Wales, you know..."

I could hear her burbling on like a frothy busy stream all the way up the stairs to my bedroom.

After they'd gone, Gran popped her head around my door. "Lorna, you were very rude."

"Sorry, Gran."

"What did you think of her?"

"I thought she was horrible."

"She never had any of my queen of puddings – said she suffered from a milk allergy – and Edna just poked it round the plate."

"I'll have some. I'm still hungry."

"Come on downstairs then."

Over the years I've tried to pinpoint what it was that Lily had to offer Edna that Gran didn't possess (apart from her knitting ability); how Edna could prefer someone silly and lightweight to Gran. OK, seventeen years is a sizable age difference, but Gran was excellent company, when she chose to talk, and so reliable – a sensible and solid woman. You'd never have a moment's worry with her at your side.

Over to you, Pat. *"Well obviously, Lorna, sensible and solid aren't the most immediately attractive qualities. Invaluable in wartime, or catastrophes, or serious illness, even minor illness, but where's the romance?"*

Why was I now visiting them? Because of Gran. Before she died she said, "Get in touch with Edna, will you? Keep an eye out for her."

"But why? She's never bothered to keep an eye out for you."

"That's not the point."

"I don't like her very much and I can't stand Lily."

"As a favour to me – you'll find life's never cut and dried." She smiled (and I might add that my grandmother was a very pretty old lady with the face of a gentle bird up till the day she died). "I don't like Lily either, but Edna always had a yen for the vacuous."

<u>*Gran's Queen of Puddings*</u>

4ozs of stale white bread, 3ozs of Quaker Quick Macaroni, 1 pint of milk (preferably on the turn), 2ozs of Anchor butter, 3 eggs, 5ozs sugar, 4 tablespoons of any jam available, grated rind of lemon, 3 old butter wrappers bearing solid traces of rancid butter.

1. Wipe one old butter wrapper around the insides of rheumy Pyrex dish.
2. Coat floor of dish with jam to the depth of half an inch.
3. Cook macaroni till spongey.
4. Crumble stale bread into... crumbs and mix with macaroni.
5. Heat milk/butter/eggs/lemon rind till warmish and form a yellow mixture.
6. Pour over... Hold everything! First put stale bread and macaroni on top of jam, now pour over.
7. Cover dish with remaining butter papers – face down to allow rancid butter to add that cordon bleu piquancy – and cook Regulo 4 for 20 minutes.
8. Serve hot preferably in a hot room on a hot day.

Their flat was on the ground floor, with a kitchen window overlooking the potholed car park and woody lavender bush. I rapped briskly, genially, on the glass before making my way to the communal door. This was a warden assisted block, yet the door always bore signs of receiving a good regular kicking by heavy boots, from younger family members desperate to get in and see what the older family members were getting up to. I pressed the buzzer and the door flew open as if Lily had been lurking behind it for some time.

"Where the devil have you been?"

"On the train. Where do you think I've been?" I said.

"None of your cheek. I rang your flat and that woman answered."

"That woman's an answering machine."

"She is not. She knew my name."

"Lily, she couldn't possibly have done."

"She damn well did. Are you coming in, or is this one of your flying visits?"

"Of course I'm coming in. I've been on the train since half past eight."

"You've been what?"

Exasperated, I tried to ease past her. She flattened herself against the inner wall and shouted, "Don't you try it, you devil."

"Lily, for goodness sake."

"Oh come on, come on. You young people have no sense of humour."

I followed her down the corridor towards their shabby internal door and as always began to see all the attributes, apart from her determined daftness, that might make Edna throw up a comfortable life in London with an older woman/house owner for a cramped little flat in a neglected block.

She was nimble, was Lily, still surprisingly quick on her slipper-shod feet. She wore a pair of dark pink woollen trousers, baggy at the back (a space which her bottom used to fill), a tie-neck blouse with a ring of orangey face powder marking the neck, her silver-blue hair quite long in what she and Edna called the Lana Turner style. "Very sexy," Edna said. Edna also said, "I was lucky to snaffle Lily – she was a beauty. Still is." I did see it, the way Lily's small sharp features and faded blue eyes could light up, as if a hundred-watt bulb had been switched on under her skin. Even I was forced to admit that Lily was 'arresting'. Exhausting, tiresome, hyperactive, childish, but 'arresting'.

"Lorna's turned up at last," Lily called out, heading briskly for the cave mouth they called the kitchen alcove. At the very moment of her disappearing into its darkness, Edna materialised from behind one of several tallboys, a grubby duster in one hand, a vinyl record in the other.

"Hello Lorna, at last the voice of youth. What do you think of Jet Harris and Tony Meeham?"

"Who?" I kissed Edna's cool dry cheek.

"Diamonds." She fanned me with the record. "Number one single in 1963 for absolutely ages. They knock spots off Segovia and his pals."

"Edna, in 1963 I was only about six years old."

Edna gave me one of her penetrating stares as if she was looking down a powerful telescope, picking out years as if they were distant stars.

"Years bunch up like buses – in my heyday I used to play in a skiffle group," she said. "Come on in."

By 'in', she meant leaving the metre of space left in the hall and entering their sitting room, which was like finding one's way around an overstocked warehouse: one false move and I'd be bombarded with clocks, trays, china ladies and Welsh dolls whose aprons predicted rain – a host of small, sharp, heavy oddments, precariously balanced like Lilliputian armies on the tops of wardrobes, previously mentioned tallboys, sideboards and stacks of packing cases. Lily and Edna were immune to attack. They had a rapport, I knew it from the way their expressions softened as they feasted their eyes on their myriad pieces of bric-a-brac.

"I thought Lily was in Cardiff this week," I said glumly. Thinking Lily was in Cardiff had been my spur to come down and see Edna after so long.

"She came back early, she was anxious." Crablike, we rounded a walnut bureau and nest of small tables.

"Oh?" Hard to imagine Lily being genuinely anxious. "How's her knitting?"

Yes, Lily was still knitting. At eighty-one she remained the top outworker for the 'famous hand-knitwear company based in Wales'. I'd never got to the bottom of what the 'famous hand-knitwear company' was called. I'd given up asking as Lily invariably tapped the side of her nose and said smugly, "Insider information," as if my knowing might cause the company's share price to take a tumble on the stock exchange.

I located a footstool and squatted down, noting that Edna was now using her walking stick indoors, which seemed unnecessary considering there wasn't enough room to fall over – even if you were determined, leaning at a sixty-degree angle would be the best manageable. She pottered off towards the kitchen and I was left alone to grow sleepy in the warm stuffy atmosphere. I began to imagine that I was locked in a bank vault or one of those giant walk-in safes. It was a bank holiday weekend just starting and I was working for a major branch of NatWest and, being so conscientious, I was the last employee left in the entire building. I'd gone to return someone's deposit box and the door had swung shut behind me. Finally, fighting for breath, I'd slither down onto the hard metallic floor… to be discovered the following Tuesday, rigor mortised into a concertina shape, which would make me the devil of a job to cram into a coffin.

"Don't nod off."

I blinked. Edna was back and sitting in the armchair; Lily and her knitting were ensconced in the corner of the crowded, rose-patterned, cushion-and-magazine-infested settee.

"Was I asleep?" I asked, surprised.

"We've been watching you for fifteen minutes – sixty-two, sixty-three – you reminded me of a statue by Rodin, only you don't quite have the bulk. Mustn't talk – counting stitches." Lily concentrated on her length of mohair spider stitch, which stretched down her bosom and over her pink-trousered knees. "Switch telly on, Edna."

"No," Edna said, "not when we've got a guest."

Lily looked left, right, lifted up her knitting and peered under that. "There's a guest? Where's a guest? Oh bum, was that two hundred and three or two hundred and four?"

"I thought you were making the tea," Edna said mildly.

"Did you? Well think again. Don't expect me to run this ship single-handed – I'm Mrs. Breadwinner, high time you accepted the pinafore."

"You're looking for a sock in the mouth," Edna said cheerfully. "Wagon Wheel, Lorna?"

Being left alone with Lily was never easy. It was like keeping company with a cobra (although obviously not exactly like keeping company with a cobra – definitely a tense situation, not necessarily life threatening). The click of her needles seemed to intensify, the way she wound her wool tightly, twice around her little finger, the quick sharp glances she darted at me... amazing how decades whizz by, yet with some people you can't move on – the two of you remain stuck in one uneasy moment in the past.

Why can't love be like that? Not progressing, not becoming familiar as it grows deeper and that intense feeling of sharing an otherwise empty conduit, with absolutely no interest in what's going on outside, imperceptibly fades. Why, eh?

I knew that when Lily saw me she too thought of my grandmother, the hot conservatory, the steaming queen of puddings and the unappreciated lilac bedsocks.

I said suddenly, "All those years ago, I shouldn't have interfered, but I knew Gran was hurt."

Lily looked at me over the rims of her spectacles. "Your gran finished with Edna, not the other way round."

"Oh. I didn't know."

"Of course you didn't. But Edna wouldn't have looked at me in the first place otherwise – she idolised Irene."

"Gran was upset."

"She was angry. I shouldn't have said that about her feet being cold but I was jealous."

"So it wasn't only my fault?"

"No dear, it wasn't."

"So you haven't borne a grudge against me all these years?"

"No. We thought you had."

"If I did bear a grudge, I don't any more."

This probably rated as the only sensible conversation I'd ever had or ever would have with Lily.

The room returned to silence except for the ticking of multiple clocks and sounds of Edna cussing and crashing around the kitchen. "I can't see a bloody thing out here. Where are the damn matches?"

"Where do you think?"

Pause, then, "Cutlery drawer?"

"Bingo."

I reached for an ancient copy of *Hello* magazine: Princess Michael with a deep crease down her middle.

"Before you get engrossed in that, you might like to know about our burglary," Lily said.

"Wait for me," Edna shouted from the kitchen. "It takes ages, boiling water in a saucepan."

"What's happened to the kettle?" I asked.

"Stolen," Lily said.

"They took the kettle?"

"Wait for me," Edna roared. "Lily, I forbid you to say another word… ever," followed by more crashing. Lily smirked with pleasure.

"Where are the damn Wagon Wheels?"

"Oh, my lord," Lily said, dumping down her bundle of mohair and going off into the kitchen. I listened to the sounds of good-natured scuffles, light laughter, the loud smack of a kiss. Golly, I thought, Gran would never have coped.

"You mean to tell me that a burglar took your kettle?" I continued.

"She did," Edna said.

"And the iron," Lily added. "Would you believe, the electric blanket off our bed?"

"No, I wouldn't believe it. Why didn't they take the video and the television, like normal burglars?"

"Lily has a theory."

We waited on Lily, who was slowly peeling wrapping off her Lyon's mini Swiss roll. "I think," she said, her eyes sparkling, "our burglar concentrated on personal electrical items as opposed to 'impersonal' electrical items." She raised her pencilled eyebrows heavenwards, then sideways, which was quite a physical achievement. I made a mental note to have a go myself, in the privacy of my homeward-bound train carriage.

I said, "Why?"

"For kicks," Lily said. Edna nodded.

"Shouldn't we just call this petty theft or a practical joke?"

"That's what the police said, but we're having none of it. We think – don't we Edna?" – Edna nodded in vociferous agreement – "that there's more to this burglary than meets the eye – it may only be the tip of a local iceberg."

"Has there been an iceberg's worth of robberies in this area, then?"

"There's been more than an iceberg's worth, there's been an absolute deluge. We're changing the locks and keeping our weather eye open for double-glazing salespersons," Edna said, pouring tea into three different Toby jugs. She flicked a glance in my direction; Lily, also, was watching my face intently. Had I missed something? Electrical goods, icebergs, deluge, double-glazing salesperson... Right.

"You think you've had a visit from a bogus double-glazing chap, is that it?"

They leant towards me like a couple of eager children, as if being burgled was the best thing to happen to them in ages. "You're heading up the wrong garden path," Lily said and tapped me several times on the head with the bobble end of her knitting needle. "I said 'she', it wasn't a chap, it was a woman. You weren't paying attention."

"I see." I rubbed my chin. "Well, she's got a nerve. Was she a proper double-glazing rep with a sample window and cross-section of UPVC under her arm?"

"No," Edna said, "but she had a briefcase and a brochure – admired Lily's knitting, had a cup of tea and a crumble cream."

"So you were able to give the police a pretty good description?"

They shook their heads. I left off rubbing my chin and scratched the back of my neck instead. They still looked devilishly animated, their lips parted – there was some response they wanted me to make.

"Did she take anything else? Small things, valuable things, jewellery for instance?"

Lily clicked her false teeth in annoyance and began knitting again. Even Edna looked disappointed, nudged the highwayman Toby in my direction and sat moodily back in the armchair. "You've completely lost the plot, Lorna, she wasn't that sort of thief at all. Anyway, anything of real value we keep hidden away where no one would ever find it – we're not stupid."

"Have you checked?" I persisted.

"No."

"Well, check now."

"You're a spoiler," Edna said, reluctantly shifting.

"I've merely put my 'David in loco parentis' hat on for a moment."

We waited, Lily knitting angrily. In the bathroom, I heard Edna lift the lid off the top of the toilet cistern, a pregnant pause and then the sounds of Edna shuffling her way back through the maze of furniture.

Lily puffed out her cheeks and stared dispiritedly ceilingwards. "Lorna Tree's hard work," she said in a sing-song voice.

Edna's head appeared turtle-like from the back of the grandfather clock; she looked old, tired and dejected.

"It's gone," she said. "Lily, everything's gone, and she seemed such a lovely young woman."

They wouldn't call the police this time – categorically refused – said they were too disheartened.

"Perhaps she'll come back," Lily said. Even Edna looked doubtful.

"Perhaps it wasn't her at all. Perhaps the double-glazing woman was genuine. Did she leave a business card?" I asked.

"No. I know she did it. She measured up every room including the bathroom." Edna sighed deeply. "The spare key's missing from under the rubber plant."

"But how would she know it was kept under the rubber plant?"

"I told her," Lily said.

"Not Lily's fault. The woman said it must be easy to lose things in here, and Lily said, anything we need like keys or Aspirin we pop under the rubber plant."

Lily put down her knitting and went through the wooden bead curtain into their bedroom.

Edna lowered her voice: "Lily thrives on attention and doesn't get so much of it these days. It's difficult having been a beauty."

I said nothing, having found it difficult enough being perfectly ordinary. I put my arm around Edna, squeezed her old sharp bones. Why would someone pick on this vulnerable pair? If J. Salter told me it was a cry for help, she could look elsewhere for her thirty pounds. Golden eagles, jokes about TSP, women with pet-carriers, that was the light side of my life. This was reality: Edna and Lily – my responsibility.

House beautiful

Saturday evening found me back in the usual swing and hubbub of London life for Lorna Tree and friends… well, Pat and her friends.

She'd telephoned in the afternoon to ask me to dinner, having finally emerged from a week-long stint in the Bermuda Triangle of Lakeside, Brent Cross and Wood Green shopping malls. She and Sandra ("Please don't call her Sandy when you see her – she doesn't like it – says it's an abomination of her real name") were comparing prices and fabrics of hers and hers three-seater sofas. "Sandra won't even look at a sofa bed, says we don't want all and sundry staying the night."

Hoped they didn't see me as an 'all and sundry'. No way would I want to stop over and witness Sandra in her night clothes, although on second thoughts she probably slept nude, padding around the new house in shorty towelling dressing gown looking permanently tussled and pleased with herself. How Pat could like, never mind love, a woman with a perpetual smirk was beyond me.

Good heavens, is that the time? I've just realised I mentioned Pat's telephone call over two paragraphs or seven minutes ago and still haven't told you why or what for. Mr. E always did say I spent more time than was good for me inside myself. Hard to do otherwise. "What's the alternative, oh great gardening guru and spirit guide?"

Pat, typically taking advantage of Lorna's sunny nature, had said, "Do you mind coming along with my colleague from work, Seymour? He doesn't know the way to our new house and has a phobia about going alone to unfamiliar destinations and being dependent on the *A to Z*."

So there we were, seven-forty-five on a drizzly Saturday evening: Seymour, Seymour's silver motor scooter and myself strolling along the High Street as best one could stroll along our High Street on a

Saturday evening. Seymour seemed impervious to the tide of revellers, late shoppers, skateboarders, baby-buggy owners and mendicants forced to step in the road or flatten themselves against shop windows so he and his motor scooter could amble along side by side.

"Where do you live as a rule?" I asked, imagining a deserted prairie with several buzzards circling over Seymour and his metal pal.

"A long long way from this godforsaken hole, I'm glad to say."

"I like it," I said. "Hackney has a very unique character and we who live here find the area possesses a rare and particular beauty."

"That's what mothers say about ugly babies."

Seymour had ginger hair. In my life I've known several ginger-haired people and never taken to one of them. I state this categorically knowing full well I may anger others with ginger hair who consider themselves fine and lovely persons, possessing friends and loved ones who also think them fine and lovely persons. Sorry, you lot – as a bunch, you're peevish and critical, often too smart by half... add smarmy to smart. Did Uriah Heep have ginger hair? If not, he should have.

"Is it much further, Lorna? I'm bursting to go to the loo."

"I told you, ten minutes door to door. We're over halfway. Third left from the next set of traffic lights."

"That far. Oh God."

"We'll be there in four minutes. FOUR MINUTES. Scooter on ahead if you're that desperate."

"No, not possible. Anyway, can hardly rush into a strange house and head straight for the toilet. Gives a bad impression. What would this Sandy think?"

"Sandra," I said.

"Don't be pedantic, Lorna."

Bloody cheek. "Actually Pat told me to emphasise the importance of the Sandy/Sandra thing. Nothing to do with pedantry," I said stiffly.

"Look, could we not talk? I'm concentrating on my bladder control exercise."

Would have liked to inquire more fully into bladder control exercise. From the tense expression on Seymour's face, it had a lot to do with holding his breath and counting. Silently we now hurried along, breaking into an easy jog at the corner of their road. It was almost pleasant. I could almost see why Pat had taken up jogging – light breeze ruffling my hair, trainers pounding the pavement purposefully. The front door stood wide open and we were able to lope straight in, with me a yard or two behind Seymour and his scooter. I caught a glimpse of Sandra, dressed in denim, with a slightly familiar, stocky, dark-haired woman, both absorbed in several zig-zag cracks in the hall plaster. Seymour rested the scooter against the wall and a chunk of plaster dislodged, falling to the floor like crumbling meringue.

No hello, no acknowledgement; Sandra was in full DIY flow: "Just a case of over-zealous emulsioning by the previous owner. Didn't give the new plaster a chance to dry out. Nothing worth worrying about." She tapped the wall authoritatively and more meringue slid onto the floorboards.

"Could be subsidence," Seymour said, taking a bottle of wine from his rucksack. "We've had a few dry summers and that's a mighty big sycamore in your front garden."

Sandra gave him a long and steely stare – still hadn't noticed me. What would Jenny Salter make of that?

"Come on in," Sandra said.

"We are in," Seymour muttered to me. "Don't much like this Sandra woman."

I warmed to him. "I think I've spotted the toilet," I said. "I reckon it's the blue door over there."

"Please, Lorna, don't fuss – I'm not that desperate."

Hard to imagine friend Pat had been a part of anything so momentous as house buying, garden landscaping and power showers. We'd always said, "That road's not for us. Don't fence us in – we're easy-going flat dwellers. Wherever we lay our bobble hats, etc." I felt almost furtive, following along the corridor, peering into darkened rooms, up a staircase, the ornate bannisters already half stripped of white paint. There was something arcane about the whole set-up that I'd never felt before. It was my entering into an area of Pat that I didn't know – hadn't known existed – her desire to share and make a house a home. There was Harry the goldfish nosing his way across the front of a small aquarium, Pat's watercolour views of Kew Gardens arranged in stylish groups on a white wall, complementing Sandra's black and white photographic studies of Hackney Marshes with a storm brewing. On a wooden coat stand at the bottom of the stairs, Pat's anorak hung next to Sandra's leather jacket, their sleeves overlapping.

This was my first visit, although I knew the house well, had passed it often enough, keeping to the other side of the road and glancing obliquely across at the blue front door with its yellow and blue setting-sun fanlight. In my head I played out two conflicting scenarios.

1. Lorna getting out of bed on the right side scenario: I'd be hurrying carelessly past, mind set on other far more important thoughts, when suddenly the blue front door would fly open and out would bounce Pat, shouting, "Lorna, you silly muggins, why didn't you knock? Come on in and have a drink, cup of tea, nose round the house – Sandra's away on a food hygiene course this weekend – you could stop for grub, we can catch up on what's been happening in your life for a change."

Lorna crosses road with bemused expression on face. "Is this your house, Pat? I'm gobsmacked. I've passed by dozens of times en route to the post office and never realised. Lead on, Macduff."

2. Wrong side of bed scenario: Lorna spends morning being ticked off by brother and the Reverend Joseph, then finally sets off for post office. This time blue front door flies open and Sandra swaggers forth – hair as always tussled from recent orgy of sex under the power shower, feeling bullish and territorial, very much the mistress of

her/their personal space, which extends to both sides of the road.

"Oi! You! It's Lorna Tree, isn't it? What you doing skulking in our road? Why don't you get a job, a life, a partner, a house of your own, you big lazy lummox, and stop sniffing around here? Next time, I'll set Badger on you."

Badger was my own invention. A small fierce bull-terrier type dog with jaws wide enough to clamp neatly around my throat even when wearing a chunky knit polo neck (me, not Badger).

"On second thoughts, let's teach Tree a lesson. Seize her, Badger! Good boy."

Out would hurry Badger at an ungainly half-run. Tree forced to take to her heels but not before she's seen best friend Pat appear in the doorway saying something along the lines of, "Sandra, you're a devilish so-and-so but I like you." Front door slams shut on happy couple making their way, entwined, showerwards. Badger chases me to the end of their road, then trails off in search of interesting smells on Stoke Newington Common.

"Everybody –" Pat was fairly sloshed – "this is Seymour and Lorna. They're not 'Seymour and Lorna', they're Seymour – full stop – and Lorna – full stop. Now, Seymour and Lorna, this is Angela and her friend – as in 'full stop' – Keith; and this is Theresa, who I think knows Lorna. Am I right?" Theresa and I nodded. "And of course, we all know Sandra, except Seymour. Phew, anyone for another drink?"

"Seymour," Sandra said as if she hadn't just met him in the hall, "Lorna – long time no see."

"Hi Sandy." Damn. "Sorry – hi Sandra."

Her eyes flickered. She didn't like me. Why didn't she like me? I didn't like her. Why didn't I like her? Answer, she reminded me of a lizard. Damn again. Mustn't think 'lizard' every time I looked at her. Replace 'lizard' with... my own eyes flickered around the room (were guests thinking 'Lorna-lizard'?)... replace with... wine glass.

"Thank you Pat," I said, taking the proffered glass of white wine.

"Don't worry," she whispered, "Sandra won't bite."

Sandra, in apparent deep conversation with Angela, still watched us from the other side of the room.

"Are you sure?" I said.

Pat, for reasons of her own, was now talking to me out of the side of her mouth like an inexpert ventriloquist. Fortunately I knew her well enough to instantly interpret.

"Gring your gockle into the gitchen."

Mr. E would have liked the kitchen. The walls were varying shades of salmon-pink plaster adorned with slivers of floral wallpaper; the floor was covered with layers of cardboard; but the real scene-stealers, which would have had Mr. E 'oh my yes Lorna'-ing and rubbing his chin with anxious pleasure, were two person-sized holes knocked into the wall on each side of the cooker, as if at some point the Incredible Hulk had burst through from the outside or burst out from the inside. One was empty; in the other a lidless toilet sat.

"What's going on in there?" I asked.

"Sandra's building a lavatory and a walk-in larder."

"Should you have a lavatory opening onto the kitchen?"

"Sandra says you should." Pat shrugged and reached for a half-full glass of red wine concealed behind the bread bin.

I put my bottle of wine into the fridge and said, "I wish you'd told me that Theresa would be here. I'd have worn something very different. And I know Angela. She's 'Ange and Baby Tonia', isn't she? We met the first time I met Sandra."

"S'right." Pat finished her glass and produced an almost full bottle from inside the bread bin.

"Oh dear," I said.

"S'right," she said.

"Do I sense a doomed evening?"

"S'right."

"Pat, could you elaborate? 'S'right' is not painting much of a picture."

"If you must know," she said, hanging on to the dusty work surface as if at any moment she might slither down onto the cardboard floor, "Last week, Theresa Stowell-Parker – who, I might add, I asked especially for your benefit against my then better judgement – last week she and Ange slept together twice. Ange's been keen on her for ages, thought it was the start of something big. Theresa has other ideas. She likes to be a free agent."

"Well, I am surprised at Theresa, and with Ange of all people," I said.

"Nothing wrong with Ange."

"She'd bore for Great Britain."

"There's worse things than being boring –" Pat finished glass – "although I do admit she's not in Theresa's league."

"So, do you think I am?" I asked hopefully.

"Course you are, Lorna." She smiled into her fresh drink, a small drunken secretive smile. "Sandra's taking Angela's side for the evening. Ange isn't talking to Theresa, although she really wishes she was talking to Theresa and not stuck with Sandra."

"Stuck?" I thought, Oh ho, all is not right in the love nest.

"Any chance of you two putting in an appearance in the other room?" Sandra's tussled head popped around the kitchen opening.

"Coming right away," I said. "Just admiring your excavations." Wrong word again.

"Yes, have a word with Theresa – she was only saying earlier how interesting it was, you being a poet." Pat twirled me round and pushed me back into the dining room.

Thinks: not impressed with polished floorboards. Felt a distinct draught playing about my ankles from large gaps in between them.

"Sea grass would be nice," I murmured.

"I adore sea grass," said Theresa, picking up my murmurance, "I've got it wall to wall in my Fulham flat."

"Really?" I said. Thinks: must not ask Theresa to my flat till something is done about nylon rubber-backed carpeting.

"We're going to need more wine," Pat said plaintively.

"I'll go!" Theresa again. "Come on, Keith, I've got another bottle in the car. See you in a minute, Lorna. Must speak about the poetry." She blew me a kiss. Her face really was charming and animated. I smiled back at her even as I recognised in my heart of hearts that my smile was probably wasted.

"Thank God they've gone," Sandra said, sitting down next to Ange. "Let's hope they get lost and don't come back." She giggled, which in Sandra's case was more of a deep 'heh-heh'.

"Or mugged and don't come back," Ange said, and they both fell against the sofa cushions laughing uproariously.

"It doesn't take much to amuse those two," Seymour whispered, passing by on his way to the bathroom. I squatted down to inspect Sandra and Pat's CD collection.

"Who's the jazz lover?" I asked.

"We both are," Pat shouted from the kitchen.

"You hate jazz," I said.

"She doesn't. Pat loves jazz," Sandra said. "Her mother brought her up on Miles Davis. Mother's milk, wasn't it, Pat?"

"Mother's milk, Sandra," Pat said.

"Don't you like jazz?" Ange asked me.

"Not a lot."

"I used to play 'Cry Me a River' on my squeeze-box."

"I don't call that jazz."

"What do you call it, then?" Sandra asked pugnaciously.

"Easy listening."

"Well, it's not."

"We're back." Theresa and Keith trooped in, saving me a tussle with Sandra, and Seymour was behind them on his way back from the bathroom.

"Love the bathroom," he said, "I'm well into chrome and stainless steel."

Sandra's denim shirt expanded with pride. "Great , isn't it? I'm not one for wishy-washy. Function and form, that's me."

Keith, Seymour and I made ourselves comfortable in deckchairs, the only seating apart from the ancient settee occupied by Sandra and Ange. Grudgingly I accepted their need for the new hers and hers purchases. One wasn't able to look like an animated intelligent guest when forced to sprawl against grubby green and white striped canvas. Keith and Seymour were bent almost double in their efforts to remain sitting upright, their chins fanning the air only a few inches above their knees.

From behind us in the kitchen we heard the loud and merry voices of Theresa and Pat, punctuated by much flirtatious laughter. I'd never heard Pat laughing like that before. *"Don't listen, don't look,"* I telepathised to Harry the goldfish. *"That is not your mummy guffawing."*

Sandra and Ange grew quiet, with Ange helping herself to more wine and swilling it down as if her life depended on it. Sandra, made of sterner stuff, tried to carry on a conversation about paint swatches with Keith while keeping an eye on the doorless doorway – a thunderous scowl forming around and above her eyes.

On my right Seymour sighed, his profile drooping and dispirited. "I'll have to be going soon," he said.

"We haven't had dinner yet," I said.

"No, but I'll still have to go soon."

"Just popping to the loo, then dinner's ready," said Pat, emerging from kitchen, flushed of face.

"Can I see your new bathroom, Pat?" Theresa was dogging Pat's heels. Exit both of them, giggling, leaving behind a room filled with silence.

Then Seymour mused, "How will Pat go to the toilet with Theresa inspecting the decor?"

Ange took a deep gulp of wine, her eyes glassy with tears, and Sandra, who didn't smoke, helped herself to one of Keith's cigarettes.

"I expect Theresa will wait outside," I said cheerfully.

Sandra stood up and went out into the hallway. "Pat, we're all waiting for our bloody dinner. What do you think you're playing at?"

"Just coming. Keep your hair on. And up here are the bedrooms –" sounds of two pairs of footsteps scuffling on the stairs.

"Wow," said Theresa, "Whew," and "Yeah," followed by whispering and more scuffling.

"I'll get them," Sandra said grimly.

I forsook my deckchair for the settee. "How's Tonia?" I asked Ange.

"Very well. Brilliant. Staying with my mum tonight. I thought it would give me and Terry a chance to be alone together." She pulled a tissue from her sleeve and blew her nose loudly.

"They're only mucking about," Keith said. "Take no notice."

"I can't," Ange said.

Enter Pat and Theresa followed by Sandra. "Everybody to the table please, now. That means you as well, Theresa. Pat, we're ready for food."

"So what's this about poetry?" Theresa smiled beguilingly into my eyes. This time I was unaffected.

"No big deal. I just write poetry."

"I used to write poetry – sonnets. My teacher said I had a real talent," Ange said.

"Do you write sonnets, Lorna?" asked Theresa. "No really, I'm interested. I think people who write poetry are fascinating."

Ange said, "I won third prize when I was seven with a poem called 'My Lovely Mum'."

I said, "I don't write sonnets, I write very long prose poems."

"That's fantastic." Theresa turned her beguiling smile towards Pat as she began to gather up the plates. "Pat darling, let me help."

"You can help by staying put," said Sandra. Well done, Sandra.

"Ange made the pudding," Pat said, taking clingfilm off a large deep casserole dish.

"It's a blend of dark chocolate, cream and Cointreau," Ange said.

"Is it a drink?" Seymour tipped his dessert bowl from side to side. "Might be better having it in a cup."

"It defrosted on my way over. It's not easy transporting so much mousse in a saddlebag – it tends to slop about. Sorry. Sorry." Ange wiped her eyes on her serviette.

"It's bloody delicious," Sandra said. I was beginning to admire Sandra.

Suddenly, out of the blue, Theresa said, "I'm all for spontaneous sex with a variety of partners – so much more exciting and fulfilling than the same old bods night after night. What do you think, Seymour?"

"Doesn't bother me one way or the other, Theresa," said Seymour.

"Well, if we must go down that path, I like the idea of going to bed with the same bod night after night because that bod is very dear to me. It's what's called a meaningful relationship," Sandra said. "Anything else is cheap and debasing."

Ange nodded her head vigorously, Keith shrugged and Seymour contented himself with more cheese and biscuits.

"But what if you aren't very successful with meaningful relationships? Does that mean you have to stay celibate?" I asked.

"You try not to hurt anyone," Ange said soulfully.

"Hurting people's half the fun," said Theresa. "What say you, Patricia?"

Pat was staggering around the table, topping up coffee cups. "S'right."

"What?" said Sandra.

For a moment Pat looked bewildered. "Sex is best within a meaningful relationship. S'right," she said.

"Nonsense," said Theresa. "You like someone, you sleep with them. No strings, no attachments. Don't get involved – got it, Ange?"

"Sandra, could we have some classical music," Ange said, tears pouring down her cheeks. "I could really do with some classical music. Got any Richard Clayderman?"

"Does Ange think Richard Clayderman is classical music?" queried Seymour.

"What about Joe Cocker or Eric Clapton?" Ange's voice rose higher.

"Does Ange think Joe Cocker or Eric Clapton are classical music?" queried Seymour.

"Shut up," I said.

"What's your hang-up with white male singers, Ange?" Theresa said nastily. "Do they turn you on?"

"Perhaps it's their talent," I said coldly. There was an awkward lull in the conversation.

"Yes, it's their talent," stumbled Ange.

"Oh yeah? Do you fancy blokes then, Lorna Tree?" Theresa and I were enemies good and proper now.

"I certainly don't fancy you," I said.

Under the table somebody gave me a friendly kick.

"More coffee, anyone?" Pat said, standing up.

"I'll do it." Sandra took the coffee pot from her and went into the kitchen, leaving Pat staring blankly down on her wrecked dinner party, Ange sobbing softly into her napkin, Theresa staring defiantly at the ceiling, Lorna pouring the dregs of Ange's mousse into her plate, and Seymour and Keith sharing out the last of the Jacob's cream crackers.

Pat came round the table and put her hand on my shoulder. She said with drunken formality, "I am sorry, Lorna, I'm so sorry."

"Don't tell me, tell Sandra," I said. "Mind if I put on some music?"

In amongst the jazz CDs I found the renegade Beethoven's Emperor Concerto that I'd given Pat for Christmas in 1993. It almost drowned out the raised voices coming from the kitchen, and the front door slamming behind Theresa.

Ange's Chocolate and Cointreau Mousse Pudding

4 stale chocolate mini Swiss rolls, 1/2 a large bar of dark chocolate, 3 separated eggs, 3 spoons of sugar, 2 dessert spoons of Cointreau, 1/4 pint of double cream, hundreds and thousands to taste.

1. Melt chocolate over a pan of boiling water.
2. Beat egg yolks with sugar till fluffy.
3. Fold in the Cointreau and sliced mini rolls.
N.B. 1. First remove purple and silver wrapper.
4. Whip egg whites and cream.
5. Stir the lot together and pour into dish.
6. Chill.
7. Sprinkle with hundreds and thousands.
N.B. 2. If transporting pudding in a saddlebag, first decant into Tupperware container.
N.B. 3. Hold on hundreds and thousands till destination is reached as otherwise they disappear into the general goo.
N.B. 4. A more sophisticated Lorna Tree touch might be to add a run of After Eight mints, cut diagonally, over the top and garnish plate with After Eight mint wrappers folded to make paper butterflies. Hmm.

*

Stood outside the health centre for some time reflecting on life, home ownership, jealousy and envy. Wondered about Jenny Salter. I imagined there would be some loving person in her background – she was very lovable; honest and lovable; reliable, responsible, honourable and lovable. Not enough Jenny Salters to go round in the world.

"I saw you outside, getting soaked – you could have ruminated in the waiting room."

"Hardly. The waiting room's full of loonies." I waited for her reaction.

"I hope you don't mind – I've changed over to peppermint," she said. She's a cool one is Jenny, always one step ahead of the game.

"What?"

"Tea bag." She raised the dripping tea bag from her cup and dangled it in the air for a few seconds.

"I don't mind," I said irritably. "After all, it's only a tea bag. Not as if it's a case of 'Hope you don't mind, Lorna, I've changed to crack cocaine.'"

"So, wherefore your anger?"

"Wouldn't it be refreshing if you counsellors could use the vernacular for a change, as in, 'What's got your goat, Lorna,' or, 'Who's been shaking your tree?'"

"What's got your goat this morning, Lorna?" Her eyes were amused.

"And it might help if I didn't always feel I was complaining to the complacently well adjusted."

We sat in silence. I was aware my eyebrows were beetling unattractively – exactly like two large hairy beetles trying to meet each other for a fight above my nose. Jenny sipped her tea, looked enigmatic. The trouble with thin J. Salter–style mouths is they always appear to be smiling as if recalling a pleasant personal memory that their client had no part in. This can breed resentment in the client who ideally would like Jenny Salter to be staring attentively at her as if her sole purpose in life for the next fifty minutes is to soothe and sympathise.

Sandals again. A different pair; mushroom-coloured suede. Pat was right – there was something not quite bona fide about Jenny. Did anyone else have a therapist who wore paisley cotton frocks with Peter Pan collars and sandals in wet weather? Unwelcome thoughts of Mum intruded. (*"Call me Della, darling. I hate to think I'm the mother of an almost menopausal child."*) Mum's sandals and frocks were a million miles away from Jenny's. Always revealing, always predominantly white or cream coloured – *"Colours that enhance the skin tone."* Was that why David and I crept about the earth in blacks and navy, rarely letting our limbs see the light of day? I looked down at my pale bony wrists and felt sorry for the way I'd denied them sunlight.

"Penny, Lorna?"

Nice of you to ask at last. Deep breath, concentrate on folding out-of-date bus pass in fleece pocket.

"On Saturday I went to dinner at Pat and Sandra's. They've bought a house together."

Jenny's perfect brow wrinkled as she kick-started the Monday morning memory banks. "Yes. That was to be a significant event, wasn't it? The first time in over a year that Pat had acknowledged your friendship?"

I nodded. "Something like that."

"How did it go?"

"Not so good. It felt strange. I didn't feel I knew Pat as well as I'd thought I did."

"Strange?"

"Her sharing with someone else."

"You felt jealous?"

"I don't know. More rejected... and then she'd asked a woman she knew I'd liked for some time, and they both began flirting with each other. Went on the whole evening. Upset everybody."

"And so then you felt...?'

"Hurt. Offended, if you like. I mean, at the moment Pat has everything going for her. What have I got? There was no need..." I swallowed.

"What do you think her motive might have been?"

I'd spent a considerable time thinking over Pat's possible motive. I'd seen her drunk before, that wasn't it. There was something else. The secretive smile in the kitchen...

"If she wasn't such a close friend," Jenny prompted, "and objectively you were asked to speak in her defence, what would you say?"

That was better. Pat in the dock. Pat shrunken in size in the dock looking frightened and apprehensive. "I'd say she was flattered by the attention. She may have been trying to make Sandra jealous."

"Anything else, about you and her, perhaps?"

"She might have been trying to make me jealous, or showing off, because perhaps you do want to show off when the ball's in your court for a change."

"Do you think she genuinely liked this woman?"

"No."

"Do you think this woman genuinely liked Pat?"

"No."

"Does Pat genuinely like you as a friend?"

"Of course she does."

"Then this is her problem, not yours. Your pain will pass. Try to get rid of your resentment. Don't expect too much from her for the moment. Your time will come. This is a time to gather plus points."

Jenny sipped her peppermint tea. Already that particular pain was passing. I resolved to bring in my own cup and tea bag next time.

Jenny was a star – a mad erratic star. I went home speedily, couldn't wait to get rid of that resentment. Enervated, I sat at my table by the window with several sheets of lined paper and listed grievances under the headings of Past and Present, finishing some hours later with "and mostly, Pat, you made a complete fool of yourself". I considered adding a scathing postscript regarding her new-found interests in herbalism, jazz and interior design; also, the advisability of building a relationship on a tissue of lies, i.e. the Miles Davis fiction; also, expecting best friend to collude. But I finally left it at "Hearts are fickle objects and not to be trusted", which I hoped was sufficiently mystifying. Of course I didn't send the letter off. That's not how it works. However, was very tempted to leave transcript on their answering machine:

"Oh hello Sandra. Pat's there, is she? No, I didn't want a word, just to

clarify a few niggling points on tape that she might like to listen to later. Switch the machine on, will you? Oh, by the by, good luck with the new lavatory – inspired siting."

Today I took delivery of the new fence etcetera, as David was at work and Julie was having a day at her Ealing beautician to 'clear her head'. The two impassive men from Travis Perkins weren't easy to charm.

"We deliver as far as the kerb – that's the agreement."

"But there's only me to carry it through," I whimpered, trying to look small and vulnerable, which I'm not.

The driver scratched his head and whistled a few bars of 'The Happy Wanderer', they exchanged shifty glances and I realised I would have to part with the twenty-pound note Julie had left to smooth her purchases from kerbside through to back garden. Next door the E family's vari-coloured net curtains twitched as they registered the delivery.

First down the side passage went the pallet of reclaimed London bricks in a mottled bluey-grey colour; then the heavy-duty, weather-proofed trellis; then the larch-lapped, weather-proofed posts with their impressive weather-proofed pineapple-shaped finials; then sacks of sand and cement, then some hardwood decking that Julie hadn't mentioned.

I paid them the twenty and they both looked disgusted. "Haven't you got two tenners?"

"No." (I squashed down an irate "I'm not made of money".)

The delivery covered the patio, spreading out as far as the fish pond. Already the garden looked different – expectant – a 'we're going up in the world' smugness about it. Nothing would ever be the same again. In a matter of days all memory of Mr. E's wire netting fence would be obliterated – the end of an era.

I'd hoped to avoid Mr. E for at least a week but unfortunately, our road being long and straight, I was spotted returning from a sortie on behalf of the *Echo*, my now *Echo*less orange bag bulging with biscuits and fancy goods for me, and prune juice for Julie.

I believe Mr. E kept lookout from the marital bedroom window. When absent, he stationed one or other of their children on watch duty; settled them down with a stock of bubble gum and a toy plastic telescope.

"Dad, Dad, come out of the lav, Lorna's just turned into the road."

Out of the lav Mr. E would pelt, still fastening his fly, his worn brown leather belt flapping. "Child, where are my secateurs? Everyone, search for Daddy's secateurs" – and all the children would scatter like mice let loose from their cage.

Four minutes later, as I briskly approached our gate, head tucked tortoise fashion between my shoulders, there was Mr. E loudly humming 'The Happy Wanderer' (odd how hateful tunes like 'The Happy Wanderer' and 'Guantanamera' stick in your head), as he continued the Herculean task of turning a feral hebe into a palm tree.

"It's a thing of beauty, Lorna."

"I couldn't agree more, that doesn't make it a palm tree."

"It's a thing of beauty, David."

"I don't think I'm a hundred percent in agreement," says David.

"Julie, this tree is a thing of powerful beauty."

"Nonsense. This bush is an eyesore and probably a hazard to passers-by of a certain height or infirmity."

At the moment, in early November, it was merely a rangy untidy mass of flaking branches angled at ninety degrees over his front wall and out into the road. He smiled brightly at me and stopped hacking at non-existent side shoots.

"Why, hello there, Lorna, long time no see," as if I'd been abroad or in prison for several years.

"Hello Mr. E. Gosh, this shopping's heavy. Better get Julie's prune juice into the fridge."

"Bowel trouble?" he asked sympathetically.

"Good heavens, no." Julie would not be pleased if Mr. E started a rumour in the street that she was suffering from bowel trouble. I'd be the first in her firing line. *"He didn't get an idea like that out of thin air, Lorna."*

"She takes it for her complexion," I said.

"Does she? I read in a book that in olden days, ladies took arsenic for their complexions."

"Yes, well, I think she'd draw the line at that." I wheezed out a nervous laugh and took another step towards our front door.

"Lorna, I'm worried."

"Yes, Mr. E."

"Worried about the wall."

I rested my bag on the doorstep and applied myself to Mr. E's worry. "Most of it will be trellis," I said. "Very attractive, is trellis. A more natural form of wire netting."

"I've done building work myself..."

"I know you have."

"I've seen the amount of brick you've had delivered..."

"Yes."

"I'm not a fool."

"No."

"I too live in the present day," which did come as a surprise to me as I'd always set Mr. E's life either in another more spiritual parallel universe or in the years when Gran was alive.

"I know all about your aspirational generation."

"Well, there you are, Mr. E. What's to be done? Julie and David can afford their aspirations – they don't want to make do and mend like Gran did."

"This is change for change's sake."

"I don't think it is," I said gently. "I think they think it's their turn now, like when you and Mrs. E first came to live here and put up the wire netting."

He began rubbing his secateurs with an old handkerchief. "It's not the same. Wire netting was all I had, and your gran wanted a divide because of the dogs."

Any second and Mr. E would have me in tears. Fortunately, at that moment when I could feel my eyes smarting, their sash window banged upwards and Mrs. E's head pushed up and under the curtains, a lit cheroot in her mouth.

"Take no notice," she shouted. "I've listened to every word that old fool's said and you tell David and Julie from me that I will crawl on my knees to thank them if they get rid of that rusty eyesore. I give them permission to demolish our entire garden.

"Edmund, Alfred is sitting by the fire again and I've told you, I won't have him sitting by the fire – his fleas get too hot and they jump off Alfred and into my rug. Rabbits live outside." Her head withdrew sharply and down came the sash.

I went inside with my shopping, leaving Mr. E thoughtfully chewing a piece of hebe bark.

I put the prune juice away in their fridge-freezer, checked their Portmeirion pottery biscuit barrel for luxury biscuits (as opposed to my custard creams and chocolate bourbons), had a look at the state of play in David's drinks cabinet... could see many bottles through glass door but unfortunately door was locked and key removed. Plodded upstairs to my own flat. Peered out of my front window – Mr. E seemed to have retired to deal with Alfred. No sign of anyone in the road. It was that quiet time of the afternoon just before the schools let out. On my desk, the small red eye of my answerphone refused to blink; no apology as yet from Pat; two large brown envelopes returning my last long poem, 'The Siege of Malta and Marianne'. I might just as well concentrate on short poems. Might be more successful dividing one six-page epic into twelve separate half-page shorties, increasing my chances of publication twelvefold. That was one of the beauties of free verse, you could find a reason for ending almost anywhere.

I glanced back out of the window and my gaze sharpened, focusing on a figure on the other side of the street. I reached for my opera glasses. Thinks: must get some decent surveillance equipment, this isn't much better than the E children's plastic telescope.

Yes. It was her. Dan. My woman in beige – wearing the same trench coat–style raincoat she'd worn on that rainy afternoon in Neville Road. Today it hung open, flying behind her like a cloak. She wore brown jeans and a creamy beige shirt, her hands nonchalantly in her trouser pockets, head thrown back as if just enjoying an unexpected mild day – however, it was obvious, to one trained as I was to observe, that she was carefully scrutinising each house. She crossed the road and stopped in front of our gate, looking fixedly through Julie and David's sitting-room window. Julie can't abide curtains or blinds, says she likes people to see what a lovely home she's created.

"It gives passers-by a dream to work towards in their own houses. It's not just about money. You know, money doesn't guarantee good taste."

Dan was certainly seeing what a lovely home they had – or was she? I'd stepped back out of sight but could still see her. She looked up, directly at my window. Her hand rested on the gate; she was coming in.

Mr. E's head suddenly bobbed into view. "Can I help you?" I heard him say.

"No. I think I've got the wrong house."

"The Trees live here," he said.

"Do they?" She raised her eyebrows. In her voice, I heard laughter, as if she knew I was watching from behind the curtain and she wanted me to know she knew and found it all a game.

"May the Trees prosper and become a forest," she said, and walked away, back towards the High Street.

Mr. E looked up at my window, then shrugged. I heard him mutter, "Bloody Alfred."

Spring 1996

Fearless women

"Why do we do it?" Della asked, offering George her open tin of blackcurrant pastilles.

"Not just now, Della." He kept his eyes fixed firmly on the road. George was a good careful driver, an unblemished licence and year-on-year no-claims bonus, yet there had been times in the past when he'd yearned to be different. His mother's refrain of "Of course, George is the late developer" hadn't helped; it had hung about his shoulders like an old shawl, ensuring his development grew even later. "He's not like my Steven was. My Steven was into everything."

He'd been tempted to say, "Which was why he drowned, Mother!" but who knew what can of worms a remark like that might open? No, he wasn't like Steven, although sometimes he wished he was – not to perish in a foolhardy escapade, but to be seen as a man who might one day perish in a foolhardy escapade, or at least a man who might *attempt* a foolhardy escapade. He sheered away from memories of Steven, which could prompt one of his blinding headaches. If only the then-youthful and not-quite-a-Reverend Joseph could have been prompted into saying, "Your George is fast turning into a tearaway – he's been seen hanging round with a nasty element at the back of the Empire." But George had had few friends – not enough for an 'element' and none remotely nasty.

After a very short time at Stamford Hill ticket office, George joined the army and trained as a chef. He'd always been drawn towards cooking, had felt there must be more to food than his mother's several tasty ways with corned beef and shoulder of lamb on a Sunday, delicious as they were. He loved being in the army, hated coming home on leave. At home his friends were married or had girlfriends and weren't inclined to meet

George for a pint in the pub to discuss army life or the film he'd been to see at the Odeon in the West End. George's film heroes took the place of friends: Marlon Brando, quiffless but mean, moody and magnificent in *On the Waterfront*; Frank Sinatra, only a mini-quiff but still magnificent in *From Here to Eternity*; and James Dean, the most perfect rolled quiff on the cinema screen in *Rebel Without a Cause*. How George hankered after a quiff, but his short back and sides refused quiffdom.

"You're classically handsome, have a full head of hair – fashions come and go," he told his shaving-mirror reflection. "One day women will fall at your feet."

Regarding George and women, his chat-up lines were not successful. Any verbal strengths lay in his ability to come out with compliments of the 'Is that thine own hair or a wig?' variety. He hardly heard the phrases spilling so easily forth, being much more aware of their effect – the glazing of the feminine eye, a swooping gesture of a pretty head as it turned to look elsewhere, with the exception of one stocky hirsute woman ("a bloody man-hating feminist" as he called her in later life), who said, "Just what gives you the right to be so damn rude, you streak of greased lightning?" Forty years on, he still hadn't come up with a suitable answer. Her parting shrugged remark of "Case of arrested development" had rankled. 'Late' was just about acceptable but 'arrested' was another matter altogether.

And then he met Della at a cocktail party in Cyprus. She was classically beautiful and had once modelled for Norman Hartnell – a brief career. George was blinded, bewitched, his river of nervous repartee quenched.

"One moment I was in demand, then overnight 'soignée' became a dirty word," Della explained over a dry Martini.

George withheld his query regarding 'soignée' becoming a dirty word.

"These days men don't want real women. They want schoolgirls in ankle socks."

George withheld "Nobody loves a fairy when she's forty."

"Real women are forced to content themselves with their own company and six ounces of knitting wool."

George withheld "Needs must when the devil drives," and said instead, "I don't think you'll ever need to take up knitting – I think you're an extraordinarily beautiful woman."

Della's eyes glazed over, she made a small swoop with her graceful classical head and looked elsewhere, followed by another small swoop as her gaze returned unbelievingly to George. "Do you really think so, George?"

"Of course. What red-blooded male in his right mind wouldn't?" – exactly the right cliché to win the hand of fair Della.

"We do it because it's in our natures," he said at last as they entered familiar Islington territory. "We don't like leaving well enough alone. Ignorance isn't bliss where you and I are concerned, we'd rather be red than dead."

"Would we?" Della asked.

"I think so."

They turned right into the Balls Pond Road and slowed to let a white van pull away from the kerb; the driver stuck his hand out of the open window and held up two fingers which immediately made George's blood boil.

"I ask you. These buggers have no manners, no education, no reason to be sharing this bloody earth with decent people."

"Better red than dead," Della warned.

"Don't be ridiculous."

George fumed along behind the white van, thinking that a young Marlon Brando would have hit the accelerator and overtaken – on the inside if necessary – mowing down women and children before careening back across the white van's path. Car door flung open and Marlon hits the ground running (a phrase George had been impressed by on a news broadcast about Paddy Ashdown in Bosnia, one of his more recent heroes). White van driver bundled out of cab before he has a chance to mumble "Fuck you mate"; Della screaming hysterically in the background, "Watch out George, he may have a gun." George smashes man against bonnet... Here George's right knee twitched at his secret aspiration to knee an opponent in the balls and/or nut them. Of course nutting would be the most personally hazardous – George stunning himself in the attempt, reeling, blinded by his own blood, out into the path of a number 38 bus...

"Shut your window, Della," George said as they crossed Dalston High Street. "God, what a dump! It gets worse every year. Why don't they sell up and find something more salubrious in the Home Counties?"

"They will eventually. Julie's a high flyer."

"You don't care much for Julie, do you?" George suppressed a grin, his mood lightening.

"I don't care much for women wearing the trousers in a relationship. David should learn to crack the whip."

"Hah – David has trouble cracking walnuts."

A mile away, David was standing at the front window watching out for their Rover. That morning, first thing, he'd put two dustbins and a plank in the road to stop Mrs. E parking her Datsun outside the house when she came back from her cleaning job; even so, she'd squeezed in by nudging the left-hand dustbin forward.

"Mrs. E is fearless," he thought gloomily, "I'm surrounded by fearless women."

He'd done his best to deal with George when he'd telephoned two weeks earlier. He dreaded George's calls – invariably they meant something was required to be done. One day soon, David was going to tell his parents that yes, Lorna did indeed have a telephone, had recovered from her inner ear problem that prevented her from listening to calls, and yes, if she refused to answer there was always the answerphone.

"Now look, David," George had said (instead of "Hello David, how are you and Julie, I just called to say I love you"), "Della's got an appointment with the specialist – thought we'd take in shopping and a show. You won't mind putting us up for a couple of nights."

David began face pulling and staccato heel tapping on their wood-block floor to attract Julie's attention. Julie was impervious for the moment, lost in the pages of *House Beautiful*, and looking fetching in black Capri pants and a tight white ribbed polo neck. Ominously, she was making notes in a pastel-coloured pad.

"I don't know what our plans are for that weekend," David said loudly, banging his knee against the cupboard doors.

"I haven't told you what weekend we're coming yet. What's all that banging?"

"The builders. They're putting in a new kitchen."

Julie looked up.

"Well, I'm talking two weeks' time – doesn't take a fortnight to put in a new kitchen."

"I'm absolutely sure that Julie..."

Julie had slid off the breakfast-bar stool and was shaking her head vehemently and mouthing "No way".

"You did hear what I just said? Your mother is seeing a bloody specialist. Or are you so caught up in your own selfish lives that you couldn't care less if your mother pegs it?"

David swallowed. "Of course I care. What's wrong with Mum?"

Julie's mouth remained open in the middle of her fourth "No way".

"That's for the specialist to decide, but we think it's women's trouble."

David covered the receiver with his hand and hissed "Women's trouble" at Julie.

"What sort of women's trouble?"

He gave her an 'I can hardly ask that' sort of shrug.

"Of course we'd love to have you both. No problem at all. Julie's here at my elbow insisting you come. Lorna will be thrilled."

"Don't overdo it. I've yet to see Lorna thrilled by anything concerning your mother and me. Thrilled's not part of our Lorna's repertoire."

"Quietly pleased, then," David muttered.

"What?"

"Nothing. We're really pleased you're coming... obviously, concerned about Mum..." His eyes followed Julie as she resumed her seat at the breakfast bar. Instead of the expected ructions, she was looking a little defeated. From her Capri pants pocket she produced a neatly folded lace handkerchief and blew her nose.

"Dad, I've got to go."

"No questions, no pack drill? Is that how the land lies?"

"The builder wants to know where the stopcock is."

"Can't Julie deal with the builder?"

"She's gone shopping."

"She was at your elbow insisting we came not a moment ago."

"She was on her way out to the shops."

"It's a bloody funny set-up you've got there."

"I'll ring next week."

"Tell your sister we'd appreciate a letter."

"I'll tell her. Bye Dad."

"Don't call me Da–"

David put down the receiver. "Julie, what's the matter?"

"Everything."

*

"Can I come in? Are you decent?" I pressed my face to the etched glass of their internal door and listened. I recognised the sound of Julie blowing her nose, the bar stool scraped across the ceramic tile floor and, surprisingly, the creak of the rocking chair. *I'm wasted on Green Bees and the* Echo – *how does one go about becoming a real detective?*

"Hold on a sec," David said from the other side of the door.

I held on for a further full minute before the door opened.

"Is something wrong?"

"Yes and no." David blinked at my red plastic mac. "Could you put your hood down please, it's unnerving. You look like the psychopathic murderer in *Don't Look Now*. I don't want Julie upset."

"Very funny. You're not the first person today to spot the resemblance – I've already frightened a woman in the post office queue. I thought Julie was made of sterner stuff."

I breezed into their kitchen, only to stop short at the sight of Julie sitting in the wooden rocking chair, dabbing at her eyes with a lace-edged handkerchief.

"Whatever's the matter, Julie? David, have you been awful?"

"David's never awful."

"Don't defend him. I know for a fact how awful he can be."

"George and Della are coming for a weekend." Julie sniffed and pulled on an angora cardigan as if she were cold, which was impossible in their kitchen.

"Oh, that is horrible. Yes, I'd be depressed."

"They're visiting all of us," David said. "Cup of tea?"

"Hot chocolate if you've got it... I may be away in the Lake District."

"You will not. Apparently Mum has to see a specialist." He looked solemn. "Dad implied it could be something serious – women's trouble."

"Probably piles."

"Piles aren't necessarily women's trouble... On the bright side –" he turned away from the kettle, a broad smile on his face – "Julie's pregnant."

"Oh." I looked around the kitchen for something to sit on and was forced to perch on Julie's vacated stool. "That's good, isn't it?"

"Yes, we're so pleased," Julie said and began to cry. "David, kitchen towel – this hanky's soaked."

"Julie's worried about how we're going to cope," explained David.

"The same as everyone else. Look at Mrs. E," I said.

"I don't want to look at Mrs. E," said Julie.

"What Julie means is, there'll be only one income coming in and she'd like to be a 'real mother' – and never having had a 'real mother' myself, I'm all for it, but it's not a step to be taking lightly. There may be serious repercussions. Nothing's necessarily straightforward."

"Well, I think it's marvellous."

"Well, you would. You don't have the responsibilities."

"David, stop hectoring Lorna."

"Not hectoring. Not meaning to hector." He turned back to the kettle and gave a muffled sniff. "Actually very happy."

"I'm very happy too. Don't fill my mug to the top – I'll just dash upstairs to get my Elmlea aerosol, to toast the good news."

"It's a secret for now, Lorna. Not a word to Mr. E."

"My lips are sealed."

"Nor Mum and Dad."

"My lips are super-sealed."

*

"Stand by your beds – here we are," George said, swinging the car into Duxford Road.

For the tenth time Della checked her make-up in the vanity mirror. "Not bad," she said approvingly.

"Jewellery?"

"Under the window shelf. It would be far safer at home in the strongbox."

"I think not. Prosperous middle-class areas are a prime target. I've no intention of leaving your hard-earned jewellery to the fate and fumblings of British Telecom Security."

"Why use them, then?"

"For when us Trees are in residence. For when we're in danger of being tied up, mugged and coshed."

Della sighed and said, "To change the subject ever so slightly, I don't mind the children now they're older. They're almost... nice."

"True. They could be a lot worse – muggers and coshers, fraudsters... That damn woman! Della, hop out and move the bins."

"George, I'm wearing cream."

At that moment David appeared. George wound down his window. "David, I thought I told you to reserve a parking space."

"You don't reserve parking spaces in Hackney. I tried but Mrs. E's a law unto herself. Don't park under the hebe, it's very windy."

"If that bush even strokes my paintwork, I'll sue. Come on, let's get the luggage indoors. Where's your sister? Titivating?"

"I shouldn't think so."

George was out of the car and throwing open the boot, looking over his shoulder as if expecting an attack at any moment. He manhandled out two large leather suitcases, Della's make-up case and a raffia snake-charmer's basket. "Handle with care! Safe place PDQ with the basket!"

"What's in it?"

"Your mother's JLY."

"Her what?"

"JLY."

David picked up the suitcases, put the raffia basket under his arm and went inside, leaving George to bring in Della and the make-up case.

"Julie, put this in a safe place – it's Mum's JLY."

"Her what?"

"Probably something to do with her women's trouble."

Julie shook it. "Sounds metallic. Should it go in the freezer? Lorna, what do you think? George says it's Della's JLY."

"Jewellery. Lock it in your drinks cupboard. Hello Dad, Mum."

"You look a pretty sight," George said genially. "What kind of get-up's that?"

"It's called trousers and T-shirt. I've told David to put Mum's jewellery in their drinks cupboard. There's a lock."

"Let the whole neighbourhood know."

"They'd need pretty spectacular hearing."

"Darlings, must use the bathroom," said Della. "Is it still in the same place, David?"

"Of course, where else would it be?"

"Me bathroom, then talk. Lap sang souchong would be nice but I'd settle for Earl Grey."

*

It was after lunch – a hearty affair where George had monopolised the conversation and David had done his best to. Della laughed at all George's jokes and Julie laughed at all David's. I'd responded to everything in monosyllables but tried to smile appreciatively for Julie's benefit. Now David and Julie were organising the dishwasher with the kitchen door firmly closed and Radio Three switched on to drown out their voices, George had gone for a lie-down in their spare bedroom (or what he ominously now called 'our room') and Della half sat, half reclined on the long sofa filling up the window bay.

She'd changed her pale wool dress for another pale wool dress, she wore fine cream stockings with a small dot in the weave, and the afternoon sunlight from the window behind her was having the desired haloing effect on her recently burnished curls and waves; her dainty high-heeled shoes of mushroom-coloured leather sat neatly discarded side by side under the coffee table... she looked perfectly at home.

I, on the other hand, sat awkwardly in the deep comfort of one of the matching armchairs, trying to balance my very full mug of hot chocolate and cream topping on my knees, well aware that any spillage would be classed as a serious offence. I didn't show up well against massed linen cushions, I spoilt their effect, and I knew Della was probably thinking precisely that.

Della frowning slightly in Lorna's direction thinking, *Why is Lorna, being the daughter of two such perfect physical specimens, so... galumphing?*

"Darling, sage green is really not your colour."

"I like it."

"Please yourself, but it makes your complexion muddy. I'm sure I'm not the first person to mention it."

"You are."

"Your friends are being tactful; it's a mother's duty to say the unsayable. Considering the pollution, your overall skin's not bad at all. You have my genes – you should choose your colours and fabric texture to enhance your skin tone."

"I told you, I like this colour."

"I'm afraid it doesn't like you."

After that we sat in silence apart from the sound of a passing car on the road and Mr. E clipping something ferociously in his front garden.

"Doesn't that man ever stop?" Della said at last.

"Mrs. E doesn't encourage him to come in the house during daylight hours."

"I don't blame her."

"When are you seeing a specialist?"

"Monday afternoon."

"Nothing serious, is it?"

Della shrugged her elegant shoulders. "Who knows? George is in absolute denial, bless him."

"How long will you be staying in London?"

"Till Wednesday at least. I'll need Tuesday to get over the trauma. I hope you'll be in attendance."

"I do my paper round on Tuesday."

"Ah yes, so tell me, how goes your work on the *Echo*?"

"I don't 'work on the *Echo*', I deliver it. I'm a hireling, the lowest of the low."

"And are the other delivery people a nice bunch?"

"Mum, I've never met them. We don't meet up in a wine bar after work and swap delivery anecdotes."

"I thought you might."

"Well, we don't." I was frowning now. Another silence – then the sound of dragging from outside. I squeezed behind the sofa and looked out of the window. "He's bringing out rolls of old lino. Bulk Waste collect on a Monday."

Della rubbed her temples then tried a brave smile. "Do you have a boyfriend yet?"

"Mum, I'm a lesbian – we don't have boyfriends."

"I thought you might have grown out of that silliness. Could you sit down? I hate the feeling of people towering over me."

I sat down and picked up my chocolate which was now at drinking temperature.

"And what about children? I mean, I'm not a complete innocent – I've read in the *Mail* about women and pastry brushes, but surely a man is the correct utensil for the job? Aren't you envious of David and Julie?"

"No, why should I be?"

"Julie being pregnant. All I can say is 'well done, David'. George is tickled pink."

"I didn't know they'd told you –" tried to lick a blob of cream clinging to the tip of my nose. "Don't you both mind becoming grandparents?"

"Not at all. George quite likes kids as long as they're well behaved."

"He minded his own."

"Lorna, you two weren't well behaved. Your grandma brought you both up to be sullen and difficult. Now, Julie will run a tight ship. I wonder where they'll move to?"

"They're not moving... are they?" My stomach dipped.

"They will, mark my words. Darling, I can hear George moving around, could you ask him for my yellow pills?"

I stood up.

"And perhaps another cup of Earl Grey and a chocolate biscuit."

I went out into the hall pulling the door shut behind me.

"Two chocolate biscuits," she called, "and tell George to come and talk – Della's lonely."

"It all adds value to the house – you can't go wrong," George was saying. He and David stood shoulder to shoulder, their hands in their trouser pockets, admiring the four-foot-high boundary wall plus further five foot of larch-lap crescent trellis with proud pineapple finials (Julie and David seemed to have a penchant for pineapples).

"I'd get some 'mile a minute' planted and blot out yon eyesore." George nodded in the direction of Mr. E's garden.

David shuffled nervously, trying to make enough bodily movement noise to muffle George's remarks from Mr. E, who was taking a breather from hauling lino, on the far side of Morris Minor.

"God almighty, David, look at the size of that rabbit. He'd feed a family of ten for a fortnight."

"That's Alfred the Great – he's a family pet – quite a character in his own right."

"Is he indeed? You sound exactly like your gran – she always insisted the E family pets were characters in their own rights, even the bloody dog that took a chunk out of Peppy 8 – Rusty the devil dog. 'He's a devil dog, George – what can you expect? Peppy's fault for making overtures.' I'd have sued."

"Mr. E's got no money," I said, crossing the patio/terrace towards them.

"Still put the wind up him."

"Dad, Mum wants her yellow pills and she said could you make her a cup of Earl Grey as nobody makes a cuppa like you do."

George gave me a long unamused stare. "Della would never use the word 'cuppa'."

"I improvised."

"For the moment I'm admiring David's barricade. I've told him to put in half a dozen 'mile a minutes' and blot out..."

"We don't want to blot out anything. We've blotted out quite enough already. Half this garden belongs to me," I said firmly, "as does half the house."

George raised his eyebrows. "Is that how the land lies? And what will madam do if her brother and his family move elsewhere? You couldn't afford to buy them out."

"Dad..." David said.

"You don't know what I could or couldn't do."

"Lorna, let's not have an argument."

"Dad's making trouble, not me."

"I'm putting forward the facts, but if facts aren't wanted I'll go in and see my wife," said George.

"She wants two chocolate biscuits as well."

We both watched George thundering back through the French windows.

"What was that all about? Now Dad's in a foul temper and they've only been here three hours."

"You said you weren't going to tell them about the baby yet – and I bet you've been talking to him about moving without saying a word to me."

"I was positing an idea."

"Oh yes? Positing an idea, is that what you call treachery? Must be just great for the two of you – baby on the way, plenty of money to posit ideas, and your locked drinks cupboard and your stuffed fridge-freezer and your overstuffed furniture..."

"Hang on a minute..."

"And your cars and your safe jobs and all this garden stuff which belittles your neighbours and Gran."

"Gran's been dead twenty years."

"We weren't brought up to this." I searched for a balled tissue at the bottom of my trouser pocket.

"Lorna, that's enough. Let's walk down to the Peppy graves and cool off. We can't be all bad – we never dug them up and replanted."

"Only because both of you were squeamish about digging up eight canine corpses."

Together we followed the meandering brick path to a wooden bench set between the composter and a circle of greying sea shells that marked out the graves. A sudden movement in the next garden and we realised that yes, it was Mr. E loitering in the shadow of Morris Minor.

"Afternoon Mr. E," called David.

"Afternoon David... Lorna."

"Hello Mr. E."

"Only two more rolls to go."

"Now listen," David said to me, "we are thinking of moving but we hadn't said anything to Mum and Dad. They just put two and two together as they do."

"And rightly came up with four. And when were you going to tell me?"

"When we'd had time to think matters through. Basically if you got a proper job and rented out our flat then you could afford a mortgage to buy us out."

"I don't want a proper job. I like living the way I do. It gives me time to write."

David kicked at one of the shells.

"Please don't do that," I said.

"Look, Lorna, nothing comes easily..."

"It does for you."

"I go out to work. I take responsibility. This may be the best thing for you. You can't go on forever writing poems nobody wants to read – and even if they did, there's no money to be made."

"And money's the bottom line?"

"Well, yes."

Julie opened the kitchen window and leaned out. "David, could you come and help, please?"

"Just coming. The important thing is to be mutually supportive this weekend – I don't want Julie upset. We'll discuss it when they've gone."

"They're staying at least till Wednesday."

"That's dreadful. Julie will have a fit."

He was halfway to the house when he turned back. "Damn, Lorna, in all the hubbub this morning I forgot to give you this."

"What?"

"Letter, delivered by hand. I found it on the hall mat when I went to let them in."

Wordlessly I took the envelope from David. "Sorry," he said sheepishly. I sat on Gran's bench. After so many years we still called it that – she'd placed it there for moments of contemplation when she'd no doubt contemplated Peppys 1–8 and how their lives and hers had intermingled. They hadn't been like Rusty the devil dog – the ones I'd known were snappy rather than devilish.

To give David his due, the bench had lasted because of his industry every spring and his conscientious wrapping it in tarpaulin every autumn. Who would tend the bench once they left? Would Lorna have to be a proper adult and find herself a job? Would Lorna have to share the garden with strangers?

But, in truth, I could see what I hadn't wanted to see: other people could have a baby here and prosper, but not David and Julie. Not possible. Not natural for them. Mrs. E would want to unload all the E family's cast-off baby clothes, the Reverend Joseph would want to baptise it, neighbours would offer it sweets and crisps and poke its cheeks with grubby fingers. Julie would hate the pregnancy horror-stories that everyone around here delighted in. In my teens I'd fainted just overhearing Mrs. E explaining to a friend how her varicose veins had been stripped out of both legs. I dimly heard, "Lorna, are you OK? Lorna?" Next thing I knew, Mrs. E was flicking cold tea from her chipped tea cup at my face...

"She's gone quite greenish."

"Is she pregnant?" Mrs. E's friend queries.

"No way – she's anti-men. You know what I mean?"

"I'm fine now. Please, no more tea. It was the varicose veins."

"Girl, you're soft. Your gran spoilt you."

"No she didn't. She just didn't talk operations."

"You shouldn't listen to other people's conversations."

"I wasn't listening. Your conversation intruded on my thoughts."

... I opened the letter. I had hopes that I was squashing down. *Lorna, it's just a letter. So what if the envelope was beige?*

"Hi Lorna – how do we make contact? I've walked down your road a couple of times – know the house but didn't like to bang on the door. I think your neighbour thinks I'm a burglar. Drink, dinner? Ring me. Dan," and a scrawled phone number.

"Ring me. Dan. Drink, dinner?" Did that mean what I hoped it meant?

"Lorna. Tea. Sandwiches," Julie shouted from her position at the kitchen window.

"I'm OK, thank you," I shouted back.

"No, I mean could you start making tea or sandwiches? I think it's warm enough for the terrace if we light the patio heater."

Surely a 'patio heater' belongs on a patio and not a terrace, oh fair and wondrous Julie?

"Coming," I said, and allowed myself five minutes more on the bench. In typical Tree fashion, my imagination took wings and flew – off with David, Julie and sproggins to their modern suburban house in a safe area; in with Dan, knocking down walls and removing locked interior doors, turning the two flats into one big home for us both.

She can come home as late as can be

"What do you think?" Julie pirouetted into the tight space at the bottom of my stairs. "Three more months and I won't be able to fit into this sort of outfit."

"No," I agreed, "you won't. Who are you supposed to be?" She wore a tight-fitting gold dress I'd never seen before.

"Sharon Stone in *Basic Instinct* of course."

"If you'd seen the film you'd know she looks the spitting image –" David caught sight of Julie's retroussé nose wrinkling ('spitting' being one of her many least favourite words) – "an exact replica of Sharon Stone, only not hard faced."

"And who are you?" I asked. David was in a black dinner suit, a brocade waistcoat and a ruffled white shirt plus false black moustache.

"Guess?" he stroked the moustache and smiled in what I knew he meant to be a roguish manner.

"Svengali?"

"Svengali? Why would I go as Svengali? Who even knows what Svengali looked like?"

"She's winding you up, David," said Julie. "He's Rhett Butler from *Gone with the Wind*."

(Jokes pop thick and fast into Lorna's head but she desists.)

It was Sunday, early evening, and we'd had a twenty-four hour reprieve. George and Della were meeting friends in town before all going to see *The Constant Wife*. They were staying in a hotel in Covent Garden, ready for the appointment with Della's specialist next morning. We were still none the wiser about the mystery ailment; Mum looked perfectly well, glowing in fact.

"You don't think she could be pregnant as well, do you?" David said jokingly, to which Julie and I gave the silent 'don't step into women's areas if you know what's good for you' treatment, and he went off in a huff to read the newspaper at the bottom of the garden.

If asked (and nobody *was* asking), I'd have said George and Della were up to something, trying to arouse our sympathy to fulfil a hidden agenda of their own. The worst scenario I could imagine would be a case of the dreaded 'thickening toenail', a fate worse than death as far as Mum was concerned, an omen of imminent senility.

"Darling, I live in fear of my toenails thickening – I couldn't bear it. So unfeminine. George would have to take me out and shoot me." I'd even thought of buying George a gun for his birthday now they were getting older.

Come to think of it, I couldn't imagine either of them with a real illness – they were too tanned and glossy and pampered, would one day walk hand in hand and unbowed by age into a glorious technicolour sunset. If David and I felt the slightest niggle of doubt we suppressed it, and when they announced their intended overnight stay in London we quickly seized up the threads of normal weekend life – David and Julie would go to their film-star fancy-dress party in St. Albans and I would attend Mr. And Mrs. E's thirtieth anniversary shindig as sole representative of the Tree family.

Pat and Sandra would be there, Pat having known the Es almost as long as I had. She still hadn't rung. I could hardly believe it – a fortnight passing without a word. For once I was determined not to be the one to make the first move.

"Do you really think I look like Rhett Butler?" David was saying, anxiously smoothing down his brocade waistcoat in front of the hall mirror.

I would have loved to reply, "Rhett Butler wasn't overweight," or "Rhett Butler had a full head of hair" (my George gene manifesting itself), but instead I said, "Of course you look like him. It's uncanny. Go and enjoy yourselves."

Julie swept a black velvet cloak over her shoulders – another garment I'd never seen before – had they won the lottery and not told me? They'd be driving around in an open-topped Rolls Royce and I'd still be pondering, *Lucky old David, they're paying him a sizable whack for being indecisive.*

"Don't forget to wrap Mrs. E's vase," Julie said, smiling girlishly from the front gate, knowing she didn't look half bad for a woman of thirty-seven and hoping the residents of Duxford Road fully appreciated what an attractive cosmopolitan couple lived amongst them.

"Clear off," I shouted good naturedly. "Stop making the front garden untidy."

I went into their kitchen to inspect Julie's purchase. As I'd guessed, she'd completely misinterpreted Mrs. E's taste or lack of it. Mrs. E wouldn't like this at all, she'd rightly think she was being patronised. The vase was from one of those pseudo antique shoppes in Camden Passage, where they display a cracked cup upside down with a limp ticket tied to its handle saying, "Early Wedgwood, £25." It was fat and pink with florid china roses and cherubs' heads adorning the sides. It was too pretty, too sickly sweet for Mrs. E. Mrs. E's vases were flamboyant; like Mrs. E, they'd seen better days and she used them for anything but flowers.

By her front door was the tall spare-key vase that David once got his hand stuck inside as a chubby teenager. "Ming dynasty," Mrs. E said. "If it weren't for the chip and the missing handle, I could retire on what it would fetch." Sometimes the spare-key vase got confused with the waste-paper and sweet-wrapper vase, which was wooden and "a present from Argentina", which still makes me think of Mrs. E as Stoke Newington's own ageing Eva Peron.

"To Mrs. E with gratitude from the people of Argentina."

"Why thank you," says Mrs. E/Peron. "This vase will always have a place in my heart and hallway, as will your love for me." Overcome, she lays a tremulous hand on her handsome consort Mr. E's chest. "Darling, I'm ready to go home now," she says huskily.

Too much daytime television, Lorna. I gave the vase a final thoughtful look and headed back upstairs to contemplate my wardrobe. This was sure to be a glitzy affair. Little glitz to be found in my wardrobe. Caught myself humming, "There's *no* people like *show* people..."

Mr. E and the children had strung fairy lights and silver and purple balloons around the front door, the gateless gatepost and the branches of his giant hebe. Mrs. E, our hostess in a silver lamé dress with stiff pleats, was resting her generous buttocks on the edge of the dustbin in the reflective process of lighting one of her cheroots. From inside I heard Aretha Franklin begging to be rescued, struggling against a slow piano rendition of 'Stand by Your Man'.

"Happy whatever," I said. "Where do you want the present?"

"Back bedroom. Who chose it?"

"Julie, with help from yours truly."

"A silk purse then?"

"Not necessarily."

"I'm thinking of giving up the vases."

"What will you put things in?"

"Tupperware."

"That won't look very attractive."

"Primary-coloured stack-a-boxes – they're all the rage."

"Are they? I hadn't noticed. I wish you'd said earlier. There's stack-a-boxes a-plenty in the Pound Store."

"Cheapskate. Your friend Pat's in the garden with whatshername... Why, Reverend Joseph, we didn't expect to see you on a Sunday!" Mrs. E switched on her warm and welcoming smile and let her cheroot fall into a disused flower pot. She was rather fond of the Reverend Joseph – after several vodka and tonics had been known to refer to him wistfully as 'the better man' which I thought very unfair to Mr. E. I hurried into the house before the Rev could treat me to one of his lengthy sermons on 'a young life wasted'. Passed the twins leaning against the central heating radiator, furiously chewing gum and awarding marks out of ten for clothes.

"Not another vase – you're so lacking," Estelle said. "Why didn't you buy Dad a new trolley or some herbs?"

"I wouldn't know where to find a trolley like your dad has."

"You could easily make one – not difficult. Mum says you've plenty of time on your hands."

"Does she? Well, the time on my hands is spoken for."

"Five out of ten," Esther said, "and that's only because you're the neighbour and we feel sorry for you. Nobody wears big collars and bust darts any more."

I caught a glimpse of myself in Mrs. E's dusty dressing-table mirror. More like an eight out of ten, thanks to the turquoise Lurex blouse I'd found in Julie and David's bedroom (thinks: must replace before they come home) plus my best black trousers, and a hint of burgundy henna in my hair. I placed the Tree family's tissue-wrapped vase with all the other tissue-wrapped vases.

There was also a smattering of pot begonias plus one large concrete rabbit: "To Edmund and Glenda, all the best, your friend Reverend Joseph." Why does anyone being thoughtful once in a blue moon bring tears to my eyes? I immediately mellowed towards the Reverend Joseph. I thought, he's not a dreary unimaginative pedant after all. However, must still keep my distance, probably won't show a spark of humanity to Lorna Tree until she's only a day or two left to live. *Enter Reverend into hospital ward bearing a leather-bound copy of the works of Radclyffe Hall: "Lorna, I have always appreciated and admired the way you've adhered to your very personal and not necessarily popular proclivities. Well done – you are a credit to your grandmother and a heroine." Lorna closes eyes and dies.*

The twins had given up and retired to the piano room. I could hear their loud argumentative voices as I made my way downstairs.

"I want to play the piano."

"No, it's my turn."

"Can't you play a duet?" some aunt said soothingly.

"I'm not sharing the stool with her."

"I'm not sharing the stool with you."

"Neither of you are playing the piano." Mr. E appeared in the doorway wearing his natty white shirt with the red and black guitar pattern. "*I'm* going to play it."

"Why should you get to play it?" they both whined.

"Because it's my piano and I know how to play ..." He began to play 'Hark the Herald Angels Sing'.

"It's not Christmas," everybody shouted – including me.

"It was Christmas quite recently."

"Dad, it's nearly April."

But the aunt had started singing in a wobbly contralto, other aunts joined in, several people began to la-la... I passed along the outskirts of the throng and noted Reverend Joseph surveying the revellers as if they were his congregation – any moment now he would give one of his impromptu sermons. I helped myself to a beaker of rum punch, caught Mr. E's eye and winked at him. He winked back and I went out into the garden where I could see Pat and Sandra sitting primly on a pair of upturned oil drums, Alfred the Great monopolising Pat's lap.

"Hello strangers," I said, meaning Pat, whom I'd hardly seen in months.

Sandra stood up and gave me a dry peck on the cheek, Pat waggled Alfred's long ears at me, saying, "Can't get up, he weighs a ton."

"Don't think much of their garden," Sandra said, "bit hazardous for children. I hope we aren't expected to dance out here with all the tin cans and rubble and... rabbits everywhere. Is that a car?"

"Half a car," I said. "They've brought up a family of five and nobody's ever hurt themselves." (This wasn't quite true; I should have said, "Nobody's ever hurt themselves much.")

"Sandra, don't worry – we certainly won't be dancing. Fill it up, will you?" Pat waved her glass above Alfred's head.

"Should you have another?" asked Sandra.

V.G. Lee

"I've only had one."

"So you say, but I'm sure you had a drink while I was in the shower."

"What? Am I a prisoner now? I'll get my own." Pat stood up and Alfred leapt onto Sandra's vacated oil drum. "Now look at me – I'm covered in white fur."

"What did you expect?" I asked. "He's moulting. It's that time of year."

"Thank you, Lorna. Since when did you become a naturist?"

"Naturalist," Sandra corrected her.

"I know what I said, Sandra. Are you going to get me a drink or not?"

Wordlessly Sandra took her glass and went into the house.

"That was a pleasant scene. What's got into you?" I asked.

"As is apparent, we're not getting on."

"I'm not surprised, if that's how you behave."

"Don't be so bloody po-faced."

"I am not po-faced, whatever that is, but since when did you become a bossy cow?"

"You would be a bossy cow if you had Sandra breathing down your neck all day. She drives me mad. They say you never really know someone till you live with them."

"*Who* says?"

"Everybody."

"I don't."

I put Alfred on the ground and sat down – we both watched him start on a large brown lettuce leaf. Pat looked sideways at me. "Aren't you concerned about your dear old friend's welfare?" she asked.

"About as concerned as you are about mine," I said. "That was a rubbish birthday card you sent: '*With fond thoughts on your special day*, Cheers, Pat'."

"It's the fond thought that counts. Lorna, you're as safe as houses, surrounded by a nauseating but loving family, fond neighbours who've known you since you were tiny and a therapist who thinks the sun shines out of your backside. Why should I worry about you?"

"Thanks," I said, wishing I could make notes to reflect on later.

"It was the DIY that started it. We could easily afford to get someone in to do the hard work but no, Sandra wants to prove to some unseen critic that she can do the lot herself. But she won't – she insists I do it with her. I can't wash my hair, read a book, take a bath without 'Can you pop down to the wood shop, just hold this, pass the white spirit, give the bloody emulsion a good stir, no that's not a good stir, a really put-your-heart-in-it good stir.' Where's the romance? I say, where's the romance?" Pat shook my arm angrily. "She says there'll be plenty of time for romance when we've finished the house, but there won't. It will be too late. It's too late already."

This was all surprising. This was all unsettling. Pat rarely made long and vehement speeches – she even sounded upset, which I found upsetting. There was something else... again I felt the flicker of unease I'd felt in their kitchen on the night of the dinner party... somehow these weren't completely Pat's words and thoughts.

"Seen anything of Theresa?" I asked casually.

"We've met a couple of times."

"Why? And why have you found time to see her and not me?"

"You're a friend and she's an attractive unknown quantity."

"I think she's awful."

"You used to find her attractive."

"Physically attractive. As a person she's hard and selfish. You must see that."

"I like what I see."

"It seems more like you like her liking you."

"Nothing wrong with that."

"Yes there is. You never used to be so... shallow."

"I did. You've always said I was shallow, or words to that effect. It never mattered. I was shallow, you were... odd."

"I quite like Sandra," I said.

"You go out with her, then."

"That doesn't mean I want to go out with her, it means she doesn't deserve you getting cold feet without at least trying to sort it out."

"It's too late."

"You haven't slept with Theresa, have you?"

"Yes. Now shut up. Here she comes – say nothing." Pat gave Sandra a wide insincere smile. "You took your time."

"I was trying to get a rust mark off my trousers – Mrs. E said she had some tetrachloride which might do the trick."

"Blimey," Pat said, "any good?"

"It wasn't tetrachloride. It was ammonia. My trousers are ruined."

"I'll just wander on down the garden," I said.

"Poor old Sandra," said Pat. "Shouldn't wear your best clothes when you're slumming it."

"Don't put words in my mouth."

"Well, see you in a bit…" I muttered.

"You're just a snob, aren't you?" continued Pat. "I must have been a fool…"

I left them to it. Horrible, I thought. Didn't like cruelty – it frightened me. All funny cheerful thoughts suspended, I felt thoroughly miserable. The fruit trees were just coming into blossom, their scent sweet and nostalgic on the chilly night air. I wished for Gran to bang heads, order socks to be pulled up and tongues to be held. Changes were occurring all around me but I stayed the same, doing the same things in the same places. Would I really ever get to go out with desirable Dan or had I chosen her because she was unobtainable? I hadn't rung her yet, waiting till Mum and Dad went home and my life returned to normal. And *would* I ring her or was it enough that she appeared to want me to ring? Could anything that happened between us equal that exciting apprehension before anything did happen, before you grew to know each other a little too well? Sandra, a whizz at quiche making and sex in the shower, becomes plaster- and paint-stained DIY bore.

With a sad sigh I peered through the trellis at our garden, dimly lit from the lamp I'd left switched on upstairs. Interesting to peer in from a different viewpoint. *Lorna watches others getting on with their lives from behind the safe barrier of a trellis fence,* I thought, then blinked. I blinked again. Had I imagined it or had I actually seen a person-sized shadow slip out of the darkness of our side entrance and take two crouched steps to the kitchen window before becoming invisible against the blue-black mass of the evergreen ceanothus that Julie was training to grow up the back wall? Were they carrying something?

Behind me a blast of Lena Horne singing 'Can't Help Loving Him' signified the party was in full swing; in front of me, I saw our kitchen window open. Quickly I worked my way back down the garden, trailed by Alfred. "Stay Alfred," I hissed. He looked momentarily bewildered, then as I moved off again, he followed.

No sign of Pat and Sandra. The guests were raucously helping Lena but "He can come home as late as can be" was drowned out by a gust of laughter – Mr. E was known as a man who never left home if he could help it, apart from his bi-weekly excursions in search of rabbit food.

I'd reached the gap in the trellis and just managed to squeeze through. I heard the sound of Julie's blouse ripping. "Damn. Stay, Alfred!" This time Alfred stayed, being far too cumbersome to leap a four-foot brick wall. "If I'm not back in ten minutes, get help."

Silently I hurried across our patio and peered into the kitchen. It was empty. A low light shone out into the hallway from the front room. I eased myself over the window ledge, surprised at how athletically cat-burglarish I was capable of being. From the wine rack I picked up a bottle of Rioja, holding it by the neck – a useful weapon. Then common sense intruded. Red wine all over the cream upholstery and oatmeal carpet? Julie would rather be burgled. Stealthily I slid the bottle back and chose a pale Chardonnay. Down the hall I padded, my heart thumping.

From the half-open door I saw a figure bending down in front of the drinks cabinet.

"Stay where you are!" I said in an authoritative voice.

The figure froze, then slowly straightened up and turned round. Behind her the cabinet door swung open and she kicked it shut with her heel.

"Oh there you are," Dan said, "so they keep the bloody wine in the kitchen, I should have guessed."

"Just what do you think you're doing here at ten o'clock at night?"

"Looking for you, Lorna."

"I don't think so. I saw you climb in through the kitchen window."

"You didn't answer the front door bell."

"We do not have a bell, we have a knocker, which is beside the point, the point being our kitchen window is kept locked which means you had to force it – and why are you wearing beige leather gloves?"

She grinned, looked admiringly at her gloved hands, flexed her fingers. "They cost me a fortune – I don't like to leave them in the car."

I was flabbergasted – horrible word but exactly how I felt – as if my flabbers, whatever part of my anatomy they might be, were well and truly gasted. Dan, on the other hand, appeared unfazed, insouciant. She might just as well have been helping herself to a drink from her own drinks cabinet except she didn't look the sort of person to own one – drinks cabinets are very David and Julie. The light from the table lamp turned the room a sickly yellow, with shadows lingering in the corners, and our encounter had the feel of a bad nineteen-fifties crime novel: heroine in torn blouse ineffectually clutching a bottle of Chardonnay while villain remains remarkably relaxed... or was she just waiting for an opportunity to spring? I touched my neck as another nineteen-fifties image shot into my head: this time, helpless woman was being bent back across a table, her blouse straining across her breasts as she struggled to reach wine bottle, fiendishly handsome woman intruder in beige fatigues lunges for her throat but instead is overcome by the terrified beauty of her victim...

"So, Lorna, are you going to call the police, hit me with your bottle, or shall we just take it upstairs to your flat and open it there? Although I think I'd prefer the Rioja."

"You've got a nerve," I said. Would that I'd had curls to toss angrily, but I made do with tossing my head, and at that instant I spotted it, tucked in next to the sofa – a pet-carrier. "Stay where you are!" I said again, but imperiously.

"I'm staying, I'm staying." She held up her hands in smiling submission.

I edged towards the settee, not taking my eyes off her, which made edging difficult as I had to negotiate around Julie's cream linen footstool and glass-topped coffee table. With my free hand I lifted the pet-carrier up on to the settee cushions. There was something furry and unmoving inside – surely she didn't travel around with a dead animal for company, a good luck talisman on her nefarious outings? Gingerly I reached inside and touched it. I don't know what I expected, perhaps an icy cold and stiffened object like Gran was when I visited her in the chapel of rest. Instead my fingers sank into something soft, like a furry cushion wrapped around a hard rectangular shape. I pulled and out it fell, giving me quite a shock. It was a fluffy dog pyjama case and inside was Julie and David's miniature carriage clock – a wedding present from me which always sat on the windowsill.

"And I thought you were a celebrity vet," I said.

"I have done a pet phone-in on Radio Margate," she said.

"I don't believe you."

"Clever Lorna."

"This is highly suspicious," I said lamely.

"This is highly suspicious, I grant you." She grinned, almost laughed!

"It's not funny. Why, you're..." *attractive, fabulous, intelligent, physically perfect...* "surely capable of holding down a good job." I sounded like David.

"I don't need to hold down a good job. I like to enjoy myself, I like excitement; this does me good, gives me a high." She crossed the room and gently took the pyjama case from me and put it back inside the carrier.

"I've had that pyjama case since I was a kid," she said and sighed – and weeks later I wondered about that sigh; whether it was for some memory in her past or a reluctance to take the next step, which was to put one arm around my waist and draw me against her.

This was not passion, not immediately – I think both of us, oddly, felt a deep sadness – and then she kissed me and her kiss was all I'd imagined it would be. And slowly as we sank into the kiss and it became passionate, so that I wanted life to stop at that very moment, the wry jokey side of my nature couldn't help registering (as she reached across to switch off the table lamp with her still-gloved hand), that perhaps this kiss was a calculated action – an illustration of how the criminal mind can compartmentalise.

I woke into darkness. In my head I was singing, "I-I-I'm just a love machine and I don't work for nobody for you," which was a song I didn't even know I knew. It was quarter to four in the morning. Dan had said to wake her at five because her pet phone-in for Radio Margate was at seven.

"You are joking?"

"Am I?"

I opened the bedroom curtains, a little light in the sky over Dalston. I could make out the E family's balloons bobbing gently, which made me think of Pat. What would she say about Dan? Two years ago, pre-Sandy, she'd have had a lot to say, but now I wasn't so sure. We'd heard her leaving the party next door just after midnight.

"And what happened to bloody Lorna?" she was saying. "I know what happened to bloody Lorna. You frightened her off, going on and on about your ruined bloody trousers."

The Reverend Joseph's stern voice saying, "Watch that language, young lady."

"Don't 'young lady' me. I don't believe in God. What do you say to that?"

"God will be most relieved."

Well done, Reverend.

"I'd have had more fun at my own bloody funeral. S'right. You know," she said as if she'd made a highly significant discovery, "I would have had more fun at my own bloody funeral."

"Please get in the car," Sandra said.

"Don't want to. Want to walk."

"Get in the car!" A sound of a scuffle, then the car door opening and slamming shut.

Dan was grinning. "She sounds a handful."

Dan slept. I didn't. In one way I was too happy, curled into the warmth of her body, her arm holding me against her as if already I mattered. I was also confused. Something should be said, surely? Questions asked? Statements taken? And I'd suddenly found myself thinking about Lily and Edna and how I'd first seen Dan on my way back from visiting them... The double-glazing saleswoman seemed the sort of daring and daft ploy someone like Dan might use – just for a laugh. *"Who'll I be today? The AA? A Jehovah's Witness? I know, it's been a few months since I've measured anyone for double glazing."* Had she sifted through my address book while I'd been arguing about bacon sandwiches in the buffet? Impossible. Why not just steal my purse? I might have noticed, I answered.

"Dan, wake up. It's five o'clock. Tea or coffee?"

"Neither. Got to go." She swung her long legs over the side of my bed and reached for her jeans.

"I wanted a word about Edna and Lily," I said, almost timidly for me.

"Edna and Lily?" she repeated, pulling on her T-shirt.

"Ridiculous I know, but have you ever pretended to be a double-glazing salesperson in the Brighton area?"

"Never."

"Does Edna, Lily and Druce Court mean anything to you?"

"Should it?"

"They happen to be old and dearly loved family friends who were robbed of their life savings plus vital domestic appliances."

She looked puzzled. "As in?"

"As in vital domestic appliances like kettles and electric blankets, also their life savings."

"Not guilty, Lorna. There's no market for kettles and electric blankets, and would I travel all the way to Brighton even for your ladies' life savings?"

"Why would you rob *me*?"

"I wasn't robbing you. Wouldn't dream of it. I took exception to your brother's Roman blinds. Whatever happened to good old-fashioned curtains?"

"Don't joke. I thought you liked me, now I don't know what to think. Did you sleep with me just so I wouldn't call the police?"

She put her arms around me and pulled me close. "Lorna, I like you very much. Will you let me off the hook? I can't explain last night – or I don't want to explain last night – but I would like to see you again."

"You promise it wasn't you who robbed my Brighton friends? I couldn't forgive that, stealing from defenceless women."

"I promise." She buttoned up her cream shirt and looked round for her socks. "Now where the hell...?"

"By the bookcase... Would *you* want a burglar finding your possessions irresistible?"

She grinned. "Wouldn't I just?"

How could I have a relationship with this woman? She wasn't even sorry – she was amused.

"You're not even sorry – you're amused," I said, handing her her trainers.

"Can we discuss this some other time?"

"Of course." My stupid heart leapt at 'some other time'. "Only I'm still so confused."

"Look, let's not spoil the night." She was no longer smiling; on the contrary, I might just as well have been a stranger – she stared right back at me, her eyes a hard green – like a cat. *This is a feral cat I've caught – she'll hurt me before she learns trust.*

"Did you put Julie's clock back?" I asked with mock severity.

Her expression relaxed, the smile returned. "I did. I am sorry. Now, can we drop the subject?"

Didn't know how much to tell Jenny Salter. She was a wise old bird when not being a heroic golden eagle. Managed to confuse her. She spent some time behind her curtain of hair, making it impossible to gauge a reaction.

"It's just one of those things," I said airily. "Whatever the real reason she had for attempted burglary, it paled in the face of our shared chemical reaction."

Was Jenny laughing behind her hair? I was sure her shoulders shook. Even to me, the shared chemistry theory was a little far fetched. I regarded my muddy trainers with dissatisfaction. Felt I did not look the kind of woman Dan would put her life of crime on hold for and that Jenny was thinking same.

"Of course, that night I wore Julie's Lurex blouse," I said. "I looked pretty..." (I discarded: amazing, fabulous, stupendous...) "different from my usual."

Jenny smiled. "I'm sure you looked lovely."

Well actually, Jenny Salter, I don't want to look lovely.

"I don't know about 'lovely', but fairly special."

"You obviously haven't had time yet to find out why Dan steals or why she was stealing from you?" Jenny had sat up very straight in her high-backed chair; for once I had her full attention.

"She said she'd taken a dislike to David's Roman blinds."

No smile from Jenny.

"She was joking," I said.

"I expect she was," she agreed quietly and sighed.

"The thing is, Jenny, I don't think she'd appreciate my inter-rogating her. What I thought was –" I scraped my chair a little closer, so that Jenny just might think the two of us were putting our heads together on my behalf and this would be a good idea – "I'd see how we go on. Give the relationship a chance to develop."

"That could work... but I don't think it's a very good idea. Wouldn't you rather give her a chance to explain, apologise, make reparation?"

These were unwelcome words indeed, coming from a woman who usually adhered to the 'Wait and see, in your own good time, and a problem deep-breathed on, often goes away' principles.

"She wouldn't want that chance. She doesn't seem bothered."

"Are you bothered?"

"I'm trying not to be."

"And just suppose she had robbed Edna and Lily?"

"But she didn't. I jumped to an extremely far-fetched conclusion."

"But Lorna, if she had."

"I'd ask her to return the goods and money."

"And that's it."

"That's it."

"I see."

Left Jenny in deep thought. Went to Best Ever Turkish Kebab and bought a hundredweight of chips. Ate them all with plenty of salt and vinegar. Felt far too ill afterwards to think about anything.

Mayday, Mayday

Mum and Dad being up in London, seeing a show with their friends, had apparently wiped Mum's visit to the specialist from our memory banks. It didn't seem a matter worth worrying about. Della seemed fine. George worried too much. This was how we'd dealt with them since childhood – out of sight, out of mind, get on with our own lives.

I was getting on with my own life that particular morning, being at that cheerful stage when someone you care about has only just left and you can happily concoct a rosy future without the torture of wondering where the hell they've gone and when they'll be back – which usually comes three days later. It was a sunny morning which cruelly showed up the dust settled atop the picture rail and pictures in our joint hallway, so I was feeling perfectly justified in using the Hoover inside the seven-day restrictions set out by David. I love the Hoover extension. It gathers dust and fluff so gratifyingly and as I gathered I hummed along to Shirley Bassey's 'What Now My Love?' which in my troubled past had reduced me to tears, especially the bit about nobody caring if I lived or died. It's a different kettle of fish altogether when you're feeling pretty certain that somebody does care, i.e. Dan of the fluffy dog pyjama case she'd nurtured since childhood.

In my enthusiasm I stretched the Hoover cable a picture rail too far and the plug popped from the electric socket and my imagined Shirley Bassey was replaced by Dad's voice shouting over David and Julie's answerphone: "Will someone pick up this bloody phone? Mayday. Mayday."

I picked it up. "Yes Dad?" I said, my heart sinking.

"Who's that?"

Is there something wrong with my voice that nobody recognises it? "Lorna."

"I wanted Julie."

"She's at work."

"I thought she worked from home."

"Only three days a week. First Monday in the month is 'Think-tank Monday', when they float new ideas."

Silence.

"Dad, are you there?"

"I'm assembling my thoughts," he said. "I'm dealing with buffoons. I need to be as lucid as possible, have no hitches, and for you to listen carefully and intelligently. Comprendo?"

"So far," I said cautiously.

More silence, then he took several deep breaths, then, "They're keeping Della in."

"I see."

"No, you don't see because I haven't told you anything yet, not given you a picture to work with," he snarled.

Oh George you can be a nasty piece of work, I mouthed into the Hoover attachment.

"This evening Della will have a major operation. Today, now, when you put this phone down, you will go out and buy three pretty nightdresses and negligées; you will pay attention to what you know she will like. You will under no circumstances 'do your own thing', impose your own rugged taste in nightshirts on her. Got it?"

"I don't have enough money."

"You will sort that out. You are an adult. I will reimburse you when I see you." His voice seemed to falter just a little, was it the thought of reimbursing me or...

"Are you all right, Dad?" I said, softening.

"Of course I'm all right. Della has the small 'c'."

"Is she very ill?"

"If she doesn't have this operation now, she will be." This time his voice did shake. *Oh bugger, Dad, don't let me down now.*

"What exactly...?"

"I've no intention of discussing my wife's medical details with someone young enough to be her daughter."

"But I am her daughter."

"Then doubly so. Over and out."

Rang David. He was at a site meeting. Rang Julie. She was a pillar of strength, agreed to meet me in front of John Lewis at lunch time and then go on to the hospital.

"Don't worry about the money. I'll pay. Your father wouldn't dare not pay me back."

"Will Mum be OK?"

"Yes she will. She's as tough as old boots Those skinny fragile sexpots last forever. Trust me."

Pondered over ringing Pat. A year ago she'd have been first on my list. My hand hovered over the receiver. In the end I rang. Answerphone. Didn't leave a message. I didn't have her mobile number. How times change.

*

"Head in sand, George. Always bloody head in sand. Mother was right." George gave the hospital cafeteria the once-over. Why hadn't they joined Bupa when he left the army? All their friends had private healthcare but he and Della imagined they were immune to illness and old age.

"You queuing?" Woman in shabby tracksuit, age unguessable, nudged George with her shopping bag.

"Would that be a question or a statement?" George would certainly have quipped had Della been nearby to appreciate his wit, but, "I'm trying to locate a tray," he said instead, and awarded her the full force of his expensively dentured smile.

"Trays are on the trolley over there." She pushed past him and joined the queue. George turned his attention to the tray trolley. For the moment it was besieged by the hoi polloi and George decided he'd hang about till the rush was over, rather than rub shoulders.

"These are just the visitors and they all look like disease carriers," he thought. "Don't let the buggers in till their clothes have been fumigated and they've been scrubbed down with a bar of lye soap."

The hoi-polloi, as George and Della laughingly called the hoi-polloi, appalled and intimidated George without Della at his side to give him confidence to swagger amongst them – if he chose, which he didn't very often. Over the years it had become increasingly easy to avoid ordinary folk, as in poorer or less well educated or badly dressed or loud of voice or... Those times when the twain met could be reserved for special occasions when George needed confirmation of just how wide the gap had grown between him and them. Irene's death and the children's animosity had helped; there was no more reason to pretend he shared common ground with the droopy-cardiganned Reverend Joseph, or to pretend to Edmund on the other side that he too felt the seductive pull of the natural world and if that included old tyres, oil drums and lengths of lead piping, so be it.

Excruciating was the memory of an afternoon during the early days of the E family occupation, he and Edmund sharing a moment of tranquillity, leaning against the warm metal side of Morris Minor, George listening patiently to Edmund's interminable silence, the two of them smoking Edmund's infernally vile roll-ups and George breaking the silence because truthfully he was not a man to enjoy a silence, saying, "You know, I take my hat off to you, Ed, you've created a paradise for the twentieth century," and being gratified that Edmund appeared gratified. Who'd have thought that thirty years later Morris Minor would still be in situ, still toy blue, still recognisable as the shell of a Morris Minor?

The crowd around the tray trolley was clearing so George sauntered across, feeling the eyes of the hot crowded room watching him saunter. George well knew that in moments such as these, crossing-the-floor moments, at weddings, funerals, retirement bashes etcetera, he radiated 'too big for his boots'. He knew because his mother had frequently told him, and all Della's assurances that "For 'too big for your boots', read, a man who stands out from the herd because he is a very special man" hadn't managed to repair the damage. He arrived at the tray trolley breathless, because he hadn't been breathing. Gingerly he removed the top tray, then the next, and the next, in search of what he liked to call 'Hornchurch clean'.

"Yes?" An aggressive-faced fellow in a grey stained overall materialised – genie of the tray trolley.

"I'm looking for a clean tray," George said.

"These are clean trays."

"Are they indeed?"

"You what?"

"Sorry?" said George.

"For what?"

"Pardon?" George, baffled, paused in his search.

"Granted, but don't do it again. Now, what are you doing with my trays?"

"As I said, I'm looking for a clean one. The soiled ones have somehow infiltrated into the clean pile – I'm sorting through."

"Do what? These are all clean, mate."

"Perhaps some are more clean than others," George hazarded, thinking, *"God almighty, under normal circumstances I'd make mincemeat of this jobsworth."*

"Either take a tray or leave them alone."

George took the next tray. It was the dirtiest tray he'd seen so far. A lesser man might have cried with frustration – not George, he squared his shoulders and said, "Look here, this tray is absolutely filthy – no way can it be classified as clean. I can clearly recognise egg, ketchup, something to do with sausages, and broccoli, although I'd be astounded if an establishment like this would know what to do with a piece of broccoli even if it grew arms and wrote its name in the grease of yon worktop… Please stop pushing, I have a right…" George was suddenly caught in a tidal wave of small people hungry for trays.

"Give me that tray," the man said.

"Why?" George clutched at the tray. All the trays were being taken – he was damned if he'd be left trayless.

"Because I'm going to wash it. OK?"

"Are you?" George's voice was surprisingly husky with emotion. "I'm really awfully sorry to make a fuss. My wife, you see…"

Gently the man took the tray from him, cleared a space amongst the dirty plates on the nearest table and from a bucket of grey and greasy water wrung out a grey and greasy cloth, rubbing the tray surface briskly.

"You're not wrong – this is pretty diabolical. Customers, they give pigs a bad name." He pulled a wad of paper napkins from the napkin dispenser and wiped the tray dry – and really it looked quite presentable, could almost be classed as clean as long as George didn't investigate the gritty patch his fingers had just found on its underside.

"Thank you," he said humbly.

Strangely soothed, he headed for the food counter. In the chrome of the hot cabinet, the tray genie was reflected, tapping the side of his head, then pointing after George and mouthing 'barmy' to nobody in particular, which in no way affected George's quiet feeling of gratitude. He was in need of kindness, was unused to it not being doled out by Della on an hourly basis.

He carried his plate of dried-out lasagna plus small carton of blueberry yoghurt over to a lone table by the window. Sighing, he brushed the resident table crumbs onto the floor before settling himself, tutted and went back for a pot of tea. The window looked out over a courtyard filled with builders' rubble, a cement-encrusted wheelbarrow, a spade stuck lopsidedly in a pile of sand. There was a stillness about the scene as if it was all that remained of an extinct civilisation. George communed with this morbid thought for several minutes before attempting his lasagna. Almost palatable – the lasagna. Such a relief, seemed like hours since he'd last eaten. Gulped tea and, feeling himself warmed, realised he'd been chilled. Feeling a little better, he leant back in his chair, no longer seeing civilisation's ruins as he tried to analyse his feelings of wretchedness.

It wasn't just the possibility of Della dying – no, he was reminded of a train of the old powerful locomotive variety, steaming out of his past, coming up behind him, intent on mowing him down. The train was the months, the years after Steven drowned; and once again, here was George in the role of inadequate bystander.

"What Mother never understood was I loved him too," he thought. "He was my brother. We got along. I didn't mind him being the favourite. I do not want to think of Steven. This is not the time nor the place."

Only it was almost, not quite, a relief from thinking of Della. Too terrible to contemplate, Della dropping through a hole in the universe, the hole closing and her disappearing. Life with no Della in the picture. He looked at his watch.

"Come back at four," the nurse had said as she drew the curtains round Della's bed. That still left half an hour. Thirty minutes. He thought of the waiting room, the long corridor; David and Lorna, who had just arrived and were larking about like kids, refusing to care, and Julie, who was playing the adult and happy to do so.

"Dad."

He started. He'd been miles away. Clumsily pushing the table away and standing up – "What's happened?" – searching Lorna's face.

"Nothing. I just came to find you. I thought you might like company."

"How the mighty have fallen, eh?"

"Not at all." Lorna sat down and George fell back into his chair.

"If you get yourself a cup, you can share my tea, for what it's worth."

"No thanks. Horrible, is it?"

"Lousy. What a dump."

"It's a hospital and a good one."

"Filled with every Tom, Dick and Harry."

"So?"

"I wanted better. She should have the best," he said almost ferociously.

"Dad, she'll be all right."

"You bet she'll be all right. Wouldn't dare leave me in the lurch." He looked fiercely out of the window. "You don't think much of your mother, do you?"

"She doesn't think much of us. You're the only one she ever really sees."

George poured more tea, blinking rapidly. "I absolutely loathe sentiment of any kind but I'll say this once, Lorna, and never again – I *need* your mother to see only me. Understand? She's the only one who ever has. You, your brother, don't need that as I do. In my way, take it as read, I'm fond of you both. Selfish maybe. So what? Worse things happen at sea."

"I think I knew that. We're very fond of you."

"You don't bloody behave as if you are."

"Ditto."

"Don't 'ditto' me." He looked at his watch again. "Time's up. Let's see how the National Health Service prepare for a major operation."

"We're a bit early."

"Early be buggered."

*

We all passed a tense couple of hours in the hospital during Mum's surgery, with David and myself glumly studying ancient copies of *Hello* magazine.

"Isn't Liberace dead, David?"

"I think so."

"Isn't Barbara Cartland dead, David?"

"I think so."

"Isn't Rock Hudson dead, David?"

"I think so."

"Isn't Red Rum dead, David?"

"That's enough, you two," snapped Julie, dressed for a possible death in the family in a shocking-pink and black candy-striped suit. Dad was saying nothing, he kept pacing the corridor, sometimes he made it to the end of the corridor, sometimes he disappeared around the bend in the corridor, sometimes he was with us, sometimes he was not. He is a big man, takes up a lot of space. Hard to understand under these particular conditions how Gran could have taken a dislike to her remaining son. In many ways he is the buffoon and there is something lovable about his buffoonery.

Finally a smiling doctor appeared and took Dad to one side for a quiet word. We watched greedily. The doctor was doing all the talking, Dad nodding. He saw us watching him and turned away so we couldn't see his face. We could see him nodding. The smiling doctor then approached us, leaving Dad to scoot off down the corridor.

"David, Lorna, your mother is going to be just fine. Convalescence and TLC is what she needs."

After he left us, Julie snorted, "That woman's been drip-fed TLC all her life. A spot of hard work..." She kissed David. Nobody kissed me.

Next thing we knew, Dad had moved out, taking Mum's JLY with him, and was staying in a mansion flat loaned to him by one of his army friends, as it was only two tube stops from the hospital – which was a huge relief to us as our house had been filled with his strident voice barking out orders to promote the welfare of George and Della. I'd begun spending longer and longer on my paper round, was even considering asking the *Echo* to extend my patch to Dalston; and David and Julie were meeting up after work and staying out for dinner.

"Lorna, where the hell is everyone?"

"At work, Dad."

"At ten o'clock at night?"

"Apparently so."

"I hope I don't detect a tone."

Oddly enough the nurses, while finding a little of Mum went a long way, seemed to love my father. I was told a number of times that "Mr. Tree is adorable."

Was inclined to respond, "You try sharing a bathroom with him, then."

I popped in to see Mum en route to the poetry class. She had some Estée Lauder colour in her cheeks at last and was loudly deploring the casual way the nurse had washed her hair.

"It looks very pretty. Curls suit you."

"I look like Shirley Temple."

"Shirley Temple's not so bad. Where's Dad?"

"He's in reception trying to get them to change my curtains."

"But everyone has the same curtains," I said.

"Exactly. If I can't be given a private room, let me at least personalise this meagre space I've been allocated. Let me bring in my own curtains. Surely they can allow a dying woman some leeway. What's that in your rucksack?"

I pulled out a bunch of drooping red and orange gerberas, a Safeway carrier bag knotted round their stems. "These are for you from Mrs. E. She said to say the E family's thoughts are with you."

Mum wrinkled her nose. "They're not even fresh. I can smell them from here. They've been standing in stagnant water."

You can see where I get my detection abilities from. Mum was quite right, they weren't fresh, they did smell of stagnant water. They'd been sitting on Mrs. E's front room sideboard since the night of her anniversary party.

"Chuck them in the bin."

"Suppose she pops in to see how you are and wants to know where her flowers went?'

"I shall tell her I'm not in the habit of accepting second-hand anything," Mum said loftily.

"Mrs. E meant well."

"She did not. It was a premeditated insult. She never did like me. None of you do. I don't have the ability to inspire love the way your grandmother could." Her eyes filled with tears but years of practice ensured they didn't spill over. "Oh God, I'm an absolute wreck."

"Trust you to make your mother cry," George said – he can move surprisingly quietly for such a big man.

"I didn't. She made herself cry."

Mum smiled bravely through her tears. "Don't tell her off, George, she doesn't appreciate the effort required to keep up certain standards. Any luck with the curtains?"

"It's all red tape and regulations. Bloody National Health Service couldn't run an ice-cream van. Lorna, haven't you got somewhere to shoot off to? You're making Della tense."

I shot off, out of the closeness of the ward. In the outer room I stopped at the desk. "How exactly is my mother, Mrs. Tree?" I asked.

The nurse sitting by the filing cabinet intent on braiding her hair exchanged glances with the nurse next to the telephone intent on scraping the insides of a Greek-style yoghurt.

"Coming along," she said.

"Will she be out soon?"

"Very soon," the yoghurt eater said ominously.

"She's not going to... die?" I swallowed.

"Not if she behaves herself and stops giving us orders."

Dan had disappeared into the wide blue yonder, her land line was always engaged and the mobile number she gave me belonged to one Mr. Cheung, an alternative chiropodist working out of Clapham Common. It was now the first evening back at poetry class, the beginning of the summer term.

"Several new people this week – Percy, is it? Have you brought something in for us?"

Percy, man with bike clips and thinly spread hair, beamed and produced a cassette player from his briefcase. "It's called 'The Plucky Pit Pony'," he said, waving a cassette at the tutor. I groaned internally. I'd sat through countless 'Plucky Pit Pony', 'Mighty Oak Tree', colliery closure, Mum/Dad/family perishing poems. You know what to expect. Tutor kept his smile in place.

"Normally, Percy, we read our poems aloud," he said pleasantly, in case Percy turned out to have a particular disability preventing his reading his poem aloud.

"I like to get the professionals to read my work," said Percy, "they'll do it justice, give it the *je ne sais quoi*."

"Ah," said tutor.

"Roy Bean in this instance. He's a conjurer chappie I know. Mellifluous voice. Superb diction."

"Good. I hope you've brought twenty photocopies in for the rest of us to study in tandem."

"No need. I can play it over several times."

"Yes, there is a need – a need for twenty photocopies please, in future. That is one of the rules we accept when joining this class."

"There go a hundred Norwegian pines to feed the greedy capitalist's photocopier," piped up Ragnar the Dane.

"So many? Good grief?" responded kindly tutor. "So, Percy, how long is your poem?"

"Thirty-two minutes, forty-three seconds."

"I see," said kindly tutor.

After three minutes, with plucky pit pony only just having been born, I tuned out and surveyed the class, saw who had dropped out and who was new, and after some strenuous manoeuvres with my head and chair I saw that, yes, that was Ange of Ange and Baby Tonia sitting next to Ragnar in the front row. Surely not a 'Baby Tonia' poem on the cards for this evening?

"I think we've got the gist of that," said the tutor, snapping off Percy's cassette. "Percy, I'm sorry but your poem is really far too dense for us to take in without reference to the written word. Perhaps next week. Lorna, glad to have you back."

There were several gratifying 'hear-hears' from Donald, Roger and Martin, and even Ragnar swivelled around in his seat and stared at me.

"Hi Ragnar," I said.

"Lorna. You're looking good."

"Thank you so much," I responded with insincerity.

Tutor was moving towards Ange with welcoming, kindly expression. "Angela, have you anything for us?"

Lorna transported into a tent on a Victorian pier; a seance is in progress orchestrated by Ange wearing a beaded shawl over her head.

"Angela, have you anything for us?"

Ange nods vehemently, "My spirit guide Grey Buzzard has a message for Lorna Tree. He sees a woman in beige. Your fates are inextricably linked. She will do the cooking and you the hoovering and let no woman put you asunder."

"My poem's called 'Terry'," said Ange, handing out her twenty photocopies. The class settled down. We emulated the tutor in our kindly, welcoming expressions.

"'Terry' –" small cough from Ange – "Sorry, bit of a frog. 'Terry'. 'She said to me she wanted to be/ close by my side. We made a promise/ but she was untrue and that night I died./ Now it's too late to tell your Ange/ how much you cared/ so I'll wait at the gates of heaven for you,/ Te-er-ry'."

Pause as class digested this. There were two other verses but I think I've given you a flavour.

"It's a reworking of a famous sixties pop song," explained Ange, wiping tears from her eyes.

"I thought it sounded a tad familiar," Roger said jovially.

"Perhaps a little more reworking," suggested tutor. "Might find yourself in copyright problems if it was ever published. What say the rest of you?"

"It's not a poem, it's a song lyric," said Brenda, who prided herself on calling a spade a spade.

"Rather too much tumpty-tum for my taste," said Donald, "but an interesting, emotive subject."

Suddenly Ragnar was roused from his slumped position over his Toblerone. "You English are all wankers. It's the best poem we've ever had here." He slapped Ange heartily between her shoulders.

"Ragnar, I will not tolerate bad language."

A smattering of 'hear-hears', and I realised the poetry class reminded me of *Yesterday in Parliament*.

"Either apologise or leave the room immediately."

We were all amazed, having never seen our tutor so incensed. Ragnar, a triangle of Toblerone an inch from his open mouth, also looked amazed.

"Wankers – is that not just a friendly colloquial English word?"

"No, it's an offensive colloquial English word."

"In that case I apologise." He proffered his Toblerone to Ange.

"No thank you, chocolate makes me hyperactive."

We moved on to Phil's maritime ballad.

Ange and I caught the 38 bus back to Dalston. I told her about Mum's operation and a little about my childhood and she told me about Baby Tonia who would be starting primary school very shortly.

"I'll miss her," she said and lapsed into silence.

This was a very different Ange from the one I'd met in the pub fourteen months earlier – obviously Theresa Stowell-Parker affected different people in different ways.

"What made you rewrite that song?" I said at last.

"It seemed to fit. Terry sometimes rides a motorbike. She looks great in her leathers."

"Do you see much of her?"

"Not enough. She turns up when she's got nothing else to do."

"That can't be very satisfactory?"

"It isn't, but if you love someone you take what's on offer."

I thought over this statement for several minutes and decided not to challenge it. Instead I said, "I can see she's very attractive but is she lovable?"

Ange's face flushed and for the first time that evening she looked animated. "You'd be so surprised. She's smashing company on her own. She and Tonia get on like a house on fire."

"Really?"

"It's this other woman. She's a bad influence."

Surely she doesn't mean Pat?

"They've lived together for years. I hate her. She says 'normal' is suburban, relationships are death-traps – and Terry swallows it all."

"Terry doesn't have to."

"She has a psychological hold over Terry. Dan says she and Terry are soul mates even though they don't sleep together any more."

"Dan?"

"Dan. The woman Terry lives with. I hate her."

"What's this Dan like?"

"Confident, attractive, bags of money…"

"Does the word 'beige' mean anything to you?" I asked miserably.

"Yes. That's her. She's known for it. Beige, always wears beige. Do you know her?"

"Slightly."

"And?"

"And nothing." I'd been about to say, "Seems like a nice woman," but hand on heart even I'd have had difficulty telling Ange that. I knew for a fact she was anything but a nice woman. "I hardly know her. She was in the pub that time when Pat started going out with Sandra."

"That's right. That's her. If she'd just leave Terry alone, I'd stand a chance."

The front door flew open while I was still rummaging for my key – it was Julie, looking furious.

"Hello Julie, everything all right?"

"No, everything isn't all right. Why was it necessary to paint moustaches on the cherubs?"

"Pardon?"

"Mrs. E's vase. Did you know that vase cost me fifty-five pounds? I didn't ask for a contribution because you're always pleading poverty, but you decided to make a contribution anyway, didn't you? A typical 'Lorna Tree non-productive make everyone look like fools' contribution."

"Steady on, Julie," I remonstrated. "Do you mind if I come in?"

David appeared in the shadows behind her. "Honestly, Lorna, whatever goes on in your head?'

"I thought Mrs. E would like it more with moustaches," I said feebly.

"Whether Mrs. E likes it more or less isn't the point; I took the trouble to buy the present as I take the trouble to do most things round here. All you had to do was wrap it up and even that was too much to ask. I thought you were growing up at long last but I was wrong."

"And the kitchen window lock's buggered." David this time.

"And I have a Lurex blouse missing and Mrs. E tells me you looked surprisingly presentable in a Lurex blouse last Sunday."

Game, set and match to David and Julie. Lorna absolutely trounced.

"Well?" asked David. "What have you got to say for yourself? Julie, go on in, I don't want you getting upset."

"Julie, I'm really sorry."

"Do you have my blouse or don't you?"

"I do."

"When did you intend to give it back?"

"Now Julie…" David massaged her neck soothingly.

"When I'd mended it."

"And the window lock? That was you as well, wasn't it?"

"Yes. I left my keys indoors."

"Mrs. E has a spare key."

"I didn't want to interrupt the sing-along."

"We despair of you. From now on you are as a pariah in this house," David said, ushering Julie back into their hallway.

"Pariah's going a bit far," I said to their closing door.

I toiled upstairs. Phew. Not a great Lorna Tree day. Message from Kate sounding subdued: "You'll no doubt be pleased to hear that Tina doesn't want us to have a litter of puppies, says I'm not ready for parenthood." Message from Pat: "I've just heard about Della being ill.

Why didn't you telephone me? I will be at your house at nine-thirty on Wednesday morning. Sometimes you are so stupid." Message from Dan: "Hello there, Lorna Tree. I'll see you very very soon."

"I won't hold my breath," I muttered; but conversely, even after Ange's information and being designated house pariah, I couldn't help my spirits rising just a little.

A lily of the field

In Julie's larger-than-life Grecian urn, purple pansies clustered around the stems of purple tulips, purple being Julie's approved garden colour this season. The urn was set on a concrete plinth and dominated our small front garden. She had also made our dustbin area a design feature with a trellis pergola set around the bins; and had instructed an evergreen honeysuckle to 'get a move on and turn this ugly corner into a leafy bower'. I was forced to admire her determination to make sows' ears into diamanté purses.

Dad on his forays in from the mansion flat at Russell Square had seen more than enough of Julie. She was the sort of woman he disliked... Hang on, he disliked most sorts of women apart from his beloved Della, but Julie types in particular, who were self-sufficient, opinionated and also physically very capable. Yesterday he had taken David aside for a man-to-man talk in the back garden.

"She's wasting your money, you know, with all her highfaluting ideas. Don't indulge her – cut the purse strings. Be a man."

David said, "It's Julie's money as well. She earns nearly as much as I do..." And then he caught sight of me manhandling my loaded clothes-airer out into the garden via our side entrance – I could see from his expression that he was tempted to appeal to me for help with Dad, but was still under instruction not to speak to me.

Dad cut in instead: "You'll be drawing a pension before you find a proper job. Aren't you ashamed of yourself, Lorna?"

"I'm a poet. A lily of the field. I neither sew nor do I spin."

Wrong response, Lorna. David immediately pounced, saying, "Well you'd better *learn* to sew! Julie wants that blouse back in immaculate condition by this weekend."

That was my reason for admiring Julie's front-garden planting – I was on my way out to the twenty-four-hour dry cleaning and alterations kiosk on the High Street, her blouse folded neatly at the bottom of my luminous *Hackney Echo* sack.

I don't think I've ever left the house without one or another neighbour harassing me. Did Gran on her death bed secure a promise from both sides?

"Keep an eye on Lorna, she's wilful but her heart's in the right place."

Mr. E with tears in his eyes at the foot of her bed, Reverend Joseph on his knees clutching the Book of Common Prayer, hopeful of administering the last rites if he hung about long enough.

"Between us, we'll keep the child on the straight and narrow."

Would they both be chivying me back onto the straight and narrow when I was fifty, sixty?

"I hear you've been up to your old tricks again, Lorna," the Reverend Joseph said, materialising from the murky shadows of his porch.

"What old tricks might they be, Reverend?" I replied truculently, feeling a slight Irish brogue was called for.

"Lorna, do you intend to argue your way into the fiery flames of hell?"

"No. I wouldn't imagine I'd get sent to hell just for arguing. Seems a little reactionary, although I bow to your greater knowledge, Reverend." Actually I didn't say any of that because Reverend J. would have been deeply offended and would probably have sent me to Coventry.

"Your sister-in-law is about to have a baby. Your mother is seriously ill. Everyone is concerned. Aren't you being a little selfish?"

"Julie's only just pregnant, and re. Mum, I'm concerned as well."

"You have a strange way of showing it."

"Still waters run deep," I said and, "I'm not one to wear my heart on my sleeve."

He sighed. "Even as a little girl you were pig-headed."

"I was not."

"You always had difficulty admitting you were in the wrong."

"I did not."

"It was always someone else's fault."

"It was not."

"There was the incident with the white mice."

"I was only nine."

"And your dolls."

"That was David's idea."

"David was away on a scouting holiday. I remember it as if it was yesterday." (Reverend Joseph has an elephantine memory.) "You broke off your dolls' arms and legs, filled the bodies with live matchsticks, then set them alight. You could have burnt down half the street."

"It was an accident."

"You see; you won't accept responsibility."

"I'll apologise again to Julie. At this very moment, even as we speak, I'm off to the shirt mender. I'll buy Julie a bag of mixed alliums from the pet shop…"

I'd lost the Reverend Joseph, his cold grey eyes had travelled above and beyond my head and were frowning at something offensive in Mr. E's front garden. "I must speak to Edmund about his palm tree."

"Actually it's a hebe."

The weight of new leaves had pulled it even further towards the pavement – pedestrians were forced to walk in the road to get around it, which wasn't easy as Mrs. E's white Datsun was hugging that section of the kerb.

"Mrs. E should move her car," I said.

"Mrs. E's car cannot be moved. It has given up the ghost. No, Edmund must bite the bullet and cut his tree down."

"But he loves it. It's a focal point."

"What benefits a man who gains all he desires, but loses his immortal soul?"

"I don't think it's come to that."

I put Julie's shirt metaphorically on the back burner for the time being and set off to warn Mr. E, whom I'd seen earlier heading for the High Street with his trolley. Finally found him looking dejected outside Costcutters, facing a mildly irritated man in a white overall.

"Look here, Edmund," said the man, "I wasn't intending to get rid of that celery today. Come back at the end of the week."

"Seems about ready for throwing out." Mr. E fingered the yellowing celery plumes tenderly.

"It certainly does." I put in my pennyworth. "I wouldn't want to buy it were I on the lookout for fresh celery."

"Oh, take it! It's only celery. Just don't come back again this week. I'm not in business to feed your bloody rabbits."

"Can we have a carrier bag please?" I asked.

"No you can't."

"Don't worry, I've got carrier bags, Lorna." Mr. E produced a bundle of creased Safeway bags from inside his ancient blue zipper jacket and crammed in the celery – which I carried as the trolley was already half full. We headed off towards Dogu Gida Turkish supermarket.

"Reverend Joseph's on the warpath about your hebe – better stake it before he organises a petition."

Mr. E mulled over this information silently. I could never be quite sure whether he'd heard me or not – he seemed to live in an almost constant reverie.

"That man lives in a constant reverie," Mrs. E had told anyone who'd listen for years and years, watching him meanly for any reaction. Whatever she said, I couldn't imagine her life would be better if she'd married the Reverend instead – his house looked ready to tumble, his garden overgrown; at least Mr. E worked hard to achieve the 'distressed beyond repair' effect.

"People are frightened," Mr. E said after several more minutes' introspection.

"Ye-es," I said encouragingly.

"They shout and holler on behalf of rainforests and giant pandas in far-off lands, but they wouldn't tolerate a rainforest or giant panda here in England."

"No-o."

"If I had my way, wild plants would take priority over wage-earners."

"Seems reasonable," I said.

At Dogu Gida we picked up a couple of pounds of split tomatoes, two pulpy swedes, a ton and a half of beetroot and as much wilting green stuff as we could carry. The trolley was full to overflowing; I had two large bags of desiccated mushrooms, one in each side pocket of my combat trousers, the swedes resting on Julie's shirt in my *Echo* bag and my head and shoulders almost completely hidden by fronds of celery and spring greens.

Mr. E was beaming. "You've brought me luck," he said – and I bit my tongue to stop the words "Must do this more often" slipping out.

It was quite warm, my face itched, I was sure the spring greens had rampant whitefly, ergo, my face, neck and hair now had rampant whitefly.

"Lorna, is that you hiding behind the shrubbery?" My fronds were parted and I saw Dan's laughing face.

"Dan," I said, "how lovely to see you." Inside my head I was saying, *Bloody bad timing, awful to see you today, Lorna looking hot and ridiculous and covered in whitefly and damn, damn, damn, wasn't that stuck-up, multi-timing Theresa and stuck-up stylish Helen in the background and does every lesbian know a lesbian who knows a lesbian you (or I) know? Answer: yes.*

"This is Mr. E," I said with manic brightness. "Mr. E, this is Dan, Theresa and Helen."

Mr. E nodded shyly and began scuffing his scuffed shoes against the kerb – he was not a social animal.

"I'll leave you to it, Lorna. Can you manage the greens?" He didn't wait to hear my "Perhaps not", just stepped out into the road and began to make his way slowly and inexorably through the busy traffic, trolley rolling drunkenly along behind him. I could have watched him fondly for some hours rather than face three pairs of curious critical eyes. I caught the distinct whiff of rotting vegetation and knew it came from me.

"Is he a fellow poet?" Theresa asked sarcastically.

"No, he's my neighbour. He keeps rabbits."

"For eating?"

"Of course not – they're pets. He wouldn't dream of eating them, in fact one of them, Alfred the Great, is almost a best friend," which didn't go down easily, from the expressions on their faces.

"*Your* best friend?" Helen asked curiously.

"No, *his* best friend."

"Poor bloke."

"So, he's a social misfit," pursued Theresa.

"He's got a loving wife and five children."

Theresa opened her mouth to say something clever but Dan gave her a slight push. "Stow it, Terry, that's enough now. Lorna, come with us for a coffee."

"She smells of rotting vegetation," Theresa said.

"I like the smell of rotting vegetation," Helen said, "reminds me of family holidays on the Isle of Wight – we had a flat above a greengrocer's. Look, I'll carry half of your veg. I used to have a rabbit called Bill – mink brown with a black nose like velvet. I loved rubbing my cheek against his nose." She pulled a designer-shop carrier bag from her designer canvas and leather rucksack.

Helen went up several notches in my estimation; not so Theresa who yawned and said, "Yeah, well, must split. No time for fluffy bunny stories," looking hard at Dan who continued smiling slightly and saying nothing.

"Seen anything of Angela?" I said sweetly as Theresa turned away.

"What's it to you?"

"I met her the other evening and she mentioned you, that's all."

"Ange is a nonentity," replied Theresa. "I see her when I've nothing better to do. I prefer your friend Pat."

My stomach dipped. I looked at my watch. It was a quarter to ten, Pat had been coming to see me at nine-thirty and I'd completely forgotten.

"You OK?" Dan asked.

"Fine. I've just remembered something I'd forgotten. Too late now."

"Shall I give Pat your love when I see her?" jeered the delightful Theresa.

"Yes, do that."

"Will do. *Ciao*, everybody." Her mood seemed vastly improved, she strode off, her hair flying.

"Sorry Dan, I know she's a mate of yours but she really is a sow," Helen said.

Pat, Theresa and the vegetables were added to the back burner with Julie's shirt. After all, it was a sunny morning and I was walking next to Dan, who was between me and Helen except when we were picking our way single file because, as I've already explained, the High Street pavement tends to widen or narrow depending on the shops: grocers and pound stores sprawl outwards; building societies, banks and turf accountants tend to keep a tidy, clear frontage.

Outside the Rochester Castle public house we had to step around an open cellar door where barrelled beer was being delivered, and Dan reached out and took my hand. Helen, looking back and seeing our linked hands, raised her fine dark eyebrows in a 'so that's how the land lies' manner. Helen, having seen how the land lay, gulped her coffee down in the Blue Legume and said she had to go immediately to Islington in search of a special jacket for a film premiere. I felt rather fond of her, the way she didn't seem to mind that her white T-shirt now had green smears down the front.

"Will you be OK with the celery?" she asked as she got up to leave.

"Don't worry, I'll carry it back," Dan said.

"See ya then."

Bit awkward after she left. The other tables filled up and everyone seemed to be sitting too near for us to have an intimate conversation, just supposing I'd been able to drum up an intimate conversation. I felt self-conscious. Were white, green or black flies even now crawling just out of my vision in my hair? Was everyone in the café thinking, "That woman smells overpoweringly of stale vegetables," as I'd have thought had I had the misfortune to sit down next to me?

Dan, on the other hand, looked completely relaxed, only a little thoughtful. Was she thinking, "Wish I'd gone to Islington with Helen, to see what's what in beige this spring"?

I tried to look thoughtful while also maintaining a vivacious sparkle in my eyes. The effort produced a sudden unwanted image of Dan's pet-carrier which prompted the sensation of my spirits falling rapidly. It was impossible. Ridiculous. I could not go out with this woman, just supposing she wanted to go out with me. I wasn't a Theresa, who thought everything was acceptable. I was Lorna of Green Bees and the *Hackney Echo*, irresponsible, unreliable – I was small-beer faults. I couldn't overlook for long, couldn't understand Dan and what made her tick. Wanted to demand, "Why do you feel the need to steal, when did you start, do you have any idea how much misery you cause, do you have an accomplice and is it Theresa, and if it is, can't you see what a horrible person she is, and can't anything be done to make your life more satisfying so you could desist, perhaps rent or buy my brother's flat and devote yourself to gardening or DIY or me or all three of us?"

"Dan, why do you wear beige?"

She smiled. Her teeth were very white in her lightly tanned face. She raised her espresso to her lips and I noticed for the first time the expensive-looking watch on one wrist, the narrow gold gate-leg bracelet on the other – were they stolen property? A sovereign on a heavy gold chain hung from her neck – was that stolen property?

"My mum wore beige. She hated bright colours and loud noise – they disturbed her. From a tot she dressed me in beige and I learnt to keep quiet around her."

"Is she still alive?"

"Yes, no, sort of."

Blimey. Yes Julie, I did take your shirt or, no Julie, I didn't take your shirt or, Julie, I only sort of took your shirt. Confusion rather than an outright lie or outright honesty. Over to you, Jenny Salter.

"Which one?" I prompted gently.

She frowned while continuing to smile. "She's still alive but doesn't inhabit the land of the living, if you know what I mean?"

I didn't. "You must find it a very sad situation."

"Yes and no," and she stopped speaking.

"You don't want to talk about it?" I said after a minute of silence.

"Better not. Tell me about your parents."

"Better not. I'll go on for days."

"I'd imagine you'd have..." she laughed slightly as if almost embarrassed, "loving parents."

"You'd be wrong. They're pretty awful," then I stopped because it occurred to me that compared to someone who was only sort of alive, didn't inhabit the land of the living and forced her child to wear beige and keep silent, George and Della were a pair of amiable characters with a few minor personality disorders.

"So?" she said.

"They like to be called George and Della rather than Mum and Dad. They are glamorous and interesting in a macabre kind of way, also selfish and greedy; however, they love and depend on each other after decades of marriage and if they weren't my parents, I'd probably find them admirable. Mum's favourite colours are cream and white which she says are youth-enhancing colours."

"Sounds an interesting lady."

"In small doses. It was her jewellery you were about to steal from David's drinks cabinet." Did I sound sour? I think I did. "Sorry," I said, and immediately wished I hadn't. She should be the one saying sorry.

"Lorna, I'm heartbroken. Having known and loved you in the full biblical sense I wouldn't harm nor steal a hair on your head, and the heads of your loved ones are also sacrosanct."

Instead she said cheerfully, "Don't be. What's her jewellery like? Worth stealing?"

"She and Dad would think so."

Dan paid for our coffees and we made our way homewards, stopping off to deliver Mr. E's vegetables – I almost forgot the bags of mushrooms which had become warm and soggy in the close confines of my trouser pockets.

Mr. E gave Dan a long stare. "Didn't I speak to you the other week? I told you the Trees lived next door."

"I didn't know Lorna's surname was Tree... then," she replied smoothly, and sauntered back towards my front gate.

"Lorna," he said out of the side of his mouth, "I don't think I like the look of this one" – as if in the past I'd paraded dozens of women for his approval.

"You don't have to like the look of her – *I'm* the lesbian."

"Your gran would turn in her grave if she heard the way you use that word willy-nilly."

"When necessary, Mr. E, never willy-nilly."

"What did he say?" Dan asked as she followed me up the stairs.

"He didn't like the look of you. He doesn't like the look of anyone unless he's seen them at least twice a week for ten years or they're carrying a small furry animal. Now, if you'd had a marmoset tucked inside your jacket it would have been a very different story."

Early the next morning after Dan had gone I remembered the two swedes and Julie's shirt – fished them out from my Day-Glo bag which

I'd left leaning against the central heating radiator – they had merged into one another.

Sometimes I could swear Jenny Salter was nodding off even while I was talking, which was disconcerting and obviously made me wonder if I could possibly be boring her. I tried not to repeat myself, not to return to the same subject more than two weeks in a row, and to make the odd encouraging comment about her clothes or an item of topical news to show I was not entirely self-absorbed, but yes, every now and then her eyelids drooped and her head did seem to nod gently. I reassured myself that she must have a hectic home life – I'd seen her bike in the corridor and the saddlebags were often bulging with grocery shopping from Sainsbury's – I imagined a male partner and several young teenagers clamouring for her attention as she tiredly wheeled her bike up the garden path.

"Mum, can we have burgers, can we have crisps?" *"Darling, I know you're worn out sitting on your butt all day but any chance of mixing me an Alka Seltzer with gin and tonic chaser? I've had a hell of a business lunch."*

Also common sense told me she must have many clients more boring than me. There was a man in a raincoat, for instance, who was generally leaving as I arrived (I was always ten or fifteen minutes early and had to kick my heels on the bench in the corridor), and he looked very boring with a long white face and thinning hair – not that those attributes always guaranteed boring but then again, sometimes they did. Always kept his hands in his raincoat pocket apart from when he had to push open the swing door. Could be a flasher trying to mend his ways. I did not like to imagine that he sat flashing at J.S. for fifty minutes while she murmured supportive small talk about his childhood in the hope he would realise how unnecessary his anti-social behavior was in achieving a meaningful relationship. He and I never acknowledged one another even though this year I'd already seen him on more occasions than I'd seen Pat. His eyes slid past me. I was not flash-worthy. Would have dearly liked to say to Jenny,

"What's matey in for?" but obviously this sort of gambit wasn't allowed.

"Can we categorise your feelings?" Jenny broke into my reverie. She had woken herself up by making a steeple with her hands – *Open the door and there's the people* – she waved her fingers at herself.

Were I in a less cheerful mood I'd definitely have said something along the lines of, "Am I keeping you up, Ms. Salter? Because I could easily take my thirty pounds elsewhere – London is full of charlatans."

"If we must," I said instead, rather pleased to be asked to categorise my feelings. I could talk to Pat and co. until my hair went white before being offered such a chance.

Jenny sat up straighter and prepared to concentrate. "Now, Lorna, pretend you're making a cake and the cake is the sum of the ingredients you feel towards and about your new friend Dan."

"She's something more than a friend," I said loftily.

"Yes, I know, but we haven't quite clarified the relationship yet, have we?"

"Fair enough."

"Take me seriously."

I wasn't really in the mood to take J.S. seriously; in fact I'd almost cancelled the appointment because for the moment I didn't feel the need to talk over my angst. My star seemed to be in the ascendant, what with Mum about to come out of hospital and be taken far away by Dad to convalesce; and Pat having met me for tea and cake in Clissold Park where we avoided any dangerous conversational territory, parting quite amicably with "Let's do this again", as if we truly believed we'd spent an enjoyable hour. Then there were David and Julie…

"The cake, Lorna."

"The cake," I repeated and furrowed my brow in earnest. "This isn't easy. I'm much better at how I imagine people feel about me."

"Love, affection, infatuation, physical attraction, tenderness, humour…"

"OK. I find Dan very attractive – physically and visually. I like her face, body, the way she walks, the way she sprawls, the way she seems so relaxed always. I like her beigeness – hair, skin, clothes, even her personality – they seem so different, so... she's like a glimpse of the sea." *Blimey, where did that come from?*

"Elaborate. I don't quite..."

"It's so noisy in London, well, in any town. I like town – love town. Colourful, dirty, frenetic, nothing and nobody stopping still..." I closed my eyes tightly trying to see the right words. "All the noise and mess and action generated by people and then as if you suddenly caught a glimpse of the sea – not a lovely blue sea – a wildish sea, yellowish and grey – the sound of unfriendly waves – uncontrollable – that's how Dan is." I didn't want to open my eyes again and see Jenny and her tiny office.

"And is this love?"

"Don't know. It's quite painful. I feel as if I'm trying to hang on to something that shouldn't be hung on to."

"Do you think you might be mirroring how you felt about your Mum and Dad when you were a small child? Choosing someone who may reject you?"

"I don't want to think about Mum and Dad today, thank you. I was cheerful when I came in here, I was bubbling over and now I feel depressed."

"Would you like to talk about something else – there's twenty minutes left?"

I opened my eyes. Jenny was wide awake, watching me with a very kindly expression.

"I don't know what to do," I said. "Dan comes into my life and goes out again like a good dream. I think it's all she wants to give – I haven't the confidence to ask for more, but I want more. I want the everyday stuff that other people have: the home-building, division of labour, supermarket shopping, weekends away. But I know that what I'm trying to do is make the sea behave like a swimming pool, and I love the sea and in reality would hate the responsibility of a swimming pool."

Jenny made her hands into fists and held them in the air each side of her head. "You choose *this* and hold tight, you'll lose *that* – and vice versa. At the end of the day 'this' or 'that' amount to the same intrinsic thing –" she opened both her fists, made a movement as if tossing two small birds into the air, turned her empty palms towards me – "Nothing."

I was thoughtful as always when leaving Jenny Salter's, glad I'd gone. The remark about Mum and Dad had hit home and it was an area I certainly didn't want to dwell on – if I was only going to fall in love with women who would reject me, then my future would seem a desolate prospect.

Think of all the people who've loved you.

Pat loved me as a friend, David as a sister, Julie as a sister-in-law, the E family as the source of amusement, Gran as a daughter and a granddaughter, Reverend Joseph as an errant lamb, Kate... yes, Kate had loved me until the day came when she found she loved somebody else. I would not follow that train of thought either.

Next stop was the social security office in Dalston Lane where I went to sign on. Whatever is said about social security offices, if you are a creative person they are a source of inspiration, great callousness mixed now and then with unexpected kindness. I had fallen on my feet with Mrs. Gordon. Signing-on visits when she was away or on holiday were flat, but usually there she was behind the counter, and from my place in the queue I'd catch her eye and wave and she'd send me a brisk nod. Had I been younger I'd have insisted she adopt me; hung around every evening at the staff entrance and wooed her with small posies of wild flowers – such things are available in Hackney, you need only know where to look.

So, I stood in the queue waiting to catch her eye and thinking, "Good old Mrs. Gordon – she'll cheer me up." I caught her eye and waved. Her nod was infinitesimal – curt rather than brisk – and when finally I arrived at my chair on the other side of her desk, her acknowledging smile was a strained, bearer-of-bad-tidings type smile.

"Lorna, before we get embroiled in our usual putting the world to rights chat, I need to tell you that you're going to have to find a proper job."

"But I'm a poet. We agreed that's job enough."

"*We* agreed – I'm afraid the social security office which I represent doesn't agree." She straightened the thick plastic folder containing my details, lined up several coloured pens in her pen tray – a present from myself the previous Christmas. As if reading my thoughts, she pushed it ever so slightly towards me: *There, take your dastardly bribe of a pen tray and go forth and find work.*

"The thing is, Lorna, although I immensely enjoy our chats, it's coming up to two years now that you've been signing on..." She looked at me over her spectacle frames as if expecting some wince of astonishment from me at such a length of time, instead I was thinking, "Two years. Is that all? I need at least a full decade to develop my poetic skills."

"So, next week you'll be reinterviewed. There's also the Job Club where you get access to all the newspapers and free stationery and postage in moderation..."

Momentarily I brightened. "Would that cover sending out my poems?"

"I'm afraid not. Job applications only."

She began repositioning my folder again. There was more to come, I knew it. I came in quickly with, "What did you think of Andrew Motion's latest? Isn't he just an embarrassment to the poetry world?" Almost said, "Why doesn't he get a proper job?" but cut just in time.

However, for once, Mrs. Gordon couldn't be tempted to chew the fat about contemporary male poets; instead, after checking over right and left shoulder that nobody was listening, she said, "It is known that you're working."

I was dumbfounded.

"The department has been informed. Forgive me, Lorna, but I'm in an untenable position."

"Do you know how little I get paid?" I whispered back at her.

"However small the amount, you should declare it."

"I can't live on fifty pounds a week."

"You could get a proper job. You are a very intelligent young woman."

"I'm middle-aged. Who'd want to employ a middle-aged woman with a gammy leg?"

"You aren't a middle-aged woman with a gammy leg. Look, I'm sorry, it's not up to me. There's a new regime –" Her telephone rang and she picked up the receiver. "If you could sign in the usual place and call at the desk on your way out for next week's appointment."

I signed and waited.

She covered the receiver with her hand. "Was there anything else?" she asked in an efficient un-Mrs. Gordonesque voice.

"Can I still come in for a chat next week?"

"No. I won't be here. I'm taking early retirement. Moving out of the area."

"That's awful."

"No, Lorna. For me, that's wonderful."

Best clothes

Mrs. E was under the illusion that I would wear anything. For over twenty years she had passed unsuitable items of clothing that didn't fit her through the gap in the wire netting fence with instructions to "Try this on now, Lorna, so I can see how you look in it – with your height you can carry it off, could have been made for you."

I'd provided hours of entertainment for her family. Even Mr. E, who was a pretty inscrutable chap, had been known to turn his head away so I couldn't see his lips twitching, or his tears of merriment.

When Gran was alive she'd step in with a brusque, "Leave Lorna alone – she has her own inimitable style, although it's not immediately apparent to the naked eye."

"But it seems a shame to throw away good clothes, Irene," Mrs. E would remonstrate.

"Then don't. *You* wear them."

I had hoped that with our new posh trellis Mrs. E would get the message, would recognise our elevating status in the Duxford Road hierarchy and desist with her charitable impulses. After her anniversary party (where, Pat told me, several guests had admired the new fence), Mrs. E went unusually quiet, which might have been more to do with the death of her Datsun cramping her boisterous style. However, on several occasions, come dusk, I saw her from my bedroom window, down in their garden inspecting the trellis as if it were a Martian spaceship that had happened to land between us. She walked the length of the garden stopping every ten yards or so to give it a good shake, no doubt searching for structural weaknesses. At the gap we'd left for neighbourly commerce to continue, her pale cardiganned arm snaked eerily through, finding the gap not big enough for a tray bearing Mrs. E's home-made rock cakes or Mr. E's diabolical home-made beer.

But then the weather worsened. Mrs. E disappeared back indoors, leaving only Mr. E in his shiny oilskin standing in the rain, communing with his rabbits – all except Alfred, who (I'd had it on good authority from the Reverend Joseph) was still hogging the kitchen fire and getting fatter and more territorial by the minute.

The weeks of rain finally passed and the sun shone on a patch of bright blue forget-me-nots, strays from under Morris Minor, which had settled themselves in the gravel area round our pond and flowered. Julie, who had only recently begun to speak to me again since the ruined blouse incident, spotted them from the kitchen window, which David had hermetically nailed shut.

"They'll have to go," she said, ironing the eighth tea towel – views of ecclesiastical buildings that the Reverend Joseph had brought back for her from his holiday in Norfolk.

(At the time, Julie had thanked the Reverend but been doubtful, told David, "I hope my dinner guests won't tar me with the same feathers as those this tea towel implies."

David looked mystified. "In what way, darling?"

"Think I've gone religious."

"It might make quite an amusing conversational motif," he said.

"Well, I suppose it is Irish linen after all. What do you think, Lorna?" This was last summer when all was well between us.

"I think it was very nice of Reverend Joseph to think of you. He never thought of me."

"He doesn't imagine you wash up, never mind bothering to dry."

"Thank you, David.")

Now Julie folded the tea towel and looked murderously at the small unassuming plants. "They'll spread all over the garden in no time."

"They're very pretty," I said cautiously.

"They don't fit in with my planting scheme."

My blood did boil a little at that but no point saying, "Let's not forget this is my garden as well," because she'd only reply, "Well, get on and do it in that case," and although I'd love to call her bluff, what if she called mine?

"Could I just move them on to the Peppy graves?" I asked.

Deep sigh, as if yet again I was proving to be an obstacle to garden-design progress. Ironing board put away and no response; iron cord wound up and iron left to cool on windowsill and no response; juicer brought out of utensil cupboard and carrots peeled for her vitamin drink and still no response. I'd forgotten my question and gone off at a tangent recalling how Julie was determined the baby would have perfect eyesight, unlike David who wore glasses – "It will see in the dark if I have my way," she'd said grimly.

"OK."

I blinked. Whatever was she OK-ing?

"Do it now while the sun's out."

This didn't fit into my immediate plans at all. "I was just going to sort my newspapers."

"Lorna, I'm not prepared to look out of this kitchen window – which, because of your earlier carelessness, has left me incarcerated in my own home – at a bloody eyesore."

"You're not incarcerated, the kitchen door opens and..."

I was drowned out by the screech of the juicer. When she'd finished she picked up her glass of carrot juice. "I'm going to have a nap – if those weeds are still there when I wake up, they're going into the incinerator." Exit Julie, curls bobbing.

And so it was that as I bent down to trowel up the cluster of pretty blue flowers, Mrs. E slid into view on the other side of the trellis and the scent of her cheroot blew towards me on the breeze.

"I was hoping to see you today," she said amiably.

"Really?" I straightened up. Mistake. First I shouldn't have straightened up. Second I shouldn't have said, "Really?" I should have remained in the bending position and said in a clipped, pain-filled voice, "Sorry Mrs. E, can't talk now – the old back's gone again – must get a cab to my local chiropractor," and rushed indoors leaving the forget-me-nots to their fate.

Over Mrs. E's free arm she was holding clothing, just like in the bad old days of, say, six weeks ago.

"Come on up the garden and I'll pass them through."

"I haven't really got time..."

"A matter of minutes."

"I'm due at..."

Already she was marching towards the gap. I sighed, threw down my trowel and marched after her.

"Here, try these on." She thrust the clothes at me. "You can't go wrong with a peasant blouse – peasant blouses do not go out of fashion," she said with authority.

"Peasant blouses have never been in fashion."

"Lorna, do you read *Vogue*?"

"No."

"Then trust one who does. Plus a pair of Estelle's leather trousers – now you can't argue with leather."

"I can and anyway they're far too small."

"Good leather – and this is very good leather – is supple. They will hold in your stomach and shape your buttocks. Put them on in the kitchen, then come outside and let me see."

By the time I'd gone back outside, the twins had joined her, their eyes wide with amusement.

"Girls, doesn't she look fabulous?'

"Fabulous." They both snorted with laughter.

"I can't do the zip up."

Mrs. E leant across the wall and pulled and pushed at the zip. "Breathe in."

"I am breathing in."

"Tense your tummy muscles."

"They are tense."

"Estelle, push Lorna's tummy in while I pull up the zip."

"She needs a girdle," Estelle said, and, "I don't like touching lesbians below the waist."

"Push hard and don't make personal comments."

"Rather you than me," Esther said, shuddering.

"There!" Mrs. E was triumphant. "Next time it will be that much easier. Doesn't she look different, sexy trousers and a feminine blouse. My girls would give their eye teeth for a bust like yours."

"We wouldn't," the girls shouted in unison.

"Thank you, Mrs. E. I'll hang on to these for that special evening out. OK?"

I went indoors. The trousers were so tight I couldn't walk properly – they seemed to be cutting my buttocks in half.

Julie was standing by the sink rinsing her glass, her face pink from laughing. "Lorna, you look ridiculous. Why don't you put your foot down with Mrs. E? She wouldn't dare try it with me. Cup of tea?"

"Yes please." I sat down and the zip broke – my stomach bulged out attractively. "That feels better. Julie, I promise to move those flowers but can I please do it tomorrow?"

"Of course. Whenever you like." A sea change had occurred. The Julie filling the kettle was a different kettle... was a very different Julie, she looked happy and relaxed.

"Lorna, I wanted to say – and it isn't easy for me to say – but I'm sorry I overreacted about that blouse of mine you borrowed. I have masses of clothes and I know you have hardly any. Last night David was telling me the story of the two of you at that hotel when you were children – I could have bawled – pregnancy seems to be making me horribly emotional."

'Showing us how the other half lived' was one of George and Della's – Mum and Dad's – favourite phrases. It was also their favourite occupation within the limited range of occupations where we and they, united as a family, were concerned.

The Strand Palace Hotel fiasco came the Christmas after Dad had vetoed Mrs. Turner's café. As always they arrived late and flushed of face because as always they'd called in first at a pub. (This was at a time when it was legal to drink and drive. In those days Della and George liked to have at least a pint of beer for him and a shandy or perhaps a dry Martini for her round about eleven-thirty in the morning.)

David and I had been ready for over an hour, sitting on the front room windowsill, dressed in our best clothes plus our navy, belted, school raincoats, which almost skimmed our ankles – prudently bought for us to grow into. Gran said it was ridiculous for David to wear his school cap and me my beret, which were the accessories we'd have liked – an ingrained influence from George and his khakis. Even now I have a sneaking desire to wear shirts with epaulettes, and I've no doubt David feels the same.

When David was a boy he was far more adventurous in his clothes than I was. The school dinner ladies – particularly Mrs. Biggington, his bleach blonde favourite – called him a snappy dresser and said, "He'll break plenty of hearts," which David accepted as a compliment even though at the time he hated girls and was set on marrying our cat Beryl when he grew up. David loved jumble sales, he loved Gran's catalogue, was never afraid of colour: red shirt, green knitted waistcoat; every item spick and span as limited Lux suds and even more limited hot water would allow. Each night he placed the next day's trousers under the mattress to press in their creases.

My own favourite outfit was a pair of men's army shorts – the waist tied with a frayed school tie – and a cream-coloured cardigan of Gran's with a ruffle down the front worn over my Aertex vest. From early on I knew it was pointless to wear dresses like other girls. Of course at school I had to wear my school dress, white with a royal blue stripe – I quite liked that, could imagine I was a trainee nurse.

Gran thought it would be a good idea if I became a trainee nurse. She said, "Taking care of the sick and elderly will improve your co-ordination. You'll get muscles where you didn't know you had 'em." Gran didn't help me to feel better about how I looked but she did make me feel I had a future.

However, with George and Della, looks were all-important – they could not contemplate having a plain child, and 'possible trainee nurse' cut no ice with them.

"I can't believe how plain she's become – she was a bonny baby – what are you feeding her on, Mother? I bet it's lard, lard, and more lard." He'd shake his head and turn to look at Della with absolute satisfaction. "She'll never be the looker you are." And Della would toss her fine curls like a thoroughbred horse and almost whinny with pleasure.

Of course I came to realise that being a 'looker' wasn't the be all and end all of life, and perhaps I wasn't quite so plain after all. David, on those scarce occasions when he reminisced, usually over the best part of a bottle of whisky on Christmas Eve, had been known to muse, "I recall a rather striking girl," (me) and then spoil this with, "I wonder where that girl went?"

I wear black now, sometimes navy, perhaps a red scarf for special occasions – oh and Julie's turquoise shirt, but I wouldn't pay good money for Lurex.

On the day in question, we were bundled into the back of the car. George wound down his window and shouted, "Are you sure you won't come with us, Mother?"

Gran, standing stoically on the doorstep wearing a faded flowered overall and fluffy house slippers, looked as if she wanted to shake her fist at him. "I prefer my own food – at least I know what's gone into it," she said grimly.

By the time we reached the hotel, George was desperate to use the gents, so he left us in the foyer taking off our coats. A hotel minion was making small lunges for Della's fur coat – she couldn't decide whether to remove it and show off her new dress or keep it on and show off the fur.

"Shall I, shan't I? Good heavens, whatever are you two wearing?"

I looked at David, he looked at me; our reflections glimmered back at us several times over from the huge gilt-framed mirrors lining the foyer walls. We looked very smart.

"Our best clothes, of course," I said.

David wore his tan suede shorts, a proud and recent purchase, teamed with a pair of brocade braces over a plum-coloured ladies' blouse, plus – a thoughtful touch – grey knitted socks which echoed the blouse with plum-coloured diamonds knitted into the rib. Nothing wrong there.

For myself, I'd chosen a blue satin shirt with a length of three-inch-wide black ribbon that Gran had tied in a fashion she called 'jabot' style, i.e. a large floppy bow at my neck; plus a pair of green and purple two-tone trousers which were catalogue brand new and my pride and joy.

Dad came towards us like a furious steam train; under the brilliance of multiple crystal chandeliers his tanned jowls had turned to an angry red.

"What the devil?" he roared from yards away. "Is this some kind of joke to make yours truly look a bloody piecan? Where did you get these outfits?"

"The catalogue," I said.

"And the jumble sale, of course," David said.

"The children are in fancy dress?" The hotel usher had finally taken charge of Della's fur and our raincoats.

"The children are not in fancy dress – the children are dolled up to make their father look like a ruddy fool. Comprendo?" George's chin thrust out pugnaciously. "We can't possibly eat here, we'll have to find a bistro." He said 'bistro' as if it were a nasty smell directly beneath his nose.

"We've booked lunch, George, I don't want to go in search of a bistro. We know nothing about bistros. Please, George."

"Come on then." He turned on his heels and walked into the hotel dining room. We followed with Della, who had adopted the role of martyred mother.

"I apologise for my children," she told a passing waiter.

By the time we joined George, he'd organised a corner table where David and I were to sit with our backs to the wall, so that most of our clothes were hidden behind the white table cloth, and our shoulders and heads were to be concealed behind giant menus.

We sat in silence, then George got up suddenly and said, "I'm getting a drink first in the bar. Coming, Della? I'll send Cokes in for you kids. Stay put or else."

"So what will it be?" asked George, three quarters of an hour later and in a much better humour. "I hear the dover sole's excellent, or the rack of lamb. Or you could have the Christmas menu – turkey's a bit bland for my taste."

We stared at the menu. Under the table David kicked me; I kicked him back.

"Dover sole," Della said, "and sautéed potatoes please." She fluttered her mascaraed lashes up at the waiter.

"Actually, after all, I think I'll go for the sirloin steak, very rare. Come on, you two, don't take all day. Sorry about this, the kids are a bit overwhelmed, aren't you, you little tykes?" George said with drunken affection.

"We'll have egg, chip and pea," I said.

"Me too," mumbled David.

"George, what do they mean?" Della asked.

George scrutinised us seriously, pushed his face into David's and said, "What exactly do you mean by egg, chip and pea?"

"We always have egg, chip and pea," David said.

"Always? Since when? I wasn't aware the two of you spent your days dining out."

I said, "At Mrs. Turner's we always had egg, chip and pea. We like it."

"Mrs. Turner's ancient history. I am trying, God help me, to introduce the two of you into the sophisticated world of gourmet food. There are plenty of things on the menu to like," George said smoothly, "so hop to it and choose."

Together we said, "We've chosen: egg, chip and pea... *please*."

The row broke over our heads but in the end the waiter produced egg, chip and pea twice, and it was very good but not as good as at Mrs. Turner's Café.

"Nice time at the hotel?" Gran asked innocently.

"It was lovely. Lights and mirrors and they gave us a jigsaw puzzle and a game of snakes and ladders," David said.

"Don't ever send them out dressed like that again," George said. "We were made to look a laughing stock."

"I have never in all my life been so embarrassed." Della tweaked her white cardigan to sit better on her tanned shoulders.

Gran's lower lip jutted. She was good, was Gran, with that lower lip to jut, and the top lip moulded into an Elvis Presley sneer – the combined weight of George and Della's annoyance would have crushed a lesser woman.

"You'll want a cup of tea, I expect," she said, and went into the kitchen and closed the door. Suddenly we heard just one shout of laughter coming from the other side of the door.

"What was that? Is Mother all right in there, George?"

"Oh, she's all right, all right. She's all right," he said grimly.

Trying to amuse the woman in beige

It was a warm, sunny morning. Usually Dan left at seven a.m. for pastures unspecified, but nine o'clock came and she was still mooching about my flat hugging a cold cup of coffee. We didn't talk much, Dan and I. I respected her apparent need for silence – her throwback to her mother thing. I'd had an in-depth chat with Jenny Salter who'd advised, "Never bombard your new partner with questions – allow them to release information as and when they feel safe in your company." So I sat at my desk and let Dan mooch and squashed down the burning question of "What do you do all day?"

"Have you read all these?" she asked, pausing in front of my bookcase.

"Most of them."

She opened the glass doors and took out a book of poems by Carol Ann Duffy. Suddenly, flicking through the pages, she grinned and started reading.

"This is good," she said.

"Which one?" (Surely allowed.)

"The Kray Sisters."

"That is good. She's a very accessible poet."

"What?"

"I mean easy to read and understand."

"Lorna, I'm not an idiot."

"I know you're not. I just meant her work's easy to enjoy." I was floundering now.

"Easy to enjoy," she repeated, almost to herself, and continued reading. Abruptly she snapped the book shut and tossed it back onto the shelf. I could have sworn... but no, nothing in the poem to make a woman like Dan emotional.

She walked away from me towards the window. "So what's cooking today, Lorna honey?"

"I didn't mean to be patronising," I said.

"That's OK. I have a thin skin. So...?"

"So what about breakfast at Springfield Park?"

She didn't look exactly thrilled but she shrugged her shoulders good-naturedly. "I'm in your hands," she said.

As we set out slowly along Duxford Road, I said, "I didn't notice your car."

"Terry's got the car today."

"Oh." Images of Pat and Terry speeding along the open road:

"Love the car, Terry."

"Great, isn't it? Does a top speed of 190 mph at fourteen miles to the gallon. We'll be in Cornwall in half an hour – I know a fabulous women-only nude beach."

"Sandra's cooking quiche Lorraine, I'll have to be home by six."

"No prob."

"Have you known Terry long?" I asked. *Sorry, Jenny.*

"All my life."

"That is a long time."

"A lifetime."

Couldn't help myself. "She's not an easy person?" I said tentatively.

"Nor am I."

"Am I an easy person?"

"Very." She smiled and took my hand. "That's what I like about you. You're uncomplicated."

I'd have liked to be a little less uncomplicated but comforted myself with the thought that, the more Dan got to know me, the more astonishing complexity I'd have to surprise her with.

It was a fair walk but with her at my side seemed to take no time at all. Springfield Park is in Stamford Hill on the outskirts of Stoke Newington and most people for some reason would rather go to

Clissold Park, trekking up Stoke Newington Church Street via wine bars, restaurants and coffee shops, finally packing into Clissold's small green space as if it were the only life raft available.

Yet Springfield Park has vistas and dips and rises and steps and paths that get lost in shrubbery. There's a sizable lake and shabby extended families having picnics on the grass, being dive-bombed by crows and cajoled by cross squirrels. The canal running through it is policed by aggressive swans that hiss and flap their wings at you as you stop on the tow path to offer them your sandwiches.

"Nice swan, good swan, swanny want a bit of bread?" And yes, swanny does want a bit of bread, swanny wants the whole sandwich, your hand and half your sleeve as well.

Pat and I used to spend cold wintry walks debating which houseboat would be the cosiest to drop in and beg a mug of hot tea from, or the most desirous should we want to buy one: *Mademoiselle* for me with its flaking blue paint, pots of herbs on the roof of the cabin and real lace curtains hanging at the tiny dusty windows; and *Neptune's Bower* for Pat, painted with dragons chasing sea-serpents from bow to stern.

"This is my favourite park," I said unnecessarily as we went in through the iron gates and the first vista of formal displays of red and pink geraniums presented itself.

"Good," Dan said.

Lorna scrutinised beloved with anxious eye; beloved's shoulders were hunched, obviously ill at ease in natural environment.

"We'll walk down to the canal and check out the houseboats." Intentionally I used the word 'check', felt it had an urban contemporary ring to it as if I might be seriously thinking of giving up my paper round for the property market. Go-getting Lorna in a sharp suit swinging her legs easily out of the passenger seat of a Lamborghini...

"Darling, we'll just check out the real-estate situation down by the canal. It really is a prime position. I can almost smell the money to be made by women with their fingers on the property pulse."

"Lead on," Dan said as if reconciling herself to a morning's boredom. I didn't want to. The path was wide enough for a small dance troupe to high-kick their way canalwards.

"Beautiful view," I said, indicating the misty fairy-tale land of distant Walthamstow.

"Walthamstow," she said flatly. Then she took off her beige cord jacket and threw it over her shoulder, snaking her other arm around my waist.

"Wish I'd brought a blanket," I said, leaning against her. "We could have had coffees and sandwiches and communed with nature."

Her arm dropped away from my waist, hand went into the pocket of her jeans and she started whistling. For a moment in the near empty park her tuneless whistling had a sinister quality, something of *The Night of the Hunter*, an old film Pat and I had watched one evening where Robert Mitchum was a murderous whistling preacher searching out Shelley Winters' children. I shivered and the moment passed.

"You don't like communing with nature?" I said.

"No point."

"It's relaxing. It feeds the soul."

"Yours, maybe."

"What do you like then?" *Mouth shut, Lorna.*

We walked a hundred yards, were almost at the canal before she answered.

"Lorna, if you're looking for a communing-with-nature type, you've got the wrong woman – I like pubs, clubs, after dark, being places I'm not supposed to be, breaking the rules – I need to feel I'm living." Phew, quite a long sentence from Dan for once.

I digested it, came up with, "Sort of a female James Dean?"

"If you like."

"Who hurts people?"

"If necessary."

"People are vulnerable."

"No. You imagine they're vulnerable. For instance, your Brighton ladies. They're not skint. For the rest of their days they'll mull over their little flurry of excitement."

"Philanthropic thieving?" I said.

"Don't take it so seriously. These people are insured."

"To me, it *is* serious. And does the charming Theresa think as you do?"

Dan grinned. "Terry told me your friend Pat said you were mad about her."

"That was before I saw her in action."

We'd reached the towpath. I'd forgotten that it took weeks of dry weather to completely dry out; there was mud and water-filled potholes and I thought of Dan's beige loafers...

"We'd better go back – it's too muddy."

"It's fine. Keep to the grass at the side." She moved past me and confidently strode ahead. "And now you know me better, how do you feel about me, Lorna?"

This took me by surprise. A single-file walk along a muddy towpath, several feet between us, didn't seem an appropriate time to elaborate on my feelings.

"I don't know."

"You must know." She stopped and turned so suddenly that I bumped against her, my feet slipped on the wet grass and I began to slither sideways towards the water.

She caught me by the elbows and held me. "How do you feel about me – I want to know?"

"How do you feel about me?" I countered.

"I asked first."

I said, "If you were just a skeleton standing here asking me that question, I'd have a very different answer."

She sighed. "Lorna, can't anything be simple with you? Just a straight answer – that's all I want."

"I'm trying. OK. I like you a lot..."

"But?"

"Not really a 'but', because even the things you tell me that are cynical and unpleasant, I make excuses for them, put them down to heart-breaking events in, perhaps, your childhood, which account for the way you are. Perhaps no one cared about you, or not enough, or in the wrong way. It makes me love you more."

Her expression was unreadable. "And supposing you're wrong? Supposing all those 'heart-breaking events' are only in your imagination and I do what I do because I want to? Don't think you're the first woman to –"

"Whatever, I'd still love you."

"I don't like the word 'love'," she said. Her hands moved to my upper arms and tightened, my body seemed to dip nearer the dark hurrying water of the canal. I closed my eyes. I wouldn't fight her. And suddenly she pulled me against her and her arms held me tightly. Behind me I heard the cheerful 'tring-tring' of a cyclist's bell, and as it sped past we stepped further up the bank to avoid the spray of mud from its wheels.

"Come on, show me those houseboats you and Pat used to talk about."

"How do you know about me and Pat?"

"Terry told me. Pat brought her down here as well."

"Terry must have been bored stiff. I expect you are as well."

"Lorna, there is nothing about countryside I like, but no way would I be standing in all this muck and filth in the middle of nowhere at this time of the morning if I wasn't at least interested in you."

We had lunch sitting at a table outside the café and I was almost content just being with Dan. My feelings were confused. I watched the canal, saw the far bank reflected in the water and how it all looked idyllic in the sunshine – but in reality the canal was deep and dirty. I didn't want thoughts like that forcing comparison, forcing conclusions, I wanted to enjoy myself, wanted life to be 'enjoyable', like it always had been.

There were several other couples sitting outside; women with children and smiling, rough-haired dogs. Dan didn't fit in. It's only a matter of clothes, I told myself, we're all human beings. But she looked bored, unimpressed by the swans, the duck families, the bouncing hairy dogs; I wondered if she even liked animals, or preferred a furry dog pyjama case to the real thing. It didn't seem like a good time to bombard her with more questions. She was restless, kept surreptitiously looking at her watch. I blinked. It was a completely different gadget from the gold bracelet watch she'd recently been wearing; this one had an expensive tooled leather strap, the face divided up into several dials. Dan leant across the table and took my hand, pushing up the sleeve of my fleece jacket. I wore Gran's old watch, with a plastic strap I'd replaced many times over the years.

"Would you like a new watch, Lorna?" Dan asked gently.

"No thank you," I said.

"That's a very old and grubby watch you're wearing."

"It may be, but it has sentimental value." I pulled my hand away from her. "Had enough?" I said brightly.

"I think so. I'll call a cab." She pulled out her mobile and sauntered down towards the boathouse where it was quieter. I watched her tap out at least three calls before the cab appeared.

"See you soon," she said, holding the car door open for me.

"You're not coming with me?"

"No, Terry's picking me up. Don't pay the driver, I'm an account customer."

Mrs. E was leaning against one of her gateposts watching a tow truck hitch up her white Datsun. "Since when did you start swanning around in cabs?" she asked.

"I'm not 'swanning', Mrs. E. I've been out to lunch with a friend and they paid for the cab."

"And we all know who that friend is – Miss Money Bags. 'Lady in beige I adore you' used to be a popular song in the fifties."

"I wouldn't know, but if I did know, it would be 'Lady of Spain I adore you'. How will you manage without your car?"

Mrs. E smiled delightedly, cheeks reddening under her tawny pink blusher. "You're not the only one with friends in high places. The Reverend Joseph's doing a deal with a parishioner – I get their old Audi Quattro, they get the choir singing 'The Lord is my Shepherd' plus a choice of three contemporary religious songs for free at their daughter's wedding."

"Audis are posh," I said.

"It's twelve years old but yes, Audis are pretty posh. The girls can't wait. I've told Edmund it's come from social services because we've got more than four children, so don't go mentioning the Reverend." She peeled herself off the post and produced a cheroot from her shirt pocket. "Now, is that your friend Pat or is it a brightly coloured mirage?"

"Got an ashtray?" Pat asked.

"You're not smoking again?"

"No, I just want to remind myself what an ashtray looks like. Of course I'm smoking again – in moderation, as a social accoutrement, but never alone or as an emotional prop."

"You're back with your counsellor?"

"I am, and a lot better I feel for it. Sandy's paying."

"Sandy?"

"Sandy, Sandra... whatever I'm happy with – although *you'd* better still stick to Sandra. She doesn't love you like she loves me."

I found a foil container from one of the previous weeks Mr. Kipling's exceedingly good Bakewell tarts and put it on the table in front of Pat. "Use this. What does Sandra say about you smoking?"

"Hmm."

"She says, 'hmm'?"

"No, I say 'hmm', stupid. You and I say 'hmm', nobody else does."

I was very pleased to see the return of the old Pat, although not ready to trust that the reversion would stick. It felt good to have her sitting in her usual chair with her tobacco tin, cheap plastic lighters and flimsy cigarette papers that seemed to turn up everywhere after she'd gone.

"Tea, Lorna, chop-chop."

"I haven't any herbal."

"Bugger herbal, break out the PG. How's tricks with the woman in beige?"

"Her name's Dan."

"I know, but we all call her 'the woman in beige'."

"Who's 'all'?"

"Me, Sandra, Helen, loads of people. She's even been called 'the mysterious woman in beige'. What does she do?"

"Don't know."

"Where does she live?"

"As far as I know, she shares a house with Theresa."

"Where?'

"You tell me."

Pat shrugged. "Haven't a clue where Terry lives. It's a different place each time I've asked her. She's had a riverside flat in Putney, a mansion flat in Kensington, a tower-block flat in Tower Hamlets... I think she says whatever comes into her head. Wouldn't be surprised if she slept in the car in somebody's garage."

"Do you see much of her?" I asked super-casually.

"No. That spark flickered for a moment and went out. Stick that in one of your poems."

"I won't, if you don't mind." I put the mugs of tea on the table and sat down.

"Biscuits, cake?" she asked.

"I've given them up."

"What? This is a pretty pickle and fine how-do-you-do. I turn my back for less than a year and come back to find you've taken religious orders. This woman's had a very unpleasant effect on you. You've lost weight. You're almost thin." Pat switched on the table light and held it up to my face. "I don't like the look of Lorna Tree at all."

I laughed, although deep down I didn't feel like laughing at all. Pat put down the lamp and returned to her cigarette making. *Dan will hate the smell of cigarettes in here, must buy air freshener and open all windows.*

"Tell me about Dan," Pat said.

"Nothing much to tell." *Nothing much I <u>can</u> tell.* "I'd rather hear about you and Sandra."

"We're all right. I've gone from besotted to irritated to rather fond and may remain at that level for some years; but you, Lorna, I want to know about you."

"I'm sorry, Pat." I suddenly found myself in urgent need of a tissue. "I'm afraid I'm not at liberty to say."

Pat stopped in mid lick of cigarette paper and stared at me in astonishment. "This is Pat you're talking to, not the police. I'm your best friend – you can tell me anything."

I blew my nose. "But I can't. You wouldn't understand."

I knocked on Jenny Salter's office door. There was no reply, which had never happened before. I knocked again. "Jenny," I called hesitantly.

"I'm here," she said from behind me – and there she was, holding a steaming Styrofoam cup of coffee. "I'd run out of tea bags and had to go down to the canteen."

"Didn't *they* have tea bags either?"

She blinked at me, an expression on her face almost of dislike. Rather unnerving. I stood back and let her unlock the door. She put down the cup, took off her cardigan, put it over the back of her usual chair and sat down. I took off my fleece waistcoat, put it over the back of my usual chair and sat down.

I said, "Sorry, Jenny, that has made me feel rather strange, meeting you out of situ – I felt you didn't like me at all. Of course it would be no business of mine if you preferred rat poison to tea... the remark stemmed purely from my feelings of disorientation."

I'm almost sure she wanted to say, "Bullshit"; however, instead she sighed, ruffled her non-existent feathers and said, "I quite understand, and of course I don't dislike you, Lorna; I also was experiencing feelings of disorientation at finding you so close to my door. Now, what has your week brought forth?"

"Not a lot. I wanted to ask you if it were possible to love somebody passionately yet be intimidated by them and also feel they were capable of murdering one?"

"Somebody, them, one? Surely after all this time, we can put names to these 'somebodys'?"

"You're not in a very good mood," I said.

"On the contrary, I'm in an excellent mood." She looked at me defiantly. What was going on?

"Jenny, I'm very confused... and unhappy."

Her face softened. She pushed a strand of hair behind her ear. "I'm sorry, Lorna. Let's begin the session again, you go out and do what you always do. OK?"

I put on my fleece, picked up my rucksack and left the room. Stood outside for two minutes and then tapped on the door. "Jenny, it's me. Lorna Tree."

"Come on in, Lorna."

She was plugging in the kettle, a tea bag was sitting in her usual cup. There was no sign of the cup of coffee.

"Have you brought your cup, then?" she asked. "I found a couple of tea bags in the filing cabinet."

"Natch," I said, and fished my mug advertising the joys of Kit Kat out of my rucksack.

The love toad

Dinner at Lorna's, 7.30 for 8pm, and this wasn't going to be just any dinner taken from Lorna's *Alternative Alternative Cookbook*. Oh no. Suddenly my cookbook didn't seem such a bright idea; guests couldn't be relied on to appreciate the irony of a curdled queen of puddings.

No point consulting Julie re. food; she'd never be able to leave matters at "Do dip into my *Dinner Party Menus for Every Occasion*. I can heartily recommend the Ascension Week goose, so tasty we repeated it in July and August and served goose chilled over rice at the September barbecue." No, she'd insist on taking over the whole menu and start talking about the imperative of a properly dressed dinner table.

Went to the local library and photocopied pages of a battered Elizabeth David, battered Gary Rhodes and a battered and wine- or blood-stained Keith Floyd which the library assistant immediately consigned to the 'All books 50p' table in the lobby.

"You don't want it, do you?" he asked hopefully.

"It's too soiled," I said.

"Sign of a good cookery book."

"Or a grubby kitchen-stroke-cook."

I invited Pat and Sandra, Dan of course, Angela – on her own or with a guest, hoping she wouldn't ask Theresa.

On the day she telephoned. "Can I bring Tony?"

"Do we know him?"

"My baby – little Tonia. I'm calling her Tony now, after a world-famous singer."

"Tony Bennett?"

"Tony Orlando. He wrote that great song about knocking three times on the pipe. It's so real, that song, I've got it on all my sing-along cassettes."

"Will Tony eat salmon?"

"No. She's completely vegetarian. She eats chips. I'll bring a bag with me. They'll just need heating in the oven."

But Ange, I silently mouthed, *my oven will be full of cordon bleu delicacies, my flat will smell of potpourri and expensive herb candles – chips will not enhance the romantic ambience I will be creating.*

"Fair enough, Ange."

David found himself just passing my first-floor-landing door. "Smelt cooking. Thought I'd better pop up and see if you were OK."

"Do cooking smells imply I may have committed suicide? I've heard of people committing suicide to their favourite music, never their favourite cooking smells."

"No need to be smart."

"I thought I was a pariah."

"Pariah or not, you're still my sister, and Julie's sister-in-law, and the aunt of our future child." He edged into my kitchen producing a bottle of wine from behind his back. "Chablis for the fish. Put it in the fridge."

"How did you know I'd be cooking fish?"

"You always cook fish."

"I didn't know I was so predictable."

"You're predictably predictable. So what else are you cooking?"

"Organic new potatoes, asparagus, salmon mousse, mushrooms and Stilton, home-made summer pudding and crème fraîche, a selection of Savoyard cheeses..."

"Come into some money?" David interrupted sweetly.

"Sainsbury's money-off vouchers in the *Echo*," I countered.

"They're for the readers, not the messenger boy."

"The messenger boy who delivers the message at four pence an hour."

"That's your choice."

"Please David, can we not argue?" I held up my hands. He recognised the gesture as his own.

"Well, you know what I think…" he ploughed on.

"I certainly do. So there's no need to repeat yourself. Look, it's not as if I have dinner parties every day of the week. Allow me some fun."

He shifted awkwardly from one foot to the other, finally muttered, "Seems like you lead a life of non-stop fun… however, it looks very nice up here. Julie says if you want to use the terrace you're very welcome."

"Thank Julie, but no, we'll be fine with all the windows open."

"Well, better let you get on," he said, making no attempt to go. "Good luck," and still no attempt to go. "Mind you, I have to say that I have my doubts about this Dan person. What exactly does she do? Where does her money come from? Why haven't you introduced her to us?"

"Because within five minutes you'd be asking her what she did and where did her money come from."

Baby Tonia (I couldn't get used to 'Tony' in less than a day), followed by Ange clutching a large bag of McCain's oven chips, a lime-green plastic potty and a bag of disposable nappies, were the first to arrive.

"Hello Ange. Hello Tony," I said politely.

Ange and I kissed the air while Tonia moved a wad of pink bubble gum from the right side of her mouth to the left, staring at me with slightly protuberant eyes – which was unkind of me to note; as Gran would say, *Let he without sin…* or more appropriately, *Ever taken a good look at yourself in the mirror, Lorna, before criticising others?* or, *You're no oil painting.*

I'm not at ease with children. I blame George and Della, for being ill at ease with me. I've never taken to the E children and I've known them since they were new-born babies, long before any nasty

203

thoughts about their neighbour Lorna had ever entered their downy heads. In those early years, when Mrs. E was taking piano and trainee deacon lessons, I'd had to babysit twice a week because Mr. E wasn't to be trusted with anything larger than a small rabbit. The house could burn down and he'd not notice once he'd entered into one of his trancelike states, reflecting on the beauty of nature.

I've since wondered if this behaviour wasn't invented by Mr. E in the early days of his marriage to ensure he avoided pram-pushing duties, grocery shopping, DIY superstores, driving family about in a car and taking said family on holidays. Gran much approved of him being not as other men, although owned to be unfailingly astonished at his assiduous manliness in producing children.

Once, I heard her say to Edna, sotto voce, "Apparently he's very fertile. Mrs. E puts it down to having worn loose trousers all his life." And Edna raised her heavy eyebrows and responded, "But surely he wears underpants. I can't imagine him in boxer shorts," and they both shuddered gleefully at the very idea.

Where was I? Babysitting the E family progeny... and now fast forward, or backwards, to Ange and Baby Tonia – who was no longer a baby but a sturdy child.

"She's not absolutely potty-trained," Ange mouthed at me. "I give her the pot and tell her, whenever you're ready, darling. In your own time."

This wasn't what I'd had in mind for my cosmopolitan evening; adult guests batting sophisticated repartee and making appreciative noises over my choice of fine wine and delicious food while, in the background, Baby Tonia sat on a green plastic potty responding to encouraging asides from her mother.

"Well done, darling. I think something's coming. Yes Lorna, I will have another spud."

"You see, she's half in, half out of nappies," Ange said in her normal voice.

"Jolly good," I enthused, "I'll show you where the bathroom is..."

"Don't worry. If you've got a towel, I'll put it down by the coffee table to clean her up."

"Better in the bathroom," I said weakly.

"Too clinical. I want Tony to have a supportive atmosphere when she's doing poos, so she feels it's a perfectly natural function – which it is, isn't it?"

"Yes, but not in public" fell on Ange's deaf ears as she'd scooped Tonia up and taken her over to the window.

"Look at Auntie Lorna's garden. Big garden."

I hoped I wasn't going to be stuck with the 'Auntie Lorna' all evening.

Downstairs I recognised Pat's particular way of banging on our front door, and heard David hurry across the hall to open up.

"Pat, Sandra, and it's Dan, isn't it?" he said.

"Yes it is."

"Is that your blue Mercedes?'

"Yes it is."

"Much trouble with car thieves and vandalism?"

"No."

"I am surprised. Julie and I have always thought twice about buying brand new while we live in London. Especially an ostentatious make."

I ran nimbly down the stairs, the welcoming hostess in her stripy cook's apron, face rosily flushed from peering encouragingly into a hot oven.

"Thank you, David. Come on up, everyone. Ange and her little girl are here already."

"You'll keep the noise down, Lorna?"

"David, bugger off," I said, and we left him fussing over the outdoor shoe rack.

"Can I have a word?" Dan followed me into the kitchen and put her wrapped bottle of wine on top of the fridge.

"I'll just check the mushrooms – garlic butter and Stilton cheese –

delicious," I said, showing off a little, wanting Dan to see what a multi-talented woman I was.

Ange came in asking for orange juice for Tonia.

"I've got apple juice," I said, "or Orangina."

"Mum, I wanted fresh orange juice," Tonia whined.

"I am so sorry, darling," I said insincerely. "Could you open this bottle, Dan, the cork's rather tight?"

She took the bottle from me, but reluctantly, almost as if accepting some unwelcome legally binding contract. She and the opened bottle followed me back out into the other room, where Pat and Ange were flopped on the settee and Sandra was showing Tonia how to juggle with a peanut and two olives. Dan put the bottle on the mantelpiece, making no attempt to offer it to anybody. It was a statement, an 'I'm nothing to do with that bottle or this woman' statement.

Pat, who has a nose for such nuances, picked it up immediately. "I'll help myself then. Anyone for a drop of red? Dan?"

"When I'm ready," Dan said. She looked and sounded surly, as if on the point of leaving.

"I think your mushrooms are almost ready," Pat said, sniffing the air. I hurried back into the kitchen.

"Lorna."

I straightened up, set the baking tray carefully on the window ledge to cool. "Yes, Dan?" I said with a bright busy smile as I snipped open Ange's bag of oven chips.

"I'm really sorry but there's another guest."

"Another guest?" I said, striving to maintain that light untouchable cheerfulness while knowing exactly who that other guest would be.

"I asked Theresa."

"And why would you do that?" Damn. Edginess creeping into my voice.

"Because she was at a loose end."

"Oh! So Theresa's at a loose end, might as well take her along to

Lorna's and spoil her evening. And are you with Theresa or me, tonight?"

She looked anywhere but into my face, finally saying sullenly, "I'm with nobody. I'm on my own. I'm sorry, but I couldn't just leave her behind."

In retrospect, I see that the heat of uncontrollable anger I felt was a totally unfamiliar sensation. *Keep your mouth shut, Lorna, hold your tongue, that's quite enough, little lady,* and Dad's ridiculous, *Softly, softly, catchee monkey,* impressed on me since childhood... I swept them all away.

I was shaken with fury; rattling frozen chips into an oven-proof dish, I said icily, "And what exactly happens to the wondrous Theresa if she spends an evening in her own company? Will she slit her wrists, turn into a pumpkin, or just be mildly bloody bored or lonely like the rest of the human race?"

Downstairs I heard the sharp rat-tat on the front door, David skating across the hall.

"She's my oldest friend," said Dan. "What harm can it do? She knows Ange and her daughter..."

"I know she knows Ange and her daughter, she knows Pat pretty intimately as well..."

"Lorna, you don't own me."

In the next room Ange and Tonia were exclaiming in delighted surprise as Theresa entered the room, while in the kitchen Dan and I stood perfectly still, our eyes locked.

I was the first to break. "You'd better lay an extra place at the table, if that's not too much of a commitment to the evening."

After she'd gone I stuck my hot angry face under the cold water tap.

Pat handed me a towel. "You OK?"

"Couldn't be better."

"Don't let the enemy know you're rattled."

"Shut up."

"I'm serious. Put on an act. Do that thing when you used to pretend to be a glamorous film star with a tragic past."

"I haven't done that since school."

"The talent's still there, girl. Tell them about when Kate left you for the kennel maid. Make yourself interesting. Smile, exude charm and sexual pheromones, inner grief... and take that bloody apron off." Exit Pat with a swagger, having for once in her life behaved like a true friend.

Oven chips into oven, salmon mouse into fridge, salad into perspex designer salad bowl, remove apron, push out breasts, hold in stomach and go for it, Lorna.

Theresa had secured my one armchair, Ange sat on its arm, and Tonia was snuggled in Theresa's lap. Very cosy.

"Terry, I'm so glad you came. I would have asked you, only I always assume you're very busy –" *clubbing, having sexual exploits with other women's girlfriends...*

Her eyes sparkled maliciously. "Not every night – like to keep my hand in with local affairs."

On the other side of the room, Sandra patted the space she and Pat had left between them for me. I glanced at Dan – she was ignoring everybody, staring gloomily at my bookcase.

"Dinner won't be long," I said brightly.

Pat nudged me sharply, turned her head in my direction and went into one of her 'gockle of geer' routines: "Undergine her, you stuckid gow."

"Actually, I'm really glad you came – the more the merrier." I made my voice ruefully confidential. "You see, this is the first time in over three years that I've asked anyone to dinner. The last time was a week before my ex-girlfriend Kate moved up to Leeds. I was very upset at the time."

From the corner of my eye, I saw Dan pull out a chair from the dinner table and sit; I had her attention.

Pat said, throwing back her head in one of those 'remembering old times' gestures, "God, I remember that. It was your birthday and you couldn't stop crying. Kate kept saying, 'It's not the other side of the world, you can visit once we've decorated the guest room.' Kate went off with a kennel maid," she explained to the others. "Do you ever hear from her?"

"Strangely enough, I do. Every now and then she leaves a message on my answerphone, about her and Tina and their clumber spaniels. It's in the past but it still hurts. Rejection is always painful."

Pat bent over to untie and retie the lace of her trainer. "Gexcellent, geek going," and I heard Sandra stifle laughter.

"I think that's really sad," Ange said.

"It was a long time ago," I said briskly. "I imagine we all have sad stories in our pasts."

Pat kicked me again. "Not as sad as yours was. Didn't she tell you she was leaving the day after you signed the hire-purchase agreement on her new car? She was a devil but extremely attractive – at times I did wonder how Lorna managed to snaffle such a smashing woman."

"Thanks Pat," I said, "I think dinner's about ready."

We sat at the table. I could only see Dan's profile. She looked thoroughly miserable. Mustn't weaken. Lorna, mustn't weaken. We are not a couple, she and I. It's been fun – has it been fun? Nothing serious. Deep breathing. Let it lie, Lorna... and suddenly, spontaneously, my mood lightened, I could take a sip of wine without fearing I might become maudlin. I thought, good old Sandra loving good old Pat, my shallow, highly amusing and dearly loved friend who, while not wanting to see me made unhappy, would always want to enjoy herself whatever the occasion – I could see Pat telling a cheerful anecdote even as I was being buried. And Ange looking as if for once, everything was working out for her. Theresa. I knew for certain that a cloud hung over Theresa. Something long term and not easily fixed was wrong. She looked up suddenly and met my gaze. Did I see something like desperation in her face?

"Sold any poems lately?" she said.

"No. That's not why I write poetry."

Ange said, "I wrote a poem about you, Terry. Lorna thought it was fantastic. Would you like to read it?"

"Not particularly. You're a stupid sod." But her voice was almost affectionate.

As the meal progressed, Dan slowly began to relax, her face lost its tight, closed expression. She said little, but that's how Dan was. Several times she looked up the table to where I was sitting and I knew that the ribbon that linked the two of us was there once more.

Later, in the kitchen, I washed up while she dried, stacking the plates neatly, cutlery clattering into the cutlery drawer.

"What was your ex, Kate, like?" she asked.

I hesitated. "She made me laugh. We had a warm affectionate relationship; the sort you think might last a lifetime."

"So?"

"So, I was wrong. The woman she settled for seemed pretty unspectacular. I still can't work out what ingredient I had missing."

"Nothing missing, Lorna." Dan put down the tea towel and pulled me against her. "Can I stay tonight?"

"Of course you can," I said lightly.

Lorna's Mushroom and Stilton starter

2 giant mushrooms per person, a lot of butter, garlic, Stilton cheese, tin foil.

1. Enjoy peeling the mushrooms. I do. (Allow time to enjoy peeling the mushrooms.)
2. Remove stalks and cut stalks into tiny pieces.
3. Chop Stilton into small pieces, which is an extremely greasy procedure.
4. Chop up optional garlic.

5. *Mix the chopped elements together and put in the bowl of upturned mushrooms.*

6. *Top with slices of butter.*

7. *Wrap in oven foil and cook until a smell of Stilton fills the kitchen.*

N.B. Do not know what temperature to cook at, as modern cookers are different from my own much-loved Baby Belling.

*

"So you see, Jenny, there's no real reason for me to keep coming here every week – my life's perfectly hunky-dory."

"I'm pleased to hear it," Jenny said, without looking up from her busy rummaging in a narrow desk drawer.

I'd expected a very different response; a concerned querying of the eyebrows followed by professional riffling through my notes, perhaps even a quickly suppressed flash of grief; but no, Jenny's arm had disappeared up to its elbow inside the drawer and the only sound was the scrabbling of Jenny's fingers against wood. Expression? Very much, *Where is that damn thingumajig?* rather than, *Is my precious fledgeling strong enough to fly unaided?*

"What are you looking for?" I glanced meaningfully at my watch – we were two and a half minutes into my official time.

"Paperclips. Ah, here they are," she waved a small plastic box of rainbow-coloured paperclips in the air. "Now, you were saying?"

"I was saying that everything's so hunky-dory I need not keep coming here each week."

"I see."

Still no eye contact, but something in the paperclip box she obviously found fascinating – carefully she began to pick out the lime-green clips.

"I'm sorry I'm distracted today," she said, sounding not at all sorry. "So, Lorna, you are saying that everything is 'hunky-dory'?"

Stifled inclination to shout, *It's me, Lorna Tree, remember? The woman whose meagre earnings probably paid for you and your family's last foreign holiday. Pay attention. You should be celebrating my hunky-doriness, not marvelling over coloured paperclips – they've been in the shops for several years now.*

"So, your dinner party that you'd set so much store by went well?'

Couldn't help a self-satisfied smirk. "It finished well."

"Good," and she lapsed into reverie.

Good. Was that it? No "Elaborate, Lorna, share the full picture. You said, then she said, and how did you feel when she said that?"

"Good," she said again, "to summarise, you are getting on with Dan and feel yourself to be embarking on a meaningful relationship?"

"Yes I do... at least, we will embark, etcetera, if Dan will let us... which I feel she will eventually... early days of course... but I'm pretty sure that whatever problems we have can be... overcome by love." Now, why had I said that? I've spent decades dying of embarrassment when I've let phrases like 'overcome by love' slip out in front of Pat.

"Overcome by love? You must be stark staring mad. Has a love toad squatted on your pea-sized brain, Lorna?"

Love toad. We'd used that all the time during our fourth, fifth and sixth years at school. Girls in our year crushing photographs of boyfriends and pop stars to their breasts, gurgling, "Isn't he lurvely?"

When I was fifteen, I became infatuated with Rod Stewart after 'Maggie May' came out. Me and Pat in the front seat on the top deck of the bus, coming back from Dalston after a Saturday morning spent mooching around Ridley Road Market; I'd opened up my minute heart-shaped locket to disclose the minute heart-shaped face of Rod Stewart wearing what looked like a hot-water bottle on his tiny head.

"Isn't he wonderful?" I'd breathed reverentially.

"Wonderful? I'd rather mate with a wallaby. I would, Lorna. If Rod Stewart and a wallaby were on offer, I'd choose the wallaby. You must have a love toad squatting in your brain to fancy him."

"Well that's excellent news," Jenny was saying. "Under normal circumstances I require a month's notice so we can work towards closure, but as you seem so happily preoccupied, I'll make an exception and we'll settle up at the end of this session."

"You mean this is my last visit?" *Hang on Jenny, I didn't truly mean there's no reason to keep coming – just a show of independence after weeks of blubbering.*

Jenny laid aside her chain of lime-green paperclips and smoothed her skirt. I hadn't seen this skirt before – it was dark brown, not a colour she usually wore, sandals again. She tucked her feet out of sight under the chair. I looked up, at last meeting her eyes, but immediately she shifted her gaze to the direction of the clock on the wall behind me. What had become of my kindly golden eagle? Jenny's face wore a closed expression I'd never seen before, as if... as if her body had been acquired by an alien – which might sound ridiculous, but one-to-one in a soundproofed cubbyhole office with very little natural light, the mind can auto-suggest the very unlikely.

"Jenny, could you please be like your usual Jenny? I feel as if a shutter's come down between us."

She blinked and smiled – I'd swear insincerely – the alien hadn't quite got the hang of human behaviour. "Don't worry. I am my usual Jenny. Look, if things go wrong, if you need to speak to me, you can always come back." This may read on the page as comforting and supportive, but had you been a fly on the wall you'd have thought, "She's not bothered. She wants Lorna to clear off, out of her office, out of her appointments book."

Chilling in a way, as if the tap of warmth had been turned off. Still, with half an hour left, I said, "I'll settle up now."

"No need," she said.

I took my three ten-pound notes from my wallet and placed them on the desk.

"Really, Lorna, there's no need, you haven't had your full fifty minutes."

I walked out of her office, let the door swing shut at my back. Not even a 'Good luck'. Bloody charlatan.

To tell or not to tell? Like Pat I never can keep my big mouth shut.

Had I, in true sleuth fashion, stopped to consider, "What was that all about? Why would someone's behaviour change so drastically?" I might have crept around the outer perimeter of the health centre to the back of the building and there located Jenny Salter's small office window some eight foot above the ground. I might then have laid my hands on three milk crates and noiselessly stacked them one on top of the other, mounting said milk crates and gingerly peering through the window. And then I might have been surprised and mystified to see Jenny still seated, with her head in her hands, a picture of misery. Had the window been open an inch or two along the bottom edge, which I think it was that day, I might also have heard the unsettling sound of Jenny weeping.

I might have, but I did none of that. I was not a sleuth on that summer afternoon, I was an angry client. I marched out onto the hot street determined to think no more of J. Salter. The slight pain I was experiencing in my chest would soon go – it was only the pain of rejection. Anyone in my position would feel the same.

1972

Followed by the squashed frogs

At least once a day, I probably thought something good, bad or indifferent about my parents, but by 1972, after they'd been stationed in Cologne on the west bank of the Rhine for more than two years, I would have told anyone who asked (although nobody did ask) that George and Della were a distant memory.

During those years we had received a total of five postcards from Della – obviously a bulk buy, as all five showed the same view of Cologne's twin-spired Gothic cathedral. I was so familiar with this view that I felt I'd visited the cathedral in a previous life.

"Pat, did you know it took six hundred years to build?"

"Yes, you've told me several billion times now."

"It's a hundred and fifty-seven metres high."

"Big deal."

"The Archbishop of Cologne became…"

"I don't give a flying bread basket…"

The above facts were garnered from the small print beneath Della's flamboyant script. "Having a terrific time. George sends his love and says noses to the grindstone – diligence brings its own rewards."

Only once did George, in his own words, put pen to pale blue Basildon Bond paper, and this letter was addressed to Gran, not us. We read it, as we read all Gran's mail, while she was out at work.

"Dear Mother, reluctantly I'm compelled to put pen to paper. Della and I are more than somewhat concerned over the children's School Reports. How can it be possible for Lorna to come bottom or second from bottom in every subject? And if David can excel in Religious Knowledge, why is he only 'adequate, disappointing, lacks application, and could do better' in all other areas? Religious knowledge will get him nowhere, he need look no further than the Reverend Joseph. Vis-à-vis Lorna, what the hell does she think she's playing at? 'Disruptive, can resort to bullying in team games.' Have I reared a pair of teenage thugs? Please emphasise that Della and I are DEEPLY DISAPPOINTED and expect to see an IMPROVEMENT.

"I enclose a clipping from our internal newspaper, rather blurred, however, Della is the woman in the elegant picture hat, and of course that's your son to the left of the flying-dolphin ice sculpture. I'm getting quite a reputation out here in the Rhineland. Della, bless her, wishes I'd followed in Henry Moore's giant footsteps. (In case you're unaware, Mother, he's the wallah that produces the reclining nudes with portholes knocked through their midriffs.) However, I'm more than satisfied with the fruits of life's harvest – which brings me back to the offspring. They are enjoying the opportunities I never had, I expect them to BUCKLE DOWN, pull up their socks, bite the bullet..."

Pat said, "Your dad writes an entertaining letter." Pat can sometimes have a satisfying way with words.

She and I had decided to form a singing duo. We would write our own songs and play our own instruments. In the interim, while the songs were being written and until the instruments and music lessons materialised (we didn't count playing the recorder which was compulsory in our school), we decided to concentrate on at least looking like a singing duo, which meant wearing roughly the same clothes and having roughly the same hairstyle – not easy given that Pat's hair was blonde and curly and mine straight and dark brown.

"What do you think?" We stood on two wooden chairs in front of David in our home-made trouser suits made from lining silk, which cost almost nothing in Chapel Market. "Imagine we're up on a stage."

"You're puckered all along the seams," he said. "I think those trouser suits are rubbish."

Pat and I looked each other over – we looked fabulous, we'd never looked more attractive.

"The seams are at the side. Nobody's going to look at us side-on." Pat and I linked arms, put our heads close together and made kissing shapes with our mouths. "Now what do you think? Do we look like a professional singing duo?"

"Like Donny and Marie Osmond?"

"Don't be stupid. They're crap. We've decided to call ourselves The Pretty Things. Sort of ironic."

"It's been done," David said, "and you're not pretty. It's all right for men to call themselves The Pretty Things and be ironic, but people will just laugh at you two. Might as well call yourselves Pretty Ugly or the Ugly Sisters."

Pat got down off the chair. "OK, Bunter, just push off now. We've had enough of you."

Apparently that was something my sensitive brother never got over, Pat calling him Billy Bunter. He could call us rude names – and once for several weeks he elaborated on us looking like accidents waiting to happen, thought himself incredibly funny: the car-crash fatalities, the unopened parachutes, the flattened hedgehogs, which spawned the squashed frogs, drowned kittens and acid-bath murders – but let Pat call him Bunter, Billy Bunter or fat face and he takes it to heart for ever and ever. Decades later he told Julie that his teenage years were blighted, self-image horribly distorted, plus ongoing repercussions affecting his social skills and job interview techniques, while Pat and I with our squashed-frog faces were expected to just get on with life.

Where was I? David's sixteenth birthday. What, it's the first you've heard of it? Well, that's where I am for the present... where I am for the past.

Although I may have described a picture of disharmony between my brother and myself, that's not the whole picture; on many likes and dislikes we dovetailed. For instance, we liked the same music, David Bowie and Rod Stewart; and we liked looking for clothes in second-hand shops and jumble sales.

Most Saturdays during autumn and winter – the jumble sale seasons – we could be found in a queue outside a church hall with our carrier bags and trouser pockets heavy with loose change. Sunday was spent washing, ironing and altering our purchases. David had a penchant for double-breasted pin-striped suits and navy denim work jeans, while I was still hooked on large men's shorts, large men's collarless shirts and large men's pyjama jackets (large men seemed to be very inattentive to hygiene where pyjama bottoms were concerned).

We no longer shopped from Gran's catalogue, recognising that Burlington's fashion pages were several years out of date, although we did both pore over the women's corset and underwear pictures, giving marks out of ten to the models. There was usually a particularly plain one and we'd hoot with derision when we found her. I think Gran vaguely disapproved of our preoccupation with the lingerie pages but felt she might be treading on sensitive ground by broaching it. To Gran, flesh was best kept covered, beds were for sleeping in, and babies were bought in from a shop up north.

By 1972, she had retired and was feeling pretty miserable about it, spending an hour or two each afternoon on fine days venting her dissatisfaction at being tossed onto life's scrapheap to Mr. E. He had consistently chosen life's scrapheap, even down to constructing his very own, rather than leaving his house for several hours a day, five days a week, and being paid money for the boon of his impassive company.

"I haven't time to turn around, Irene, what with the rabbits, Rusty and the garden." No mention of his own five children, Mrs. E, the dismantled kitchen, the built-in wardrobes lying on their sides on the top landing like three open coffins.

He always had time for tea and a little conversation at the fence; Gran on her yellow Formica chair with its black and grey Chinese character pattern, Mr. E squatting on an oil drum or a splintering orange box. David and I were as used to their gently murmuring voices, the sight of Gran's thin curved back and hunched shoulders under one of her many Courtelle knit cardigans, as we were to Rusty's endless snarling and the E children fighting over whose turn it was to go first.

Phewee. It's hard work this thinking back. The more you think, the more you remember. So it was that Gran decided (because she was bored and because, I think, she saw in David something of her drowned son Steven) to give David a birthday party he'd remember all his life. We'd never had a party before. We were not a gregarious family, however, we took up the party idea with enthusiasm. There would be cheese and pineapple chunks on cocktail sticks, cheese and party pickled onions on cocktail sticks, cocktail chipolatas on cocktail sticks, devils on horseback on cocktail sticks. Moving on from the cocktail section to sandwiches: egg and salad cream, grated cheese and cucumber, ham, and tinned pink salmon – cut into triangles, crusts removed. Onwards, to more hard-boiled eggs than we had ever dreamed of, sliced Scotch eggs, mini pork pies, quirky morsels (to be decided) on Ritz crackers, and giant jars of Branston pickle and piccalilli. Drink would be Cydrax, shandy and ginger beer.

David and I recognised that, like Gran's catalogue, this didn't quite answer our modern-day requirements for what constituted a teenage party. Not easy to get drunk on Cydrax or shandy, but we didn't mind. Pat or somebody would bring in 'the hard stuff', we told each other.

Gran was to go bowling and promised not to come home before midnight; David could invite twenty guests and I could ask Pat. It was only when we sat down one Saturday afternoon in September, David with a large sheet of paper and fresh Biro, that we faltered. He wrote, PARTY at the top of the page and then GUESTS.

"Pat," I prompted.

He wrote PAT, and then laboriously wrote out the names of six boys who were in his school swimming team. Sitting at the other side of the table I read the names upside down.

"Do you actually know any of these people?" I asked.

"Slightly." He stared down at the piece of paper.

"Leave him alone," Gran said. "Now, what about a few more girls?"

"He only knows me and Pat."

"You're not yet on the list and you won't be if you don't pipe down," Gran said.

"There's Janice Sharp," he said hesitantly.

"Janice Sharp! She's 'orrible."

"She isn't."

"She sings flat in assembly – got a voice like a foghorn."

"Not a hanging offence," Gran said, her own voice not being up to much.

"I know, Gran, only she's dreary and old fashioned and smelly."

"We do not make personal remarks. Put her on the list. Now, Lorna, is there anyone apart from Pat you'd like to ask?"

"No. I hate everyone."

"Well, we've got a possible ten people – a small select group," Gran said brightly. David looked at me from under his eyelashes, profoundly glum.

"You say something," I said.

"No, you say something," he said.

I said, "Gran, it's a lovely idea to have a party, but couldn't we just have people we know, like you and Mr. and Mrs. E and the Reverend Joseph and of course Pat?"

"David wouldn't want that. He wants friends of his own age."

David was chewing the Biro and the whites of his eyes were reddening. Firmly I said, "No, he doesn't. He wants us and the neighbours."

"Do you, David?"

"As Lorna's pointing out – I don't have any proper school friends – any friends at all."

"Of course you have," I said. "You've got us and the neighbours."

"I'm like Dad."

"You're nothing like your dad," Gran said. "What about if we dressed up as well? Something a bit different?"

OK. Small beer. A pathetic, stay-at-home, unadventurous pair of teenagers. No true desire for sex, drugs and rock and roll. Both of us happy to daydream about a world outside our soft, cushioned home; David, at sixteen, content to spend evenings teaching the budgie to say "Hello Gran" in return for a wad of fresh chickweed, rather than going out meeting the opposite sex.

I was still at the stage of staring at girls who attracted me in the hope they'd find me fascinating rather than weird, which was why 'bullying' had turned up several times in my school reports. My adjunct to staring: give my chosen loved one a sharp crack on the knees with my hockey stick, or a poke in the ribs with a descant recorder, and run off shouting, "You can't catch me," in the hope that she would catch me and a fight would turn into a romantic encounter.

"Take that and that, Lorna Tree –" rains body blows with own hockey stick on Lorna Tree. Tree felled, crumples to her knees, a purple bruising appearing on ashen temple. "Lorna, darling, I never meant to hurt you, only to teach you a lesson. Jesus, I've never realised just how beautiful, amazing, intriguing, fragile and sensitive you were until this very minute." Fade on Lorna and assailant in loving tangle on hockey pitch, hockey sticks, descant recorders cast aside.

"We could go as our favourite singers," I said. I'd go as Ziggy Stardust. I loved David Bowie.

"I'll go as Ziggy Stardust," David said.

"I wanted to go as Ziggy Stardust."

"You're a girl. Be Olivia Newton-John. It's *my* birthday."

"Couldn't you both be this Ziggy Stardust?" asked Gran diplomatically.

"What about Pat?"

"She could be Marc Bolan. She likes him."

"Or that ugly blonde bloke in Sweet," David said, sniggering and risking one of Gran's 'we don't make personal remarks' remarks.

"You don't like Pat very much, do you?" I said, and David's face turned scarlet.

I do believe it was at that exact moment that David decided he liked Pat hugely.

"She's all right," he mumbled.

But when we saw Pat, she wanted to be David Cassidy.

Gran was secretly relieved about the party. She confided in me, as we cleaned out the budgie's cage (the budgie being known affectionately as Budgie), that the thought of David's swimming team had made quite an adverse impression. For some reason – and she had nothing she could put her finger on against male swimming teams – she'd kept imagining six sixteen-year-olds dressed in skimpy swimming trunks, goggles, snorkels, possibly flippers, dancing suggestively in her living room, and sprawling semi-naked across her hoovered upholstery.

"And it's not a pleasant image, Lorna. I like my men fully dressed these days and preferably with a hammer or paintbrush in their hand."

Pat and I were relieved we wouldn't have to dance with the opposite sex or be either up- or downwind of Janice Sharp.

Regarding 'dressing up': after much discussion it was decided that Gran would be Margaret Rutherford in *Passport to Pimlico*. She bemoaned the fact that in her heyday – of which we'd heard much of over the years – she would have passed for Margaret Lockwood, a British film star specialising in wicked women roles in historical costume dramas. "Just a pencilled-in beauty-spot and I was a dead ringer for her."

"But Margaret Lockwood was hardly Marilyn Monroe, Gran. She was never internationally famous."

"Margaret Lockwood was huge in Britain, had an enormous following. Marilyn Monroe was a one-string fiddle by comparison."

Reverend Joseph had become almost animated when told he had to dress up, as opposed to his everyday dress-down. His lugubrious bloodhound features rolled themselves into a smile – fascinating to watch. I don't think I'd ever seen him try to smile before. Odd to realise that the Reverend looked old even then, yet he must have been not much older than David and I are now – no more than forty.

"I'll let Edmund know about the fancy dress," Mrs. E called through a mouthful of clothes pegs – she was hanging her generous underwear up on the whirly line. "At the moment, I talk and he communicates with nods or grimaces. The silly arse has taken a vow of silence and wants the whole family to follow his example – says we should listen to ourselves think – as if we've all got time to go around thinking."

"He spoke to me this morning," Gran said.

"Did he indeed?"

"Oh yes."

"Wasn't it yesterday morning?" I said. In those days Mrs. E was notoriously jealous of Gran, and Gran either knew it and liked to be aggravating or she was wilfully obtuse over interpersonal relationships.

"No, definitely this morning. I mentioned our party and he said he might come as a beech hedge if he can find enough leaves."

Must say, the picture of Mr. E edging into our living room dressed only in leaves wasn't reassuring, I'd have almost preferred David's swimming team. Mustn't let Mr. E hover near Gran while she was puffing a cigarette, or near Mrs. E (not that he often hovered near Mrs. E) while she smoked a cheroot. Mr. E starts off evening as a beech hedge, goes home as an autumn bonfire.

"We'll see about that," Mrs. E said grimly and, bosoms heaving ominously, she gathered up her plastic washing basket and went back indoors.

David's party was on the day of his birthday. I'd bought him Rod Stewart's *Every Picture Tells a Story* album; Pat gave him *The Electric Warrior* by T. Rex. From Gran he got a novelty clock with Mickey Mouse ears that vibrated when the alarm went off; also two pairs of socks in lime green and shocking-pink. He seemed surprisingly pleased with them, although up till then not a hint of lime green or shocking pink had entered his clothes cupboard.

There was not even a card from George and Della. While David riffled through the post in search of an envelope with a German stamp, Gran and I exchanged tight-lipped glances.

She said, "George is probably on manoeuvres and your mother's got a head like a sieve, and by the by, I've bought you both a can of silver hairspray."

The afternoon was spent helping Gran prepare the food. We must have used five hundred cocktail sticks. David said he was going to collect them all up at the end of the evening and make a model of the Cutty Sark.

Cocktail-stick jokes abounded. Death by a thousand cocktail sticks. Pat falls forward onto a plate of cheese and pineapple chunks, Mr. E, leaning across the chipolatas to reach the Cydrax bottle, is inadvertently pierced in his privates, putting a stop to the E baby production line, or Mr. E loses several crucial beech leaves when they are impaled on the chipolata sticks, and has to wear Gran's apron for the rest of the evening.

"It would ruin the chipolatas," David said.

"That's enough, you two. Go and get ready," Gran said, feeding the last of the Christmas tree lights through the Venetian blinds.

What did we wear? Did we look good or did we look great? Definitely great, as we vied for room on Gran's spindly dressing-table stool so we could see ourselves in the three-way mirror.

The silver hairspray made the most difference. We sellotaped greaseproof paper to each other's faces and necks to give our heads a thorough saturating, then we used Vaseline to make our hair stand up like a hedgehog's – not that a hedgehog has hair, or does it? Answers on a postcard... Not quite David Bowie's technique but astonishing. Talcum powder dusted over any areas of visible skin, a lipstick lightning flash across our foreheads and purple Rimmel eye make-up; Pat provided glitter. We'd made ourselves skin-tight silver bodysuits in yet more of that good old lining silk – and this time the puckering along the seams only added to what we saw as the surreal effect.

"Gran, we look like alien twins," I said.

"Oh my God –" Gran almost dropped her bucket of fruit punch on the way through to the dining room – "One of these days, you'll give me a heart attack." She put down the bucket and peered closely at us. "You certainly do look like aliens."

"We do, don't we?" And David and I smiled in mad, alien fashion at each other.

What to say about the party guests? Pat decided against David Cassidy as he was too normal. She made herself a wig from six ounces of black poodle wool and said she was Marc Bolan; Gran wore a grey dress with a lace collar from the jumble and a beaten-up man's hat; Mrs. E was impressive in a blonde wig but not immediately recognisable as Diana Dors; Mr. E disappointed by wearing his usual baggy cord trousers and only stapling a few leaves to a Grateful Dead T-shirt; his children were the singing children from *The Inn of the Sixth Happiness*, which meant they didn't have to dress up at all, just sing, "Knick knack, paddy wack," whenever anyone asked them who they were meant to be; and the Reverend Joseph was Bing Crosby as the priest in *The Bells of St Mary's*, although quite early on in the evening he sang a selection from *White Christmas*.

We were all so pleased with one another, so pleased with the passed round plates of cheery bits, so happy to knock back fruit punch and agree that, 'yes, it was pretty potent stuff,' even though there wasn't a drop of alcohol in it.

"It's the sugar from the fruit," Reverend Joseph said sagely, jiggling Diana Dors up and down on his knee – and nobody looking surprised, least of all Mr. E, that a Reverend or Bing Crosby would behave in such a manner.

"Guess my favourite fruit?" Mrs. E shouted, pouting her bosoms in his face.

"I've no idea."

"Melons! Let's have Chubby Checker on again."

Pat, David and I groaned. The E family had taken over the music, bringing in their LPs, *Twist with Chubby Checker* and *More Good Old Rock'n'Roll* by The Dave Clark Five.

"Or something smoochy," yelled Mrs. E, and she put on Gran's *The Magic of Val Doonican*.

I danced reluctantly with Pat, she then danced with David, I danced reluctantly with David, Mrs. E tried to dance with David and, when he shied away, face sweating under the talcum powder, she shouted, "What's up with the little tyke, never got to grips with a real woman before?"

Reverend Joseph said, "Calm down, Glenda," and shepherded her out into our garden.

Finally Pat managed to put on *The Rise of Ziggy Stardust and the Spiders from Mars*, and we and the E children started dancing our ideas of wild and weird dancing. Distantly I heard the front door bell ring.

"You didn't ask Janice Pooey Sharp, did you?" said Pat.

We turned up the volume and I made several dramatic and pseudo-drug-crazed passes with my hands across my eyes, saw myself reflected (eerily) in the mirror above the fireplace. *God Lorna, you don't half look weird. Wish I could look like this every day. Who the hell's that in a white turban?*

The music stopped abruptly, switched off by a bloke dressed up as a soldier, and I turned around and it was Della wearing the white turban. ("Actually, Lorna, this is called a toque amongst the European fashion cognoscenti.") And the soldier was of course George – with Margaret Rutherford, a little flustered, trying to flap him away from the turntable with an oven glove. For once, Mum and Dad didn't look out of place, almost underdressed next to the rest of us.

"Lorna, is that you?" George barked. I stepped forward to kiss his cheek, he stepped back sharply. "Whatever you've got on your face and hair, I don't want it smeared over your mother and me."

He looked around the room, as if we are all subordinates being insubordinating. Della only pretended to hide her amusement as Mrs. E came in from the garden with Bing Crosby's arm draped around her bare shoulders.

"Bit of an orgy?" George said sarcastically.

"It's David's birthday party," said Gran.

"More like a bit of an orgy to me."

"That's rubbish. You wouldn't see Margaret Rutherford at an orgy. Why didn't you tell us you were coming?"

"Birthday surprise for our son," Della said, brushing the folds of her cream chiffon skirt as if a layer of dust might be forming on it. "We thought we'd arrive unexpectedly and whizz the children off to The Talk of the Town in Hanover Square. David's first nightclub... but obviously this is more fun than any nightclub." She laughed affectedly and I found myself thinking, not for the first time, *I do not like my mother. How can this woman even be my mother?*

George was getting his second wind, ready to show these buggers he was as good a sport as the next man. "So," he roared jovially, "who the hell are the pair of you togged up to be?"

"We're Ziggy Stardust," David said, suddenly looking embarrassed.

"Who the hell's he when he's at home?"

"He's David Bowie, Dad. He's famous."

"Oh yes, I've heard of David Bowie. As far as I'm concerned he's a bloody pervert. And as far as I know – and your old dad's open to contradiction here – but he's a man, and aren't you a girl, Lorna?"

"George, it's a fancy-dress party," Reverend Joseph remonstrated.

"Look, Bing, I'm having a word with my daughter, thank you very much."

"He's androgynous, Dad."

"Exactly, and I'm not having any daughter of mine being androgynous – or son. Wash it off, both of you. I want you down here in ten minutes flat, looking normal."

"George, leave them alone. You will not give orders in my house."

"Mother, they are my children."

We all felt it. The good sport had been superseded by George at his nastiest.

"Better do as George says, darlings," Della said.

And we did as George said, and I swore to myself up in my bedroom – as I wiped away my lightning flash, hearing the front door shut on a subdued E family, Reverend Joseph and Pat – that this would the the very last time I would do as George said.

We were longer than ten minutes. It wasn't easy washing out the silver spray and Vaseline. I put on my baggy khaki shorts and a clean white shirt, clattered down the stairs behind David, who'd changed into his grey school trousers. In the living room, Gran was dispiritedly tipping plates of food into a bin bag while George and Della had appropriated the armchairs and sat in an aggrieved silence.

"I'll help you, Gran," I said.

"No you won't, madam. We've come all the way from Germany to see you both, you'll sit and talk to us," George said. Critically, he looked us up and down. David passed – just.

Quietly George said, "Lorna, I want you to go back upstairs and put on a skirt or dress."

"You'd look so much nicer, darling..." added Della.

"No," I said.

"If you don't do as I say, you won't be coming out with us tonight."

"Fair enough. I'd rather stay in with Gran."

David said, "Please Lorna, I don't want to go on my own."

"You'll just have to," I said, but my voice shook.

Gran trailed her bin bag towards us. "It's David's sixteenth birthday, Lorna, what about a compromise? Those blue sailcloth trousers you got at Christmas?"

"I want her to wear a dress," George said stubbornly.

"It's your son's birthday, I think you could afford to compromise rather than spoil it any more than it's been spoilt already."

"George." Della sent George a message with her eyes: *Go on darling or we'll never get out of here.*

"Very well."

So we compromised. We left Gran to the cleaning up and we motored into the West End where Danny La Rue was appearing, and yes, he was very funny. He made us laugh, Mrs. E would have loved his dresses, wigs and false eyelashes, but there remained something sour and unhappy about the whole evening.

With that annoying clarity I had even as a child, I could hate Dad for spoiling the party and trying to belittle our friends, while part of me understood that he wanted to be the best, the best liked. He used all that gloss and glamour to hide his own inadequacies and the knowledge that his children and mother were happier sitting conversing with Mr. E, any day of the week, their faces pressed against that wire netting fence.

High hopes

I have high hopes for my 'I'm No Angel' poem, although reluctantly I've been forced to pare it down and increase the quotient of gritty realism and self-parody, to pass the criteria of gritty realism and self-parody necessary to win the National Poetry Competition. Am still unsure of the title. Should I be more specific? Display an intimate knowledge of the angel hierarchy? Perhaps 'I'm No Cherub' or 'I'm no Archangel'. Asked Pat what she thought. She shrugged and said, "Search me."

At the moment am running two categories of daydream. There's the personal, centred around Dan and where our relationship might be heading – will she ever reveal her hidden sorrow? Then there's the professional daydream (with which I'm more comfortable, it being pure fantasy), where I win the National Poetry etc. and am fêted by publishers and media alike. I already have an award acceptance outfit of best black trousers and white linen Nehru shirt. In this daydream I'm in a darkened auditorium, the rows of seats filled with numerous high-ranking poets who have gathered from the four corners of the earth, having heard a rumour on the poetry grapevine that this year a truly outstanding poem, something on the theme of angels, has won.

"And the winner is... Lorna Tree."

I'm hit by a blast of spotlight as I stumble my way to the end of the row, lope athletically down the aisle to a rustle of head turning and whispers of, "Who is this woman? We don't know her. Doesn't look much of a poet."

As I reach the stage there is a whoop of applause from my poetry class, gentlemanly calls of "Bravo. Well done, Lorna." I see the glint of Ragnar's Toblerone held aloft in salute. David, Julie and Pat stand at the back of the hall, having decided belatedly to come. In a small cubbyhole office in deepest Hackney, Jenny Salter raises a peppermint teabag...

"An amazing debut for Ms. Tree, opening a new chapter in the annals of free verse." *Independent on Sunday*.

"Lovely luscious lesbian babe rocks stuffy poetry world." *Sun*.

"The National Poetry Prize was today awarded to a surprisingly youthful thirtysomething. Literary unknown Lorna Tree has upset many a popular stereotype of the female poet. Out with wooden bead necklaces and eco-friendly sandals – here we have a smart, infinitely attractive north London lesbian whose cool laconic delivery belies the depth, breadth and womanly insight of her work. What say you, Germaine Greer?" Radio Four's *Front Row*.

Pat arrived for one final reading before I posted off my entry. David and Julie were away in an isolated area of the Costa Brava for a fortnight, so we had the patio and Julie's sunbeds to ourselves.

"You're asleep," I accused, pausing at the foot of the first page.

"Just resting my eyes."

"Sit up and keep your eyes open."

Pat sat up and put on her sunglasses.

"I know your eyes are shut behind your sunglasses. Surely you can stay alert for three pages."

Pat took off her sunglasses and folded her arms. "There. Satisfied?"

"OK. I'll go back a bit."

"You don't need to. I remember it as if I'd heard it twenty times already: 'the devil dog belongs to me'."

"Most amusing. Pay attention.

> *The devil dog belongs to me*
> *the white-eyed horse,*
> *the curtained hearse…"*

"Don't like the sound of a 'white-eyed horse', couldn't it be wild-eyed?"

"No. Poetry's littered with wild-eyed horses. 'White-eyed' is eerie."

"It's a bit sick-making."

I threw down the poem in exasperation. "How can a white-eyed horse be sick-making? It's just a horse with white eyes. Alfred is a rabbit with red eyes, you don't feel sick about him, do you?"

"I don't feel too good either. I'd much rather Alfred had the usual brown or navy blue eyes. Eyes being an out of the ordinary colour makes me feel queasy."

We were interrupted by Mr. E's chesty cough from the other side of the trellis.

"Afternoon, Mr. E," I said brightly.

"Good afternoon, Lorna. Pat. Lorna, your mother and father are trying to open your front door."

"What? Did you tell them I was in?"

"No. I've been watching them from the front bay. George will break the door if you don't open up – he's using his hip."

"Couldn't you call the police? Say you've spotted intruders."

Mr. E sighed. "I'm looking for Alfred" – and he merged back into the tree trunks. We heard him rustling his way through the long grass towards the bottom of the garden.

Pat and I looked at each other in consternation. "What shall I do?" I asked her.

"You'll have to let them in. I hope Alfred's all right. Do you think he heard what I said about his red eyes?"

"Pat, does it matter? Is it likely? Aren't there more pressing concerns?"

I weighted my poem down with my Diet Coke tin and went indoors. From the kitchen doorway I could see the shadow of George's head making angry jerking movements on the other side of the dimpled glass.

"George, that must be the wrong key." Della's fretful voice.

"It's the right bloody key. I used it when I stayed before."

"Perhaps they've changed the locks?"

"Why in tarnation would they do that? I will get in."

I could hear him tugging at Julie's pineapple, as it were, then suddenly the letterbox flew open and George's angry eyes blocked out the daylight. Too late, I stepped back into the kitchen.

"Lorna, is that you lurking in the shadows? Open this door at once."

"What do you want?"

"I want to come in. What do you think I want?"

"Tell her I'm dehydrating," Della said.

"Your mother's dehydrating in this sunlight. She will die if she doesn't get a glass of water now."

I drew back the bolt and George came tumbling into the hall. "The door was bolted," I said.

"Why the devil was it bolted?"

"So people can't break in while I'm alone in the house."

George, Della, three large suitcases, Della's vanity case and the snake-charmer's basket carrying her JLY crowded into the hall. I stood my ground; flared my hips, stuck out my elbows, filled up as much space as I could.

"So what's going on?" I said sharply, as if I wasn't their disenfranchised daughter Lorna, but a zealous member of the Duxford Road neighbourhood watch.

"We're staying for a day or two," George said firmly.

"I thought you were taking Mum on a cruise."

"Lorna, please let me sit down, I'm dead on my feet," Della wheedled.

"You've only walked up the path – I can see the car." But I was wavering, because Della was clinging onto George's arm as if she were truly ready to drop. Damn, damn, why could I never tell whether the two of them were acting or for real?

Pat came into the hall and gently took my arm. "Let them in, Lorna. You're being silly."

"Never mind 'let them in, Lorna'," George said briskly, "we're in. Della, go and put your feet up immediately. By God, you're a daughter and a half, I don't think."

They pushed past me, heading for David and Julie's kitchen.

"Does David know?" I shouted after them.

"David wouldn't see his old mum and dad out on the street. Pat, you seem to know the ropes around here, we wouldn't say no to a pot of tea and a slab of something delicious. We've driven all the way from Heathrow today."

Fuming, I went back into the garden, passing the sitting-room door where Della's stockinged feet rested on Julie's white leather pouffe.

"Grub up," Pat said to me, coming out into the garden fifteen minutes later bearing a loaded tray. "I thought we might as well help ourselves to a bite of lunch. You can blame the two of them."

She'd brought salmon and cream cheese sandwiches, plus a bowl of kettle crisps and some black olives, two mugs of tea and two flutes of something orange and sparkling.

"What's that?"

· "Bucks Fizz. George made them."

I sipped it gingerly. "He's used champagne!" I said.

"He has. Said Della needs champagne to invigorate her circulation."

"David and Julie will be furious."

"Why should you care?"

But I did.

After Pat's second visit to the kitchen for more Bucks Fizz, I began to calm down.

"So what's the story?" I asked her, through a mouthful of salmon and cream cheese.

"They were supposed to fly out to Madeira this morning to pick up their cruise ship but at the airport George realised both their passports were out of date."

"Why didn't they go home to Hornchurch?"

Pat chuckled. "Didn't feel like it. George said he wanted to take Della around his old haunts, and with D and J away, seemed sensible to use their flat as a base. You have to remember that this was George's home once."

"It isn't now."

"To George, it still is. Your parents are like a couple of anarchic kids. Amazing you and David turned into such a sensible pair."

"Nothing wrong with sensible. Sensible doesn't go round upsetting other people's apple carts, treading on everyone's toes."

"Now you sound just like your father. Just get on with your own life. It isn't as if they're squatting in *your* flat and eating all *your* food."

"They've got more sense."

My eyes caught a flicker of movement from the house and George materialised, bare legged but for a pair of leather flip-flops, and wearing David's shorty towelling bath robe – or dressing gown to you and me.

"Any more sunbeds, girls?"

"In the shed," I said.

Pat pinched my arm. "Help George."

"Why should I?"

"Because he's your father."

"Technically."

Pat got up. "You are a miserable devil sometimes. Where do you want them, George?"

"On the lawn."

I couldn't stop myself. I was on a mean and nasty roll. "We're not allowed to have garden furniture on the lawn area," I shouted.

"*You're* not allowed," said George. "As a parent I can sit where I like. Della, are you coming out before sundown or what?"

Della popped a towelling turbaned head out into the sunshine, "Are we overlooked?"

"Not much. Park your bum on here and stop dithering."

"George, I don't think I will." However, she emerged fully onto the patio and minced towards George's sunbeds, looking like a model for Saga holidays.

I could almost feel the movement of the E family's eye sockets widening behind their net curtains, Mrs. E pulling deep and disbelievingly on her umpteenth cheroot of the day and saying, "Mutton dressed as lamb. Children, if you ever see your mother prancing about the wilderness wearing a white chiffon sarong scattered with gold appliquéd flowers, lock me in the bedroom and telephone the loony bin."

That evening I rang David and Julie's hotel.

"You've just missed them," the tour guide said, "they're visiting a twilight market for handicrafts and local produce."

"Tell them Lorna called – urgent. Tell David, 'The eagles have landed'," I said.

The next morning I rang again. They were out. The tour guide was in.

"They're visiting a museum commemorating Salvador Dali and his wife Gala."

"Did you tell them Lorna rang and the eagles have landed?'

"David looked bewildered and said he didn't know of any Lorna."

"Impossible. Lorna. L O R N A. Tell them again. Urgent."

That evening I rang again.

"Are they out?" I asked the tour guide.

"They are indeed. Tonight it's a romantic donkey trek through the sunflower fields at dusk."

"Did you tell them again?"

"David said, 'Don't call us, we'll call you.' OK?"

Two days later David rang, sounding as if he was phoning from inside an airing cupboard.

"Lorna?"

"Yes."

"Is it awful?"

"Pretty awful. Tonight they're entertaining a Captain Bill Simpson and his wife Muriel. George has bought a CD of *Sweet Charity*, and they've warbled along with Shirley MacLaine singing 'If They Could See Me Now' four times in the last half-hour."

"Have they bought their own groceries?"

"No. They've bought CDs, a new shoulder bag for Della and some hand-rolled Cuban cigars for George. Grocerywise, they've pillaged your freezer and food cupboards. Dad says to say that your choice of fine wines is superlative and he's been pleasantly surprised."

I heard a muffled groan as if David was pressing his face into a pillow.

"David, are you in an airing cupboard?"

"Actually yes, or as near as they get to airing cupboards in Spain. I'm hiding from Julie. She doesn't know. Good thinking on 'the eagles have landed'. I don't want her upset. She's in a very fragile condition."

I was inclined to snort at Julie's 'fragile condition', say something pithy of the 'like mother-in-law, like daughter-in-law', variety, but instead said, "Della's found that satin robe with the maribou trim you bought Julie for Christmas, she's been swanning around in it like a forties film star."

"Oh God."

"Are you going to phone and tell them to clear off?"

"They wouldn't clear off."

"They might."

"No. George would say something sarcastic, finishing off with 'blood's thicker than water' or 'I can see who's paying the piper' and I'd be forced to back down, as I've always backed down."

Tempted to say, "Are you man or mouse?" Felt it would not help the situation or improve David's feelings of low self-esteem.

"We'll be lucky if we get our flat back at the end of the holiday," he said dolefully.

"Julie will get them moving in no time."

"Am I man or mouse, Lorna?" His voice became muffled again.

"You're not trying to smother yourself, are you?"

"Of course not. I was just resting my face against a duck down pillow. The surface feels nice and cool against my sunburn. How's your woman in beige?"

I hesitated before replying. But why lie? David had his problems, I had mine.

"Haven't seen much of her this week. She says George's deep baritone is disturbing and the house reeks of cigars and cigarettes."

My old man said

"This room could be lovely, George," Della said – she was propped up against pillows in the guest bed in the guest bedroom. The latest copies of *She* magazine and *Woman and Home* lay open on her lap. George came in from his station by the kitchen door where he'd been listening for sounds of Lorna leaving the house.

"She's gone," he said with satisfaction. "She's wearing her Green Bees overall, so we've got the house to ourselves for the day."

"I was just saying, this room could be lovely. We could put in French windows and make it into a dining room leading out onto the garden."

"Don't count your chickens. David may be a slice of cake but Lorna's another matter." He sat down on the edge of the bed. "Will we pull it off, Della?"

"We can do anything we set our minds to, darling" – and she squeezed his hand – "I think softly softly catchee monkey, as you always say, would be the right approach."

George looked ill at ease. "I know I always say 'softly softly, catchee monkey', but *you're* better at the softly softly routine."

"You'll have to make an effort; stop bossing Lorna about, show interest in her, I mean she has a few friends, she can't be all bad. And *I* must appear vulnerable."

"You are vulnerable."

"Not underneath. Not where you and me are concerned. They must see us in a different light; as old folks in need of care and protection."

"Julie'd have us both in a nursing home PDQ." George stood up, stretched and marched out into the passage. "Do you know how many bloody halogen lights David's set into this ceiling? Twenty-two including kitchen and bathroom. It's going to cost a fortune taking them out and replacing the ceiling roses. Mother used to have a pair of fabulous chandeliers... Della? Della?" He hurried back into the bedroom. "Della, answer me when I speak to you – I keep thinking you've died."

"Don't be silly, George. Chandeliers are just right for that hallway, although whatever you say, this house will never have the light the Hornchurch bungalow has."

"But it's my family home. By rights it should have been mine." His lower lip jutted aggressively. Della smiled. She particularly loved George in boyish sulky mood, he seemed so... boyish and sulky.

"Suppose I get ill again?"

"You won't."

"But suppose I do?"

"I can't allow myself to suppose you do. Positive thinking. We have a battle on our hands. Can't afford to shilly-shally over illness. When are you getting up?"

"Now."

"Good girl. I'll start the breakfast."

Della got up slowly. She felt very tired. She studied her face in her silver-backed hand mirror and could have cried. Instead she smiled, opened her eyes wide and batted her eyelashes several times; whites of eyes still clear, eyes a merry brown. On the back of a chair, neatly folded, were the clothes she'd worn the day before. She was tempted to put those same clothes on – George would never notice... but what if he did notice? She crossed to the wardrobe and unhooked the cream Aquascutum skirt, her new peach-coloured blouse with the pleated Ascot tie-neck. From her suitcase she sorted fresh creamy underwear, a pair of sheer stockings. She moved about the bedroom, her confidence increasing; she began to sing quietly at first and then louder so that George could hear her out in the kitchen:

"My old man said follow the van
but don't dilly-dally on the way.
Orf went the van with my home packed in it,
I walked behind with my old cock linnet.

But I dillied and dallied, dallied and dillied,
lorst me way and don't know where to roam..."

The kitchen door flew open and out bounced George, wearing one of Julie's candy-striped aprons and waving a spatula. Together they sang at the top of their voices, *"Now who's going to pull out the old iron bedstead, 'cos we can't find our way home."*

Life becomes idyllic

There was no reason for Dan to fall in love with me, was there? It's not as if I was scintillating company. I didn't go to clubs, was not a night person, delivering the *Echo* was the nearest I got to a walk on the wild side. I was not part of any scene, unless you counted the Duxford Road scene, rubbing shoulders with reverends, eternal trainee deacons and red-eyed rabbits. And where would the Duxford Road scene have been without my very own brother and his wife; the only Tory voters in the entire street – Julie the iron maiden displaying a 'Vote Conservative' poster in the front window and adorning the door with blue rosettes come election time, and nobody daring to tamper with her rosettes. Yes, Julie, incomer of only seven years, was held in higher regard than Lorna Tree, of whom all the neighbours were fond because she'd lived here all her life but who they feared would turn into yet another batty old biddy who sat on random front walls and harangued passers-by.

Once, in the old days, when Gran was alive and before the house was split in two, Gran and David and I looked out of the window on a summer's afternoon and saw a large woman wearing a dusty black hat and coat, sitting in our front garden on a fold-up chair, eating a sandwich. I might explain that Duxford Road front gardens are small, the width of the house by about five foot, so the woman and her chair were quite cramped, fitting in between two dustbins, a rhododendron doing very well for itself, and two blue hydrangeas.

"She's got a bloody cheek," I said. "Our garden's not a picnic area."

"Language, Lorna." Gran looked thoughtful.

I kicked David, whose voice had recently broken. He'd begun insisting he was now the man of the family, should have the final veto on all television programmes, chips whenever he felt like them, and should be waited on hand and foot.

"Stop kicking me," he said.

"Aren't you going to take charge of the situation?"

"What do you suggest?"

"Go out there and tell her to clear off."

He looked uncertainly at Gran. "I don't think it's up to me, it's Gran's house," he said.

"Chicken," I said. "Shall I go, Gran?"

She was looking fondly at David. I think he was the favourite. Perhaps because of that resemblance to Steven, the drowned son.

"You stay where you are, madam, you'll put your oar in once too often," and she left the room.

We heard the front door open and then the murmur of voices. Gran passed in front of the woman, who immediately lumbered to her feet and offered Gran her chair.

Gran said, "Don't mind if I do. My feet are killing me."

Before sitting down, she turned towards us and rapped on the window. "Two cups of tea, one with, one without, and the bourbons." And she started a conversation with the interloper on foot problems.

"It's just the arch in the left foot – it's put my whole leg out of kilter."

"I wish I had a mother like you," the woman replied.

"You get the tea," I said to David.

"No, you get it."

"No, I got it last time."

Still arguing, we went into the kitchen.

"You take it out to them, then."

"No, you take it out."

"You're the same sex."

"You're the man of the family."

In the end, because I was curious and David wasn't, I took out the tea tray – not the Coronation one with the Queen's head that had been put away as an investment for our future, or so Gran said; no, we now used 'The Last Supper', a present from the E family the previous

Easter. Fortunately, Jesus's face was quite small and we didn't mind putting hot crockery on the disciples.

The lady in the hat had moved over to the wall – her solid legs either side of a hydrangea – and she and Gran were both eating what looked like corned beef and mustard sandwiches. Gran had always told us never to accept food from strangers, so I personally thought she was being foolhardy, but she threw me a warning look that said, 'Button it'. I rested the tray between the two dustbin lids.

"You're very lucky to have such a lovely mother," the woman said, "I wish I had a lovely mother like that."

"She's my gran, not my mother," I said.

"Lorna, don't argue."

"I wish I had a lovely mother like that. I wish you were my mother, Irene."

Blimey, first-name terms in under fifteen minutes.

"We get the mothers we are born with," Gran said obscurely.

"Think yourself lucky to have such a lovely mother" – back to me.

"I do," I said.

"I wish I had a lovely mother like that."

"I wish you had as well. That will be all, Lorna."

I made a small sarcastic curtsey but Gran was back talking about illness, she'd moved up to her lumbar region and the woman was getting in her fourpence-worth of 'what a lovely mother you are Irene'.

Me and David kept a watchful eye from the front room. A little later Mr. E joined them on his way home from walking Rusty the devil dog.

"That's a lovely dog you've got there. I wish I had a lovely dog like that."

"Never had a dog with a sweeter temper," Mr. E said.

"Beats Peppys 1–7 hands down," Gran said generously.

"They are so boring," David said. "I'm going to watch television."

I waited for Gran to come in. We watched the woman meander off down the street, her chair under her arm.

From time to time after that we saw her again, but she passed us by as if she didn't know us at all; and one day, a couple of years later, I saw her sitting on her chair eating sandwiches in a front garden in Leswin Road. She looked contented. Seemed quite silent. I wondered if it was her garden.

Remembering this had given me a ten-minute respite from thinking about Dan and the futility of nurturing 'hope'. I asked myself, how could I be sure the feeling I felt was love, when I knew so little about her? I didn't know Dan and yet I thought about her all the time. She just wouldn't let me in to know her. Disappeared for days and days. What was she doing? Putting up shelves, building a roof terrace, looking admiringly into friends' front rooms to size up future pickings?

I found myself scouring the local papers, the *Echo* included, for reports of burglaries. None of the reports sounded amusing, or exciting, or a worthwhile project. Nothing where I could at least grimly say, "Huh, he or she got their come-uppance, no mistake." Impossible to paint Dan as a modern Robin Hood.

The other night over drinks with Pat to christen Sandra's newly turfed lawn and solar-powered lighting, I had almost said, "Pat, she's doing my head in," which was a phrase I never imagined in a million years I'd ever use. I was not a person to say or experience such traumas. Lorna was cheerful, loving, with fleeting bouts of introspection. I needed to regain cheerful Lorna. Reasons to be cheerful:

I have my health.

*

Life was idyllic. Life was going my way at last. Which way would that be? Up, up, up. Did I say life was lousy? Ignore that. Cancel that out. My head was full of fresh air and goodwill towards everyone, even George and Della. Let them reposition the furniture in D & J's flat, let them gouge holes in the lawn dragging the sunbeds back and forth chasing the sun, let George put the stubs of his cigars out in the pond and leave them floating unpleasantly on the surface, and let Della leave a trail of pink make-up tissues – I didn't care. It was none of my business. Lorna had her own fish to fry.

Having got all that *joie de vivre* out of my system, life was not without complications... but no, I'm not going to dwell on complications – complications must be overcome.

It was Tuesday afternoon – another day of fine grey drizzle – and I'd just come in from my newspaper round to find the house for once completely quiet and deserted. For one minute I thought Della and George might have had enough of living in somebody else's home and gone back to Hornchurch. No sign of their car outside, their jackets were missing from the hooks in the hall. I peered into the downstairs kitchen. A leg of lamb was defrosting in a tray on the draining board, peeled potatoes waited in a saucepan of water at the back of the Aga, and broccoli and a carton of organic green beans sat on the chopping board. Credit where credit's due, George was remarkably organised. In no time at all he'd transformed D & J's kitchen, even down to changing the tea towels to his own brand – starched white cotton with a red border.

I investigated no further, not putting it quite past the pair of them to be only pretending to be out, hiding in a wardrobe, to see what Lorna got up to when she thought she was unobserved. Instead I went upstairs to my part of the house, slowly, doggedly – at this point I was still entrenched in my 'where will it all end if not in tears?' mood.

Outside the sky was darkening, the rain settling in in earnest; my landing was gloomy with shadows, the sound of rain drumming against the windows. Usually I appreciate bad weather, once I'm inside, making the flat cosy. That Tuesday I was... disconsolate. Felt thoroughly sorry for myself, emissary of the local paper that nobody wanted to read but was useful for lining cats' litter trays etc. No messages on my answerphone. I walked into my study and over to the window. Nothing doing along Duxford Road – although I don't know why I expected anything to be doing, having only come in myself three minutes earlier when nothing had been doing.

"Tea, chocolate, wine, coffee?"

I almost jumped out of my skin. There in the gloom on the far side of my desk, Dan sat, in Pat's chair.

"Dan," I said, "how did you get in?"

"Ways and means" – which was good enough for me.

"I'm so pleased to see you. I didn't spot your car outside."

"It's parked behind that old red Audi. Sit down."

I sat. She came and knelt in front of me, began to untie the laces of my soaking wet trainers. I let my *Echo* bag drop to the floor and ruffled her hair.

"You should give up the newspapers. It's hard work, no money and you could get mugged," she said.

I sniffed. Felt tearful. Said nothing. She eased off my shoes and socks.

"Lorna, your feet are freezing. I'm putting the kettle on and getting you some warm socks."

"But it's still summer."

"It's cold today."

I listened to her rattling about in my kitchen, then the drawers opening in my bedroom. She brought in a mug of chocolate with its pyramid of cream on top just as I liked it, my socks and dry trainers.

"Drink this." And while I sipped at the chocolate, she chafed my feet till they were warm, before slipping on the socks.

"This is the plan," she said.

"Yes?"

"You will finish your drink, then you will pack what you need in a rucksack and you'll come and stay with me until Friday."

"What about Green Bees?"

"I'll ring them and say you're ill."

"Are you sure?"

"I'm certain."

I was pleased. I was thrilled. Even so, that wretched little demon, jealousy, wanted to ask a question: *"What's happening Friday?"* For once I kept quiet.

It wasn't a long drive – walking distance, not even as far as Springfield Park – but by car, there was the traffic on the High Street, the one-way system to be considered... I gazed out of the window, a casual smile on my face, just in case I saw anybody I knew or, more importantly, they saw me.

"Good God, isn't that Lorna Tree in that Mercedes? I thought she was one of those earnest, penniless poets who never went anywhere."

"Hello Sandra, you know Pat's colourless friend Lorna? Well, a friend of mine saw her this evening cruising along the High Street in a fabulous top-of-the-range car, looking cool as a cucumber. Wonder where she was off to?"

"Pat, you didn't tell me Lorna was going out with some woman who drives a Bentley – she was spotted heading towards Heathrow..."

We turned into Evering Road and after a couple of hundred yards took a sudden left into a quiet cul-de-sac which I'd never noticed before on my various and extensive wanderings. There were five pairs of towering Victorian houses, each with their own driveway, and Dan's car was making for the one facing us at the end of the small road. The Mercedes purred in between open wrought-iron gates, the tyres crunched over gravel. It was almost dark, still raining. I had an impression of wet laurel branches brushing against the car windows like grasping hands and then the shadow of the house seemed to block out the remaining light. For a moment I wished I'd left George and Della something more enlightening in the way of notes than "Gone out. Back in two days."

"Here we are," Dan said with satisfaction. She leapt out of the car and hurried round to open the passenger door for me – a first in Lorna Tree's lifetime. "Want me to carry you over the threshold?" she said with a grin.

"I'm OK," I said rather primly, as if women were always opportuning me with offers to carry me over thresholds. I grabbed my rucksack and made a mental note to buy or borrow a smart travel bag if this kind of outing became routine.

A light shone through the vertical slats of stained glass on each side of the double-width front door, at the top of a flight of stone steps. This was not what I'd expected. I'd expected loft development, Canary Wharf perhaps. This was more like Dracula's castle – which was an ignorant uncharitable thought, to be discarded immediately. There was no denying, regardless of the light shining out to welcome us, that my first impression of the house was of sadness and gloom.

Added to that I was thinking, more prosaically, "Please God, make Theresa be out."

Dan's house was about twice the size of our Duxford Road house, although initially it seemed much bigger. Inside, it was grand in the aforementioned Dracula's castle style, with wall hangings, large pieces of ornate dark furniture and a fine layer of dust. I could tell immediately that this wasn't the home of occupants who liked daylight. Outside it might have only been six o'clock on a wet summer's day, but indoors I soon found it stayed at anything between ten in the evening and three a.m. Morning and midday didn't exist. The curtains were of heavy brocade and never fully open, the lights were table lamps or were concealed behind intricate plaster cornices, shedding a sinister yellow glow. Only the bathrooms and kitchen were modern and free of dust. The kitchen was free of most things expected in a kitchen, like food.

"Make yourself at home, put the kettle on, you'll find everything you need – I just want to put the car in the garage."

I peered in the fridge; there were three pints of semi-skimmed milk and a boxed Sainsbury's cheeseboard selection. I looked in the cupboard above the Alessi kettle and there were three marble containers: tea, instant coffee and a new packet of... hot chocolate.

Four mugs, so clean, they looked as if they'd never been used. No teapot. I made the tea and took the used tea bags over to the gleaming chrome pedal bin. It was pristine, a fresh bin liner, it seemed almost a crime to drop the tea bags into it.

"It won't bite," Dan said, coming up behind me and putting her arms around my waist.

"I could cook us a meal if you show me where everything is," I said.

"Everything isn't. I don't want you to cook – you cook for me when I'm at your place. We'll go out about nine. There's some biscuits somewhere for now."

I can't say Dan *rummaged* through her cupboards on the lookout for biscuits, because most of the cupboards were empty. She opened and shut several cupboard doors and eventually there they were, half a dozen packets of chocolate biscuits.

Now, I've not been an aspiring detective for much of my life for nothing. My mind was boggling, as detectives' minds do boggle, at the strangeness of it all. Why was there no food? Why didn't Dan like daylight? Why couldn't we just order a takeaway and cuddle up together and watch television like other couples did?

"You've put the car away," I said.

"We're getting a cab."

"Oh."

She picked up the mugs of tea and tucked a packet of biscuits under her arm and I followed her down a long passage into a room lined with books. I immediately thought of my little bookcase and how I'd somehow imagined her not to be the type who read books.

"Have you read all these?" I said, smiling.

"Most of them. Don't look at the books, sit down and talk to me."

I sat down next to her on a heavily cushioned settee. She took hold of my hand. "Leave the tea for the moment, I want to talk to you. About what I said earlier – I want you to give up these insane jobs of yours."

"But I like them," I said. This wasn't exactly true, but they did reflect an area of my personality of which I approved.

"How much do you make?"

"Not a lot... but enough" – which wasn't exactly true either.

"Now, don't get angry, but what if I gave you, say, call it 'housekeeping', each week. You could keep things stocked up here and there would be plenty left over to live on."

I felt hot and a little sick. I looked into her face and saw kindness and... concern?

I said, "Dan, there are probably things I can't change about you, and you must accept it's the same with me. I know I don't earn much, they aren't exactly status jobs, but I like the variety, being out on the streets or in the packing fertiliser environment. Particularly at Green Bees, there are a lot of people like me."

"Misfits?" she said, but not nastily.

"If you like." Somewhere in my head I could hear George's booming baritone, saying, *"Pot calling the kettle black here, Lorna. Asking you to give up honest toil and take tainted money – be a glorified housekeeper."*

"If I promise you the money's legal?" she said.

"No. I wouldn't take money from you. I'd organise your kitchen, help you in any way possible here, but because I care about you. Money doesn't come into it. I'm good at organising, not bad at cleaning and tidying. Excellent with a Hoover. I can do all that plus Green Bees and the *Echo*."

In the end we didn't go out for a meal, we went to bed with a bottle of claret, the Sainsbury's cheeseboard selection and a fresh packet of chocolate biscuits – discussion deferred to another day.

"Is there a garden?" I asked the next morning (which was almost lunch time).

"We don't talk about the garden," Dan said.

I opened one of her bedroom curtains.

"The light. I can't stand the light," she shouted, and hid under the duvet.

A storm was still raging from the night before; I saw shrubs and small trees, overgrown and entangled in one another, buffeted by the wind. It was a sizable garden, stretching away towards a line of conifers. Later, when the rain finally stopped, I went out to investigate. Paving stones ran all the way along the back of the house, with no pots or ornamental urns, nothing except leaves and a few branches broken off in the storm.

"Come back in, Lorna," Dan called from the open doorway. "I could lose you forever in that wilderness."

But it wasn't a wilderness. It was nothing like Mr. E's garden. Once upon a time, someone had planted the garden out carefully. It made me think of Gran taking David and me to Kew Gardens every spring to see the rhododendrons flowering. She'd known all the bushes, taken us round pointing to this and that, telling us names that meant nothing to us: Japanese dogwood, viburnum, clerodendrum, Obviously Dan and Theresa didn't like gardening.

Theresa. Happy as I was to be with Dan, Theresa's presence haunted me like Bluebeard's locked room. Where did Dan end and Theresa begin? Who had chosen the furniture? Had they chosen it together? Someone must have said, "We'll have this green and white patterned wallpaper of shepherds opening five-bar gates for shepherdesses in the main sitting room." It looked brand new although I appreciated it was supposed to look old.

"Who chose the wallpaper?" I asked innocently, on coming in from the garden.

"Terry. Great isn't it? It's a toile de Jouy paper."

"Really?" I said. I fear my tone was sour. "It's very busy."

"Terry felt the room could take it."

"So, why didn't Terry stock the kitchen cupboards?" I said sharply.

"Terry doesn't care about food. Look, I've a few calls to make. Back in a minute."

So, Terry didn't care about food, Terry cared about wallpaper. How had I ever thought for one minute that Terry was attractive? I hated her. I sat down. I was hungry but determined not to eat another chocolate biscuit for at least a month, and then Dan came back and said, "Are you ready? We're going to have lunch at a restaurant overlooking the Thames."

I woke up in the night. Had no idea what time it was. Dan's side of the bed was empty and from downstairs I heard the muted sound of voices. I went out into the passage; it was just Dan's voice I'd heard. I listened intently.

"Terry, I'm sorry. I can't collect you at this time of night. Like I said, I'll see you on Saturday."

I padded back to bed and feigned sleep when Dan came in.

"Lorna," she whispered, "are you awake?"

Unintelligible mumble from me. Dan burrowed down inside the bed and tickled my toes. We both started laughing.

I said, "I woke and you were gone so I got up and heard you talking on the telephone, so I came back to bed."

"Why did you pretend to be asleep?"

"So you wouldn't think I was eavesdropping."

She was quiet for a moment, then she put her arms around me. Sleepily I said, "Who laid out your garden? It must have been lovely once."

I felt her body stiffen. "It *was* lovely. My mother did the garden. It was her obsession."

I sat up. "So this is your family home, like mine is?"

"Not quite like yours. Yours seems as if it was a proper home. You all seem cheerful, as if, although you argue, you still get on."

"Not always. We've had our ups and downs."

"Better sleep now," Dan said.

"But I'm wide awake."

"Lie down and try to sleep."

I lay down and closed my eyes, my head buzzing. I said, "If you've lived here all your life, why have I never seen you round and about?"

"I didn't say I've lived here all my life. My mother lived here. I lived here as a child but I've lived in other places. Last stop Clapham, then back here."

"And Terry comes too?"

"Terry comes too."

Eventually I slept but I had bad dreams. I think I cried out once. I think I heard Dan say, "It's OK, Lorna, I'm here."

The next day, Friday, Dan drove me home. As we waited for the lights to change at the beginning of the one-way system on Evering Road, Jenny Salter stepped out into the traffic. I hadn't thought of her in weeks and yet, seeing her again, all the animosity I'd felt at our last session disappeared.

I opened the window and shouted, "Jenny, it's me, Lorna."

She hesitated and as she did, the cars began to move and she was forced back on the pavement. Dan's car passed her, me waving and smiling maniacally. She seemed to raise her hand to shield her face but not before I'd seen how sad and drawn she looked. I turned in my seat, fighting the seat belt. She was walking away from the crossing.

"That was Jenny Salter, my counsellor," I said.

Dan smiled briefly, saying nothing.

"She looked unhappy, I wonder what's wrong?"

"*She's* the counsellor." Dan turned into my road.

As I got out of the car she said, "Present for you, Lorna," and took a small box from under the dashboard. "Don't worry, it's not stolen. It belonged to my mother."

It was a gold ring with a small sapphire in an old-fashioned marcasite setting. I tried it on but it was too small for any of my fingers. Gently she unclasped the chain I always wore, removed Gran's St. Christopher and slipped the ring onto the chain instead.

"It's lovely. Are you sure?"

She frowned. "I wouldn't give it to you if I wasn't sure."

It was only after the car had gone and I was searching for my key at the gate that I realised the St. Christopher was still in her car.

"It doesn't matter," I told myself, "she'll give it back to me when I see her."

But supposing she didn't? Gran had given it to me just before she died... And then, behind me, a car pulled up at the kerb and Dan shouted, "Lorna, your St. Christopher. You left it on the dashboard."

Later, as I sat at the back window watching (without really seeing) George getting the barbecue ready, I suddenly remembered Jenny and how she'd looked. Death in the family? Husband trouble? No point in worrying about her. She didn't want to see me, why should I care about her? I returned Gran's St. Christopher to its small velvet box. Felt a twinge of guilt but pushed it away. Complacently I fingered the sapphire ring at my neck. Things were hunky-dory, and hunky-dory made me, for a time, quite smug.

Pat is a pathetic excuse

Five more days to go before David and Julie got home, and still no sign of Hornchurch-bound movement from the squatters downstairs; however there was a marked change in the squatters' manner towards me. On Thursday, when I came in tired and a little subdued from Green Bees, George was waiting for me.

I'd walked down the road with Mr. E and his trolley. He was also subdued, but then, that's a natural state for Mr. E. He and I had exchanged very few words:

"Hello there, Lorna."

"Hello there, Mr. E."

"All well?"

"Not bad. And Alfred?"

"He's a rascal."

"As always. Well, good night."

"Good night. I see George is at the window."

George obviously didn't want to be spotted at the window – was no more than a retreating shadow, who then whisked the front door open before I could find my key.

"Ah, Lorna, we wondered if you'd like to join us for a gin and tonic?" He ignored Mr. E, who was loitering near his giant hebe, but gave me a wide ingratiating smile.

"Fair enough."

I could see this wasn't as enthusiastic as George had hoped, because his forehead puckered into the frown usually worn when contemplating me; and then, as if somebody had pinched him hard in his nether regions, his frown disappeared and the smile returned.

"Hello darling." Della appeared from the section of the hall that George's nether regions occupied. In the amber light of early evening,

Mum looked tanned and fit and years younger than her age. She wore a short white tennis dress, white trainers and ankle socks, plus a green sun visor.

"We've been watching the early evening news," she said as if that explained her sporty outfit. "Drinks on the patio, George?"

"Julie calls it a terrace," I said, not for the first time.

"Sheer affectation. However, it is a superb area for social intercourse. We're thinking of buying a gas-powered barbecue."

I followed Della outside while George shot off into the kitchen. More surprises. On Julie's terrace were two unfamiliar sun loungers.

"You do intend to go home at the weekend? David and Julie will definitely be here by Monday midday."

Bright laughter from Della. "I hope we're not folk who overstay our welcome," was all she replied.

I chose an uncomfortable ornate metalwork chair, feeling I would need my wits about me. We sat in silence, Della looking pensive. She was never completely happy in a one-woman-to-one-woman situation, particularly if that woman happened to be her daughter.

Finally I said, "Is there a particular reason for you to be wearing a tennis dress?"

"We went for a game in Clissold Park. George said he once beat Reverend Joseph at tennis in Clissold Park, before the courts were laid."

"I'm not surprised; Rev. Joseph's only about half his height. I'm astonished he even had a tennis racket."

"He didn't. Nor did your father. They used table-tennis bats."

"You don't look very... disarrayed."

"Some petty-fogging official said we should have booked! To be honest, we lost heart when we saw the sort of person those places attract. I'd thought it would be like the tennis club in Hornchurch, a standard of dress, at least clean..."

I interrupted her. "But are you well enough to play tennis anyway?"

"A gentle game."

"How are my two best girls getting on?" George said heartily.

Della smiled gaily. "Mother and daughter doing just fine."

We drank our drinks and George passed around olives and crisps, bemoaning the fact that he couldn't find Smith's crisps for love nor money these days, everywhere was common or garden Walker's or Phileas Fogg.

The amber light turned to a deep blue, several tiny bats criss-crossed the garden and made Della shriek. George lit a pleasant-smelling mosquito candle and replenished our glasses. We could hear the comforting sounds of the younger E family members arguing over whose turn it was to use the bathroom, Mrs. E clattering away in the kitchen, Mr. E moving invisibly through his shrubbery with the hose, every now and then a gentle, "Get from under my feet, Alfred." It was a benign evening. I looked at George and for once his expression had genuinely lost its angry desperation; he kept looking up at the sky and smiling to himself.

I said, "You like it here, don't you, Dad?"

"Yes, I do."

"Better than Hornchurch."

"Your psychotherapist wallahs would call it imprinting," he said – which made me look at him in a very different light. Della stared admiringly as if he'd just discovered a miracle age-defying moisturising cream.

"Lorna," she said – and I knew immediately that they had been building up to whatever was coming next, probably for some time. "We wondered if we could take a peek around your flat. Your father would love to see his old boyhood bedroom. At home he's still got the same bomber squadron he made from construction kits up in that very room. Haven't you, darling?"

"Call me sentimental," George said.

I smelt a rat. In twenty years, George had never shown any inclination to visit his old boyhood bedroom.

"It's all a bit of a mess up there at the moment. Perhaps the next time you visit."

"A bit of mess won't harm us, no time like the present," George said jovially. "Eh, Della?"

Several mad but useless thoughts occurred to me: were they going to share out the squatting between them – Della downstairs while George overran the two top floors? Before I knew it their suitcases would have penetrated the loft space...

Or was George only drunk and sentimental, bored or curious about the calibre of his daughter's decor...

Or did he really want to see his boyhood bedroom...

Or were they going to...

And anyway, should I ring Dan and tell her where I was, and if I didn't ring back by ten p.m. she must come immediately? But where was Dan? I'd already rung three times in the last twenty-four hours and encountered Theresa in a nasty mood. "She's out," she said, as if through a wad of gum – or was it a wad of surgical dressing? Perhaps she'd had a wisdom tooth removed. "She's out where?" hadn't seemed an option. Theresa would be circulating rumours that "Needy Lorna won't let Dan out of her sight without having a hissy fit."

"Well?" prompted George.

I drank down the last of my third gin and tonic. "It's a bit of a mess up there," I said.

"We dealt with that ten minutes ago. We expect nothing less."

"I've left a sealed envelope with my solicitor and if I don't ring a certain number within the next hour that envelope will be opened and your foul deeds made public."

"Lorna, you're mumbling."

It was Della who clinched it for them. Out of the corner of my eye, I saw her start to lever herself off the sunbed. This wasn't Della, my mother, the woman who would walk into the technicolour sunset hand in hand with George. George was watching me. I was watching him, but registering Della's tired face without her sun visor and her painful awkward movements. She would do anything for George. On her deathbed she'd be putting on her Estée Lauder slap and insisting she'd be right as rain in no time.

"Come on, Della," I said, taking her by the hand and helping her to her feet.

"Yes, come on, chuckles, let's black our noses, as they say oop north." George leapt boisterously to his feet and suddenly I realised it was the house – his boyhood home – that they were after, and strangely enough I didn't mind.

"Actually, you two go on up. I'll help myself to another drink and commune with nature." I handed them my keys.

They looked quite troubled. "Are you sure? We don't intend to pry?"

"A quick dekko and we're out."

"Take your time," I said, "no hurry." Everything was starting to make sense.

"Not long now?" Pat observed from the canvas depth of George's newly purchased steel-framed hammock.

I was seeing a lot more of Pat since Sandra had begun excavations under the kitchen for a wine cellar. Sandra had so much in common with Mr. E; they should be brought together – he had a wealth of experience in subsiding floors and which supporting joist to remove to cause the most damage.

"What can I do?" I asked Pat. "We're getting on so well. I almost prefer them to David and Julie. They don't argue, George can do no wrong as far as Della's concerned, and he's very generous with his gin and tonics."

"That's because they don't belong to him. To change the subject ever so slightly, I noticed Mr. E's palm tree is becoming quite a hazard to negotiate. One of the branches got caught in my handle bars. It was like being attacked by a triffid. I've noticed Mrs. E parks her Audi on the other side of the road these days."

"It's not a palm tree, it's an out of control variegated hebe."

"From a distance it does quite resemble a palm tree, bent forward by a strong wind. Reminds me of that film when a typhoon strikes the tropical island and the man in a jeep whose hat never blows off has to save the lone woman daft enough to be out searching for a lost child and its puppy."

"I've never seen that particular film."

"You must have. There's been at least seven versions. What does Dan say?"

"About what?"

"About your parents squatting in the downstairs flat, of course."

"She offered to have a word with them."

"What did you say?"

"I said I'd think about it."

Not strictly true. In our last telephone conversation, some seventy-three and a half hours earlier, I'd said, "Don't worry, I'll handle them." Something inside me couldn't bear Dan to fail – as I believed she almost certainly would, against such a long-standing team of con artists. Conversely, I couldn't bear the spectacle of Della and George being vanquished and retiring to Hornchurch with their tails between their legs. (Note: am increasingly using phrases like 'tail between legs'. It's George's influence and a nasty one. Must not allow this to become a habit. Must fight habit tooth and nail, if necessary use a sledgehammer to crack a nut and remove the mote from my own eye.) Besides, I was intrigued. Did they want to buy the house or didn't they? What would they offer? Fresh dreams of Dan and me and a house on the coast...

"So when are we going to be allowed to meet Dan again?" A curl of smoke from Pat's roll-up wafted skywards.

"Eventually. She's not much of a social animal."

"Theresa says different."

I watched Pat's smoke. No smoke without fire. Bugger. I itched to know what Theresa had said. Knew Pat knew I itched to know. Think of something else, Lorna.

"You wouldn't like to hear the first draft of my latest poem? It's still quite short?"

"No, thank you. I expect you're wondering what Theresa said?"

"You obviously want to tell me, so go ahead. I'm really not very interested in Theresa's opinions."

"I absolutely agree. She's horrible, mad, weird, nasty, but you must admit she's quite interesting."

"I don't."

"Anyway –" Pat's curly blonde head popped up over the side of the hammock; she had a merry little face, particularly vivacious when chewing on a tasty morsel of gossip. "Theresa says, under the right circumstances, Dan can be a lot of fun."

"Is that it? Sounds a bit tame for Theresa."

"Words to that effect."

"And I suppose you all think, 'What's a woman who's a lot of fun doing with our Lorna, who isn't?'"

"Don't sell yourself short."

"Just because I like to have quality time with those I care about and don't want to be affable to people I don't know, who don't want to know me unless miraculously I turn into 'a lot of fun'."

"You are taking things seriously."

"That's what women who aren't a lot of fun tend to do."

"I was only saying…"

"Well, don't. There must be some reason why Dan prefers my company to the blessed Theresa – and I could ask why your Sandra, excellent cook and committed DIY-er, not to mention kind person, might want to go out with a lazy and obtuse pain in the neck like you."

Pat started laughing. The hammock shook. "Because I'm good in bed, of course."

"How do you know I'm not bloody brilliant in bed?"

"I'm sure you are, but more in the comfy cosy line."

"That is so insulting. Dan wouldn't settle for comfy cosy."

"She might if she had a comfy cosy fixation."

"So what exactly has Theresa said?"

"Nothing. I wouldn't believe her anyway. I've told you, she's mad. I'm sure half of what she comes out with is just a pack of lies. Shouldn't have said anything."

"What did she say? I want to know."

"It's not pleasant."

"Tell me."

"She said you were anally retentive."

"What?" I shot out of my deckchair, reached Pat in a split second and tipped her out of the hammock onto the grass.

"Steady on!" Pat was half laughing but rubbing one reddening knee. "*She* said it, not me."

"And what else?" I stood over her, ready to shake out every drop of Theresa's bile.

"She says Dan's stringing you along because she finds your oddball innocence refreshing in small doses."

"What a vile thing to say."

"Exactly what I said. Take no notice. I tell you, she's as mad as a hatter. You wouldn't take it seriously if I told you some famous mad person like… name a famous mad person?"

"No." I walked away from her. "Theresa isn't a famous mad person – she's a sane and calculating woman and you're a pathetic excuse for a best friend."

I slumped down into the deckchair again. Pat crawled across the grass towards me; when she reached my chair she undid my laces and tied each trainer to the other as we used to do at school.

"Say I'm not a pathetic excuse! Lorna, don't cry. I didn't mean to upset you. I knew I should have kept my mouth shut."

"Lorna, your telephone's ringing." George appeared in the kitchen doorway wearing an ample pair of bathing trunks and carrying a brightly coloured parasol.

Even Pat's mouth fell open. Under George's ministrations, the garden was beginning to resemble a Riviera-style mini-playground for the rich. If David and Julie didn't come back soon, he'd have a swimming pool or jacuzzi installed. As I feverishly untied my laces and made for the house, I was dogged by unwelcome images of George and Della frolicking half naked with their friends, Captain Bill Simpson and his wife Muriel, where once Julie's koi carp had innocently swum.

Oh, make it Dan on the telephone, I prayed. Make it all right with us. Make Theresa fall down a black hole and let my hastening figure, laces flapping, not look too desperately over-eager to Pat's cynical, gossip-gathering eyes.

"Lorna, is that you?"

My heart sank. Edna, sounding upset.

"Yes, Edna. What's the matter?"

"Could you come down?"

"Are you and Lily OK?"

"Not really. It's Lily. I can't talk on the phone. Could you come now?"

"Edna, I can't. I'm at Green Bees for the next three mornings. What about Sunday?"

"I'd appreciate it."

It was all nonsense. Take no notice. Theresa was jealous. I must believe that. I looked down into the garden. Della was out there now with George. She wore a towelling scarlet kaftan splattered with white orchids – a definite departure, colourwise, for her. Pat was telling them some story and making them laugh, and next door in Mr. E's garden I could see he had paused to listen and was smiling also. No sign of Alfred, who was probably snoozing in the cool shadows of Morris Minor.

I wasn't worried about Edna and Lily – probably some minor catastrophe they needed to share with one other – it was Pat I was thinking about, and how she'd really hurt me this time, listening to

Theresa and then hardly able to wait to spill out the nastiness. Dan wasn't stringing me along, whatever Theresa said. I was sure that, perhaps against her will and better judgement, she cared what happened to Lorna Tree. I wouldn't use the word 'love'. Stuffy I may be, but I don't use that word easily and I can't easily put it into Dan's mouth. These thoughts of Dan steadied me. I stroked the sapphire ring on its chain around my neck.

Pat was standing on her head in the middle of the tiny lawn and George was roaring with laughter. I heard Mrs. E fondly say, "That daft girl's going to make herself sick in this heat."

I took one of the brocade cushions from my bed and threw it out of the window. I'm a good shot, even with a cushion. It went flying down, hitting Pat in her upturned midriff. She keeled over, gurgling with laughter.

Della picked up the cushion and said, "My children have very good taste when it comes to home furnishings."

"Tree," I said, "L. Tree," although there was no need. He knew L. Tree because he and L. Tree had often locked horns on points of principle during the two years I'd been collecting my benefit at this same mean cashier's grille. I was tempted to say, "Good weekend?" just to annoy him. I bore a grudge and I rarely bear a grudge which means that when I do, look out!

Several months earlier, he'd refused to tell me his Christian name on the initial grounds that familiarity bred disrespect.

"But you know my Christian name," I'd pointed out, "You know all our Christian names," waving at the queue behind me. They shuffled irritably. All they wanted was to get their giros and hop it – no inclination to show solidarity with their fellow signees.

"We can't be too careful when handing out government money," he'd said pompously.

"It's not government money, it belonged to the taxpayer."

"You're not a taxpayer."

"That's not the point – but if you want to argue on that level, there are four taxpayers in my family, which must more than cover my paltry fifty-two pounds. I don't even get milk tokens, and I'm nearing the brittle bones stage of my life."

"Milk tokens are for families."

"Sign and take the fucking money," a leather-clad man immediately behind me had hissed. A hard object had been pressed against my spine – could have been a knife, a gun, was probably a mobile phone, but no point in taking risks, so reluctantly I had given way over the Christian names...

"L. Tree," I said again, back in the present. The cashier was looking at me as if I were a complete stranger who might suddenly develop anti-social habits. His right hand rested innocently enough on the old wooden ruler used to keep his place in the cardboard box of giros, but his other hand was out of sight under the counter, possibly poised over the panic button should L. Tree suddenly turn rabid.

"I've nothing here for Tree," he said truculently.

"You must have. Lorna Tree of Duxford Road."

"Nothing here for Lorna Tree of Duxford Road."

"Lorna Tree of any other road?"

"No."

"Could you telephone the office and check?"

On this occasion I had a tall man in leopardskin trousers and several mobile phones at my back. Men have no patience. Can't allow even thirty seconds to pass without something having to happen in their lives.

"Look, I've got business to attend to – can't hang about here all day," he said to the back of my head. I had at least two smart answers ready but as he was a foot taller, I decided they'd be better delivered from a distance.

I turned my attention to the cashier who was still watching me impassively. "I'm sure there's been some mistake," I said, "please could you phone the office?"

The queue groaned, maybe growled, with impatience. They all had business meetings to get to, coffee or lunch dates to keep in Church Street, a holiday to book, a novel to write – we jobless knew how to fill our time. Reluctantly the cashier slid off his chair and went behind a screened partition and, as far as I knew, pretended to phone the office. He sidled back five minutes later, chewing and carrying a sheet of paper.

"You've been deregistered."

Shock. Horror. A ripple of gasps ran through the queue. These were the words we all feared.

"I can't have been."

He studied his sheet of paper. "You've failed to turn up to two appointments at the Job Club, failed to notify anyone if this was due to extenuating circumstances, failed to respond to two letters. Yes, you've definitely been deregistered. To reregister, you'll have to fill in a new set of forms, attend an interview, provide written proof of attempts to find work, details of last place of employment, a year's bank statements…"

"What do I do now? I haven't any money."

"As I said, you'll have to reregister."

"And as I said, I haven't any money."

"Well, you'll have to reregister."

"And in the meantime, how do I eat?" I forced my eyes to well with tears, sucked in my cheeks and shoulders.

He almost smiled. A nasty, self-satisfied, almost smile. He put his face just close enough to the grille so that I could hear his quiet words, not close enough for me to, say, poke a pen through the wire and up his nostril.

"You'll have to get one of those four taxpayers in your family to sub you. I don't suppose they'll let you starve."

George allows himself to dream

"We'll have to go home soon, George." Della watched George as she applied her rehydrating moisturiser. "I swear by Estée Lauder," she said, smoothing cream into her neck, "I think my jaw line's finally going – do you think we could run to a mini-tuck?"

Normally George could be depended on to reply reassuringly, "When your jaw line drops as far as Muriel Simpson's has dropped, i.e. she resembles a bloody bloodhound, then we'll start talking tucks," but today he remained silent and morose.

"George," Della repeated.

"I know we've got to go home, damn it, doesn't mean we have to rush off like a couple of frightened rabbits. We're not doing any damage, on the contrary I think they'll be rather impressed at my improvements in the shed and kitchen. Then we'll bring out the big guns."

"What if they don't want to sell to us?"

"They will. We're in a position to be a cash buyer. They could be settled in the house of their choice before the baby's born."

"What about Lorna?"

"If she won't sell, we don't buy, but we don't let her know that. She'll go, in the end she'll go. High time she went out into the real world. We'll be doing her a favour."

"Will we, George?"

"You tell me."

Della wiped her fingers on a pink tissue. "I know nothing about her. She's a mystery. I did try to give her some pointers on clothes and make-up the other day and she became very unpleasant."

"Perhaps we're out of touch?"

Della took up her comb and began to tease her hair into the required shape: widow's peak over her left eye, two glossy wings each side of her impressive cheekbones. "Must get my roots coloured. George, we are not out of touch. Our children are, always have been. They've been cosseted all their lives. London's wasted on them. I mean, Lorna hardly ever steps out of N16. Now please, George, I can't listen to any more on house buying, I need to concentrate." She flipped up the lid of her vanity case and began to match up eye shadow, eye pencil and lipsticks for the day.

"Glad we're not going out tonight – dreadful weather," George called from the next room. A moment later, his head appeared around the bedroom door. "Della, I keep telling you, answer me when I say something."

"George, I'm concentrating."

"What's to concentrate on? You know your way around your make-up blindfold."

"George, decaf, PDQ," she snapped, but lovingly.

George filled the kettle and plugged it in, then took up his favourite position by the kitchen window. The wind was sending Della's underwear, pegged to Julie's state-of-the-art washing line, round and round like a lacy carousel. In the background, on the other side of the trellis, Edmund was making his slow way down his own garden. What did Ed make of Della's tiny smalls? George had seen Glenda's underwear and been unimpressed. Told Della, "You ought to go out and have a look – they're twice, maybe three times the size of yours."

"Some men like a fuller figure," Della had said flirtatiously.

"Not me. She'd frighten the living daylights out of me. I bet she frightens Ed."

George left the kettle and went out into the wind. "Edmund."

He turned. "George."

"We're off at the weekend. Back to sunny Hornchurch... for the time being."

"I see," Edmund said.

George waited but Edmund said nothing further. George had never quite decided whether Edmund was thick or deep – certainly thick in matters of the world such as house buying and selling, stocks and shares, cars, holidays abroad – the list was endless of the subjects Edmund knew nothing about. Keep ahead or get left behind, George thought, pushing his chin out pugnaciously. God, Edmund was hard work. George stepped over the pond, which brought him nearer to the trellis fence. Alfred the Great was sitting on Edmund's foot munching on a stick of celery.

"Any plans for Alfred?" he asked.

"Plans?" Edmund looked bewildered.

"In the pot? Jugged rabbit? Winter mitts for the wife?"

"Would you eat a friend?"

"Well no, but I'm not talking about homo sapiens, this is a rabbit. Not even a cat or dog, wouldn't eat a horse for that matter. Rabbits are semi-wild, eat everything they can lay their paws on and cover the ground with smelly pellets. And after all, you don't want to spend the rest of your life tied to that trolley with the need to beg, borrow or steal food to fill the little blighters' bellies. Have you ever thought that you're sitting on a goldmine? It's a desirable piece of real estate you've got. Once the kids are off your hands, you could clear the garden, gut the house and you've got a des-res worth nigh on half a million smackeroos."

"I don't follow you, George."

"I'm not going to repeat my bloody self. In a nutshell, no room for sentiment. Time to look after numero uno, money in bricks and mortar, cash in bank, bird in bush."

"How's Della?"

George gave Edmund his steeliest of stares. Did the bugger undermine him every time intentionally? Some subterfuge the lower orders had picked up to make gutsy characters with get-up-and-go feel like big-mouthed braggarts? Was Edmund actually saying, in his "How's Della?", "All that you've said, George my old pal, is surely as nothing set against your wife's health"?

"She's much better. Not quite out of the woods yet. She's a brave woman, is my Della. That's her underwear on the line."

Edmund smiled and said gently, "I know, George. It's admirable."

George discovered he needed to blow his nose loudly. "Only joking about Alfred and the pot. Of course you love him. He's a fine animal. Damn sight quieter than Mother's Pomeranians."

They stood in amiable communion for some minutes: Edmund looking down into the swaying green gloom of his fruit trees, George surveying his own side of the fence, how it would be if only... Extend the patio, get rid of pond and take lawn right down to the Peppy graves. A wide herbaceous border, hollyhocks, delphiniums, foxgloves, as it had been in his childhood. They'd buy a dog. Della could have the cat she'd always hankered after. They'd stay put.

The wind blew harder, the sun disappeared behind dark clouds and the trellis creaked.

"I reckon we're in for a storm," George said, but Edmund had disappeared, merged into his own greenery. Alfred stared up at George. George detected amusement in his stare.

"Vamoose!" he hissed, and Alfred turned tail and scampered in the direction of Morris Minor.

Pom. Pom-pom, pom-pom, pom-pom

Time was getting tight – or, in a phrase popular with David and Julie, apparently much used in their alien world of commerce, George and Della were pushing the envelope, while I was doing nothing to stop them. By Monday evening, whatever happened, I would once again be a pariah where my brother and his wife were concerned, if I hadn't cleared the house of parents and removed all evidence of their occupation.

It couldn't be done. Polishing door furniture and a once over with the Hoover wouldn't shift them – there was too much to shift – and I didn't much care. I had my own problems to mull over. Maybe Reverend Joseph would swear on a bible that Lorna Tree had always been selfish and self-absorbed, but Lorna Tree didn't think so. She/I thought we'd spent far too many years being selfless. Very clearly I saw my alter ego: tallish woman with straight, no-nonsense hair, a fine wide forehead denoting courage and wisdom, fearless grey eyes – *Say what you like about Tree but she's as honest as the day is long, absolutely no flies on Tree* – which was all well and good, but high time this Tree character began working on her own behalf, sorted herself out a partner with whom to go donkey-trekking in Spain, a partner with whom to discuss sunbed upholstery. Tree deserved 'Should we go for tartan rather than floral or is floral so out, it's due back in at any moment?' type conversations.

A windy Saturday evening blew Captain Bill Simpson and his wife up Duxford Road. I tut-tutted from my station at the front window. They were dressed for an afternoon of shopping in, possibly, Knightsbridge, wearing matching Burberry raincoats, Bill sporting a maroon paisley silk scarf and Muriel something pink and gauzy at her neck. Bill carried a rolled umbrella and a small leather attaché case, Muriel a stylish envelope bag tucked under her arm; both were an absolute gift to any passing muggers – I feared for their safety once night fell.

"Good evening," Bill said to Mrs. E, who was lounging in her dustbin area. Had he worn a hat, he'd no doubt have raised it in salute. Muriel looked awkward, registering the great divide between her impeccable raincoat and patent shoes and Mrs. E's tight-fitting satin dress worn with muddy trainers and sports socks. I darted quickly from the window to my darkened landing, just in time to see George stride across the hall below and fling open the front door to his visitors.

"Where's the car?" He must have been watching them from the window.

"Buggered. New clutch and two new tyres needed or no MOT. We used public transport. Suprisingly speedy."

"Apart from close encounters of the whiffy kind," Muriel said, slipping off her coat. "Surely these days everyone has access to soap and water?"

"Ignorance is bliss," said George. "Better get a taxi home – I wouldn't fancy your chances on the 149. Come on in, I've left Della in charge of the hob and she's not to be trusted."

They went into the kitchen. I returned to my flat. What to do now? Had no desire to read a book, write a poem, watch television. Downstairs I heard the sociable tinkle of glasses and the low drone of serious conversations. Nothing doing out in the garden, the wind was tugging at Julie's newly planted honeysuckle and a renegade plastic flower pot, surely not one of ours, was rolling across the terrace. I stared at the telephone, willing it to ring. I considered a spot of Buddhist chanting. Years ago, when Pat had been briefly into Buddhist chanting, I'd done it with her for all of one morning.

"Just keep imagining an envelope with a thousand quid inside is coming through your letterbox, and if it's meant to be and you really concentrate while chanting – it'll happen. Happened to me."

"A thousand pounds dropped through your letterbox?" I said incredulously. "You didn't tell me."

"Not a thousand pounds. Pam Peters. On day six I met her in the street and we went for lunch at the Blue Legume."

"You can't stand Pam Peters."

"*Now* I can't stand her. Then I was mad about her. It was the lure of the unknown."

What was the chant? Couldn't remember. "Pom. Pom-pom, pom-pom, pom-pom," that's how it sounded, but what did the 'poms' represent? Could I ring Pat? No, she'd guess and add another snippet to her file marked "Best friend's sad and desperate behaviour". Wondered if chanting "Pom, pom-pom, pom-pom, pom-pom," would work equally well, but couldn't bring myself to spend the evening sitting cross-legged and chanting "Pom-pom" at the telephone, especially if it didn't then ring till day six. In the end, went to bed early to finally sleep and then be woken up by a cab collecting Bill and Muriel. Fell asleep again and woke late into a grey morning of sheet drizzle.

No sign or sound of movement from below until suddenly the radio was switched on and the omnibus edition of *The Archers* blasted up through my floorboards. For the umpteenth time Kate Archer told ex-boyfriend Roy that she wanted nothing more to do with him and whether he liked it or not she was taking their daughter Phoebe out of the country.

I heard George exclaim, "She's a little bitch," and Della countering with "So-and-so's so much nicer, darling," and I found myself reluctantly smiling. Against all common sense and unpleasant historical experiences, I was growing fond of them and their continued presence downstairs. Increasingly, it was hard to imagine David and Julie as real people, it no longer seemed credible that they'd ever lived here. I imagined George in shirtsleeves, meeting them on the doorstep, being jovial, "Had a good holiday, you two? Clock those tans, Della. Where do you intend staying while you're in London? Flying visit or what?"

Despite this new warmth of feeling, I locked all windows and doors before heading off to Brighton, just in case – can't be too careful – know thine enemy.

From some distance away I spotted Edna. She sat on the low wall in front of Druce Court, framed by leggy lavender which was now in full purple flower and busy with bees. She was leaning forward, hands and chin resting on the crook of her walking stick; the expression on her lined leathery face was wistful. I thought, *Past would be better for you now than future,* and wished I hadn't had that thought, because like a line of dominoes falling in my direction, the words bounced back towards me, making me see the passing of time, opportunities lost...

"Hello Edna," I said stooping forward to kiss her.

"Lorna?" She lifted her face, squinting up at me. Nothing left of the jolly tanned pirate, she was pale and gaunt, her blue eyes sunken into dark hollows. I pretended not to notice the change, the difficulty she had pulling herself up from the wall; instead I sniffed the lavender, admired the fat-bodied bees. She snapped off a flower head and crumbled it into her pocket and we made our slow progress inside, shutting out the blustery sunshine. She led me down the dingy shared hall with its piles of unwanted local newspapers and advertising flyers, and dusty letters for residents dead or gone away. My spirits dipped. This was not to be a sparring visit, with Lorna required to give as good as she got; there was no energy in Edna, no animation or enthusiasm, she seemed exhausted.

"Bought any records lately?" I asked as she rattled her key in the lock.

"Don't get out to the charity shops any more," she said flatly.

Inside were the same chaotic ranks of furniture and bric-a-brac, with perhaps a little more dust; all Gran's bits and pieces, candleless candlesticks, clock faces that told every different time of day, the china ladies with their crinoline skirts, engaged in a still dance on top of a walnut bureau. The flat was silent. I'd been there often enough to hear behind the ticking clocks and dripping taps, and today there was nothing – no sound of Lily's clicking mules or knitting needles, no noises from the kitchen – the bead curtain parting or rattling in the breeze from the one fanlight window that still opened.

"Where's Lily?" I asked.

"Asleep."

I followed Edna on our winding crablike journey between the tightly packed furniture until we arrived at the centre of what always seemed like an ornate maze: Edna and Lily's cramped five foot by five foot of space, containing settee, armchair and the Formica table with the black and white drawing of the *Golden Hind*.

"Sit yourself down. Tea or Nescafé?"

"Tea please."

She shuffled away, leaning heavily on her stick. For a minute I felt dismayed, a little frightened. There was something serious on the cards that wouldn't turn into an amusing anecdote about my family and other animals for me to chortle over with Pat.

There was Princess Michael, even more creased than before, face almost unrecognisable, half stuffed down the arm of the settee, Lily's op-art plastic knitting bag, the ends of several pairs of knitting needles protruding from between the rope handles, discarded tissues, Lily's frayed pink mules. From the kitchen I heard the distinctive sound of water being run into a kettle.

"So you've bought a kettle?" I said brightly when Edna returned unsteadily, balancing the tray with one hand.

"No, it's our old one," she whispered.

"The police found it?"

"I found it. Could you keep your voice down? Lily –" she nodded towards the bedroom.

"Sorry. Where did you find it?"

"In the Borneo chest."

"Ah," I said, having nothing better to say.

I hadn't seen the Borneo chest for twenty years but I remembered it well, it being the last major purchase Gran ever made. It was a large and heavy, carved wood chest, not from Borneo at all, made in Manchester for Fishpools Furniture Store in Waltham Cross during the early seventies, especially attractive to customers who'd never been out east but liked to look as if they had. Gran had said, "It's exotic, Lorna. I need some exoticism in my life," and I'd agreed, in fact been rather proud of the chest, it being enormous and impossible to miss in our front room. When school friends visited, I'd say, "It's an antique, you know. From Borneo," and Gran never corrected me, just smiled and nodded and sometimes took a duster over its highly carved surface.

"Follow me," Edna said in a low voice, "While the tea's brewing," and off we went again, this time towards the back of the room – an uncharted place for me, as I only knew my way to the armchair, the bathroom, and back out to the front door.

Now the Borneo chest truly looked like an antique. Dust had built up in the indentations between the clusters of pomegranates and long-stamened flowers, much of the marquetry beading had broken away and there were deep scratches on the lid as if a wild animal had used it to sharpen its talons.

"Tous les object je trouve dans là," Edna hissed.

"Par-don?" I too, for some reason, slipped easily into a comical French accent.

"Oublier," she said, "ne c'est pas ici." She stared at me intently. "Tu comprends, les objets that disparu."

"You're learning French, Edna?"

Edna almost stamped her good foot in frustration. "Non, non, non. Secret. Ouvrez la porte."

"Open the door? But the door is already open."

"Ouvrez la bloody porte!" She pointed to the trunk.

"Oh, open the lid."

"Oui. Doucement. Lily est là." She nodded her head and I realised that we were now only a wardrobe away from the bead curtain dividing this room from their bedroom.

"Lily ne connaît pas French," Edna said.

With difficulty I heaved up the lid of the trunk. There was the electric blanket tucked around a milk pan, the rusty cheese-grater, a heap of necklaces and bracelets all tangled together, a sugar bowl, the silver condiment set, the Toby jugs, boxes of pills, rolls of bandages...

I lowered the lid. "I don't understand," I said.

"Lily," Edna whispered.

"But why?'

"Elle vieux fou."

"She old mad? Can't we please speak English?"

"Lily has incredible hearing." Edna's eyes filled with tears.

I took her hand and squeezed it. "Then let's leave this and sit down – the tea must be ready to drink by now. Any Wagon Wheels?"

"No. I'm sorry. There's Viennese Whirls but they may be stale."

"No harm in stale biscuits," I said cheerfully, "Gran always said, you eat a peck of dust before you die. I'll find them."

They were very stale and the kitchen was grim. Edna and Lily had never put food hygiene at the top of their priorities but now the mess was almost frightening. The microwave looked as if many things, possibly including a human head, had exploded inside it, likewise the fridge – only make that countless human heads. The work surfaces, which Edna had years ago introduced as, "My own handiwork, Lorna, beech-effect laminate of the highest quality," were engrained, encrusted, engulfed by crumbs and other less easily namable detritus.

Edna ate three biscuits with relish, I swallowed most of own without chewing, hurrying it on its way with a gulp of tepid tea (milk on the turn). Edna was wiping away more tears...

"And the money? Have you found that?"

She nodded. "Rolled up and tucked inside a ball of wool in Lily's knitting bag. It's so sad. Some days it seems we're back to normal and then it starts again. There are other places now, not just the chest, and she gets so angry, accuses me of stealing from her. She's bewildered – thinks I've turned against her because she's old. As if I would."

Suddenly she brightened. "The good thing was, the double-glazing salesperson came back with a quotation on our windows. Lily wants to have them done, just so we can see a bit more of her. I've half a mind to go ahead just to keep Lily cheerful."

"Edna, who's there with you?" Lily's voice. Did I imagine it, or was it not quite Lily's voice of old, more querulous, more genuinely angry?

"Come and see. Lorna's here."

"Lorna who?" The bed creaked, the curtain rattled, the sound of Lily's pattering feet came towards us. Suddenly her head emerged from behind the grandfather clock, her face flushed, silver-grey hair tangled.

"Hello Lily," I said, "it's me – Lorna Tree."

"Irene's granddaughter," Edna prompted.

Lily eased herself down onto the settee. She was wearing the same pink slacks, with a grubby satin nightdress tucked haphazardly into the drooping waistband. "Never heard of her. What's for dinner?"

"Not dinner time yet. It's lunch. I've got honey-roast ham sandwiches – your favourite."

"Yeuch."

"You love ham."

"I hate it. I won't eat it. Give me a lemonade."

Edna limped kitchenwards. "You'll have a ham sandwich, won't you, Lorna?" she called back over her shoulder.

"I had a sandwich on the train," I said quickly.

"Give her a ham sandwich – a refusal often offends," Lily shouted.

"No, really."

"Too bloody late," Lily smiled smugly. "Did you know Edna's going senile? She keeps talking in tongues. I heard her rattling away to you. My old dear's as nutty as a fruitcake." And she relapsed into silence, eyelids closing. Then they snapped open again, watching me beadily. "I know you," she said.

"You should do."

"You're George's daughter."

"That's right."

"He drowned his brother."

"He did not."

"You'd be surprised."

"I'd be astonished."

Edna appeared with the sandwiches.

"Didn't George drown his brother?" Lily said.

"He didn't drown Steven," Edna replied. "He just didn't manage to save him."

"What?" I was astonished, always thinking the story about George and Steven and river-drowning was more fiction than truth.

"Steven was a good swimmer and also Irene's favourite, although she always denied it," said Edna. "She told me that somebody had thrown a sack containing a mother cat and her kittens into the canal, and the boys spotted it while they were out fishing. It was on the opposite bank, caught in weeds, and they could hear the cries.

"Anyway, Steven went in to try and save them and got into difficulties. George followed him, but George was never much at swimming – he managed to save the cat and her kittens but Steven went under and disappeared. He was found several hours later, a mile down river. George and his mother never got over it – George always thought his mother wished it had been him who'd drowned, and Irene was full of guilt because in her heart of hearts, she did feel that."

"Poor George," I said.

"Yes, poor George."

"But he saved the kittens."

"Yes, Reverend Joseph took the mother," Edna recalled, "and the kittens went to the pet shop. Of course, he wasn't Reverend Joseph in those days."

"Where's my knitting?" Lily's plate slid off her knees and landed on the carpet.

"In your knitting bag."

"Where's my knitting bag?"

"Sitting next to you."

"What are you knitting, Lily?" I asked.

"None of your business."

The piece of knitting Lily produced was a jumble of dropped and added stitches, so many stitches that they were falling off the blue plastic needles. Lily, the elderly femme fatale I'd spent so many years resenting. I thought, *I'll never spend time resenting anyone again, never judge, never insult, never think uncharitable thoughts…*

I helped Edna clear away. Shoulder to shoulder – no, Edna's shoulder against my elbow, she'd grown so small and bent – as she washed and I dried.

"Is there anything I can do?"

"No dear. I just wanted you to see her before things got too bad. In so many ways Lily's a lovely human being."

Only ten minutes away from my fine resolutions, and I was already thinking, *Well I wouldn't go as far as that.* Aloud I said, "Yes, she is. She's made you happy."

"I've had a wonderful life."

"Not over yet."

"We're closing down, Lily and me. I'm none too well, don't know how much longer I'll be able to cope."

"You'll go on forever."

"I wish. I want you to know that what little we have goes to you."

"Edna, don't."

"Edna must. You're our family – all that's left of it. You're like your gran – a loner – nobody to look after you because you're so busy looking after. We both appreciate how you've visited us in spite of the past. Do you know, you've been coming to Druce Court for over twenty years? You're a good girl."

She squeezed my arm affectionately. I left them both watching *Ready, Steady, Cook*, Edna concentrating on the recipe, making notes in the margin of an old newspaper, and Lily, her knitting forgotten, laughing, "Crème fraîche, my eye. Who makes up these ingredients?

Do they think we're made of money? Tatty-bye, Lorna, see you anon."

She was back to normal, as comfortingly, cheerfully daft as I'd always known her to be.

I hardly thought of Dan as I sat on the train, even when it stopped at Clapham Junction. I thought of my twenty years of visits to Druce Court and how in those twenty years I'd passed from being a teenager into early middle age, and what did I have to show for it? I didn't want to be a loner like my gran. That wasn't how I'd seen myself at all.

And so I sat, in a brand new Connex train with air conditioning, tables and a brand new red, blue and gold upholstery, but I had no heart to colour it into my notebook. My train upholstery spotting days were well and truly over.

The Good Samaritan

By the time I got home from Brighton I was too tired for my usual investigative mine-sweep of the communal hall. One message on the answerphone, David sounding plaintive: "Lorna, I'm depending on you – Julie will be livid. I think Dad's vetting incoming calls and they've changed the phone message to the final bars of the Warsaw Concerto, followed by 'George and Della Tree are busy enjoying themselves elsewhere – please leave message after the beep'."

I mooched from room to room, half hoping Dan would suddenly materialise as she'd done once before, but no Dan, just empty rooms, stuffy from their windows being locked all day. I pushed up the kitchen sash; the force of the wind sent the blind flying inwards.

Tried Dan's number. No reply. No message. I let it ring for a count of twenty, and then another ten. Took a long hot bath with the bathroom door open so I would hear the telephone ring. Lit a herb candle: rosemary, one of twelve different herbs – present from David and Julie on my last birthday. Imagined Dan letting herself in... sniffs air approvingly, *Gorgeous smell,* and there lies Lorna, picturesque water maiden, islands of inviting flesh visible in a sea of soapy bubbles, plain features softened by candle glow. Topped bath up with hot water twice but when skin began to appear red and shrivelled even under flattering candle-glow conditions, got out of bath, lotioned and powdered and put on very best polycotton pyjamas.

That night I slept fitfully, dimly aware of the storm raging outside. It even entered into my dreams, but now the thrashing trees were leafless and threatening, tormented shadows reducing Lorna to a small child wearing shorts and Gran's frill-fronted cardigan. "Gran, don't leave me. Where are you?" I was crying, as I tried to get into our house; and then I was inside and all the doors were locked, so many doors, splintered and dull wood, not polished and bright like they were now. I woke suddenly as if someone had laid a firm hand on my shoulder. I wasn't calling out "Gran" – it had somehow changed to "Dan, Dan," and Dan's voice was saying soothingly, "It's OK, Lorna, I'm here." She held me tightly until I stopped shivering.

Incoherently I blurted out all manner of hidden hopes and fears as we lay curled into one another listening to the storm raging, the hiss of tyres on the wet road outside. She stroked my hair and hushed me when I came to the final part about Edna and Lily, and Edna seeing me as a loner like my gran. "Alone and unloved," I said, "growing old with nobody caring about me or wanting my caring for them."

"Lorna, everybody loves you. You're surrounded by love and affection: neighbours, family, your weird parents in their own weird way, your friend Pat."

"But nobody loves just me," I wailed.

"You can't ask that – perhaps you get lots of medium-sized bits of love, while some people get one large piece but some poor sods get nothing at all. *I* love you."

"No you don't."

"I do."

"Theresa told Pat…"

"Theresa tells Pat all sorts of garbage because she knows Pat has a big mouth and it will get back to you. Would I come out on a night like this if I just found you an interesting curiosity? Lorna Tree, attractive friend to rabbit and human alike."

The bed shook agreeably with our laughter.

"Thank you for saying you loved me," I said.

"Don't thank me, just be patient. Life's not straightforward. I have commitments."

"Theresa?"

"Theresa. I can't turn my back on her. That's not how it works for me."

"Can you talk about it?"

Then she stiffened, but not for long. Gradually her body relaxed again and she hugged me against her, murmuring into my hair, "Not yet. If things work out – then maybe. These are nice pyjamas. I don't recall seeing them before."

"Polycotton," I said.

"Is that good?"

"Just a light iron, and stays colour fresh." The bed creaked again with our muffled laughter.

And then in the calm of the next morning that followed the previous night's storm, all hell was let loose.

First, let's deal with the calm, because I do believe that truly happy moments in life are rare and need remembering – so speaks Lorna Tree, wise woman and know-it-all.

We woke late. It was already mid-morning; half an hour of further snuggling until it dawned on me that it wasn't just mid-morning, it was mid-Monday morning and David and Julie were due back at two. From downstairs came sounds of leisurely movement: George opening a window, saying, "Good grief, Della," and shutting it again, the intermittent rush of the shower, the sound of Radio Four.

"What am I going to do about them, Dan?"

"It's not your problem."

"But David can't handle George on his own."

"Time he learnt… and anyway, there's Julie."

On a Monday nothing much happened to me workwise. About tea time the *Echo* usually delivered the newspapers and I sorted them out for Tuesday's paper round, having first spent a pleasant half-hour reading the local news and personal ads. As a rule, I worked on a poem during the day or sometimes concocted a recipe for my Alternative Alternative Cookbook, which was progressing very slowly indeed. On my desk one Monday, for instance, was a small tin of ravioli – a product which I liked but felt to be hugely neglected, only ever being eaten once or twice in most lifetimes. Bright orange, comfortingly gooey, *Sorry darling, found this at the back of the cupboard.*

All there is till Sainsbury's tomorrow – let's have a bohemian evening.

Candle stuck carelessly in a Sarson's vinegar bottle, what's left of the stale walnut bread crisp and toasted, *Yum, yum, now I remember ravioli. It's delicious. Why doesn't some bright spark rebrand it?*

Answer: because it tastes like papier-mâché, is packed with unspeakable additives and is bright orange.

Hey, I like the taste of additives.

How did tinned ravioli manufacturers keep going if they were only able to shift a couple of dozen tins a year? Were the employees forced to accept cans in lieu of wages, sign an agreement that their children would be reared on a staple diet of ravioli, under threat of forfeiting occupational pensions? Let me tell all you many tinned ravioli pooh-poohers that it can transform a salad from run of the mill to absolutely delicious and an object of admiration, forcing guests to ponder, *Wherever did she find fresh ravioli in this area? Your own home-made tomato sauce, I don't doubt – absolutely ravissant.*

Lorna smiles demurely.

Anchovy and Ravioli Salad

12 mashed anchovy fillets, a fair few mushrooms. (I do like mushrooms – you can't have too many), 1 large tin of ravioli, chives or spring onions, lemon juice and olive oil

1. Mix the mashed anchovies with lemon, oil, and as much pepper as you like. DO NOT USE SALT!
2. Slice and add mushrooms.
3. Heat ravioli and allow to cool. Remove evidence of the tin.
4. Mix the whole nasty mess together and put in an attractive blue dish to set off the tomato red of the ravioli sauce.
5. Garnish with chopped onions or chives.
N.B. Lorna's garnish: Nasturtium leaves. Warning: check underside for blackfly.

*

You see how easy it is to drift completely off the subject, because that Monday morning, no thoughts of tinned ravioli entered my head, nor thoughts of my other tinned favourites, rice pudding and macaroni cheese. No, I was lightly boiling organic free-range eggs and setting out my Kermit and Miss Piggy egg cups – items I'd kept hidden long enough for them now to be considered fashionably kitsch.

Dan was dressed and assessing the storm damage from my front window.

"You've lost your dustbin lids."

"I'll find them later. Probably only a couple of gardens down the road."

I felt truly happy, wondering how to hold on to it. Dan was at ease in my flat where curtains were never pulled against the daylight and windows were flung open most of the year round.

"Your sister-in-law's urn has taken a tumble – must have been quite a gale."

"Breakfast in two minutes." I set out cherry preserve and marmalade.

"Ah."

This wasn't a slightly rural (sorry, rural readers) ah of agreement, as in 'oh ah', meaning 'you're not wrong'; this was an ah intimating all was not as it should be, an 'I don't quite know how to tell you this' ah.

Carefully I placed an egg into each egg cup and a second on each plate next to it, then cut the buttered toast into trim soldiers.

"Ready now," I called in a carefree, 'nothing and nobody will spoil this precious morning' voice.

Dan appeared in the kitchen doorway, thumbs tucked into the belt loops of her jeans. "I'm really sorry, Lorna – bad news."

"I suppose you've spotted your dear friend Terry sauntering towards the house," I said sharply. *Button it, Lorna.*

An expression of offended surprise on Dan's face. "No, the bad news is that Mr. E's palm tree's fallen across your mum and dad's car and smashed the windscreen – they won't be going anywhere this morning."

"That's terrible," I said.

"And the even worse news," and she started laughing, and as one does in the face of genuine bent-double laughter, I also started laughing in anticipation of, say, having the roof blown off number thirty-eight where the man lived who kept chows that always had an urgent need to defecate in front of our gate.

"Your brother and his wife have just got out of a taxi."

I looked at my watch in disbelief, looked at the clock, went to the front window – yes there they were – the taxi had been forced to park quite a distance down the road because of the amount of debris from the storm.

Quietly and firmly I said, "We'll continue as usual, only silently."

"Why?"

"So they don't know we're in." Already I was whispering.

I opened the stair door and peered down into the hall – no sign of parents. Quickly I ran down, opened the front door, then slammed it shut and crept back upstairs. At the top, Dan stood, looking profoundly bewildered.

"G and D will conclude we've gone out to a café for breakfast," I explained.

"My car's parked outside."

"They'll assume we've walked – not everyone automatically drives from A to B," I said with mock severity.

So we sat at my tiny table quietly tapping the tops off our eggs. Not so easy to grill toast quietly as the grill pan had a mind of its own. No matter how steady I held its handle, I couldn't control its natural desire to bash its metal sides against the grill walls.

A key in the front door and Julie saying, "Just as I predicted, that hebe has fallen on someone's car. Thank God we had the sense to leave ours in the garage." And then a sharpening of her voice. "Isn't that George and Della's car, David? Whatever is it doing here?"

David: "I just need some change to tip the taxi, darling."

Sounds of angry handbag-unzipping and coins changing hands – not easy for Dan and me to muffle our giggles. David set off back down the path towards the bored taxi driver, Julie stormed across the hallway, her heels making the sound of machine-gun fire as they hit the quarry tiles. The taxi paid, David broke into a run towards home while Dan and I vacated the chink in my curtains and took up our position on my side of my internal door.

"Why, the travellers return." This was George's cheerful, hearty baritone; he was no doubt trying to crush Julie into one of his all-encompassing bear hugs which Della had convinced him was a charming and love-inspiring action (as opposed to patronising and suffocating). "I'm afraid you've caught the pair of us still in our dressing gowns."

"David's dressing gown – towelling robe," Julie snapped accusingly.

"Yes, well, David's dressing gown. If you'd telephoned, we'd have laid on a welcome."

"I do not need welcoming into my own home. What are you doing here?" A no-holds barred, clipped tone from Julie. Dan took my hand and kissed it.

"Julie –" David was breathing hard. I did not allow myself to feel sorry for him, told myself he would not feel sorry for me – "I don't expect they're stopping, probably their holiday fell through. Mum's not ill again, is she?"

"What's wrong with their own home?" asked Julie.

"Didn't you say something the other week about having the roof space converted into another bedroom, Dad?" David asked desperately, but George refused to take the obvious way out.

"First I've heard of it! There's not room to swing a proverbial in our roof space. Della, what's this about an extra bedroom?"

"That's enough." Julie's voice was like the crack of a whip. "In the kitchen, now!" And George and David were herded inwards and the kitchen door closed.

Dan looked at me. I looked at her and knew that I was a warmer, nicer woman when she was around and my family became endearingly amusing rather than irritating. For a moment all our dark clouds were pushed aside – and might they never come back.

She said, "Come on, let's go now, while they're arguing."

I grabbed a jacket and my rucksack and stealthily we made our way downstairs, eased open the front door and closed it ever so quietly behind us. We got as far as the gate. The bristle head of a large yard broom shot across our getaway path, the broom handle being attached to Mr. E, intent on sweeping up leaves and bits of branch. He turned a face of deep tragedy towards us.

"Excuse me, Mr. E, we're in a hurry." I kept my voice low. Too low. He didn't hear me.

"Push past," Dan hissed.

"My palm tree," he said brokenly.

Couldn't help it, had to say, "And George's car, Mr. E."

"Lorna." Dan grabbed my arm and tried to hustle me around the broom but Mr. E was an old hand at manipulating a broom to cause the most inconvenience.

"George will be insured," he said.

"He'll be furious."

"Leave it, Lorna."

Reverend Joseph's front door flew open, revealing Reverend Joseph in pyjama trousers and a vest. "Lorna, does your father know what's happened to his car? I warned you, Edmund, pride comes before a fall."

"I'm just going out, Reverend," I said. "David and Julie will deal with it."

"Whatever happened to the Good Samaritan?"

"Don't answer," said Dan.

"Will you pass by on the other side? Go and do as he did."

"It's only a car, it's not a person lying in the road," I said.

"Edmund," said the Reverend, "you've set up a false idol of plant and small mammals."

"I can't believe this," Dan said, "this is chaos. Please Lorna, come now…"

Truly too late. The Tree family's highly polished front door opened and the Tree family erupted out into the front garden like a small horizontal volcano: David and Julie still in their shorts and his and hers T-shirts with sunflower motif, Della in a blue satin nightdress, Julie's maribou-trimmed bed jacket about her shoulders, and George in David's towelling robe, genial bonhomie put on hold as he rampaged past us towards his car causing Mr. E and yard broom to flatten themselves against our hydrangea hedging.

"My bloody car! Edmund, you are a damn fool. This is London, not even Torquay. Palm trees don't flourish here, nor do damn hebes masquerading as bloody palm trees."

Della tweaked the hem of my T-shirt. "Lorna, my JLY's disappeared. It was in our drinks cabinet yesterday evening and now it isn't."

"*Our* drinks cabinet," roared Julie. The volume of her roar impressed everybody, unnerving some, and sent Reverend Joseph rushing back inside to search out his moth-eaten cardigan.

I caught a glimpse of Dan's tense face in the narrow gap between George and Mr. E, and had an odd impression of a white blur receding into a darkening tunnel; no longer loving, no longer amused.

"I'll leave you to it, Lorna," she said.

"I'm coming with you."

"Little lady, you're going nowhere." George had an iron paw on my shoulder, holding me steady as Dan crossed the road towards her car.

"Dan!" I shouted. She ignored me, climbed in and gunned the engine.

"Someone help me lift the tree," Mr. E said. "We may be able to save it."

"Never mind saving the bloody tree, let's call it getting the damn thing off my car," George said. I twisted out of his grasp.

Dan's blue Mercedes sped past us; her face grim, she stared straight ahead.

"You'll need a thick rope," said David.

"David, it's none of our business," said Julie.

"Mr. E is our neighbour, Julie."

"Damn bloody ridiculous. I don't hear any apologies coming thick and fast." George was disentangling branches from his shattered windscreen.

"George, your dressing gown," Della said.

"David's robe."

"Never mind whose robe it is, Julie." Della pulled the maribou trim closer to her neck. "I don't want George displaying his credentials to the whole street – and what about my JLY?"

George gently turned Della housewards. "Go indoors, darling. First things first. Let's shift Edmund's bloody palm tree."

George was making one of his lightning temper recoveries, beginning to see the humour of the situation. Re-enter Reverend Joseph, fully attired in dog collar and weekday trousers, rolling up his cardigan sleeves apropos of manly tree-winching business.

"After all, I'm well insured." George smiled expansively at all us little people waiting in the street to do his bidding. "We've got the lot: car, house, holiday, death, critical injury, arson, flood and terrorist attack. You name it, we've signed up for it." He double knotted his towelling sash.

Julie was unimpressed, she stood hands on hips on the front step. "David, if you don't come in right now, I'm leaving."

"Please, Julie, go inside with Mum if you don't intend to help."

"Help? Intend to help? Are you out of your tiny mind?" Her voice rose magnificently.

The E family children, assembled to witness the raising of the tree, widened their eyes admiringly.

"You *are* very strong," I said to Julie.

She hesitated, considering all our eager faces and Mr. E's despondent one.

"Just a minute." And she darted back into the hall, kicked off her sandals and slipped into a pair of green rubber wellingtons kept especially for impersonating a genuine country person when visiting garden centres and stately homes.

"David, get the rope," she barked, and the E family gave her a round of applause.

"Lorna, stand on Mr. E's wall in lieu of a ladder. Mr. E, this is the last time…"

Together we raised the tree. It took all our efforts and forty-five minutes. George, David and Mr. E knocked two sizable stakes into the ground each side of it and tied it securely. Mrs. E brought out strong coffee in a variety of chipped utensils and George discovered that his radio cassette player, map books, tissues and tissue-box holder, plus scented South Park Kenny, had disappeared overnight.

"They'd steal the fillings off a dying man," he said several times.

"Lorna, I'd like a word," Julie said – which didn't bode well. I had hoped that the energy expended in raising the tree, and the good feeling it had engendered, would smooth my path out of the house, but Julie's voice said otherwise.

"Now, I don't intend to lose my temper because the accompanying adrenaline rush is unhelpful for a woman in my condition. Do we understand one another?"

"So far," I said cautiously.

"Good. Briefly, I want to say that I hold you personally to blame for allowing those incubi into our home. Not just allowing them in, but aiding and abetting. Della tells me that you haven't been averse to helping them eat and drink their way through our hard-earned food and wine."

"On one occasion, two at the most."

"Apparently you frequently accepted offers of gin and tonic, crisps, Greek-style yoghurt dips, stuffed olives, and salmon and cream cheese sandwiches."

"That was very disloyal of Della to tell you."

"And not disloyal of you to eat and drink at our expense and by omission grant them approval to squat, to wear our clothes, play our music, entertain under our roof?"

"Please don't get annoyed, Julie."

David came out of their front room. "Julie, take it easy."

"It never occurred to you to even telephone us at the hotel? We would have caught the next plane home."

Only I seemed aware of the anxious current pulsing through David's body, his Adam's apple yo-yoing above the rib of his crew-neck T. He said feebly, "You're being too hard on Lorna. It's not easy to resist George and I expect she didn't want to spoil our holiday."

"She *has* spoilt it. Its memory is forever tarnished, cancelled out, ruined."

"I'm more concerned about Mum's jewellery," David said, changing the subject adroitly.

"We must call the police." Her voice switched from dynamically furious to dull and apathetic. "There'll be police, insurance assessors, we'll never get them out of here. I'm reduced to being a stranger in my own home."

"Don't call the police. I might be able to find Mum's jewellery."

Julie's eyes flickered over me. "That wouldn't surprise me in the least," she said sourly, as if we'd never been friends, never rubbed congenial shoulders as we drank wine at her kitchen table. "Well, back into the fray."

She opened the kitchen door. There was George at the sink filling the kettle. "Cup of tea, Julie? I'm making one for Della, she's putting her feet up for half an hour."

The door slammed shut.

"Thanks for not dropping me in it," David said.

I shrugged. "No point in Julie feeling disappointed in both of us."

I turned to leave, hesitated and turned back. "Actually, Mum and Dad aren't so bad. I don't think this parasitic behaviour is real, it's just a cheeky game they're playing, they like to stir us up. I don't believe they'd do it if they thought you really needed the food and drink."

"It's the invasion of our privacy," he said pompously.

"Look, they seem to want to move in, you want to move out. Where's the problem?"

"Are you joking? It's *our* flat."

"They're getting old. They haven't masses of time left. George loves this house and you don't."

"I do."

"You don't. If you offered to sell to them, they'd pack up and go home, get their bungalow spruced up for selling and start dreaming dreams."

For some reason, the phrase 'start dreaming dreams' had the power to upset me, and I was glad of the hall gloom.

Suddenly David saw the beauty of the plan. "But what about you, Lorna? You do love this house. You always did."

"Well, if I do, I don't want to. Dad has Della, you've got Julie and a baby to look forward to, I want a flesh and blood person in my life, not picture rails and door furniture." I unlatched the front door. "Don't let anyone ring the police till I get back."

I hurried down our front path.

"Lorna..."

"Not now, Mr. E," I said firmly, crossing the road.

I heard Mr. E say, "Well, Alfred, she's in a mighty hurry."

Couldn't help looking back. There was Alfred sitting in the trolley on top of a pile of greens, a red neckerchief tied around his fat fluffy neck.

"He likes it," Mr. E shouted delightedly, "he likes the attention."

The unmasking

As I charged along Evering Road, the sky began to darken ominously. All I was wearing was a T-shirt and baggy shorts, on my back I carried my rucksack – don't know why I'd taken that with me. Something to do with delivering the *Echo*, got used to carrying a bag. It gave me a purpose, a reason to be beavering around the back streets. As I reached the tamarisk tree in one of the few pretty gardens on that road, I felt the first spots of rain. For once I didn't pause to admire the imaginative planting and the original stained-glass fanlight, I rushed onwards, because now it was really raining. A roll of thunder, a zig-zag of lightning; I dodged nimbly around each sodden tree – I wasn't ready for death, particularly not by electrocution. Headline in the *Echo*: *Lorna Tree, Hackney's roving reporter, struck down while sheltering under namesake*. The skies opened – no time for sheltering or even coherent thought.

I reached Dan's cul-de-sac. There was her car at an untidy angle in front of the house as if she'd parked in a hurry. In the strange grey-green light the house looked deserted. I rang the bell twice, pressing long and hard, peered through the heavy Victorian letterbox, shouting, "Dan, Terry. Anyone at home?" The hall was in semi-darkness. I put my ear to the aperture. I could hear faint voices and scraps of unrecognisable music. I rang again, rapped on the door with my knuckles. Gave up and went round to the side gate. This was set into a brick wall, about eight foot high, with barbed wire above the gate and vicious-looking broken bottles embedded into the top of the wall. The gate was heavily padlocked, so nothing doing there.

In one corner of the wall, ivy had been allowed to crawl nearly halfway up and was thick and knotted. I'm not a natural athlete, not good with heights or even faintly interested in pitting myself against the elements, however, as I'm sure George would say, needs must when the devil drives. Awkwardly, I climbed into the soaking wet ivy. It held my weight. I climbed higher. I couldn't have been wetter, and the palms of my hands and my chin scraped painfully against rough brick.

At one point I did think, *Why am I doing this? I know they're in the house, surely it would be so much easier – don't you think, Lorna old chum – to just telephone them: Hi, it's Lorna, could I have a word? I'll keep it brief.*

Oddly enough, I felt invigorated by the sense of unaccustomed adventure, Lorna getting to grips with life for a change. By the time I ran out of ivy, the upper part of my body was above the wall. I could see Dan's overgrown garden beaten down under the force of rain, and the path of wet paving stones leading round the outskirts of the house.

I slipped off my rucksack and laid it on top of the immediate glass; I then lay across the rucksack so that my head and shoulders hung over Dan's back garden. Losing my ivy foothold, my legs now stuck out almost horizontally into Dan's front garden. I had reached a physical impasse. Looking downwards, I could appreciate that the ground reached higher up the wall on this side, giving me a drop of only say... seven foot. This might not be much under normal circumstances, i.e. being the right way up, but to take a header into an unknown bank of slimy mud was surely foolhardy. For a start, how would I clean myself up to make an impressive entrance? *I unmask you, Theresa Stowell-Parker, for being a spiteful conniving bitch – and Dan, you will return Mother's jewellery forthwith or never darken my bedroom doorway again.*

I tried to wriggle backwards, just to see if I had any options, but unfortunately the leg of my voluminous shorts had snagged on the uptilted neck of a bottle. Options: I could stay stranded on top of the wall till somebody spotted me and helped me down, I could stay stranded on top of the wall till somebody spotted me and called the police, or I could go forward.

I've heard there's a trick to jumping off walls or out of high windows, or preserving life and limb inside a plunging lift – a relaxation sequence – bend at the knees, tense ankles, stretch neck and back, keep chin tilted upwards... This was not easily applied to nose-diving. I visualised a plane in a black and white war film... *A stormy sky, out of the clouds comes a Spitfire, black smoke curling from its tail. "We're losing altitude, enemy flak over the Dordogne, I'm going to try to bail out. Aargh –" as plane hits hillside and explodes.*

The rain began to ease off. Soon people would be out and about. Did I want to be found in such a ludicrous position, particularly by Dan and the noxious Theresa? I'd never live it down. *What that Tree woman will do to get Dan to take notice!*

I thought, *Think Count Dracula swarming down the wall of his castle like a giant bat.* Gingerly I leant forward, searching the brickwork for cracks to hold on to. I told myself in a reasonably non-panicking tone, *Lorna, you can't possibly hurt yourself, your head is only about five foot from solid ground,* and Lorna replied in an unreasonably panicking tone, *I could possibly break my neck,* and thus it was that as the debate continued between brave and fearful Lorna, my rucksack suddenly came adrift, the legs of my shorts tore free and I shot off the wall, performing an almost perfect somersault – *nine point eight for the English girl, neuf virgule huit pour la femme Anglaise* – landing on my back, legs in stingy nettles, the back of my head hitting the wall. For some minutes I lay quietly, admiring the flickering stars in the afternoon sky, then the rain resumed and it seemed important to at least make an effort to stand up.

My legs shook, my head hurt when I moved it, various parts of my body registered pain. I stood still until my knees stopped twitching, checked limbs, nothing broken, a fair amount of bruising. Retrieved my rucksack. *Did you know there is a right of way through your garden and I was merely exercising my right to use it?*

I made my way around the back of the house. As usual, all the curtains and blinds were drawn; no one could see out, I couldn't see in, not a chink of light was showing. I reached the kitchen door. From inside came a rich manly voice singing, "Oh my baby, my curly-headed baby," accompanied by a small orchestra. The voice warmed and cheered me. I recognised that voice, one of Gran's favourites, Paul Robeson. Surely this was a good omen?

I tried the door handle. It turned. I pushed the door open and stepped into light and warmth and Ange sitting at the table chopping carrots. She stared at me, face registering fear and horror as if I were indeed Count Dracula.

"Tony darling, come to Mummy now," Ange shouted, standing up, her chair falling over as she backed away from the table. Tony/Tonia scuttled across the kitchen to her mother, her eyes enormous, a balloon of bubble gum deflating over the lower half of her face.

"It's OK, Ange. It's me. Lorna."

"Lorna." She peered hard at me, still clutching her vegetable knife in a threatening manner as if I might only be a Lorna impersonator. "Have you been in an accident?"

"Sort of," I said. (So tempted to say, *"Pranged the plane, damn parachute refused to open and I came down in a tree to the left of Dan's garden shed. Any chance of a good old English cuppa?"*) "Any chance of a good old English cuppa, Ange?"

She said, "Tony, make Lorna a cup of tea while I sort out her cuts and bruises. Lorna, sit down before you fall down."

I sat down. Through a trickle of blood I watched Tony. She was a remarkably efficient five-year-old. Seemed to know her way about the tea-bag jar and kettle. Meanwhile Ange produced cotton wool, disinfectant and an ancient bottle of calamine from one of Dan's pristine half-empty cupboards. She filled a bowl with warm water and began to dab at my face.

"You look dreadful," she said cheerfully.

"Thanks. Is Dan here?"

"She is. Sit still. You've got several rather nasty cuts. If I were you I'd take that chin to hospital – it needs stitching. And you might have concussion or a fractured skull."

"I don't feel as if I've got a fractured skull. I want to see Dan," because as kind as Ange was being, it was Dan I wanted fussing over me.

"Not possible at the moment. She are Terry are in the middle of a major row and I've been told to stay in the kitchen."

"What are they arguing about?"

Ange shrugged. "Terry up to her old tricks again."

"What tricks?"

From the hall came the sound of running feet and Theresa burst into the room. "Who the hell's this?" she shouted. She looked furious, her face flushed with anger and her eyes red as if she'd been crying.

"It's Lorna. She's had an accident."

I felt at a subtle disadvantage – covered in mud, blood, bruises, filthy wet clothes, defiling Dan's spotless kitchen – in front of Theresa, who was sharp as a blade in black jeans, black vest, trainers that looked as if they'd never been out on a London street.

She smiled nastily. "You look a fucking wreck," she said, circling me (or to be accurate, semi-circling me, as the table was against the wall). "How did you get in here?"

"I climbed over the wall. I did try conventional approaches but nobody answered the door."

"It didn't occur to you that we didn't want to answer the door? We wanted you to fuck off."

"Not in front of Tony," Ange said.

"No, it didn't occur to me."

"Well, now you know, out you go and don't be slow. See, anyone can write bloody poems. I don't want you in my house."

"It's Dan's house," I said.

"It's *our* house, smart arse, and you're sitting in our kitchen on *our* chair. Dan's and mine."

Wincing with pain, I stood up. "Thank you, Ange, you've been very kind. I want to speak to Dan. If *she* tells me to go, then I'll go."

"Don't you understand, she doesn't want to see you. Can't you get that into your thick, ugly head?"

"Terry, that's not very nice," Ange said reproachfully. "You're setting Tony a very bad example."

"If you don't like it, you can go as well."

I'm taller than Theresa and a fair bit wider. I felt I must look quite intimidating; I'd managed to frighten Ange and Tony. She stood between me and the hall door – I would walk round her or through her.

"I'm going to see Dan," I said.

"You're going nowhere," she snarled.

"You wanted me to leave, so I'm leaving."

"You can go out the way you came in."

"I don't think I can actually. It was a one-off."

"I'll unlock the back door."

"I'm sorry, Terry, I intend to see Dan."

"You're going nowhere," she snarled.

"You've already said that. Dialogue a bit limited?" I took a step towards her.

She pushed me surprisingly hard, and I staggered back against the edge of the table. I saw RED! I saw my enemy in her smart black outfit, like a slim matador, and I was the furious wounded bull. Head down, I rushed at her. She stood her ground – well, good, I'd ram her in the solar plexus. Just as my head was about to hit her hard in the stomach, her arm flashed upwards to administer a deft karate chop. Somebody grabbed her arm and I rammed into that somebody as they pushed Theresa out of the way.

"That's quite enough," Dan said, her voice cold and angry. "Fighting in front of a child. Ange, what sort of a mother are you, letting Tony stay here while this is going on?"

Ange batted not an eyelid, looked happily complacent. "The best sort of mother. You can't wrap kids up in cotton wool. When I was a child my father used to take me to world-class boxing matches..."

"I don't want to hear one of your interminable stories." She turned to me. "Lorna." She held me by my damp shoulders and, as she took in my state of disrepair, her anger faded. She looked concerned. She looked half amused. She said, "Terry, run a bath for Lorna. Ange, when I've sorted Lorna out, I want you to bring tea and whisky into the front room. Terry, leave a blanket on the settee and make up the fire."

"I will not."

"Yes, you will."

I lay on the sofa. I felt so much better. Up to my chin was a tartan blanket, in the grate a fire burned brightly. Ange rested the tray on a footstool.

"Thank you, Ange," Dan said as if very used to Ange waiting on her. Had Ange taken on the housekeeping job Dan had offered me?

"I suppose you've come to collect your mother's stuff?" Dan asked me.

"Not just that. I wanted to see you."

Dan stroked my hair, her face tired and drawn. The clock on the mantelpiece said ten past seven. It seemed impossible that, only that morning, I'd been boiling eggs and cutting soldiers for us, thinking how happy I was.

She poured tea, poured whisky into two tumblers, before pulling up an armchair close to the sofa.

"So here I am. You've seen me. Now what?"

Let me emphasise, Dan didn't say this flippantly. Not at all. Her voice was subdued, sad.

"Can I ask some questions?"

"Ask away."

I sighed. Was there any use in asking questions? I should have asked them weeks ago instead of always being afraid of losing her.

"Go on, Lorna, ask your questions," she said gently.

"Why did you steal from my family – not once but twice? After all, I know you care about me – it doesn't make sense."

"I didn't steal from your family. Why would I do that, particularly the second time? Use your head."

I tried to use my head but my head wasn't working. Surely Della's jewellery being taken unlawfully from my house and arriving at Dan's house while Dan had spent the night in my house could be classed as 'stealing', and Della as 'family'? And if Dan hadn't stolen Della's jewellery, who had?

… I said, "Terry?"

She closed her eyes, said, "One, Terry needs to be liked. She thought you liked her, then, very obviously, you decided you didn't. Two, Terry is possessive and jealous. She knew I was interested in you; you didn't notice her but she saw you in the pub that evening when I was playing pool; she recognised you when you tried to give me a *Hackney Echo*, and after that she knew I was trying to find out where you lived. Three, in a way, I'm all the family that Terry has and we don't make friends easily. She knows that you have friends and family – Pat goes on about you all the time. So, this was her way of hurting you."

I muttered, "She's got Ange and Tony."

"She doesn't see it as quite the same. The power is with you and you don't realise it – you've got everything going for you and we've got very little. It's made us weak and you strong."

I didn't want to hear those we's and us's. I said, "So Terry steals?"

"Yes. From time to time. She doesn't need to. She just likes to cause grief, it's her way of getting even with the world."

"Why should she want to get even? No, don't answer that." I didn't want to hear any more about Terry either – soon I'd be feeling sorry for her, putting her first. I said instead, "But what about that first time? I caught you actually taking things out of David and Julie's drinks cabinet."

"No, I was putting stuff back. That night, Terry had already broken in through your kitchen window. I was too late to stop her. There was just the clock to go back when you came in with your bottle. Terry was behind the door."

"She was there all the time?"

She nodded. "That was why I switched off the light."

"And kissed me?"

"Yes. I had to distract you – and then –" she smiled her old sweet smile – "then it was irresistible, I had to take it further. You're very lovable, Lorna, with your quirky courage. I've never met anyone quite so... so..."

"Entertaining?"

"Let's stick with lovable."

"And what about those times I spotted you with the pet-carrier?"

"Drink this whisky." She supported the back of my head and held the tumbler to my lips.

"Fire water," I said, laughing and coughing. She sat back in her chair. I felt as if I were a child again, in bed and just a little unwell, with Gran nearby telling me a rather thrilling story.

"When you saw me that time on the train, I'd been returning some Clarice Cliff pottery that Terry had stolen from my then girlfriend."

"And in Neville Road? The envelope?"

Dan smiled. "A birthday card for Terry."

"But why the pet-carrier? The pyjama case? It's so unnecessary. Why not something unremarkable like a supermarket carrier bag?"

For a while she was silent. I glanced across at her; she wasn't watching me, she was staring into the fire seeing some memory from the years before we'd known each other. She folded her hands around her glass and began:

"When we were kids, Terry and I, we had a Highland terrier. I really loved him. Called him Angus – not very original. He was a funny little dog, very playful –" she smiled at me – "and each night he slept on my bed and I could reach out my hand and know he was there. One afternoon I came home from school to find that Mum had given him away. She said having a dog was unhygienic and too much trouble. She said it was unnatural my being so fond of a dumb animal. I was heartbroken. Couldn't get over it.

"Whatever your opinion of Terry, in her funny warped way she really loves me. Terry was never jealous of Angus because she knew how much he meant to me. That pyjama case was the first thing that Terry ever stole. She saw it in a shop and it looked just like our dog. I used to keep it next to my pillow and put all sorts of secret things in it.

"After that, Terry began hiding Mum's earrings, scarves, small things that were hardly noticed – I think she wanted to punish her. I'd find them and put them back. Then she started at school, taking other children's sweets, pens, rubbers; she's never ever stolen money. At school she could have got into serious trouble, but I made a joke of it. Anything she took, I'd bring it back in my dog pyjama case. It became a habit, a laugh. As we grew older, we added to the joke by putting the pyjama case into a proper pet-carrier.

"She only ever steals from people we know, and somehow, me carrying the stuff back in the carrier makes it almost funny and endearing, so it's not taken seriously. It doesn't happen often, Lorna."

I said quietly, "So Terry's your sister?"

"My half-sister. We share the same mother."

"She needs help, Dan. Her stealing isn't a joke. There's nothing funny about it, whatever you bring the stuff back in."

"She's getting better. One day she'll stop. We've come this far."

"Does Ange know?"

"She does now."

"Why did you and Terry both pretend that you used to be, might still be, lovers?"

"It protects us. Nobody gets near."

"Did I get near?"

"Yes."

"And where does that leave us now?" My voice surprised me – no hint of pleading, just cards on the table.

"I can't offer you anything. I couldn't share your life. It's tempting from outside looking in, but it belongs to you. I need to be needed."

"I need you."

"Terry needs me more."

"Weren't you the wild at heart one?"

"I always come back here to Terry. There are times I wish I didn't have to, but I can't make the break. She depends on me."

What more could I say? I loved and needed her but I wasn't dependent – that was very different.

She said, "Lorna, I'm being torn in two," trying to blink tears away. I was off the sofa and holding her close, pulling the blanket around both of us.

I said, "I'm so sorry, Dan. So very sorry," because I was torn in two as well. I knew I couldn't make the jump from my life into hers. One or both of us would be destroyed.

Early the next morning, she dropped me home. We sat outside my house, in her car, for nearly an hour. She said, "I love you, Lorna," and I said, "I love you Dan," and I thought, *She only lives a mile away. I'll see her again. It can't be over. There are other ways of making a relationship work if the love's strong enough.* I thought about Terry. I could manage Terry, couldn't I?

Finally she said, "Lorna, I want to say something and I want you to really listen to me. You and I have both let ourselves become trapped. There's nothing I can do for myself but you're different. Don't commit yourself to that house and your family, or to staying in the area in the hope of us meeting again. Do something. You might come back like your dad is coming back, but go away and do something else first."

"I don't want to go away."

"Then you will end up like your gran."

"I loved my gran."

"She had the two of you to look after. But you'll be on your own."

We said goodbye and I watched her drive away before I crossed the road. As I opened the gate, our front door opened and I was surrounded by David, Julie, George and Della.

"What the hell are you playing at? Didn't you see me pulling faces at the window?" George bellowed.

"Your jewellery, Mum." I handed her the snake-charmer's basket and walked past them into the house.

"What's happened to you? Those aren't your clothes. Oh my God, George, Lorna's been in an accident."

"I'm OK, Mum."

"Young lady, we'd like a word with you."

"Not now, Dad. Tomorrow or the next day."

"Look here, Lorna..." David began.

"Leave her." Julie took my arm and said, "Go on up. You look exhausted. Is there anything you need?"

"A bloody good hiding," George shouted.

Two weeks passed. George and Della went home to Hornchurch after David and Julie had agreed to sell them their half of the house and I'd agreed to lease my half to them on a ten-year lease.

Having got his own way, George was in excellent spirits. "Ten years is all I ask," he'd bellowed triumphantly, "not that we've any intention of dying but don't worry, I'll go quietly when the time comes."

I doubted it. I said nothing.

Five years later

What happened next

I arrived at Abney Park Cemetery at four-thirty on a May morning for the Dawn Chorus Walk which Pat had booked. No sign of Pat, just twenty shivering strangers, several hyper children, one coughing baby in a rucksack... and then there she was, ambling through the cemetery gates looking very pleased with herself. She'd cut the curl out of her hair, it was white-blonde, she wore a double-breasted leather coat, several sizes too big, with epaulettes on the wide padded shoulders, plus epaulettes plus buckles on the cuffs that covered her hands down to her fingertips; from her buckled belt hung a Simpsons key ring with at least a dozen keys.

"Like it?" she asked.

"What about, 'Hello Lorna, long time no see'? And no I don't like it. You look like a member of the Gestapo."

"Hello Lorna, long time no see. Sorry I'm late, had to see a man about a dog."

"Don't be ridiculous."

"Quiet please." A youngish woman in jeans and a T-shirt that proclaimed 'Give it up. Tobacco kills' had appeared amongst us. "Silence is the essence. Geoffrey is your guide this morning. Keep to the path. Don't trample on the grave stones. Mini-doughnut and coffee will be served back here at base camp in fifty minutes."

"Good-oh," said Pat, "I'm starving. Want an Opal Fruit?"

"Shh," I said.

We shuffled along behind Geoffrey, a youngish man in shorts who looked like an extra from *The Sound of Music*. Every twenty yards or so, he signalled for us to stop and we shambled to a halt, staring hard at the shrubbery while listening with our heads on one side and nature-loving smiles plastered on our faces. We saw and heard nothing – well, almost nothing – on the third stop, Pat was asked if she could keep her coat quiet and stand further back. Geoffrey told us that apart from Pat's jingling and creaking coat we could hear woodpeckers, wood pigeons, black caps, territorial robins, jays and a song thrush.

"Look, there goes a wren. Second smallest British bird," he whispered excitedly.

What, where, how? We all stared frantically into dense woodland. (As a town person, three trees equal one wood to me, and two woods equal one forest.)

"I think I see it," said the man in the K2 anorak and walking boots.

From Pat at the back came a creak, a jingle, a click and a small flash of light from her camera.

Sound of Music pushed manfully through our group and said sternly, "A flash is absolutely useless out here in this light. All you've achieved is frightening the birds."

"Actually, in the past, I've taken some very good outdoor snaps with this flash, haven't I, Lorna?"

"No," said Lorna.

"Will you please keep your voices down," Geoffrey whispered loudly.

"I want my money back," Pat said. "I haven't seen a single bloody bird."

"That's because you've frightened all the birds away," said Geoffrey.

Pat took a snap of Geoffrey's furious face and he stepped towards her threateningly. "I want you out – now. I do not intend to lose my temper."

"Good. Glad to hear it. We'll leave you to it then. Come on, Lorna."

On our way out, we saw a fox nuzzling the rubbish in a waste bin. Pat and I stood quietly some yards away. The fox looked at us and then continued. Pat unwrapped an Opal Fruit and tossed it to him. Unfortunately, and typically for Pat, the Opal Fruit hit the fox behind the ear and with a low growl he bounded away and was immediately lost from sight.

I said, "Pat, you are the most appalling person," and started to laugh.

Laughing uproariously, we left the cemetery. All around us birds began to sing. Pat said, "I can hear a black cap, wren, ostrich, flamingo, gorilla and wallaby."

We found a café that was just opening up on the High Street.

"We're just opening. Not quite ready," the waiter said.

"Can we come in and sit?" Pat asked and he shrugged which we took as a yes. "Full English breakfast when you're ready. One with two eggs, one with no meat, ta very much," and we sat opposite each other at a table by the window.

"So?" said Pat.

"So?" I said.

"We bought one of Kate's clumber spaniels."

"You didn't?"

"We did." She looked shifty. "I might as well tell you now, we called it Lorna."

"Was that supposed to be a joke at my expense?"

"I thought you'd think that, but no. Only, after you left London, I quite missed you, and Sandra said, 'If we ever get a dog, let's call it Lorna, so there's still a Lorna in your life.' Sentimental, aren't we?"

"Has it got a nice nature?"

Pat looked irritated. "A nice nature? No, it hasn't got a nice nature. Since when did I like things with nice natures? If you think you've got a nice nature, you're very wrong. You've been vile to me for five years and yet here I am, arranging dawn chorus events and treating you to slap-up breakfasts, telling you I've even named my dog in memory of our friendship..."

Pat looked as though she was going to cry, which was terrible as Pat didn't cry. Pat bragged, lied, got drunk, insulted people, double-crossed her friends, but she didn't cry.

"Don't cry," I almost shouted. "Tell me gossip. How's Kate? What's Sandra's latest project?"

"Kate's very well." Pat dabbed at her eyes with her paper napkin. "She's not with Tina any more, she's with a Moira who is Scottish and apparently looks like a clumber spaniel. Sandra will tell you all about her latest project. I must say you look very well, although, never mind my coat, nobody wears baggy T-shirts and leggings any more in London."

We were back to normal. The full English breakfasts arrived, and as often happened, it was my breakfast that had the large thumbprint pressed into the egg white.

Pat heroically leant across and cut off the print and ate it, saying, "I'm doing this for friendship, Lorna, I wouldn't eat a thumbprint from just anybody's egg."

"I'm sorry about Edna and Lily," Pat said, pushing aside her empty plate and lighting a cigarette.

"Edna was lost after Lily died, I think she pined away."

"And you're happy living on the coast."

"Yes, I love my little house at Pevensey Bay."

"Only, you don't seem very happy."

"I'm OK. I don't miss London."

"What about Dan? Are you over her yet?"

"I think so. Why? Have you seen her?"

"Never. We move in different circles. You knew Ange went to live with Terry, didn't you?"

"Yes."

"I never see them either. Not a great loss."

Pat was so... obvious. I could see she was itching to tell me something, the way she kept looking at me, then looking down at her cigarette butt, and that suppressed smile she had when she was biting back some news.

"You are absolutely over Dan?" she said.

"Listen," I said, "years ago I fell in love with Jean Simmons, who starred with Kirk Douglas in *Spartacus*. Not my type at all, but so sweet natured, courageous and loving that I couldn't help but love her, while knowing someone so special would never be for me."

"You're not going to tell me Dan was like Jean Simmons? She's more like Kirk Douglas."

"No, I'm absolutely over Dan. It's years ago, and anyway, it was madness, a path to unhappiness. I'd have lost everything – you can't love for long in a vacuum."

"Then what's with the Jean Simmons story? Is the sea air interfering with your brain cells?"

"No. Listen. I was going to tell you that Jenny Salter had very similar qualities to Jean Simmons in *Spartacus*."

"Jenny Salter?" Pat sat back in her chair as if stunned.

"You remember, the charlatan. My counsellor."

"The golden eagle?"

"That's right."

"In that case, let me tell *you* a story. Just over a year ago, Sandra and I went to a party in Shoreditch. It was rather crowded and noisy – the way I like parties to be, but living hell for Sandra. Anyway, after a couple of drinks I was looking around for someone to impress with the full weight of my fabulous personality and I spotted this woman, sitting on her own reading a paperback. Of course I thought, she'll like me better than any book, so over I sauntered. I got her a drink and then another, bothersome Sandra joined us and led the conversation off on a totally non-productive tangent about conditions in the National Health Service..."

"Is there a point to this story?" I asked.

"All in good time. To cut to the chase, this woman turned out to be a counsellor – which isn't uncommon in this part of the world, probably half the women at the party were either counsellors or being counselled... or nurses..."

I sighed.

"Anyway, the story was that this woman had been married, and then one day she realised she was in love with one of her clients. Unfortunately, quite apart from the ethical question, that client had just met the love of her life and didn't want to be her client any more."

"Is that it?"

"Don't you get it?"

"Get what?"

"When I saw this woman sitting in an armchair engrossed in her book, I thought, 'Bloody weird, but that woman has something of the golden eagle about her.'"

I looked at Pat. She looked at me with a wide, clever-dick smile on her face.

I said, "And?"

"And? What more do you want? Jenny Salter was the woman with the book; you, unbelievable though it is to me, were the client she'd fallen in love with."

"You're making this up."

"I'm not."

"Did you say you knew me?"

"I did. I offered her my hand to shake and said, 'I'm Pat. Did Lorna by any chance mention me in her ramblings?' I've still got her phone number somewhere."

"Why didn't you tell me?"

"Because, stupid, I didn't know you liked her. You were the swan that mated for life. Remember?"

"She's probably met someone else by now."

"She hasn't. Sandra's kept in touch with her. Jenny Salter's a bit too serious for my taste."

"You mean you're a bit too puerile for Jenny?"

*

Companionably, I walked Pat home. It was only seven a.m. and the previous night's litter bowled merrily along the pavement. Sandra was up and making fresh coffee and we sat in her rose arbour.

After a while I checked out her kitchen *en suite* toilet and found the plasterboard walls and concertina plastic door very inhibiting, but said, "Fabulous lavatory, Sandra, must have added thousands of pounds to the value of this house." Behind her, Pat made a thumbs-up sign.

"I'll be starting on the loft come autumn," said Sandra. "Any plans to move back?"

"I'm very fluid," I said enigmatically.

The High Street was much the same; a few new shops had opened but they'd taken the precaution of retaining the old fasciae so that now a Turkish baker operated out of Tarts for Hair, Beauty and Perfect Nails; and another shop promising it stocked everything for newlyweds was still called the Amigo Café. I turned into Duxford Road which was as usual jammed with very old cars and more overflowing dustbins per square metre than any other road in Hackney. However, the council in its wisdom had planted trees, erecting protective tubes of wire netting around each sapling which in turn were being filled up by the residents with beer and soft-drink cans. George had been initially pleased with the tree planting, but was incensed with the cans.

"What kind of mentality do these bloody hooligans possess? If I lay my hands on just one of them, he'll get the thrashing of his life."

So far, nobody had been thrashed by George.

Mr. E had taken it upon himself to give special care and attention to the robinia planted equidistant in the pavement between his and George's front gardens. Regretfully, he was using it as a test case for a fertiliser made from rabbit droppings that he'd been fermenting all winter. The robinia looked on the point of death, whereas the can-encased trees were thriving.

As I dawdled up the road, I could see George and Mr. E lounging, arms folded, in their respective gateways, George's voice booming above the noise of the traffic.

"Why don't you just leave the poor thing alone? It might at least stand a fighting chance."

Mr. E was silent, looked troubled. They both spotted me.

"Lorna, your opinion required. Over here. Chop-chop."

Rebelliously thought, *Women in their forties don't appreciate "Chop-chop."*

"Look at this tree," George instructed. Unwinding himself from the comfort of the gatepost, he took hold of a puny branch and shook it. A new leaf already turning yellow spiralled to the ground. Mr. E visibly winced.

"Is this tree dead or is my name Billie Piper?" George grinned, pleased with himself. He liked tossing in the odd contemporary reference to upset any preconceptions that might be developing regarding him, Della and senility.

I ignored this, working on the principle that George was unbearable enough without encouragement. I looked at the tree. It was dead. Looked at Mr. E. Couldn't bear to see him glum.

"Perhaps a shop-bought tonic?" I suggested. "All the other trees do seem healthier. Even the vandalised ones."

"There you are, Edmund, from the horse's mouth. Never mind the mindless vandals, you're an eco-vandal! I notice you don't try your rabbit's muck on yonder hebe. I'm telling you, if I see one drop of that stuff falling on my hydrangeas, I'll sue."

"I'm going in," I said.

"Yes, you go on in, dear, and give Della a hand."

"I'm not going in to give Della a hand, this is my holiday."

"So you think I should stop using it?" asked Mr. E.

"I do. Lorna, your mother could die at any minute. She's living on borrowed time."

"But it's starting to bubble and make hissing sounds," said Mr. E.

"God give me strength, you're going to blow up the whole street. Next thing we know we'll have the bomb squad down here and you'll be had up for urban terrorism – and don't think for one minute you can rely on the big fellah, i.e. yours bloody truly, to bail you out..."

I closed the door on them both.

"Cup of tea, darling?" Della called from what was now the back sitting room.

"Don't mind if I do."

"Well, make it in the pot. I've been sitting on my own in here for hours."

Had a philosophical thought about people not changing for the better as they got older, just becoming more polished at being aggravating. Prepared tea tray, just as Della expected: bone-china tea service, milk in jug, sugar cubes in sugar bowl with tiny silver tongs, five plain chocolate biscuits arranged in a crescent on a pink paper napkin. Had another philosophical thought: that as I'd got older I'd become more philosophical.

Mum had taken to the role of semi-invalid like a duck to Springfield Park. For years she'd been declared cancer free, but she still referred to her operation as if it were the previous week. In retrospect it had also grown in severity. She endlessly implied that hers was a life due to be blighted in its prime. Saw herself in the role of Cathy in *Wuthering Heights*, with George a distraught Heathcliff: *"Do not leave me in this abyss, where I cannot find you!"*

However, she and George had visited me twice now in my little house by the sea; we'd congregated for Christmas in David and Julie's brand new ranch-style home on an executive estate in the suburbs of Norwich – or, as Julie unfailingly called it, "the Cathedral City of Norwich". We hadn't got on badly. As you may have gathered, George, under strict control, can be amusing, and we found that even Della possessed a small ironic sense of humour and could sparkle brightly on social occasions when she knew she looked her best.

"It's lovely outside, Mum, definitely springlike," I said.

"Would I need a blanket for my knees?"

"Absolutely not."

"How was the dawn chorus?"

"Disappointing."

"Pat's a nice girl."

"Isn't she?" I said, knowing that Pat and Sandra relished the task of spying on my parents for me.

"George dotes on Sandra. Apparently she's a mine of useful information. In my day, that would have been the kiss of death. Women were enigmatically silent – keep the man in a state of perpetual uncertainty."

In the past I would have explained yet again that women like us didn't need to keep men in a state of perpetual uncertainty, but instead I said briskly, "I'm taking the tea into the garden, now."

"Wait for me."

"No. Come when you're ready."

Della never moved fast. She was languorous. It took her five minutes to get her feet into her shoes. I wanted some time to myself for a really good think, rather than the constant drip-drip of small talk.

I put out the sun lounger for her, deckchair for myself, positioning them in the sun, in a corner of the large lawn George had laid a while back. No more pond – he'd even dug up and turfed over the Peppy graves. "Only a few bones left, nothing to write home about," he'd said.

Poured tea for myself and prepared for an in-depth thinking bout: the Dan versus Jenny Salter debate, and how during the intervening years I'd managed to turn Dan into a monster and Jenny a saint.

The longer I'd stayed out of London, the more I'd felt relief – even feeling that I'd had a narrow escape, that the difficulties and darkness surrounding life with Dan would have far outweighed any chance of happiness. What did I mean by happiness? Happiness was Pat hitting the fox on the ear with her Opal Fruit, happiness was sitting with Julie watching my little niece Jessica playing in her sandpit, happiness was sitting on a bench with friends seeing the sun dip into the sea. I needed friends, family, affection, humour – Dan had offered me none of these. And yet... Pat would think me mad, I would think me mad, but I had to see Dan, my woman in beige, one last time, otherwise the feelings, good and bad, that I still felt for her would haunt me for the rest of my life.

Later that evening I tried to telephone, but there was no answerphone and no reply.

Pat turned up, or Pat bounced in, just as I was setting out at about eleven the following morning.

"Have you rung her yet?"

"Yes, no."

"Yes, no? Have you or haven't you? Or are we talking at cross-purposes?"

"We are."

"I hope you don't intend to visit Desperate Dan?"

"I do."

"Bad idea."

"In your opinion."

"But Lorna, that woman has spoilt years of your life. Because of her, you've exiled yourself to an obscure seaside resort, cut off communications with friends and loved ones, missed the chance to be a godparent to Alfred and Eva's babbies."

"I don't want to be a rabbit godparent."

"Come and have a drink at the Rochester."

"It's mid-morning."

"This is London, not the back of beyond."

"I don't want a drink."

"Time was when you were gagging for a drink mid-morning."

Smiling, I said, "I gag no longer."

"Do you realise that if you choose Dan you're opting for Kirk Douglas rather than Jean Simmons?"

"Dan hasn't got Kirk's hair or cleft chin."

"She's got his torso."

"Don't be ridiculous."

"Can I come with you?"

"Definitely not."

"I'll say hello to Della and George then. By the way, if you're still in the land of the living, i.e. London, on Saturday, Sandra and I are doing an Easter barbecue. No histrionics this time, mind – I'll never forget that Easter brunch party."

I left Pat to mull over past social disasters and went on my way. How did I feel? Apprehensive, excited, negative? None of these. I realised how much I'd changed. I knew I'd never felt better, or looked better. Finally I'd renounced my penchant for men's baggy shorts. I liked jeans and brightly coloured T-shirts with short sleeves. I was tanned all year round now, the sun and sea had bleached gold streaks into my dark brown hair.

I took my time, chose a long winding route through the back streets, reacquainting myself with the area I'd spent most of my life in. I loved it still, its familiarity, but felt no desire to move back. From some distance away I heard noise – bangs, crashes, the rasp of a lorry reversing. I turned into Dan's cul-de-sac. Her house and its garden were now a building site. The house had been gutted, not a window frame or door remained, all that stood were the walls and roof inside a cage of scaffolding. The garden fences lay broken in a skip, and behind the house I could see the flattened garden.

"Hey, where do you think you're going?" a man in a hard hat shouted as I picked my way forward amongst the debris.

"I'm looking for Dan Carson. She used to live here with her sister."

"She's round the back. Be careful."

At first I didn't recognise Dan. She too wore a hard hat and unfamiliar dark blue shirt and jeans, her hands pushed inside her back jean pockets.

"Dan," I called.

She turned, wiped a hand across her eyes as if her sight were blurred. All she offered me was a slight smile of welcome.

"What brings you here?" It was said so casually, as if I hadn't been out of her life for five years.

Lightly I replied, "I've been staying with George and Della for a week, looking up old friends."

She made no movement towards me. We didn't kiss or even touch hands – her hands remained firmly in her pockets.

"What's happening to the house?" I asked tentatively.

"We're turning it into flats." I noted the 'we'. "Our mother died last year and left the house to us. We've had planning permission for a two-storey building in the garden, as there's direct access to the street. I'm helping with the building work."

She had lost weight, grown sinuous and muscular.

"Really?" I said politely, "And where will you live?"

"Not here. Terry and I have bought a place in Hoxton. Ange and her daughter live with us."

"I'm sorry about your mother."

She shrugged. "I'm not."

"How is Terry – and Ange and her daughter?"

"Do you really want to know?"

"No," I said.

"How about you?"

"I teach English part-time and live by the sea."

"And the poems?"

"And still the poems."

So odd, having been that desperately involved with each other, to come to this banal exchange. Or had it just been my involvement? For her, no more than a stream surfacing, then returning underground, unreachable again? I breathed out, only then realising I hadn't been breathing at all. We looked steadily at each other. I felt the tension leaving me. Couldn't deny that I liked what I saw. In a phrase of George's, Dan was damnably handsome, only I no longer needed to have this physically magnetic, damnably handsome woman. It wasn't enough to satisfy Lorna Tree.

"We had some fun, didn't we?" Dan traced the line of my cheekbone with a dusty hand.

"A little," I said. *A very little.*

"Dan, telephone call!" someone was shouting from inside the house.

"Could we meet tomorrow, perhaps?" Dan said.

"I can't. Pat and Sandra are having a barbecue and I go home on Sunday. I just wanted to make sure you were... OK."

"I'm fine. We're fine." She leant forward and kissed me lightly on the forehead. "Love you, Lorna," she said, very quietly, then strode away towards the house, without once looking back.

I walked down the long garden to where it opened into the next road. I walked quickly, and behind me the hum of the building site grew fainter.

"Aye-aye, kissie-kissie." Pat appeared from behind a laurel hedge.

"Have you been spying on me?" I said almost angrily.

"I have. Couldn't quite hear what you both were saying, but think I lip-read the gist of it, plus I'm ace at reading body language."

"Oh yes?"

"In brief, Dan's become a property tycoon and you, who prefer to live at Nature-on-Sea, find her still damnable attractive but too square a peg for your... er... um... round hole, if you'll overlook the familiarity."

Couldn't help laughing. "You read my mind. Those were the very words. Do you think she thought I was a fine-looking filly?"

"What, you?" Pat paused, scrutinised me carefully. "She might have done. You've stopped wearing those dreadful baggy shorts. What was that all about?"

Pat and Sandra's Easter barbecue

As I mooched around George and Della's tastefully appointed best guest bedroom, getting ready to set off for the barbecue, I couldn't help but recall the previous Easter celebration to which Pat had referred. I thought back over the years to that brunch party. Kate had only just left me for Tina and Poppy the clumber spaniel...

I'd looked dreadful – exactly like a woman recently spurned – face pale and puffy, eyes dull and watery, hair lank. Downstairs, David and Julie were singing, "We're all going to San Francisco..." at the tops of their voices – which they were, leaving me as always to mind the house. Everyone else was making progress with their lives except me, I'd thought grimly. The last thing I wanted to do was go to Pat's, but I'd promised, and as Reverend Joseph and Gran had drummed into me and David since we were children, a bloody promise is a promise.

"It will do you good," Pat had said. "Kate wouldn't want you to mourn..."

"Kate hasn't died, Pat, she's gone off with a kennel maid. She couldn't care less if I mourn. I hope they both contract hard pad, rabies or dysentery."

"That's the spirit. So you'll come."

Kate had left loads of her stuff behind. She was a great one for buying ointments, lotions, potions and unguents which were supposed to have a miracle effect on her appearance. In the chest of drawers I found a tube marked Bronzer. On the side it said, "A light coffee gel giving a realistic natural tan and flawless golden finish." Just what I needed.

I would march into Pat's bloody Easter brunch: *"Kate? Kate who? Oh that Kate. Thank God she's gone at last. Personally, I feel the relationship had far outlived its sell-by date. Champagne? Yes please, I'm celebrating my singledom."*

I ignored the blob of gel I'd squeezed out onto each wrist for the minute, it was too thick to be going anywhere fast, instead I rubbed the tint onto my face and neck. At the back of my head, flashing lights started signalling: *Alert, warning, Mayday, Mayday. Stop now, Lorna,* as the front of my head, particularly my nose (red already from crying) became the colour of cooked lobster. The more I rubbed, the worse it became. No way would it turn into a 'flawless golden finish'. Too late, I remembered my wrists; the immediate goo came off on a tissue, leaving behind two burgundy marks resembling stigmata – most appropriate for an Easter brunch party. Would guests think I'd done it on purpose as an ironic gesture or would they be too concerned about my deep scarlet face?

Put on jeans and light blue, long-sleeved shirt in the hope that the blue would counteract the red.

Met David in the hall, who said, "Heavens, Lorna, what's happened to your face? Julie, come and look at Lorna's face."

"No, don't bother," I said sharply, and slammed out of the house.

The brunch party had been terrible. For a start, nobody was drinking alcohol.

"It's alcohol-free," said Pat blithely, ignoring my widening eyes while still accepting my bottle of sparkling wine. "I'll hang onto this for another occasion. Is it hot in here?"

Actually it was chilly. I sat in the only vacant chair by the open kitchen door. Guests kept tripping over my feet and rucksack on their way in and out from smoking cigarettes in Pat's small garden. Everyone asked, "Where's Kate?" and when I told them, they hovered uncomfortably for a minute or two before sidling away muttering, "Must check out the blueberry muffins/blinis/bagel situation. Be right back." They didn't come back.

"Do try and cheer up," Pat said, "you're having a negative effect on my guests."

"I didn't ask to come."

"But as you're here, at least make an effort. You're not the first woman who's been dumped over a bank holiday." She switched on a gracious smile and darted off, carrying a small dish of caviar on a large tray. "Caviar anybody?" she trilled in a false, unPatlike voice.

There were Easter eggs everywhere. Why didn't I think of bringing an Easter egg? Every time the fridge was opened, I wistfully saw my bottle of wine squashed in between a bowl of cold pasta and a bunch of spring onions. I was thoroughly depressed. Couldn't decide whether I was being avoided, whether I was being avoided because of Kate leaving, whether I was being avoided because nobody wanted to mention my high colouring, whether I was not being avoided at all per se but might be sending out 'avoid me' signals.

Suddenly I was prompted to shout, "I'll die if I don't get a Scotch pancake," and several women turned and stared at me as if I must be mad. Who in their right minds would die for lack of a Scotch pancake?

Where was Pat? There was Pat, talking animatedly to a short squirrel-faced woman. Typical. What sort of a friend was she, not to be here at my side, being supportive? I watched her making a note in her page-a-day diary, before lifting a saucepan off the stove and pouring something the colour of old spinach into a jug. "That's a date," she said to squirrel-chops and made her way through the crush to me.

"Lorna, you must have a cup of this – it's a mixture of leftover spinach and seaweed, it will bring your temperature down."

"I don't have a temperature."

"Oh, I think you do. You're the colour of a beetroot."

She poured me a cup. I took it reluctantly and said, "Pat, I wish people wouldn't keep asking me about Kate."

"Fair enough. Don't blame you." She put down the jug and picked up a spoon, rapped loudly on the table. "Everybody, I want to make an announcement." The room quietened. "Regretfully, as you probably know by now, Kate has left Lorna. Very bravely, Lorna has turned up today, and I want us all to make a special fuss of her. Show her it's Lorna we love – Kate was only ever superficially brilliant... and vivacious... admittedly fearless when I had an invasion of flying ants last summer."

"Thank you, Pat," I said grimly. I would have said more but suddenly I was surrounded.

"High time you and Kate made the break. So where is she this fine morning?" someone asked.

"She's gone to a barbecue with Tina, her new girlfriend."

"God, look at your wrists, you haven't tried something foolish, have you? Pat, I think we need two plasters over here, Lorna's tried to kill herself."

"I have not. They're bruises. I caught my wrists in a car door."

"Of course you did. Pat – plasters, possibly a bandage."

As my wrists were being bandaged, someone else said, "I bet she's awful."

"Kate doesn't think so. I do know she's a Gemini, which is the last star sign Kate should go out with, and she owns a clumber spaniel."

Someone else asked me what colour schemes they would have in their new home; someone else told me she'd seen Kate several times in Springfield Park with another woman and a clumber spaniel and *had* wondered; someone else told me she knew Tina, and she realised the situation must be very difficult, but Tina was an extremely witty woman with an almost uncanny rapport with dumb animals. This last someone I pushed hard, my bandages unravelling. The woman staggered back and, in an attempt to avoid landing in the dish of caviar, fell instead into the profiteroles.

There was a deep uneasy silence apart from sounds of woman being helped out of profiteroles. I was sorry about these because I had had my eye on them as a follow-up to the Scotch pancakes.

"Have you gone mad?" Pat asked.

"For the time being," I replied. I unwound the remainder of bandage and dropped it into the jug of spinach and seaweed. Reclaimed my wine bottle from the fridge and went home.

Phew! Would my Easter pattern repeat itself today? I hoped not. My future had looked bleak for months after that.

I knew she'd be at the barbecue – the inimitable Jenny Salter. But would another, even bleaker future be staring an older, sadder L. Tree in the face by the end of the day? Or was there hope? I felt incredibly shy, had a pain in my chest at the way I'd so easily dismissed Jenny from my thoughts in that hunky-dory moment when I'd seen her from Dan's car.

She wore what I can only describe as a paisley pantaloon outfit. I cannot say it was a stunning ensemble; Jenny Salter's clothes had never been stunning, they were the tinned ravioli of the clothes world, clothes that nobody wanted or that they regretted buying almost immediately. I imagined that she must go on pilgrimages to distant towns and villages untouched by fashion and progress, to discover such items. Even so she looked... wonderful, heart warming, loving-smile-provoking, as she stood framed by Sandra's driftwood rose pergola. ("Driftwood's not easy to come by in Hackney," Sandra had informed when I'd murmured a query. "I'm watching and waiting for some more to turn up.") Jenny was eating a tofu and red pepper kebab. I'd never seen her eating anything before (couldn't count dunking tea bags). It was a first for our relationship. She hadn't seen me. I thought, I'll just mosey up and surprise her with a casual, *"Hi Jenny, how are you doing? Long time no see."*

"Hi Lorna, how are you doing? Long time no see."

Had to hand it to Helen, not only was she always impeccably dressed, she could also read minds. She wore some sort of a cool grey biking trouser, exposing tanned biker's calves, with a white T-shirt which bore no resemblance to the white T-shirt I was wearing. Put me in mind of an old Persil soap-powder advert from my childhood where two children are standing next to each other, dressed identically – child with the smug smile is the one in the whiter white.

Squashed desire to quiz Helen about her choice of washing powder and said, "I'm doing very well, thank you."

"On your own?"

"Sort of."

She raised a trim eyebrow, "Sort of?" Her face registered the storing of information – *Lorna Tree's on the verge of bagging a partner at last.*

"Well, not really 'sort of'. There is somebody I very much like but it doesn't do to get one's hopes up."

"Jenny Salter, is it?"

I felt the red rushing up from the neck of my T-shirt and said in a strangled voice, "What makes you say that?"

"Just a hunch. Don't we all fancy our therapists? Better circulate," and she sauntered barbecuewards, leaving me looking desperately around for Jenny.

I spotted paisley fabric in a small group gathered around – good God! – Mr. E and Alfred the Great. What were they doing here? Alfred sat on his trolley. Want to know what he was wearing? A neckerchief printed with guitars. I think it was a remnant from Mr. E's party shirt. Will draw a veil over Mr. E's clothes. Shall just say, they were nothing much.

As I neared the group I heard Mr. E say, "Alfred is the best damn rabbit in the world. He and I are soul mates. If we'd met up years earlier I wouldn't have bothered with marriage," which was the longest and most enlightening sentence I'd ever heard from him.

"Hello Mr. E," I said.

"Lorna," he nodded.

"Hello Jenny," I said. Damn. Forgot the *"How are you doing? Long time no see."*

"Hello Lorna." Jenny turned to face me.

My head moved forward to kiss her cheek but with literally inches between my puckered lips and Jenny's face, Sandra suddenly bobbed up between us waving paper cups of white wine. "Jenny's got a cellar," she shouted.

"Really? Congratulations," I said.

"Plenty you could do with a cellar," Mr. E said.

Sandra continued, "Pretty good ventilation by all accounts. A window with a top-of-the-range Ventaxia fitted."

"You could keep livestock down there," Mr. E said thoughtfully.

"I can't imagine Jenny would want to do that," I said.

"Or grow mushrooms. Ideal conditions for fungi."

"Sound-recording studio," suggested Sandra. "Therapy room. Yes, you could work from home. I could give you some advice on getting it tanked. Alfred want a sip of wine?"

"Actually Sandra," I said, "I think Pat could do with another glass."

Sandra looked less than pleased. "Pat's had too much to drink already. Why is it that she always has to overdo things? Really, Lorna, I'd be interested to know?"

"It's her nature," I replied weakly.

"Then I don't like her nature. Her nature stinks. Could you take over the barbecue for me while I check out just what state she's got herself into? Jenny, one of these days I'd love to hear any thoughts you may have on excessive social drinking." She handed me a plastic spatula and marched off Patwards, wiping her hands on the tea towel attached to her belt loop.

"I'm so glad to see you," I said to Jenny.

That was as far as I got. Sandra, from ten yards away, turned back and bawled, "Lorna, barbecue! Make sure the briquettes don't go from white to dull grey. Dull grey means loss of heat."

"Sandra's very authoritative," I said, and, "Jenny, could we go somewhere quiet and talk?"

"But the barbecue. There's a queue."

Looked at queue. Queue looked hopefully at me. Wanted to say, *"Sod the queue. What have they and Ventaxia windows to do with the likes of us?"*

Problem: Jenny seemed ready to look disappointed at my careless attitude; and Mr. E's comment re. Alfred – "He's a reliable little fellow you know. Always at my side in an emergency" – was definitely loaded. I did not want Jenny to witness an instance of me being less reliable than a rabbit, so smiled reassuringly, tossed my head insouciantly, and smiled... cheerfully, bravely, with aplomb... in a womanfully sheepish manner?

"Well here goes. OK, everybody form an orderly line."

"We're already in an orderly line," Seymour said. Remember Seymour? Of the carrot-coloured hair and eyebrows.

"How are you doing, Seymour? Long time no see." Bloody hell, what a waste of a good line.

"Be doing a lot better once I get my laughing gear around a burger or three."

"Coming right up."

I shall never own a barbecue. If any of my friends see me pondering over them in B&Q, may they hit me hard with the nearest power tool. They are nightmarish, a symbol of much that is wrong in the western world; and my T-shirt – maybe it wasn't the pure white of Helen's Muji T-shirt, but now it was ruined. Every item of food took it into its silly vegetable head to spit fiercely at me. And the pressure! The barbe-queue become a faceless, demanding rabble waving floppy, plastic-coated paper plates and shouting impossible requests.

"Having fun?" This was a tipsy Pat at my elbow.

"No, I'm not. Can you take over?"

"Not allowed. Sandra says I'm a fire hazard. Shouldn't really be standing within twenty yards."

"You are a disgrace to your… profession," I said, which made us both laugh as Pat hadn't had a proper profession for years and years. "By the way, what's happened to Lorna, the clumber spaniel? I'd expected a formal introduction."

"She's indoors. Alfred lunged at her. Mr. E said Alfred has a phobia about anything that isn't a rabbit or a human." She nodded at the next person in the queue. "Customer for you. Must press more flesh." Pat has an unpleasant way of combining certain words and phrases with a salacious wrinkling of her whole face. At least I think it's unpleasant. I have been told by less discerning women that it's rather seductive.

"I want two kebabs, one burger in a bun, one without a bun but topped with onion and ketchup and a dollop of coleslaw to side."

I said severely, "Seymour, this is your third order of food."

"So?"

"Some guests haven't had any food at all yet."

"So?"

Behind Seymour and four other people clutching plates I could see Jenny with Mr. E, nodding and gesturing out into the road as if she were about to leave.

"So?" Seymour said again, pushing his chin truculently towards me. And there his chin was, blotting out the fair Jenny. For her to be supplanted in my vision by Seymour's large, red, greasy chin was too much to bear, Your Honour. I am truly not a woman of violence. I am a woman of jape and jest but there in my hand was an equally greasy plastic spatula and there in front of me was Seymour's chin. Thwacked is the word I'll use because that was the sound the spatula made. Not a hard hit – sharp and sudden. *Thwack!*

"Oh Seymour, sorry. Accident. My hand slipped upwards. You must never thrust your chin over a lighted flame."

"She hit me," Seymour said, rubbing his chin vigorously and spreading more shiny grease, wiping his hand on his trousers – and yet more grease. Impressive, how far a small amount of grease will go.

"You hit me," he shouted, red-headed temper revving up. "My trousers are ruined. You'll pay for this."

I appealed to bystanders. "It was an accident. You all saw what happened. This spatula has a mind of its own – it is a tool of Beelzebub." I waved it in the air and miraculously the queue diminished, dwindled and disappeared. Nobody wanted to get involved with a tool of Beelzebub – apart from Pat who reappeared pushing a bottled beer into Seymour's hand and dabbing at him with a soiled paper napkin.

"Come on, Seymour, it's only Lorna getting out of hand. It's living on the coast – she's forgotten how we behave in the city."

"I'm never speaking to her again. Do you understand, Lorna, I'm never speaking to you again?"

"Most decent of you. I wouldn't speak to me again either."

Pat led him away towards the house.

"Could I possibly have a baked potato?" someone asked.

"No, you can have this spatula and this tea towel. Don't let the briquettes go grey." And I raced after Jenny, who was now out on the pavement.

"Jenny, wait!" I yelled.

She turned, retraced her steps. "I'm coming back," she said. "Sandra's sister's coming with her four children so I was going to Woolworths for Easter eggs."

"I'll come with you."

"There's no need."

"There's every need."

Behind Jenny, Pat's head bobbed up above the fence. "Watch it. Gangra's ong de gor gath."

"What?"

Out of the gate erupted Sandra, brandishing a pair of gorilla oven gloves. "You are a menace."

"Jenny's not so bad," I said.

"*You*. I'm talking to *you*," and another truculent chin was pushed into my face. No way would I dare to tamper with Sandra's chin. Sandra does body-building. According to Pat, Sandra is capable of carrying items like boilers, cast-iron toilet cisterns and fridge-freezers on her back.

"For years," she said, "I've tried, for Pat's sake, to find something likable about you, but you don't make it easy, do you? You have assaulted a dear, dear friend, and as if that wasn't enough, you've let the barbecue go out. Dead. Kaput. Happy now?"

It was wonderful walking along the road with Jenny. I thought of the times with Dan and how I was never at ease, always worrying what she was thinking, aware that we liked very different things, anxiously searching for common ground to build a relationship on. Somehow I knew without asking that Jenny liked spring sun on her head and shoulders, liked the idea of buying Easter eggs for Sandra's nephews and nieces, liked Alfred the Great, front gardens, cats on steps. Most of all, she liked me.

Epilogue

Did I ever see Dan, my woman in beige, again? Well, yes, I did. A few months ago. I was staying with Jenny in her house in Dalston. A car pulled up at the lights where Church Street meets the High Street. It was a silver-grey Mercedes and somehow I don't think I'll ever lose the habit of looking at a Mercedes and feeling a pang. Theresa was behind the wheel, next to her sat Dan, and in the back a beaming Ange and pre-teen Tonia. The lights changed and the car passed us, Dan staring straight ahead, her face impassive. From the back window, Ange and Tonia blew kisses, and I blew kisses back.

"How do you feel?" Jenny asked me, slipping her arm through mine.

"Fine," I said. The wound had healed. I do believe that Dan had been a book I'd only ever been allowed to peep inside, not very much to do with love. Jenny was different.

"I am a swan," I said. "Whatever Pat says, when I love, I mate for life."

Jenny squeezed my arm. "And I'm a golden eagle, what I have I hold on to."

"Golden eagles devour their prey."

"Let's not be too literal, Lorna darling."

I liked that 'Lorna darling', hoped I would become that for all time, that friends would joke, "Here comes Lorna Darling, otherwise known as L.D. Tree, writer of lengthy poems."

We turned into Church Street, stopped at the first estate agent's and perused the window display.

I said, "I love London, and if you want to stay here, that's fine by me, but if you decide you could bear to live by the sea…"

Jenny turned her back on the estate agent's window. "Lorna, we can live wherever we like – we can do whatever we like."

"Well, today we could go to Springfield Park and feed the swans," I said.

"Or we could catch a train to the seaside and feed the seagulls."

"We could visit the E family and feed Alfred and his progeny."

"Or we could go back to my house and feed ourselves, and sit in the garden and make plans and lists and drink wine as the sun sets behind the flats opposite, and then tomorrow we could..."

"We could," I agreed.